# Blood Moon Over Aceh

Arafat Nur
Translated from the Indonesian by
Maya Denisa Saputra

Dalang Publishing

*Blood Moon Over Aceh*
Originally published as Lolong Anjing di Bulan in 2018 by Sanata Dharma University Press,
Yogyakarta, Indonesia
(ISBN 978-602-5607-43-1)

Copyright © 2018 Arafat Nur
Translation copyright © 2018 Maya Denisa Saputra

Cover design: Herfitrisna Yulianti Asnar
Book Production by Cypress House
Editor: Elizabeth Ridley
Indonesian literary advisor: Manneke Budiman

All rights reserved. No part of this book may be reproduced or transmitted in any form or by any means now known or to be invented, electronic or mechanical, including photocopying, recording, or by any information storage and retrieval system without written permission from the author or publisher, except for the inclusion of brief quotations in a review.

Dalang Publishing LLC

San Mateo, California

www.dalangpublishing.com

dalangpublishing@gmail.com

ISBN: 978-0-9836273-4-0

Names: Nur, Arafat, author. | Saputra, Maya Denisa, translator.
Title: Blood moon over Aceh / Arafat Nur ; translated from the Indonesian by May Denisa Saputra.

Description: San Mateo, California : Dalang Publishing, [2018] | "Originally published as Lolong Anjing di Bulan in 2018 by Sanata Dharma Press, Yogyakarta, Indonesia (ISBN 978-602- 5607-43-1)"--Title page verso.

Identifiers: ISBN: 978-0-9836273-4-0 | LCCN: 2018956957

Subjects: LCSH: Indonesia--Politics and government--1966-1998--Fiction. | Soeharto, 1921-2008-- Fiction. | Aceh (Indonesia)--Fiction. | Insurgency--Indonesia--Aceh--Fiction. | National liberation movements--Indonesia--Aceh--Fiction. | Indonesian fiction. | BISAC: FICTION / Historical / General. | FICTION / Political. | FICTION / Cultural Heritage. | HISTORY / Asia / Southeast Asia.

Classification: LCC: PL5089.S4835 D3713 2017 | DDC: 899/.22133--dc23

Printed in the United States of America

# Blood Moon Over Aceh

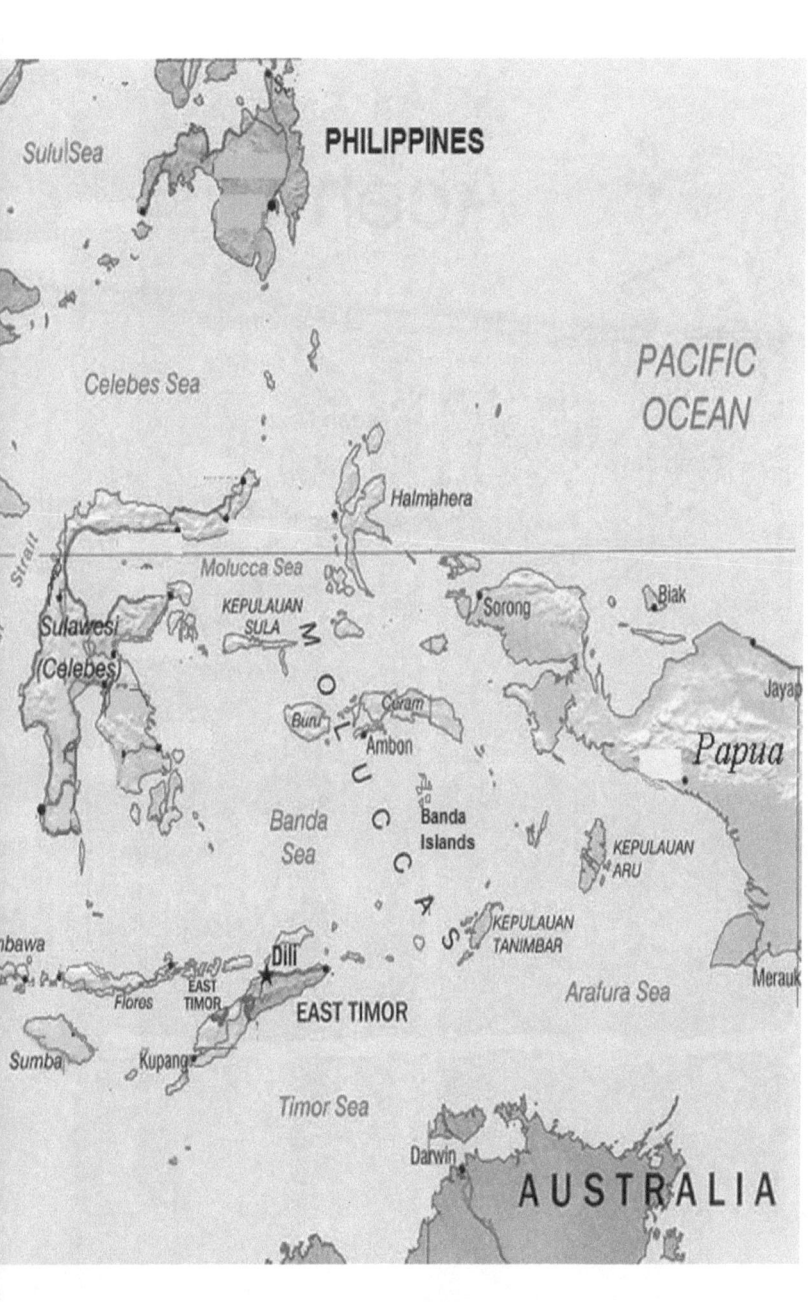

# Aceh

# Buloh Blang Ara District

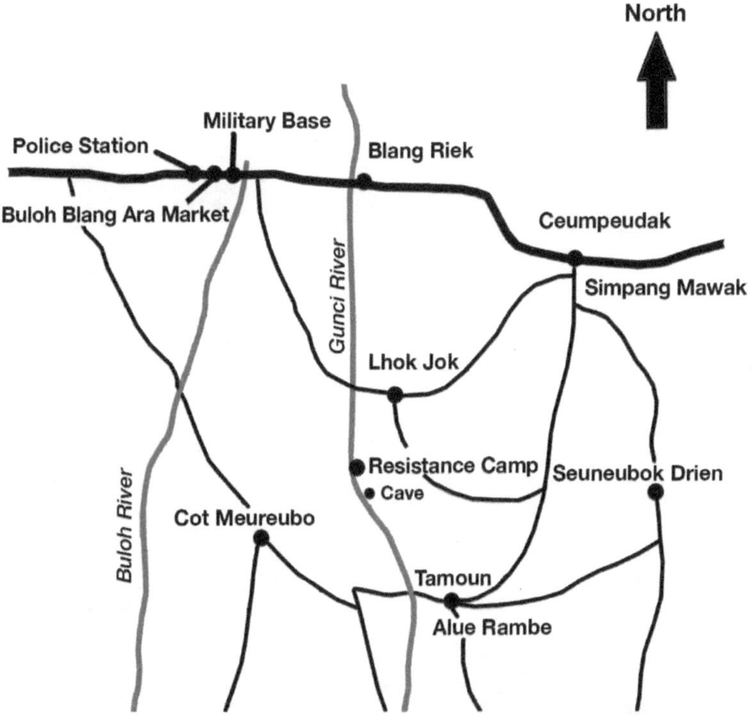

North
Military Base
Police Station
Blang Riek
Buloh Blang Ara Market
Ceumpeudak
Simpang Mawak
Gunci River
Lhok Jok
Resistance Camp
Seuneubok Drien
Cave
Buloh River
Cot Meureubo
Tamoun
Alue Rambe

Blang Ara
Alue Rambe
NISAM
Simpang Keuramat
Nisam Forest
Buloh Blang Ara Forest
Simpang Keuramat Forest

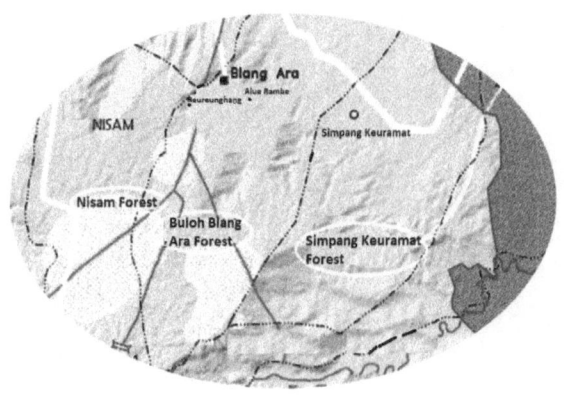

# TRANSLATOR'S NOTE

When I started working on the translation of *Lolong Anjing di Bulan*, I had no idea how much the powerful narrative of lives ravaged by a thirty-year-long war between the Free Aceh Movement and the Indonesian military would impact me. The gripping scenes depicted with straightforward and simple words transported me to Aceh during those years of terror to become part of a farmer's family in rural Aceh. Like most Acehnese, their life was greatly affected by violence and poverty resulting from the war. While working, I tried to recall my vague memories of the shooting incidents that headlined the newspapers in the eighties and nineties, which eventually led to the ceasefire agreement signed by the representatives of the Indonesian government and the Free Aceh Movement in December 2002. As I then lived in Bali, at the opposite end of the country, I could only follow the news from afar. Working on this novel has rekindled my interest in the conflict.

*Blood Moon over Aceh* is rich with details about the daily life of the Acehnese. It was exciting to learn new things about the Acehnese culture and language. The novel has shown me the unimaginable atrocities that humans are capable of and the terror of living in a war zone, fearing every second for one's life. I hope my translation provides an insight on the years of unrest in Aceh and serves as a reminder that any kind of warfare scars the lives it affects, regardless of the cause.

My gratitude goes to Lian Gouw and Retna Ariastuti for another opportunity to work with the wonderful Dalang Publishing team and also to Arafat Nur for writing a compelling novel. And last but not least, I thank Elizabeth Ridley, whose editing skills transported my translation to this publication. I feel much honored for having been given the chance to translate *Lolong Anjing di Bulan* into the English *Blood Moon over Aceh*.

Maya Denisa Saputra

July 2018

# Blood Moon Over Aceh

# Chapter 1

One evening in July of 1989, Leman's coffee stall at Tamoun quickly filled with cheering villagers. The crowd suddenly fell quiet when my uncle, Arkam, started speaking. Arkam's loud voice could be heard outside of Leman's stall.

Drawn by the unusual activity, men and women, dressed in their dirty work clothes, kept coming to the stall. Meanwhile, the sun moved towards the western horizon. Its shape resembled a circle of light stuck between the buds of the candlenut trees. Half of the light poured onto the Tamoun market, casting long shadows on every object and a few people walking to Leman's stall.

Arkam showed a piece of red cloth with a star-and-moon motif, which he referred to as a flag. That kind of flag had never been flown in Alue Rambe. I had heard that the Commander of the Pereulak Region, Ishak Daud, was the first person who raised that flag in one of the high schools in East Aceh.

Everyone silently paid attention to Arkam's stern face.

Pacing in front of the crowd, Arkam continued his speech with fervor. His face tensed, and his arm showed bulging veins when he folded his fingers into a fist. He repeatedly touched his red cap — as if he wanted to take it off, but never did.

"We've been living under oppression for too long. We are being repressed and tyrannized. We can't live like this any longer or we'll be slaves forever. Where's our dignity? All of us are dignified people. Our grandfathers were great fighters. We shall not fear. We must be brave and fight against this injustice and tyranny. Are you brave enough to fight against this cruel regime?" he shouted and shook his fist in the air.

"We are," the crowd answered passionately.

The thundering voices were deafening.

Arkam kept talking. He reiterated the original reason for the uprising Hasan Tiro initiated thirteen years ago at the foot of the Pidie mountain. However, the army had destroyed these initial small attempts to rise against the unjust government. A lot of Hasan Tiro's followers were shot, while the rest were detected by government agents and finally captured, kidnapped, and killed. Meanwhile, Hasan Tiro and a few of his followers fled overseas, seeking political asylum and international support.

During that period, the rebels were amassing power overseas. Some went underground for training in Libya. Others smuggled weapons to Aceh and buried them in the jungles or farmland.

They were the youths who believed they could rebel against the central government in Jakarta under the regime of Soeharto, who had already brought much suffering to his people. His oppression and injustice not only targeted the people of Aceh, it was also inflicted on many segments of our society.

How could it be possible for a nation rich in natural resources — including crude oil and natural gas — to be forced to live in poverty?

"Now it's time for us to rise and fight. Take what is rightfully ours. We can live prosperously and in dignity by taking charge of our own land. Long live the fighters," shouted Arkam. His face was tense and red.

"Long live the fighters," the crowd answered, shaking their fists in the air. "Long live Aceh. *Allahu Akbar.* God is The Greatest."

Arkam was Ibu's brother. At that time, my mother's brother was in his thirties. After he stayed in Malaysia for six years, he joined a military training camp in Libya for another year. Now he was back, looking taller, his raised cheekbones accentuating his taut expression. His mustache was still thin. Apparently, he had developed a habit of wearing a red cap.

Arkam and his seven friends often wandered around the villages to solicit the villagers' support and recruit new followers. Aside from Arkam, only two of these men were armed. Two operated a handheld radio, and the other three were empty-handed.

They mostly wandered around the villages that were under Arkam's command as Panglima Sagoe, a rank of an insurgency fighter in a subdistrict. Alue Rambe, my village, was located in a remote mountain area of North Aceh, south of Lhokseumawe. Our village fell under Arkam's jurisdiction.

The main road in the village was a gravel road. Passing motorcycles and delivery trucks created large dust clouds. However, in the rainy season, some parts of the road were flooded and became very slippery.

I was among those who congregated outside Leman's stall. Mingling among the men, women, and children, I leaned on an open clapboard so I could see what was going on inside.

Men filled every seat on the benches. Those who did not get a seat leaned against the poles; others squatted on the bare ground. Two long-barreled guns and a revolver lay on the only empty table. It seemed those weapons were purposely put on display to fuel the crowd's rebellion against the central government in Jakarta that mistreated the people of Aceh.

Arkam picked up an AK-47. Waving the gun at the crowd, he assured them that the weapon was made from metal, not wood or plastic. His friend held up another AK-47 and arrogantly loaded and unloaded it. Someone else held an Italian-made pistol and tried twirling the Beretta by placing his index finger inside the trigger loop. The gun did not rotate properly and almost fell. When Arkam glared at him, the man looked away.

I knew what the different kinds of weapons were because Arkam repeatedly explained each of their functions to the people surrounding him.

All that time, a muscular man stood guard beside the table. The young men among the crowd seemed reluctant to leave. They continued to stare at the weapons as if they were the world's most magical objects. It was true that such objects had never been seen in this village.

Yasin had been looking silently at the guns. Without paying attention to Arkam's explanations, he suddenly touched the AK-47 that had just been laid on the table.

Arkam immediately slapped Yasin's hand, shocking him.

"This is a dangerous weapon. You can't touch it," Arkam snapped, alerting his three friends.

One of them pushed Yasin away from the table. Some rowdy youths moved towards the back of the stall.

Arkam continued his scolding. "Do you think this is a toy? Only after you join us and are trained to shoot, then you can hold it."

Some people laughed and supported Arkam's firm statement by nodding their heads.

Yasin's face reddened. He seemed to be ashamed of his carelessness.

Arkam also boasted about his skill in long-range shooting. The rebels' military training was better than that of the government's army. Those soldiers were outfitted with used World War II weapons, which often had jammed barrels and an inaccurate sight mechanism.

Leman, the coffee stall owner, was mostly silent while faking a smile. More than half of the villagers had gathered around his coffee stall. Some of them crowded the shop; others loitered around it.

I was certain they did not come to drink coffee, but merely to take a closer look at the deadly firearms that Arkam and his friends had brought. Before this afternoon, the existence of weapons was only mentioned as a boast by people who dreamed about reaping the benefits of Aceh's rich natural resources. In this country, there was no civilian who dared to touch such a thing, let alone have one at home. The punishment for illegal gun possession was the death penalty, or at least decades behind prison bars.

Some people in the coffee stall, especially the youth, were impassioned and seemed convinced that the resistance movement would be able to fight against the injustices of the central government. I saw a glint of worry on the faces of some older people who were present. They must have been worried about the dangers that currently lurked in the villages.

War never seemed to end in this land. There had been war ever since the arrival of the Portuguese, followed by the Dutch, the Japanese, and then the Communist Party and Darul Islam rebellions, and now the once-weakened Aceh resistance movement was on the rise again.

Meanwhile, Arkam's friends and the young men in the crowd yelled curses about the government military, as if their enemy stood in front of them. Their frenzy irritated others, causing them to leave the scene and follow the women who had already left Leman's stall to return home.

"Trust me!" Arkam's roar silenced the stall.

Leman, who was filtering coffee, was caught holding a coffee can by its handle with one hand, while his other hand held the filter.

"Trust me." Arkam repeated his words with great confidence. "We'll be able to chase away those soldiers. Our weapons are far more powerful than theirs. They only use worn-out M16s that belonged to the American soldiers in the Vietnam War. The triggers are often jammed and won't fire the bullets." Arkam's laughter was met by cheers of other passionate youth who didn't seem to want to leave.

Leman turned pale and his hand holding the coffee can shook when the boisterous laughter broke out. He looked as if he wanted to drive out his rowdy visitors, who displayed guns in his stall without his permission.

Other kids and I were anxiously waiting for Leman to turn on his television. Leaning against the open clapboard, we stood outside the stall while looking inside the room. Every evening, after performing the Asr afternoon prayer, the other kids and I would watch television for a while, before Leman chased us away with shouts ordering us to take a shower and go to the Quran's recitation class. Watching television in the evening was such a pleasure. It was an unmatched enjoyment for us children, and perhaps even for the adults who were free to watch it until late at night.

Leman's fourteen-inch television was the only television in my village; hence, his stall was always crowded after the Asr prayer time, when the television broadcast began.

That evening, we were really disappointed. Arkam's gun show had prevented us from watching television. About twenty young men remained seated around the table where the three firearms and their bullets were laid down. It was as if Arkam were the greatest and most powerful rebel leader in Aceh.

Three of Arkam's new followers were unarmed. He said they'd be given weapons at a later time.

After Arkam finished talking, a villager asked one of the unarmed men, "Why don't you carry a gun?"

The slim man answered awkwardly, "It's on its way from abroad."

In order to convince the villagers, Arkam, who apparently had overheard the conversation, nodded his head. He seemed tired and looked tense. He sipped the cooled coffee that he hadn't had a chance to drink earlier. After just one sip, he quickly ordered Leman to take it away and replace it with a fresh, hot cup.

Leman quickly poured the coffee and served it.

Only a few people had left Leman's stall. Most of them still hung around Arkam, who ordered everyone to go home.

---

By the time I reached home, Ayah was sitting on the long porch bench catching a breath of fresh air. My father smiled, watching Ibu, my mother, hanging the laundry to dry.

At that time, I was unable to understand how complicated happiness could be for adults.

Ayah's smile immediately vanished when Ibu turned around and said, "Arkam was asking a few times to see you. Have you two seen each other?"

"Not yet." Ayah frowned and asked, "What does he want?"

Ibu shook her head. At times like these, when they were discussing other matters, my parents would usually exchange smiles. However, since Arkam and his rowdy friends showed up and showed off their weapons at Leman's coffee stall, my parents smiled less.

Ayah was from Kuala Simpang, a more developed area located near Medan, which was very far from here. He used to be a clothes vendor who peddled his wares every day of the week wherever his travels took him, especially at the small markets in North Aceh. During a week he was in Buloh Blang Ara, Ayah met Ibu, who was shopping. They became acquainted and, after several more meetings, married.

After marrying Ibu, Ayah sold all his inventory at ridiculously low prices. With the proceeds of his last sale and his savings, he bought a parcel of land and built a small house on it. From that time on, he lived as a farmer in this village. He never mentioned his parents and relatives. They never visited us, nor did we ever visit them.

It was early in July 1989; I was thirteen and a middle school student. Every day, I saw a group of soldiers roaming around the streets near Buloh Blang Ara, which was a marketplace and the center of the district. Day by day, the number of those soldiers increased. I knew they were spying on us and hunting down people who were involved in the rebellion, like Arkam and his followers.

Every morning, I put on my school uniform: a white shirt and navy-blue shorts, a pair of white socks, and black shoes. I rode my bicycle north across the gravel road. After Simpang Mawak — which was the center of Ceumpeudak village — I turned west, past the dense housing complexes, with rambutan, mango, and water apple trees in their gardens. Then I rode for about three miles across a paved road that was flanked by rice fields until I arrived at the bridge of Buloh Blang Ara. Near the bridge were the military headquarters of Buloh Blang Ara and a row of two-story stalls. At the center of the market, I turned south onto a narrower gravel road. After passing the police station, which had a wide ditch in front of it, I arrived at the front of my middle school, which had been built three years ago.

There was a total of sixty students from seventh to ninth grade. On its north side, the school building bordered a primary school building, an overgrown empty lot, and rice fields that ended in the Pipe Line Road. The road had been built by Mobil Oil, an American gas company, for the purpose of transporting gas as raw material from Lhoksukon through metal pipes that were installed along the roadside, until it reached the Arun gas liquefaction plant in Rancung.

The large refinery by the beach was equipped with tall, straight chimneys with flames at their tips. Next to it were two fertilizer factories and a perfume factory. Farther away, southwest of the plant, in a hilly area some distance from the sea, was a paper mill. All those factories needed gas as one of the raw materials to operate their engines.

There were rumors that the rebellion of Hasan Tiro was triggered by the establishment of factories that began in 1976, the year I was born.

Just like what Arkam said in one of his speeches, almost all of Aceh's natural resources were sent to Jakarta, and Aceh never shared in any of its profits. The government drained Aceh's natural resources with policies that turned Aceh into their cash cow. Despite Aceh's wealth in natural resources, the people of Aceh lived in destitution. The Arun gas field is one of the biggest natural gas fields in the world, but the Acehnese could only watch, dumbfounded, while they were robbed of their natural resources.

I never saw the raging flame that the gas liquefaction plant produced. I only heard about it. Those plants had attracted the rebels from Pidie and East Aceh to come here to attack the military bases. They hoped to attract international attention. According to Arkam, at that time, the other countries were more concerned about other matters they deemed more important than the underhanded massacre that the central government afflicted on the Acehnese.

---

In school, I learned new things that made me reflect and think. My friends were not interested in learning; they were more interested in playing pranks on others. I was sometimes a victim of their pranks. Some of the boys liked to stick chewing gum on the wooden seat of my classroom chair. The stain it made on my navy-blue shorts was very difficult to clean. On another occasion, they flattened my bicycle's tires, and I had to walk my bike to the nearest coffee stall to borrow their air pump to refill the tires. I learned to overcome these unpleasantries and ignore their teasing.

"You're too weak, Zir," a naughty boy yelled at me because I avoided being involved in a fight. "You'll become a slave if you're too weak."

I stayed quiet. I did not understand why boys liked to fight, oppose the teachers, skip school, and not do their homework. Some kids fought until they bled, and the headmaster then had to call their parents. However, fights continued to occur. They were often triggered by small things, such as unintentionally bumping each other.

Once in a while, I would wander around the market after school. I was attracted to the performance of the medicine vendor who showed up every Saturday. On market days, about thirty vendors crowded both sides of the road. This narrowed the road substantially, especially when a car pushed its way through.

Once I was amazed by the performance of a traveling medicine man who cut himself with a sharp knife, yet he was not hurt at all. The longhaired man also cut his hair, but not a strand fell to the ground. People in the audience said that he was invulnerable, meaning his body could not be hurt by any kind of weapon.

I came home late because of watching that performance.

Ibu scolded me. My punishment was to fill up the water barrel in the kitchen. After that, I rarely spent time at the market, especially after a couple of soldiers, armed with long-barreled guns, were seen wandering in the Buloh Blang Ara market, extorting money from every vendor. Of course, people tried to avoid them after that.

At that time, my fear of soldiers had lessened. After all, not all of them looked grim. Some of them were friendly and had conversations with pedestrians. To make sure the villagers did not carry any weapons, the soldiers summoned them and conducted some basic checks for gun possession.

One morning, when I had just started the seventh grade, I saw hundreds of soldiers set up tents around the Buloh Blang Ara Military Headquarters. Later on, I found out that they were a special, well-trained army unit sent by Soeharto's regime. During daytime, they subjected the villagers to forced community service while looking for those who were involved in the rebellion. Rumors said that at night, a group of soldiers often sneaked into Alue Rambe village to spy on the villagers' houses. They were known to prowl around the forest like ghosts.

---

One night, when everyone was asleep, I left the house through the back door to retrieve the money that I had hidden behind a rock. I had hidden the money there before taking a bath in the stream and had forgotten to fetch it before I went home. It was a substantial amount — the hard-earned money from my peanut harvest and my monthly school tuition — and I was unable to fall asleep. Even though it was very dark outside, I worked up the courage to leave the house alone without waking up the others. If Ayah found out, he would surely scold me for my carelessness.

Before sneaking out, I looked for the flashlight that usually hung on a wall in a corner of the living room. I groped around in the dimness of a small oil lamp whose glass chimney was covered with soot. I startled when passing Muha and Raziah's — my brother-in-law and eldest sister's — room and could hear them panting. I wondered how someone could be so tired while sleeping. Were they dreaming of being chased by a ghost or a mad dog?

Unable to find the flashlight, I finally decided to leave quietly through the back door. Outside, it was pitch black. The only light came from an ember in the burning trash pile near the goat shed behind my house. The smoke filled the air and warded off the mosquitoes. Every so often, I heard the goats move around their pen, while the chicken coop next to it was very silent, as if it were empty. In the silence of the dark night, I could hear my own heartbeat.

I never knew that the Earth could look like a black shadow. Only ghosts and those who wandered around late at night would know what the Earth wrapped in bleak darkness looked like. I couldn't hear a single drop of water fall, and there was no breeze at all. Even the nighttime insects were silent; the only thing I heard were my own footsteps as my bare feet crushed the fallen tree leaves.

I was very worried that someone had moved the rock, which sat between the brush and the big tree branch that bathers used as a clothes and towel hanger. Unfortunately, I had combined my spending money with the school tuition Ibu had just given me that afternoon. I cursed my carelessness. To redeem myself, I now had to fetch the money in the middle of the night, before someone found it in the morning — that is, if the money was still there.

I took a shortcut through an orchard of candlenut and melinjo trees. Relying on my hunches, I felt my way between the trees and bumped several times into one. Meanwhile, mosquitoes followed me closely with a loud, irritating buzz.

After I managed to pass through the dark orchard with much difficulty, I came to a wider gravel road that led to the stream. I searched for the rock between the bushes and found that the money was still there. Relieved, I smiled. I was so happy that the thought of encountering snakes or other wild beasts never entered my mind.

As I walked back using the same pathway, I felt a different kind of fear. I realized something I had never thought of before. Walking in dense shadows of the trees, I suddenly thought of Muha's crooked mouth, which supposedly was caused by being slapped by a ghost. What would happen if a ghost stopped me in the middle of this orchard and slapped me for no reason? Does a ghost need a reason to slap someone?

Even though the night air was quite cool, I broke out in a sweat. My heart raced, and I could hear my own heartbeat. I barreled through the orchard until I finally reached the road in front of my house.

In the dim light, my house appeared like a dark shadow, a house in the middle of a forest. When I looked behind me, the candlenut and melinjo orchards were swallowed by the darkness.

All of a sudden, a dark figure appeared. It stood, slightly bent, staring at me.

At first, I thought it was a ghost, the kind of ghost who had slapped Muha.

"Where do you come from?" a friendly male voice asked, as if we had known each other for a long time.

My throat felt dry, but I immediately answered, "From the river. I went to pick up my money. I left it there this afternoon."

"Do you know Arkam?"

"I do." I answered naively without any to-do.

"Where is he now?"

"I haven't seen him for a long time."

"Where did he go?"

"People said he went back to Malaysia."

During the long silence that followed, I wondered why there was someone prowling around like a ghost in the middle of the night and why he approached me to ask questions about Arkam.

"You haven't seen him?" he repeated.

"No," I answered.

"How long has he been gone?"

"About a month."

There was another long silence. I had no problem answering the stranger's questions. It was as if it had not been me who had answered — instead, it was the guardian angel whose duty was to protect innocent children.

Teungku Imam once said, "Allah sent angels to watch over those who pursue knowledge, so there's no need to be fearful." However, that night, I was not on my way to school but to collect money I had left on the riverbank.

"When will Arkam return?" The man stood still like a statue. My eyes had adjusted to the darkness, and I could see the long-barreled gun he held with one hand, the base resting on his shoulder. A part of the gun's barrel was parallel to his head, near his ear.

"I don't know," I answered flatly.

A moment later, other figures appeared from behind the bushes and between the trees. I vaguely saw their painted faces. They looked like the soldiers I had seen on television who were going to combat. There were about seven of them. They came out of nowhere and departed without making any sound or leaving a single trace. Even though I realized they were soldiers, they moved more like ghosts.

Perhaps they had thought I was innocent and naïve. Perhaps they were also amazed that, as an Acehnese youth, I could answer all of their questions smoothly and fluently in Indonesian, the official language they mostly used, aside from the Javanese they spoke among themselves.

Later on, I found out that they were a well-trained special army unit that had infiltrated this village like ghosts, in search of Arkam.

Through Kakek — my grandfather — and his followers, Arkam spread the news that he had gone back to Malaysia.

I treated that night's incident as a secret and kept it from everyone else. Months later, when there were no more soldiers spying on my village, I assumed they left because of that night's incident. I supposed they became tired of spying on Kakek's and other villagers' houses, while Arkam was nowhere to be found. I suspected that there was a traitor who had divulged my uncle's involvement in the rebellion. Arkam was the first person among the villagers who made the blacklist of those who were to be eliminated by the government's army.

# Chapter 2

After disappearing for more than three months, Arkam appeared with his seven friends at Leman's stall on a Sunday. He only dared to appear in public again after he had made sure the soldiers had stopped searching for him. A number of his followers in this village, who lived along the road to Simpang Mawak and had never given a hint of their involvement with the rebellion, had been watching the movement of the soldiers based at Buloh Blang Ara Military Headquarters.

Just like before, only three men carried weapons. The rest were either busily talking into a handheld radio, which emitted a lot of noise, or were empty-handed.

A young man whom Arkam had sent to pick up Ayah from home returned to the coffee stall, sweating.

I followed him to confirm that Ayah was not feeling well. I knew that Ayah purposely avoided attending meetings like these after finding out that soldiers had started to hunt those who were involved in the rebellion.

That morning, Leman's stall was once again crowded by the villagers who came to listen to Arkam. He called on the young men to take up arms against the unjust government. He said, "Who else but the people of Aceh will fight for Aceh? Only the people of Aceh can free themselves from oppression and the exploitation of our natural resources." He pointed out that this struggle was an honorable aim to improve the prosperity of the Acehnese, and free the population from all kinds of oppression.

Arkam delivered more of his advice. He continued with a presentation of Aceh's history. He pointed out that Aceh was once a sovereign empire that fell victim to the greed of the central government in Jakarta. He talked, pacing in front of a dozen young men who hung on his every word, just like the kids in Leman's stall when they watched a Si Unyil movie.

"We must take back our land," he shouted, waving his fist in the air. "According to international law, we have the right to rule Aceh. Don't allow Jakarta to rob us of our oil, gas, wood, and other wealth. If we don't revolt, we'll always be oppressed, live in misery, and languish in poverty."

During that time, there was always someone spreading news of attacks launched by rebels in other areas. The attacks were aimed at police stations and military bases spread across East Aceh, North Aceh, and Pidie.

The disgruntled soldiers then hunted down a group of people they perceived as troublemakers and threats to the country's sovereignty. They engaged their spies and captured anyone they deemed suspect.

Almost every night, I heard of people who were kidnapped. Later, their murdered bodies, with eyes poked out, were found at the sides of the roads.

While these actions were meant to spread terror among the villagers, the rebels were not weakened by such actions. The District Commanders had issued an announcement that anyone who would seize the enemy's weapons and then kill them would immediately be promoted. Arkam repeated that edict with fervor in Leman's coffee stall. "Anyone who's able to seize weapons and kills a soldier, will be immediately promoted to Panglima Sagoe," he yelled.

That announcement was the main cause of attacks and murders of careless soldiers who patrolled the markets by themselves or with only one companion. After a series of events, I heard that Ibrahim Hasan, the Governor of Aceh, reported the uncontrollable rebellion to President Soeharto at the presidential palace. As a result, Jakarta declared Aceh a war zone known as *Daerah Operasi Militer* (Military Operation Area), DOM for short, and in early 1990, sent thousands of soldiers as a backup military support to squelch the Aceh rebellion.

"In the near future, we'll be kicking those monkeys out of this land." Arkam's exclamation was followed by cheering from people who crowded the coffee stall and those who stood outside. Arkam added, "You'll see that we're mightier than them."

A man who had been busily talking into his radio hurriedly entered the stall to see Arkam, who immediately halted his speech and turned to his friend.

"Those monkeys are on their way here, Pang," the young man screamed, looking worried.

*Pang* was short for Panglima Sagoe, an honorable title for Arkam, who had been formally appointed as the leader of some forty rebels.

"How many are there?" Arkam asked.

The young man relayed Arkam's question to his friend who was keeping an eye on the soldiers at Simpang Mawak.

"Four monkeys, Pang."

Arkam paused for a moment, then asked, "Where are they now?"

The man returned to his handheld radio.

"They've passed Simpang Mawak, Pang."

"How are they getting here?"

After checking with his radio contact, the man answered, "By motorcycles, Pang."

"With motorcycles?" Arkam jumped. "Why didn't you tell me sooner, moron!"

Arkam screamed at his followers to evacuate immediately. Soon, the sound of roaring motorcycles leaving Alue Rambe and heading for the Nisam Forest came from the foothills.

Not long after, two motorcycles carrying four soldiers appeared and headed for the village chief's house at the alley next to the closed bicycle repair shop.

Meanwhile, the crowd at Tamoun had returned to their respective houses.

No one dared leave their house. The village looked uninhabited.

At that time, I was inside a villager's house, located near the intersection. The owner kept me from leaving.

From the yard, I saw the motorcycles stop at Leman's stall, perhaps to ask some questions. A few moments later, they drove off.

As soon as the soldiers left the area, people flocked to the streets again. The village chief, who joined the crowd, immediately issued an announcement stating that no one was allowed on the streets after *Maghrib*, the sunset prayer time. This was a new curfew law. Now the *Imam*, the worship leader of the mosque, had to cancel the evening Quran studies at the mosque, and the children were overjoyed when they heard the announcement.

Late one night, not long after that incident, after everyone had gone to bed, Ayah sat in the living room smoking. Ayah always sat up smoking nipa palm cigarettes when he could not sleep.

That night, I too had trouble falling asleep and lay listening to the regular night sounds when there was suddenly a soft tapping on the front door. I jerked up but relaxed when I heard Arkam's voice softly call out a greeting.

I wondered what had brought him here this late while there was a curfew. I imagined him standing by the door, wearing his black jacket, his usual red cap, and leather shoes.

"I'm sorry, I know it's late." Arkam sounded uncertain and apologetic.

Ayah grumbled something; the front door's hinges creaked as the door opened and Ayah said, "It's all right. I'm still up."

My room was located between the living room and the kitchen. In the cold and silent night, even whispers behind the walls could be easily heard.

I heard another door opening — Ibu had probably awakened. Her voice sounded hoarse and heavy, like someone who was forced to wake up from a short nap. A brief chat between Ibu and Arkam was followed by the soft clinking of glasses in the kitchen as the conversation moved to Ayah. Carefully eavesdropping on their conservation, I learned the gist of it.

Arkam lamented about how the resistance movement occupied all of his time; there were too many things he had to take care of. After he returned from Malaysia, he never had a chance to visit relatives. He could not even stay long enough to chat with Kakek and *Nenek*. During his stay in Malaysia, he had met with a lot of resistance fighters who had run away from Aceh but were determined to return and free Aceh from the central government's shackle.

"I spent a year training in Libya. I learned to shoot and also learned a few things about war tactics," Arkam said.

During the brief pause that followed, I heard Ayah clear his throat. Then Arkam continued in a lowered voice, "I came here because of something important."

"What is it about?" Ayah asked.

"All right, then," Arkam started his explanation. "I need to tell you that the government of the Free Aceh Movement has been established. It actually has existed for a long time but wasn't complete yet. Besides the *Wali Negara,* the highest leader, there are also ministers. The Minister of Home Affairs has already appointed a number of governors, and they in turn have appointed *bupatis*, county managers. Only some of the district supervisors haven't been appointed. We, the military, are ready to support." Arkam paused to clear his throat. "Once the cabinet and army of the movement are operational, we'll be enjoying a more comfortable and prosperous life." Arkam continued by explaining that due to uncertain circumstances, he was tasked with various jobs, ranging from training the military to assisting in the establishment of the civil government of the Buloh Blang Ara County. He said he was under direct orders of the Area Commander of Pasai and council to the governor while partaking in their meetings at their secret base in the Nisam Forest, the location of which was known only to them and to God.

In regard to the organization's strategy to attack the army bases and police stations, he was assigned to look for opportunities and the right time to launch the attack. Previous attacks by rebels in Peureulak, East Aceh, Pasai, North Aceh, and Pidie resulted in the dispatch of a number of troops to hunt and capture the rebels, whom the government accused of disrupting order and peace.

"In actuality, they are the ones who are disrupting the peace by inflicting so much fear on the people with their kidnappings, murders, and robberies," Arkam declared with a choked voice.

"I agree." Ayah cleared his throat again.

"This time, our organization is more organized; we've even established a complete government," Arkam said.

Another silence was broken only by the sound of crickets and nightingales.

"Aside from having to take care of military affairs, I'm also tasked to recruit civilians to serve as government officials in our guerrilla movement. At least there should be supervisors for the districts. If nothing else, I like to have leaders for the districts of my jurisdiction. We should support each other by working together and exchanging news," Arkam ended.

Ayah coughed. He often coughed whenever he smoked too much. After his coughing stopped, he replied, "I'm happy that you told me about the progress. I'm only an ignorant farmer. I didn't even finish my basic education. I rarely go to the city, and I don't even know what kind of place Lhokseumawe is."

"That's no problem," Arkam replied. "I was asked by the Area Commander to select the candidates for the position of *camat* (district supervisor) of Buloh Blang Ara. I should know the person really well, and he should be cooperative. If you'll accept the position, you'll soon be formally appointed by the bupati at the temporary, secret location of the resistance's base. You'll also have a chance to become a bupati in only five years. And, if we're successful, it's not impossible that you'll immediately rise to the rank of governor or even minister. This is a very good opportunity."

After a long pause, Ayah asked, "Are you offering me the position of camat of the Buloh Blang Ara district?"

Arkam cleared his throat and said, "I don't know anyone who's as smart and as wise as you are."

Ayah chuckled. He must have found Arkam's explanation ludicrous. As far as I knew, Ayah was not the type of person who would be interested in joining any kind of organization, especially not one that was illegal and engaged in very dangerous activities. A movement that resisted the government would incontrovertibly have to face a large army, and if those government soldiers were killed in battle, Jakarta would simply send another batch.

"When will you get married?" Ibu suddenly cut into the conversation.

Apparently, Ibu's question disrupted their conversation.

Arkam didn't say anything for a long time, and Ayah only coughed a few times.

"I'll get married as soon as this mess is over," Arkam replied.

"It's weird." Ibu's voice was accompanied by the soft clink of glasses. Maybe she was serving cups of hot tea. "You're purposely calling for danger. Our mother complained to me a few times about your attitude. You come and go as you see fit and don't seem to think about your future."

"It's difficult to explain this to our mother. She won't understand that right now I'm not only thinking about me. Instead, I'm fulfilling my responsibility towards our nation. If it's not us, who else would do it?" Arkam parried.

"I don't know, Arkam," Ibu replied quickly. "I've grown up in this village, and I don't understand your way of thinking. What I know is that this movement, led by people like you, has brought armies to Aceh."

After a long pause, Arkam said, "How about this: The sooner we're able to live in peace, the sooner I can get married."

"And when will we live in peace?"

"Trust me, it won't be much longer. We've gained full support from the international community."

It turned out that what Arkam said, I would hear repeatedly from other rebels. The country that had supported the rebels' struggle during the last five years was Libya. The rebels impressed upon the villagers that support from other countries was on its way. Once the Islamic countries on the Arabian Peninsula were on board, the European countries would follow suit. When that time came, Aceh would be freed from the government's oppression.

I did not hear how the conversation between Arkam and my parents ended, because I fell asleep. The next morning, I woke up to a bright and clear sky. I hurried to the stream to take a bath. After I got dressed in my school uniform and had breakfast, I took off on my bicycle.

The birds in the trees flitted from branch to branch, chirping.

A black dog crossed the road, trotted by the coffee stall, and headed north. A flock of chickens busily pecking crumbs on the road quickly moved aside when the dog passed. A small girl, about six years old, picked up a rock and threw it at the dog when he passed her. The rock missed the dog and dropped not far behind him. The dog turned, glanced at the rolling stone, then continued trotting away.

---

It was late in September 1989 when rain started to fall once in a while at night, and it often drizzled in the afternoon. I went to see Ayah, who was fixing the floor of the goat pen behind our house, where the goats slept and ate during nighttime. A small stack of burnable trash was piled up in the center of the pen and would be ignited around Maghrib. The swept dirt floor around it was marked with broomstick strokes.

Nono, our black dog, appeared from the bushes. Panting, he looked at Ayah. Nono acted like a spoiled kid looking for attention. Sometimes, I was jealous of Nono. He always seemed to receive special treatment, which was more than Ayah gave me.

"Nono," Ayah called from inside the shed.

When Nono came, wagging his tail, Ayah scolded, "You're disobeying me. Why did you come home while I fed you already? Stay at the *dangau*; don't let the monkeys destroy the young cornstalks. Go on."

I did not know how a dog that was only an animal and could neither talk nor think could understand Ayah so well.

Nono lowered his head looking guilty, then trotted back to the field in the valley that was divided by the small stream we used as a bathing place.

Nono was only close to Ayah and did not care about me.

While waiting for Ayah to finish his job, I took the ax, the blade of which was wedged between a stud and the kitchen wall, and chopped up two sago palm stems for the chickens to eat.

We had about a dozen chickens. As if they knew there would be food for them, they came in from the yard where plenty of crickets and small worms hid under the small bushes. Crowding around the two small piles of chopped-up sago stems, the chickens pecked away happily.

I grabbed my straw hat and a small hoe from the chicken coop.

Meanwhile, Ayah had made himself ready. He looked so handsome wearing a straw hat, a hoe handle on his shoulder, and holding a small plastic bag in one hand. He glanced at me and said, "Let's go, Zir."

I nodded and followed him. Behind me, the house, with all the doors closed, looked very empty. Only the breeze blew gently. Some chickens returned to the yard. Perhaps they were tired of pecking at the sago. They must have been full. Some settled in the shade. Flapping their wings against the ground, they scattered the dust around it. I wondered why chickens liked to bathe in dust instead of water.

The wild grasses in the field grew tall very quickly. If we didn't get to them on time, they would turn into a thicket. The same was true for the grasses that grew knee-high between the cornstalks.

Overwhelmed, Ayah asked me to help him after school. Meanwhile, I was excused from having to fill the water barrel in the kitchen.

Baiti, the youngest of my older sisters, replaced me. Between her tasks in the kitchen, after she came home from gathering candlenuts in our backyard, she had to carry the buckets of water from the river to the kitchen.

Muha, Raziah's husband, joined us. His face hidden under the rim of his straw hat, he uprooted the lush green grass stems, creating a scraping sound as he ran his hoe across the ground.

As soon as Ayah arrived at the dangau, Nono came to greet him. Barking and wagging his tail, he circled Ayah, who carried a coconut shell with leftover rice mixed with bits of mackerel's head — just like Ibu did when she fed Manis, our cat. Nono looked at Ayah gratefully.

Behind us, the weeded rows of corn looked as if they now breathed the air around them more freely. The uprooted grasses looked wilted in the scorching heat from the sun that hung in a cloudless sky.

After hoeing a few more rows, I took off my straw hat and wiped the sweat from my face. I was wearing shorts, and the tips of corn leaves scratching my thighs and calves made me itch.

"Pak Camat," a young man yelled. He ran toward Ayah while trying to avoid stepping on the corn plants. "You're asked to come to Leman's stall, sir."

Ayah jolted; he seemed shocked and irritated. "Don't call me Pak Camat, asshole."

"Oh, I'm sorry," the man, called Mahmud, corrected himself, nervously. Wiping the sweat off his face, he continued, "Commander Arkam asked you to come to Leman's stall."

"What for?" Ayah asked quickly.

The young man fumbled and finally said, "How would I know?"

For a moment, Ayah silently leaned on his hoe handle. He seemed to be in doubt.

Finally, Ayah let his hoe handle go and left hurriedly without looking back.

I picked the hoe up and tried to straighten the crushed cornstalk.

Nono started to run after Ayah, then stopped for a moment before running to the end of the cornfield.

"Go back to the field," Ayah shouted.

The dog hung his head, then obeyed Ayah, whimpering.

Muha and I continued our work without enthusiasm. After all, the corn was our livelihood aside from the betel nut and candlenut, whose prices often fell. But planting corn in a field like this would always attract troops of monkeys and therefore needed to be constantly watched. The farmers often tied their dogs under the dangau. When monkeys or boars came around, the tied dog would bark fiercely and chase away the boars and monkeys.

However, Ayah never tied Nono up in the field. He trusted the dog. Nono was, indeed, an obedient dog; even when he went home, he would soon return to the field without being ordered. Because he was untied, Nono could roam the fields freely, while making sure that no monkeys sneaked in. As long as there was no female dog in heat around him, Nono was the most vigilant watchdog. Ayah had most likely trained him. The dog understood Ayah fully.

Muha and I left the field at dusk.

Nono circled us. He probably wanted to go home with us. Usually, monkeys did not come at night, especially not now that the young corn was only knee-high. Usually, Nono was allowed to come home in the evening. After he was fed, Ayah would send him back to the field to keep the weasels away. Sometimes, we could hear him and other dogs bark in the middle of the night.

Since it was still light, I did not go home immediately. Instead, I quickly went to find Ayah at Leman's stall.

It was crowded around the coffee stall. Arkam and a few other armed men were surrounded by many people. Ayah sat inside with a man who was about his age. Later on, I found out that he was the bupati who had installed Ayah in the Nisam Forest.

I watched Arkam, who always allied himself with a handsome and fair-skinned man who looked a little like Ayah. He was probably two to three years older than Arkam, but much younger than Ayah. He wore a black cap, a long-sleeved shirt, black jeans, and a pair of leather boots. A handheld radio was attached to his left shoulder, and he carried a rifle on his back. He must be Ishak Daud, the one who had drawn the crowd to Leman's stall.

When it turned dark, I remembered my chore to light all the oil lamps and quickly went home.

We had dinner without Ayah, who came home after Maghrib, looking pale. He still wore his working clothes, but had taken off his straw hat. His thin, white hair clung to his scalp. Grumbling, he fetched an empty bucket and went to take his bath in the river.

"I don't want to be camat anymore," Ayah told Ibu after he came back from the river. "I will turn in my resignation to the bupati."

The way Ayah talked gave an impression that this ugly, old, wooden house was the house of a government official. A government official was surely a rich and honorable person. Imagining myself to be the son of a government official made me laugh. *Forget about wealth; even my pocket money was too little.*

"Didn't you meet with the bupati earlier?"

"I did," Ayah replied without looking at Ibu. "I spoke with him at length."

"Thank God you resigned," Ibu said happily.

"I didn't make that a priority." Ayah sounded as if he was irritated by his own weakness.

"How did that happen?" Ibu seemed puzzled. "Didn't you speak to him for a long time? Why couldn't you mention something that simple?"

"It isn't as simple as you think," Ayah replied. "The situation was difficult. They were gathered to entice folks to join the rebellion, hoping to increase the number of followers, and then, suddenly, I decide to resign. They'd think all sorts of bad things about me. They could even suspect me of being a spy."

"So?"

Ayah cleared his throat. After pondering for a while, he added, "I don't know."

"You've never done anything for them, have you?" Ibu probed.

"But I'm still a camat," Ayah said, depressed. "My name's still recorded as a camat."

"That's also your fault; why did you accepted the offer?"

"It was your brother who kept on persuading me," Ayah answered sharply.

Even though Ayah had not done any of the work other people did, and he always found many excuses for not attending any of the secret meetings, being a camat made him miserable.

After finishing his dinner, Ayah remained seated at the kitchen table, rolling himself a nipa palm cigarette. The light from a big oil lamp that hung on the wall next to the table fell on his face. He still looked pale and irritated as he glanced at Mother, who lifted a pan with leftover fish stew from the stove that was still lit.

I tried to solve some mathematical equations the best I could and was occasionally distracted by my parents' conversation.

"If that job is stressing you out this much, you should just quit," Ibu advised, while putting dirty spoons and bowls into the dishwashing pail.

Ayah chuckled. "You're talking as if I held a real position. Can you think of anyone in this world who holds a public office and whose life is as miserable as mine?"

"Won't it change, once we achieve peace?"

"Do you think it's easy to achieve peace?" Ayah watched Ibu tending the fire in the stove. "I support the rebellion. But I don't want to be a part of their government. I've never liked working for the government. That's why I never became a civil servant. That's why I chose to be a street peddler, and now I'm a farmer."

"As I said before, just quit." Ibu grabbed a rag and started to wipe the table.

"That's the problem." Ayah sighed. "I have been persuaded by Arkam. I thought I'd be just a puppet, who served to complete the notion of some make-believe government. I never thought I'd be expected to attend all sorts of meetings and have to listen to their senseless babbling. I'm not a part of the rebellion in Aceh."

"Then, just quit," Ibu said impatiently.

"That's the problem," Ayah repeated. "I should've never let your brother persuade me. I have no idea why he involved me in this rebellion business."

"Did you tell him that you want to quit?" Apparently, Ibu had not paid any attention to Ayah.

"I did," replied Father.

"So, what happened?"

"That's the problem," Ayah said. "I indirectly resigned. I told them that I'm not suited for the position of camat for Buloh Blang Ara. Of course, I didn't say that there's a camat in Buloh Blang Ara who has been appointed by the Indonesian Government. I know it's impossible to say that."

"Of course, that's impossible," Ibu retorted, glancing at Ayah. "And what did Arkam say?"

"Well, that's the problem…"

"What *is* the problem, what really is the problem?" Ibu asked, frustrated.

"That is the problem," Ayah replied, annoyed. "Your stupid brother didn't understand what I meant."

"Why didn't you just come out and say it? Why do you talk in riddles?" Ibu, seemingly unwilling to lose the argument, pulled up a stool next to the table.

"I'm not being evasive," Ayah defended himself.

"Explaining yourself straightforwardly will clear up the matter."

"That's the difference between an educated and uneducated person." Ayah tapped his cigarette.

"If you know that Arkam has no education, you should talk straightforwardly."

"Talking straightforwardly is dangerous and diminishes me. They'll think I'm a coward, even too scared to serve as a civilian official, while those directly facing soldiers in combat never complain."

"Argh, this is giving me a headache," Ibu replied.

"How do you think I feel?" Ayah glared at Ibu. "The problem is that my situation is very different from that of the Acehnese rebels and their organizers. It's different — very different. I have a field and a family to take care of. I can't just leave when something happens. Unlike them, who don't have similar responsibilities, I can't just pick up and leave."

Ibu did not respond. She rose and checked on the leftover fish stew she was heating to keep it from spoiling. After she removed the pan from the stove, she poured some water on the fire. The remaining embers sizzled as the fire died, and Ibu took care of the remaining chores.

Noise coming from the chicken coop made Ayah hurry outside. A weasel could be prowling around. Nono was gone watching the field. Whenever the dog was not around, something always prowled around our house, including a group of soldiers who sneaked around like weasels. When home, Nono barked fiercely at anything and anyone who dared to enter the yard.

---

Just three days after Ishak Daud and a group of his followers came to visit Alue Rambe and neighboring villages, there was a great commotion in North Aceh. On September 26, 1989, Ishak Daud, together with dozens of rebels — including Arkam — launched an attack on a group of military soldiers who were in the midst of forcing the villagers to perform community service around the Krueng Tuan area, some twenty-two miles southwest of our village. The number of casualties on the enemy's side was unknown, but eleven guns and hundreds of bullets were successfully looted from the soldiers.

Not long afterwards, the remaining military units that were scattered around the Balang Ara Military Base were instructed to pursue Ishak, who always moved from one place to another in a very short period without leaving a single trace. It seemed that due to the incident, President Soeharto had secretly dispatched additional units. All those soldiers came and infiltrated every village almost every night.

Ayah, who had yet to wrap his head around the incident, was even more burdened by his position as camat, even though he was never assigned a task other than attending the secret meetings, which he recently chose to ignore.

When Muha returned from the coffee stall and said that Ishak Daud's troops had attacked a group of military soldiers in Krueng Tuan on September 26, 1989, and seized a lot of weapons, Ayah was stunned. He stood frozen like a statue, holding a machete that he had used to rib coconut leaves in a corner of the yard.

"You're not lying, right?" Ayah asked, as if to reassure himself.

"Everyone said so." Muha looked shaken. "Actually, I'd rather not believe it."

All of a sudden, Ayah tossed his machete aside and hurriedly headed for the road, as if he wanted to see everything Muha had told him for himself. I followed him and tried to mimic his behavior.

Before long, we arrived at the road, and much to our surprise, people at Tamoun Square welcomed Ayah excitedly. The laughter coming from the youth was everywhere, as were the mocking, insults, and cursing at the soldiers, whose whereabouts were unknown. The crowd praised and worshipped Ishak Daud and his troops.

"This must've been the army's first time to fight a more powerful opponent," said a man who walked toward Ayah to shake his hand. Confused, Ayah returned the handshake. "Congratulations, Pak Camat," the man continued.

Ayah pulled his hand back and his face dropped. "You don't need to call me that." Ayah restrained himself. "For your information, I was still in my cornfield when the attack occurred."

"Ah, don't be so modest about it, sir. Whatever it was, you must have had a hand in that attack," the man uttered earnestly.

"What am I supposed to be modest about?" Other men, who were unaware of the problem, came to Ayah and happily shook his hand. They wanted to hear from Ayah, who rarely showed up in public but who was known and accepted as someone who worked most of the time in his field and spent a lot of time thinking about the rebellion at home.

"Of course, we're talking about your modest attitude, sir."

"Listen," Ayah replied. "I was not involved in that attack. I didn't give any advice or voice an opinion. I was in the field when everything happened. I do not know anything."

"Pak Camat," another man interrupted. "We know that the attack wasn't only planned by the rebels. The governors, the bupatis, and camats have all contributed a great deal and so have you. Didn't you?"

"You're all crazy," Ayah cursed. "And don't call me *camat*." Ayah turned his back and immediately left the scene.

The men who were left behind were confused. One of them asked, "What's the matter with him?"

The others shrugged and shook their heads.

That night and many nights thereafter, I often found Ayah sitting alone in the dark kitchen.

When I was younger, after I stopped wetting my bed, I began waking up in the middle of the night to urinate. I'd walk to a spot behind the house, near the chicken coop. Ayah, standing by the back door, would shine his flashlight on the pail hanging on a tree branch so it would be easier for me to get a scoop of water to wash myself.

After I returned to my room, I would peek at Ayah in the kitchen. His shadow slithered against the wall, and then he peeked outside through a gap between the planks of the wooden wall, as if there was someone outside watching him. Then, he would slip into the living room and dim the oil lamp.

Ayah's behavior affected me. I, too, became paranoid. No one else knew about Ayah's behavior except for Ibu and me. Ibu often stayed with Ayah in the kitchen. When their whispers woke me up, I'd put my ear against the wall. Lately, however, Ayah was often alone. After *Isha*, the night prayer time, Mother went to bed immediately. Maybe she was too tired to stay up to keep Ayah company. Meanwhile, Baiti did not seem to be aware of anything.

Muha was kept busy tending to Raziah's complaints as she tried to overcome the anxieties of her first pregnancy. He looked depressed when he heard the rapidly spreading news about the kidnapping of civilians by the soldiers.

In the aftermath of the attack by Ishak Daud's unit, there were a lot of people who became victims of kidnapping and murders. People who died, their bodies riddled with bullets, were never identified as being rebels or not. Strangely, none of those who died had been involved in the attack on the government's army in Krueng Tuan.

One morning, Arkam appeared at Leman's stall. He assured everyone that all the rebels were safe and sound, and cursed the government's army for continuing to kidnap and murder the villagers in the middle of the night. Arkam, who was accompanied by a number of his followers, promised that he would take revenge on those murderous soldiers. He said that all soldiers from Jakarta should be banished from Aceh.

After the attack on Krueng Tuan, none of the Alue Rambe villagers were hurt. The soldiers were deployed to the western regions where the attackers were supposed to be hiding. Due to the absence of military power in the Buloh Blang Ara area, Arkam appeared at Leman's stall and arrogantly stated that he was not afraid of the soldiers.

"I'll soon attack the Buloh Blang Ara Military Base," he shouted.

A cheering crowd supported Arkam's dangerous action. Two dogs passing by the coffee stall were startled by the outcry and quickly moved away.

---

The rim of my bicycle wheel became bent when I drove into a ditch after school one day. I took the bike to a repair shop in Tamoun. Basyah, a man in his fifties whose hands were always covered with grease, lamented that he had to replace the rim. He said he could not make the repair without a down payment.

When I told Ayah about needing a down payment for the bike repair, he said that the money from the corn harvest and the sale of three sacks of cheap candlenuts had already been spent.

Ibu suggested selling one of our nanny goats, but Baiti refused. Because she was the one who mostly took care of the goats, she insisted that she had the most say in the matter.

Ayah asked me to be patient. He wiped off a roadster bicycle that was leaning against the kitchen wall. The bike was usually only used during harvest time, but for now, I rode the bicycle to school. When I passed the Buloh Blang Ara Military Base, I greeted the guards.

In early 1990, hundreds of soldiers were ordered to return to Jakarta, and were replaced by less violent troops. Ayah was able to relax some and fell asleep earlier. At sunrise, he called Muha to help him harvest betel nuts in our backyard and, on another day, to help him cut down the brush that grew tall too fast.

One afternoon, when I came home drenched in sweat, Mahmud was approaching the house, wanting to visit Ayah. The bupati, Mahmud told me, wanted to see Ayah. This time, it had nothing to do with Arkam. It was the bupati himself who asked Ayah to come to a place in the Nisam Forest, some eighteen miles southwest of our village.

Their meeting place in the Nisam Forest would be a former rubber and oil palm plantation that belonged to businessmen in Medan and Jakarta. I even heard that parts of those plantations were owned by Soeharto's family. I wondered why President Soeharto's family, who lived on Java, would own factories and plantations in places so far away from the palace.

Nono barked when Mahmud entered our yard, and Ayah did not try to stop him. Without anyone telling him to stop, Nono kept on barking fiercely at Mahmud.

Meanwhile, inside the house, Ayah stalled for time; after motioning me to get into my room, he tried to look busy and pretended he did not have time to entertain a guest.

Apparently, Ayah already knew the visit had something to do with him being a camat.

Nono's continuous barking made me curious, and I peeked out of my room's window.

Baiti was on the porch. She sat on a large log, shelling areca nuts. Her machete carefully sliced through the fruit's skin before she cracked the nut on the thick *broti*, a giant wooden nutcracker. Even though she pretended to be indifferent to male visitors, I was certain she intentionally showed off her beauty every time a young man came over, especially if he was handsome.

From under a coconut tree in the corner of the yard, Mahmud watched Baiti. When he moved toward the porch, Nono quickly blocked his way and made him return to the coconut tree.

"*Adik*, little sister," Mahmud called, "can you please tell that dog to be quiet?"

Baiti bowed her head. Hiding her smile, she ignored Mahmud's request and allowed Nono to continue scaring him. Even though Nono acted aggressively, Ayah had trained the dog to never attack or bite humans.

"Why is that dog so fierce?" Mahmud asked.

"He hasn't had supper." Ayah appeared on the porch, and Nono ceased barking. But as soon as Mahmud took a few steps toward Ayah, the dog started barking again.

"Ah, he hasn't eaten. No wonder," Mahmud replied with a grin.

"What do you need?" Ayah asked, without inviting Mahmud to come in, as was customary.

"There's something important the bupati would like to discuss with you, Pak Camat." Mahmud tried to keep away from Nono, who came after him while Ayah pretended not to notice it.

"What's the problem?" Ayah asked.

"The usual." Mahmud sounded a bit tense. "Financial matters of the rebellion and, perhaps, some other important matters."

"Oh."

"Sir, can you please tell your dog to be quiet?" Mahmud asked cautiously.

"I told you, he hasn't eaten yet," Ayah snapped. He threw Mahmud an annoyed look and said, "If he hasn't eaten, he doesn't have to obey any kind of order, even if it comes from the Area Commander or Prime Minister."

"Oh, all right." Mahmud looked perplexed. "I'll excuse myself now, sir. I'll come back tomorrow and make sure I come after mealtime."

After Mahmud left, Ayah said to Nono, "Why didn't you bite him? I hate everyone who calls me Pak Camat."

Ayah ignored the bupati's summons. Once the sun moved to the west, wearing his straw hat and carrying his hoe on his shoulder, Ayah walked to the field with Nono. The plot that was previously used to grow corn was now planted with turmeric. This root crop required less care than corn or peanuts. It would take almost a year before the crop could be harvested, so Nono was often home. During the daytime, he was free to follow Ayah wherever he went, either to the field, Kakek's house, or Leman's stall to buy cigarettes and other items. At night, Nono watched over the chickens.

Every time I went home from school, I saw my bicycle lying among other broken bikes. The pile of broken, abandoned bikes made Basyah's small repair shop look even more cramped.

When the owners of the broken bikes passed by his shop, Basyah glared at them. One day, he called out to me and asked when I would give him the money to buy a new rim. I was not sure if he was merely joking or if he really meant it when he said, "Isn't your father a camat? Why don't you have the money?"

Some people who overheard Basyah smiled, while I only bent my head, blushing.

Somehow, his words reached Ayah's ears. And Ayah, who lately was often short-tempered, almost hit him.

I felt awful. Basyah must have thought that I was the one who had reported his sneer to Ayah.

Finally, Ayah sold the remaining candlenut harvest, which was stored on the porch, and bought a new rim himself in one of the stalls that sold bike parts in Buloh Blang Ara market.

In addition to someone calling him camat, something he really hated, Ayah would also get angry whenever anyone mocked his son-in-law's crooked mouth. At times, when Ayah was in Tamoun, some young men mimicked the way Muha talked. His crooked mouth made it difficult to pronounce words correctly and made him involuntarily spit when he spoke.

Whenever Muha came to the coffee stall, people intentionally engaged him in conversation and laughed derisively at him when he tried to speak. This angered Ayah. He knew that they were entertaining themselves at someone else's expense.

The teasing about Muha's crooked mouth came to an abrupt end when a man in his thirties, who was one of the teasers, was struck by a disaster. One afternoon, after fishing in the river, he went to defecate near a big rock, east of the public bathing place.

Someone said that spirits dwelled in the huge rock, which was as big as a goat shed. The man squatted next to the rock while looking at the flowing water that sent his feces to the Seuneubok Drien River, near Ayah's turmeric field.

When the man washed himself, he found out that his testicles had swollen and were as big as a fat man's fist. He was forced to keep his legs spread widely while walking home.

When people found out that spirits had grabbed him by the balls and caused them to swell like that, they burst into laughter.

After this incident, Muha's crooked mouth was no longer the main object of people's ridicule.

That man's fate was surely better than Muha's. After a week or so passed, the swelling of the teaser's testicles went down, whereas Muha's mouth never straightened. However, the man was too embarrassed to hang out in Leman's stall and never teased Muha again. He now spent most of his time working his field. People who watched him commented on how lucky he was to have the spirits grab his testicles and thus teach him that his time working the field was better spent than making fun of other people's handicaps.

## CHAPTER 3

One afternoon in early May 1990, a small group of soldiers suddenly appeared in the alley in front of our house, just as I returned from the field.

I was shocked, and my heart throbbed as I saw them. For a few moments, I just stood still, feeling awkward. At first, I thought they were a family of farmers who were also returning from their field. Their footsteps sounded like those of farmers who wore boots. Three soldiers quickly looked away when our eyes met. It was as if they wanted to say that they had nothing to do with me.

Raziah stood behind our home's partially opened front door. Her look told me to leave the yard immediately.

I saw fear in her pale face. Her bulging pregnant belly made it difficult for her to move. She shifted her buttocks, hiding her body behind the door. As soon as I came to the door, Raziah pulled me inside so hard, I fell.

Kneeling, I peeked out the window to watch the soldiers walk to the main road.

Ayah appeared from the candlenut and melinjo tree orchard across from our house. A towel still wrapped around his waist, he had just returned from taking a bath in the stream. He nodded at the soldiers, who stared at him grimly. When he raised his head, he looked even more pale than Raziah.

Lately, this group of fifteen soldiers often appeared suddenly in the villages, to show that those places were still under government jurisdiction.

For a while, Ayah sat on a bench near the dining table with his towel still wrapped around his waist. According to rumors, the soldiers patrolled the villages to scare the rebels and their families, who were sure that their rebellion would be victorious.

---

A few days before Raziah's due date, Muha rode the roadster bicycle to Buloh Blang Ara to buy miscellaneous supplies for the baby. On his way home, a soldier, who thought Muha was mocking him, slapped him across the mouth. Strangely, the repeated, firm slaps on both cheeks only caused bruises and a nosebleed but did not straighten Muha's mouth. It seemed that the result of Satan's slap was more permanent than that of the soldier's.

Raziah kept complaining about her sore body and did not have time to tend to the wounds on her husband's face.

Meanwhile, Ayah's distress was on the rise. He was haunted by fear lest the soldiers recognize him as one of the rebellion's officials, even though he had never touched a gun, let alone used one. Ayah lamented that if some handwritten notes were found during raids, or if Arkam's carelessness proved he was a camat of the rebellion, his life would be finished.

After some small-scale shooting incidents, followed by the kidnapping of civilians by the military, Arkam and his followers disappeared from the village.

Ayah did not want to get caught by following the bupati's messenger to attend a secret meeting.

"The bupati and those rebels are crazy," Ayah grumbled to himself in the kitchen. "They're trying to involve me in their madness."

"It's okay," Ibu hushed. "Just be honest with Arkam and the bupati and tell them you need to quit."

"That's what I will do when I see them," Ayah grumbled. Unsure of himself, he added, "But with all these soldiers roaming around, how will it be possible for me to go see them?"

Actually, if Ayah were as brave as the rebels, he could have sneaked around to attend their secret meetings and gatherings. The soldiers would not have been able to peg him as a rebel. What distinguished a farmer from a rebel was that a farmer carried a hoe and a machete, while a rebel carried a gun or a handheld radio.

One morning, Raziah, with the help of an old midwife from Cot Meureubo, gave birth to a healthy baby boy.

Zuhra, my four-year-old baby sister, was very happy with the birth of her nephew.

Muha named his son Akbar, which means *great* or *big*. I thought the baby was small. Only his head was big. His big head was not due to some medical condition; it looked bigger in relation to his small body.

Before leaving the house, I visited my sister, who lay on her bed with outstretched arms. She stopped her muffled groaning when she saw me and threw me a shy look.

Baiti helped with everything that Ibu prepared, while Zuhra leaned against Ibu's shoulder as she was sitting down.

"Nazir, don't forget your water bottle," Ibu reminded me.

"I didn't get my pocket money, Bu."

Ibu was opening a package of new diapers on the living room table. She quickly walked to her room and returned holding a fifty-rupiah coin between her index finger and thumb.

"I can only buy a popsicle with this, Bu."

"Are you going to school to study or to eat snacks?" Ibu turned. She walked to the dining table and busily tended to her tasks. "You don't need to buy popsicles. Can't you just drink the water you bring? You're a big boy now; don't act silly. With that money, you can buy cakes or some other food that won't give you a stomachache."

A few other kids and I rode our bikes along a pebbled road. After riding a little over a mile, we passed Simpang Mawak. A high school building was being built on an empty lot nearby. The construction was supposed to be completed in another two years, and I could continue my education there after I graduated from middle school. It was much closer to home. At that time, kids who wanted to go to high school had to go to the one in Lhokseumawe. It was the only high school in the region, more than fifteen miles away. There were only a few kids who continued their education after graduating from middle school.

Even in Alue Rambe, it was only I who continued to middle school after graduating from elementary school. Other kids, including Raziah and Baiti, were only elementary school graduates. It was too troublesome for girls to travel such a long distance. The roads were so bad that everyone had to ride their own bicycle. It was impossible to ride with another person on the passenger seat. And then there was always the concern about the kidnappings and murders that started in early 1988.

"You're a boy." Ayah spoke to me the way he spoke to adults. "You should be strong and study well."

I understood that what Ayah had said was not only applicable to boys, but to girls as well. He only talked in accordance with someone's perception, and the perception in this kind of village was that no matter how wise a human is, it is not always possible to speak about something similar to his or her son. During that time, people would begin to understand something different after it had passed a long time ago, and the memories were erased like puddles on the streets that were baked dry by a long drought. Who would have been able to understand why someone who could not even bring himself to snarl at a cat stealing fish, would one day be able to kill humans? That time was the beginning of humans turning into animals.

Very early one morning in May 1990, after I finished my final exams in middle school, there was a bustle inside my house. Ayah had butchered three cocks. Ibu, Nenek, and Baiti were busy in the kitchen.

Raziah occasionally visited the kitchen, helping as much as she could. As soon as Akbar cried, though, she quickly returned to her room to breastfeed him.

I was excused from all duties, including carrying water from the stream. Ayah and Muha did not go to the field that day and took care of everything.

The chickens had been fed plenty of sago palm to keep them in the backyard. Ayah had also built another coop for some laying hens so they would not nest in places that hindered us.

At dawn, Kakek came over, smoking a rolled nipa palm leaf cigarette. He chatted with Ayah as if they were friends. I had never seen that in Ayah and Muha's relationship. Kakek greeted Muha, who passed them carrying two pails of water.

Muha put down the pails to shake hands with Kakek.

After taking a bath, I put on a white shirt and a new sarong. All the living room furniture had been moved to the kitchen, and I sat down on the *sajadah*, a prayer mat, that was unfolded on top of the pandan mat on the floor. A big plate of *pulut*, glutinous rice, and a smaller plate of grated coconut and brown sugar sat next to a bowl of water that held some wild grasses and various flowers.

Nenek took a seat opposite me. She held a small bowl with *beras-padi*, a mixture of rice and unhulled grain, and read a prayer and *Salawat*, a special prayer asking blessings for Prophet Muhammad. Then, she took a pinch of pulut mixed with grated coconut and palm sugar and fed it to me. Another pinch of the rice mixture was placed on both of my earlobes. She took the small bowl of beras-padi and, after whispering a prayer and Salawat over it, she scattered the grain on my body and all over the room, sprinkling some on Kakek, Ayah, Ibu, Raziah, Baiti, Muha, and Teungku Imam Masjid — my Quran recitation teacher — who rushed into the room after saying a greeting.

Nenek borrowed the golden ring from Raziah's dowry. After dipping the ring into a bowl of water, she touched the middle of my forehead and my chest with it while chanting, "May your mind shine as this gold, and may your heart be pure and beautiful as this gold." Nenek's words truly touched me, and people were listening solemnly.

After Nenek took some of the wild grasses and threw them on me; everyone else in the room did the same. This was the *peusijuek* ritual, which asked for blessings and protection during the next stage of life I was about to embark on.

Ayah took a bundle of the grasses and hung it on a nail on top of the doorframe, together with the bundle of grasses from Raziah's wedding peusijuek.

Shortly afterwards, dozens of people came to eat chicken curry and pray for the deceased ones, for my future, and also for the family of Dahli and Hamamah — my father and mother.

The next morning, Ayah took me on his roadster bike to the Buloh Blang Ara market.

In one of the two-story wooden stalls, a rather stocky man welcomed me. He gently told me to lie down on a bed so he could circumcise me.

I was circumcised a few days before Ishak Daud and Arkam suddenly appeared again. The attack on the military base on Monday afternoon, May 28, 1990, shook the entire Buloh Blang Ara area.

The distance between Buloh Blang Ara and my village was almost four miles. As Alue Rambe was nestled between densely forested hills, the loud artillery noise easily penetrated the silence and could be heard clearly.

Still wearing a sarong, I went outside my house and, with great effort, climbed a small hill. Many people stopped whatever they were doing, trying to determine where the gunshots came from.

Not long afterwards, Ishak Daud and Arkam's troops swarmed the roads with dozens of motorcycles. Shouting victoriously, they waved the weapons they had seized from the Buloh Blang Ara Military Base. News spread quickly. During the surprise attack, which lasted less than an hour, two soldiers were killed, while the rest scattered and hid outside the market. Blood from the dead soldier lying in the base's yard spilled all the way to the gates. A middle school student, who lived near the base and happened to be on the street, was shot dead.

Because many of the soldiers were not at the base at the time of the attack, it was easy for the rebels led by Ishak and Arkam to claim absolute victory, without a single casualty. However, soon after the rebels retreated into the foothills, hundreds of soldiers filled the roads around their base.

The soldiers roamed around in small groups and attacked everyone they met without any explanations. Most of the victims came home with broken arms and legs or vomiting blood. The soldiers were taking revenge on the rebels who had gone into hiding. The innocent people now became the victims of the soldiers' wrath.

# Chapter 4

After the attack on the military base in Buloh Blang Ara, Ayah became even more anxious and fearful. He was unable to sleep, and every night, he felt that soldiers were prowling around the house, ready to capture him at any time. As usual, the main problem was his being a camat in the resistance movement that the government referred to as the Free Aceh Movement, also known as GAM. If he could have held that position in his hand like an object — such as a hat, a belt, or a stone — he would have thrown it in Arkam's face.

When the attack in Buloh Blang Ara occurred, Ayah and Muha were working in our turmeric field. When Ayah heard the gunshots, he ran home.

Nono and Muha had followed him.

They gathered with other confused villagers on top of a small hill in front of our house. Some people who had just returned from Simpang Mawak said that the rebels led by Ishak Daud had ravaged the military base and killed two soldiers.

The real threat for Ayah was not the government troops. His appointment as camat was what was killing him slowly and quietly. When I went after him, we watched dozens of rebels on motorcycles racing through the roads of Alue Rambe. Without stopping even briefly at Leman's stall, they headed straight for the forest.

I imagined they'd use the small country roads until they reached a wider road. The soldiers who were newcomers to the area would not know their way in that terrain.

Some young men, who always joined Arkam whenever he entered the coffee stall, came to shake Ayah's hand.

Ayah looked gloomy, confused, and doubtful. He repeatedly wiped his face while people around him engaged in lively conversation. Some asked questions, and those who had the answers repeated their stories over and over again.

On our way home, Ayah grumbled and cursed. He stated repeatedly that being a camat was actually shortening his life. He flinched every time someone passed us and greeted him cheerfully, "This time our movement was truly successful, Pak Camat."

Ayah could no longer contain himself and flared at one man, "I'll punch you if you call me Pak Camat again."

Perplexed, the man looked at him.

Ayah did not care. He turned around and rushed home.

I had to run after him or be left behind.

Without bothering to clean himself, Ayah walked into the house and went straight to the kitchen.

Mother greeted him with a question. "Why do you look so pale? What's actually happening out there?"

Ayah snapped, "Ishak Daud and Arkam attacked the military base."

The following days were filled with news about soldiers frisking and attacking people on the streets of Buloh Blang Ara. Some Alue Rambe villagers who went to the Buloh Blang Ara market came home with bruised faces and stories of people who had been assaulted. The soldiers apparently vented their anger on everyone, regardless of them being a rebel or not.

The roads remained deserted for weeks. The few people who happened to travel became victims of the soldiers' violence. It seemed that the soldiers, who were mostly Javanese, really hated anyone who had an oval-shaped face with a sharper nose than theirs — the type of face that marked a rebel.

The mini trucks, which usually came every two or three days to transport betel nuts and other agricultural products, no longer entered Alue Rambe. The farmers who had harvested their corn, peanuts, and mung beans were unable to sell their goods.

During that month, the fish peddlers did not make their rounds, so there was no fresh fish available, and the price of salted fish sold in stalls at Tamoun soared. When the kerosene supply ran out, we could only use a small oil lamp, even during dinner.

Baiti complained about her dark room. She was really scared of the dark and unable to sleep.

Ayah grimly rubbed his face and turned to Zuhra, who played in a corner of the room. "Zuhra," he called, "go sleep in Baiti's room."

"I'm scared, too," Zuhra replied.

"Come on." Ayah held back his anger. "Everyone sleeps in the dark. There's no kerosene for sale anywhere."

"Baiti," Ibu chimed in. "You're grown up. Don't act childish."

Ayah rose and walked to his room while grumbling, "Instead of helping me stay calm, everyone in this house keeps adding to my worries."

I also rose and walked to my dark room. Stumbling through the darkness, I lay down. This whole world was a dark place; very dark, indeed.

*Arafat Nur*

Not long after the unrest from the attack on the military base in Buloh Blang Ara had died down, I noticed Mahmud following Baiti as she walked home from washing clothes at the stream.

Baiti, now a sixteen-year-old, shyly responded to the curly haired young man's questions.

Nono met them in front of our house with barking that stopped Mahmud in his stride.

Ayah, who was smoking on the porch, greeted the young man without inviting him to come in. Making small talk, Ayah asked what brought him here again.

Mahmud lowered his head and rubbed his arm.

Nono kept on barking.

"Has that dog not been fed yet?" Mahmud threw Nono an anxious look.

After Ayah hushed Nono, the dog quieted and lay down near him.

Relieved, Mahmud smiled. "That dog certainly obeys you, Pak Camat."

Ayah chuckled then, holding the young man's gaze, and said, "I don't like to be called Pak Camat. No one is allowed to call me that. I want you to tell the bupati that I'm resigning."

"You can't do that, sir," replied Mahmud cautiously. "I apologize. As far as I know, in every government, there are rules to follow. People can't just resign from their jobs without good reasons."

"Hey, young man," Ayah snapped, "who's making those rules? I have my reasons."

"I'm sorry, Pak Camat," Mahmud continued awkwardly. "If you do have a good reason, you need to submit it yourself. You can't do it through me."

"Eh, why does it have to be so difficult?"

"I don't know," answered Mahmud nervously. "But, as you know, everything has to be done by the rules. Moreover, this is concerning a government position. You can't consider it a joke."

"Who's joking here?" Ayah asked angrily.

"I know you're not joking, Pak Camat."

"Hey!" Ayah shouted. "If you call me Pak Camat again, I'll punch you in the mouth."

"Oh, I'm sorry," Mahmud stuttered, stepping back. While keeping his eyes on Ayah's balled-up fist, he said, "I'll excuse myself then, Pak Camat — er, sir."

"Damn," Ayah cursed, turning his back.

---

When school started in June 1990, I was in eighth grade and going through important changes in my life as a fourteen-year-old teenager who was already circumcised and growing a mustache.

School was not going well. Teachers were often absent. Standing in front of the class, they only advised us to be careful and not do stupid things that would provoke the soldiers.

Because there were still a lot of soldiers roaming the streets, I skipped school several times. However, on that day, after concluding that the soldiers were not going to move away but would continue to protect their base from future attacks, I decided to go to school.

When I arrived in Simpang Mawak, a group of soldiers were checking on everyone who went to and from the market. Suddenly, I was attacked by great fear and regretted my decision to go to school that day.

One of the soldiers walked up to me and asked, "Are you the son of a rebel?"

"No, I'm not," I stuttered, shaking my head.

I wondered if I looked like the son of a rebel. My cheeks felt numb. I had not exactly been truthful, but I hadn't told a lie either. Even though Ayah was a camat, he did not want the position. And, as far as I knew, Ayah never participated in any rebellious activities, either. He was just an ordinary man trapped in unfavorable conditions.

The soldier moved his gun barrel, gesturing that I was free to move on.

During the entire trip to school, I kept thinking about Ayah's problematic appointment as a camat. Lately, Ayah always looked pale. He always seemed tense and unenergetic. I remembered him flinging his machete into the trunk of a coconut tree and shouting, "You're an asshole, Arkam. You want your sister to be widowed soon and your nephew and nieces to be fatherless."

When he was with other people, Ayah always put up a good front. He only complained to Ibu, who was always busy with various chores and surely bored of listening to him. I did not know if he told Muha anything when there were only the two of them in the field.

A couple of times, I heard about Ayah's plan to ride his roadster bike to the plantations at the foot of the mountain to meet the bupati. However, the increasing number of soldiers patrolling the area kept him from following through. He did not know the back roads that the rebels used.

And even if he knew the secret shortcuts, it did not mean he would be safe from the soldiers, who always lost their temper whenever they saw someone suspicious wandering around. Maybe they wondered where these poor and weak Acehnese found the courage to fight against fully armed government troops.

I remembered when Ayah finally mustered the courage to go to Leman's stall and announce to the crowd there that he was no longer the camat and forbid everyone from calling him Pak Camat. "Call me Dahli, just like you used to," he said firmly.

The announcement surprised many people, and quite a few among them regretted Ayah's resignation. But some who were Arkam's followers knew that Ayah's resignation was invalid and that he was still legally a camat.

Despite the fact that after this no one called him camat anymore, Ayah was still plagued by anxiety. Every night, he paced the living room, which was only lit by a small oil lamp that hung on the wall. He calmed himself by smoking nipa palm leaf cigarettes, and every morning, his tin ashtray was filled with cigarette butts. Because he always went to bed late, he often overslept and only went to the field at noon. He worked listlessly, and most of the fieldwork was done by Muha, who understood his father-in-law's predicament.

After his announcement at Leman's stall, Ayah repeatedly mentioned his regret for not having firmly rejected Arkam's request in the first place. Now he was overcome by fear that the military would find out that he was a camat. A situation he had regarded as some pretense was now threatening his life. There was no other punishment than the death penalty, even for those who were unarmed. Ayah was fully aware of the statement that the central government had issued regarding the necessity to eradicate rebels and, if needed, their entire families so there would be no future generation of rebels that could threaten the unity of the country.

Every night, many unidentified round-faced people with flat noses roamed around the villages, while during the day, they passed themselves off as peddlers of various household items such as pots and pans, plastic containers, toiletries, or even kitchen knives. Many suspected they were disguised spies who tried to gather information while peddling their wares.

The repercussions of the rebels' attack on the military base continued to the end of 1990. Sometime at the end of October, the villagers of Alue Rambe were awakened by gunshots shortly after daybreak. The noise that traveled through the cold morning came from around Tamoun.

I jumped out of bed and went to the living room. Ayah walked in and, keeping close to the ground, he whispered, "You stay home."

Scared, I nodded.

Ayah walked to the kitchen.

During a short pause in the shooting, Mother and Raziah, both looking disheveled, rushed in. Screaming, they dropped to the floor when the next round of fire started.

Zuhra, bewildered, stumbled out of Baiti's room and ran straight into Ibu's outstretched arms.

Muha, carrying his baby close against his chest, crept toward us without noticing that the baby was urinating on his blue T-shirt.

A round of explosions kept us all huddled, close to the ground.

The baby began to cry and Raziah took him from Muha's arms.

Akbar quieted as soon as he latched onto his mother's breast.

The house was wrapped in a tense silence. After the noise of artillery fire died, the day moved on. Birdsong filled the air like any other morning. It was as if nothing had happened.

I suddenly noticed Baiti was missing. When I went to check on her in her room, she was still sound asleep.

For a while, the rest of us huddled together in the living room. Whispering, we tried to guess the source of the explosions, and foolishly kept questioning each other.

It was not until noon, after a troop of soldiers was seen leaving the village, that people flocked to a house in an alley behind the mosque.

In the living room lay a man's dead body covered with a long batik cloth. His wife, who had just given birth two months ago, wailed like a wounded animal. Some teary-eyed people who surrounded her tried to comfort her, but to no avail. When her baby cried, she turned toward the wall and breastfed him, sobbing.

Apparently, her husband had been shot when he walked out to the yard after he finished his *Fajr*, the dawn prayer. Hearing a gunshot, the woman ran outside and saw her husband sprawled on the ground. Blood spurted out of his wrist.

Three soldiers and a stranger stood around him. One of the soldiers aimed his revolver and fired on the man, who lay cringing. The bullet hit him in the side.

The wife rushed to embrace her husband, but a soldier pushed her away violently and she fell.

Not long afterwards, the man's mother-in-law appeared. Wailing, she rushed out but was prevented by the soldiers from getting close, and then she was beaten into silence.

One of the soldiers picked up a machete that was lying nearby. He cut down a banana tree growing near the kitchen and placed a part of the trunk under the victim's head as a pillow. The three soldiers then stepped back and riddled the man's body with bullets.

The two women covered their faces with their hands, screaming. The man was known to have attended the secret meetings with Arkam, but had not been involved in the rebels' attacks.

The incident shook Ayah so much that he no longer wanted to stay home. He took his pillow, sleeping mat, and a mosquito net to the dangau near the turmeric field. Meanwhile, the rebellious attacks on patrolling soldiers intensified.

# CHAPTER 5

On my way to the turmeric field, I came upon a new dangau. It was built in the shade of a candlenut tree. The bamboo mat walls were covered with plastic rice bags that had been cut open to keep the wind out. Judging by the presence of a pandan mat, an old, crumpled-up mosquito net, along with a pillow and a sarong, I figured this must be the place where Ayah had been hiding out during the past week.

I could only imagine how Ayah spent the night here, worried sick, anxiously scanning the area to make sure no one was approaching the dangau. Meanwhile, the cold December wind that chilled the bones brought rain.

I noticed a wooden log, the width of an adult's knee, coconut shells, and husks that could be used to make a fire that would not only warm up the dangau but also serve as insect repellent. Rain often fell in the middle of the night, and although the heavy rain soaked his mosquito netting and disturbed his sleep, it also must have made him feel more comfortable. It was unlikely that soldiers would be prowling around in the heavy rain. Moreover, Nono's constant presence kept him safe.

Nono would immediately bark when there was any movement near the shack. His bark could be heard all the way to the house and would surely awaken Ayah. In the event that soldiers were indeed coming, Ayah would run to a hideout he had already prepared in the woods.

Ayah's pale face and red, heavy-lidded eyes clearly showed his lack of sleep.

I turned around and started weeding the turmeric field while straightening stems that had collapsed during the night's rainstorm. The lush green grasses would quickly take over if not tended to immediately. Their roots would spread rapidly and rob the soil of its nutrients, thus stunting the growth of the turmeric plants. The parts of the turmeric field I had worked looked nice and clean.

When the rain started to fall heavily again, I went home. On a bench under the porch's overhang, I saw Ayah's mat, pillow, and batik blanket. Ayah must have come home.

"What's the reason behind his persuasion? Just think about it."

I could hear Ayah yelling in the kitchen.

"Don't you already know the reason?"

I slipped into my room, where I eavesdropped on my parents' conversation.

"Your brother is possessed by the devil. Yes, Satan," Ayah exclaimed. He seemed unsatisfied with Ibu's answer and continued, "It must have been Satan who told him to see me."

"Then you don't need to blame him. It's all Satan's fault."

"No. That's not the way it works," Ayah retorted. "He's Satan himself."

"I don't understand what you mean."

"I also don't understand your brother's intention."

There was a silence. Ayah seemed to try to overcome his anger. I had just taken off my soaked clothes and was pulling a dry shirt over my head when I heard Ayah holler, "If he ever shows up, I'll kill him."

"You don't need to kill him." Ibu sounded terrified. "You can talk to him civilly."

"Your brother is truly damned."

"He is," Ibu scoffed. "But you don't need to kill him."

"Why don't you ever understand what I mean?" It seemed Ayah had shifted his annoyance to Ibu.

"Didn't you say that you'd kill him?"

"I did," Ayah railed. "But of course, I didn't really mean it."

"Oh, you were just joking?"

"No, of course not."

"Then what do you mean?"

"Oh, my God, how do I explain a hyperbole?"

"What's a hyperbole?"

"It's fine, just stay quiet," Ayah snapped.

---

The soldiers stationed at Buloh Blang Ara usually rotated every six months. Ayah continued to worry that his name was listed at the military base and police stations in Buloh Blang Ara. The authorities obtained names from their secret agents — or from the screams of a rebel, whose toenails and fingernails were pulled out one by one with pliers, before he was killed. It was a known fact that the names of Arkam and some of his followers were listed by both organizations as dangerous rebels they needed to eliminate.

Ayah would have been arrested a long time ago if his name had been listed. Even though Ayah's involvement as a camat only amounted to occasionally attending secret meetings, he would still face grave consequences.

However, it turned out that Ayah's name was never listed, and he did not need to run away and hide. Moreover, Arkam had openly declared himself the enemy of the central government, while Ayah was merely an undetected civil official, who never carried arms or boasted about his connection to the rebellion.

But Ayah could not tolerate living in constant uncertainty. Something unexpected could always crop up. A group of soldiers could suddenly appear to arrest or shoot him on the spot, making his wife a widow and his children fatherless.

Ayah wanted to tell his brother-in-law that the post he held made his life miserable; it could cause him to get killed anytime, just like the man who lived behind the mosque and was shot to death a few months ago.

---

Lately, Ayah split his time between waiting for Arkam at Leman's stall and working in the field. In the morning, he'd frequent the coffee stall and have long conversations with anyone who could relieve his anxiety. After he made sure Arkam would not come that day, he'd amble home.

Ibu had left with Zuhra to do the laundry at the stream. Baiti was tethering the goats in the backyard while collecting firewood and fallen candlenut, while Muha had already gone to the field. Raziah and her baby were the only ones home.

In the rainy season, the roads were usually covered in mud. This made it difficult for vehicles to pass through, even bicycles. Every day after school, I had to wash my shoes and school uniform at the stream where the water now had turned brown and murky. If by the next day my uniform had not dried, I'd have to skip school.

Just like any other young couple who found it difficult to live on their own, Muha and Raziah depended heavily on Ayah.

However, in times like these, Muha was the one who did most of the work.

Ayah never instructed him directly, but Muha already knew what needed to be done. When he was eight years old, his father died, and then Muha lived with his mother and younger sister until he married Raziah.

Ayah continued his daily routine. In the morning, he'd visit Leman's stall and chat with some people while waiting for Arkam. Then he'd briefly go home to have breakfast before heading to the field.

Ayah never asked me to come along to the field anymore. He didn't seem to care whether or not I helped him take care of the turmeric plants. I understood and accepted the changes in his behavior.

Usually, after noticing I did not wear my uniform for a few days in a row, Ayah would ask, "Why are you not going to school today, Zir?" and pay attention to my explanation. Lately, though, he seemed to ignore me.

As time passed, his conversations with people at the coffee stall managed to calm him down slightly. He noticed that people he met didn't seem too worried about kidnappings or murders, which were still happening in several villages.

Only once in a while would people be gripped by anxiety.

Baiti proved her point that Ayah's fear was unreasonable when Ayah began to realize that being a camat wasn't as life-threatening as it seemed, especially after he noticed some young men who had attended Arkam's meetings laughing carefreely in the streets.

When the women gathered in front of their houses, they only fleetingly mentioned the kidnappings. Even though they were still worried about the situation, they still loved to talk about family problems, clothes, furniture, and their dislike of someone.

Ibu did not like to gather with other women to gossip, and she forbade Baiti to do so. However, my sister often went visiting to one of the houses after she finished tying up the goats. When she returned without carrying any firewood or candlenuts, Ibu would question her.

"I've not been gossiping, Bu," Baiti protested.

"Then, what did you do?"

"I was just socializing."

Ibu did not respond. Her quarrel with Baiti would make the situation at home only more uncomfortable.

Usually, when Baiti was upset, she did not want to do any of her chores. She would lock herself in her room all day.

Ibu would have to tether the goats, wash the clothes, and collect the firewood to cook for two or three days. When Baiti no longer had the heart to let Ibu do all the housework, she'd slip into the kitchen after Maghrib.

Everyone had their own problems, and Raziah could not be relied on to do anything because she was busy with her baby, who often cried at night. Akbar's cry bothered everyone. But, there was nothing we could do except bear it, because he was a baby. Baiti simply covered her ears with a pillow when he screamed.

Muha did not always stay in our house. For two or three days every month, he would take Raziah to visit his mother in Cot Meureubo. When Muha was not around, Ayah went to the field and cleaned up the backyard by himself, and I would accompany him in the evenings.

Arkam visited Kakek and Nenek a couple of times around noon. After meeting with some people at Leman's stall, he'd take off on his motorcycle. Heading south, his roaring bike would disappear in the foothills where the rebels hid. He never came to see Ayah. Maybe he did not know Ayah was looking for him, or maybe he did not have a chance to visit. He also might consider Ayah unimportant.

Arkam always seemed to be high-spirited. He continued to spread propaganda for the resistance movement and recruit followers everywhere he went. Thus, the number of his supporters kept increasing in Alue Rambe, Lhok Jok, Blang Riek, Ceumpeudak, and other villages.

Most of Arkam's followers were not equipped with weapons or radios. Arkam tasked them to find out the recent moves of the soldiers. Some young men in my village often disappeared for two to three days. People assumed they were attending meetings with rebels who came from different places.

Arkam never seemed to involve Ayah in these meetings or respond to any of the messages Ayah left for him with Kakek.

"He said he can't meet with you right now," Kakek said when Ayah visited him.

"But this is very important."

"I heard that you're no longer a camat." Kakek glanced at Ayah.

"That's correct. I resigned. But Arkam needs to tell the *gubernur*," Ayah said, irritated.

"Okay, I'll tell him when he comes next time," Kakek replied.

After he came back from Kakek's house, Ayah smiled again. He no longer seemed to be haunted by worries about being a camat, and he began to live his life like he used to.

In early 1991, Arkam and some of his friends appeared in Leman's stall. Their number had increased. From just eight of them at first, there were now a few dozen of them. They enjoyed their morning coffee as if nothing had happened.

*Arafat Nur*

Yasin, a quiet boy who lived on Kakek's street, had joined Arkam's troop. At first, he was equipped with a handheld radio and tasked to report on the soldiers' movement. Some other youth, who lived along the road to Simpang Mawak, were handed a similar radio. They were to report immediately when they saw any military heading for Alue Rambe.

One day, I saw Yasin carry an M16. The weapon had been seized during one of the attacks on the military. His radio had been assigned to someone else. Yasin, who was well built, proudly carried the weapon. Being a soldier was his childhood dream, and he never once missed any of the war movies that were shown on the television at Leman's coffee stall.

Because Yasin did not graduate from elementary school, he definitely could not be accepted into military school. Even if he had finished high school, his father would not have had the money to bribe the officials. At that time, it was no secret that anyone who wanted to work as a soldier, police officer, teacher, or civil servant had to bribe officials in charge of the hiring. It did not matter how smart or qualified you were; without the bribes, it was impossible to get accepted for these positions.

"I'm a soldier now," Yasin proudly exclaimed.

Arkam slapped him on the shoulder and said, "In times of emergencies, your ability to handle the gun is more needed than merely operating a radio. But don't be careless. Learn to shoot well. Never treat your weapon as a toy, like you did when we first met, a year ago."

Yasin blushed.

Arkam usually divided his unit into small groups of three to four people. This made it difficult for the soldiers to chase them. After they attacked a patrol, the small group of rebels would run for cover in the jungle, which was unfamiliar terrain for the soldiers. The rebels could easily disguise themselves as farmers and hide their weapons anywhere in the fields.

The palm, areca, candlenut, and cacao farms around Alue Rambe became the safest hiding places for the rebels. The vast, uninhabited areas dotted with neglected, damaged dangaus provided Arkam and his friends with a perfect hiding place.

Cloudy morning skies often wrapped the village in a solemn atmosphere. Once the sun moved west, the sky cleared. A couple of Arkam's followers were sent to Simpang Mawak to harass some soldiers on patrol. The random shots created chaos among the soldiers, whose only combat experience was the training they had received in military school. It galled them that the Acehnese, who were ordinary villagers without any kind of power, had the courage to attack them.

Arkam staged these attacks to scare off the soldiers and also to tire them out.

Because the attacks often occurred in the areas around Simpang Mawak and the villages behind the Buloh Blang Ara market, the soldiers who patrolled those areas often struck out in blind anger.

Every time an attack on the military bases or police stations occurred, the school automatically closed, because neither teachers nor students would come. When Arkam attacked the base at Buloh Blang Ara, my school shut down for almost a month. Later on, I discovered that during that time, only the schools in Lhokseumawe could continue their activities in accordance with the academic calendar.

Then news spread that soldiers started to kidnap people of Simpang Mawak who were suspected of supporting the rebellion. During a sudden street search, a young man, caught holding a handheld radio, was shot in the head.

No one dared to claim the body, until his father came and quietly took his son's corpse home. Not many people attended his funeral, and no one came to mourn. The military did not allow any gatherings. It did not matter what the gathering was for, whether it was a festivity or a study group.

One evening, Ayah went to visit Kakek and asked, "Did you give my message to Arkam?"

Kakek looked puzzled at Ayah's pale face. "What was I supposed to tell him?"

"I told you a month ago, I don't want to be camat anymore," Ayah replied, fastening his eyes on Kakek.

"Goodness," Kakek said pensively. "I forgot about it."

"How could you forget about it?" Ayah asked, annoyed.

Kakek was quiet for a while, then said, "Isn't he often seen at Leman's? Why don't you just tell him yourself?"

Ayah's face dropped. The matter of his camat position was actually still unresolved. He walked home, grumbling. If Kakek were not his father-in-law, he surely would have punched him in the face.

One afternoon, Nono and I followed Ayah to Yasin's house.

Yasin was often seen with Arkam, but unlike the other rebels, he always returned home at the end of the day.

Ayah tried to persuade Yasin to tell the gubernur that he no longer could act as a camat.

"I don't even know what he looks like." Yasin threw Ayah a puzzled look.

"You never met him?" Ayah looked confused.

"Until the day he died, I never met him."

"He died?"

"You didn't know that, Pak Camat?"

"Don't call me that," Ayah snapped, as his jaw tightened. "How did he die?"

"Gubernur Yusuf passed away a few months ago."

Yasin continued to explain that the gubernur was shot to death by soldiers not far from the rebels' base. A bullet went to his neck, and two others hit his chest. The soldiers captured his guards and seized all his files that related to their secret meetings.

Perhaps Ayah's preoccupation with himself had caused him to miss the news of the gubernur's death among the regular reports of arrests, shootings, kidnappings, and murders.

That night, Ayah returned to the field with his mosquito net, pillow, and sarong.

Nono went with him.

## CHAPTER 6

In early March 1992, there was no more rain, and by noon, the hot sun wilted the young corn, long beans, mung beans, and mountain *padi*. Dirt roads started to solidify. Farmers' fields were no longer muddy, and shrubs welcomed Arkam's troops with soft pricks of thorny branches. The warm, dry weather made it easy for Arkam and his friends to intercept military convoys that travelled on the main roads between districts.

Compared to the earlier massive attacks led by Ishak Daud, Arkam's small assaults were insignificant but enough to overwhelm and anger the government's army.

Two days before the month of *Ramadan*, the Muslim fasting period which, that year, fell in mid-March, Arkam and five of his subordinates held up a small military unit near Lhok Jok and Ceumpeudak.

I was out of school for the Ramadan holiday and with Ibu, who was doing the laundry at the stream, when we suddenly heard the artillery fire.

Ibu immediately grabbed Zuhra and rushed home, abandoning her laundry, while I ran to the turmeric field where Ayah and Muha were working.

I found them standing near the dangau. Ayah stood in the scorching heat, holding his straw hat in his hand. His head cocked, he looked up to the bleak, cloudless sky filled with the rattling of gunshots.

The noise came from the west, around the bridge of Buloh Blang Ara, and slowly moved east, toward us.

"This place doesn't even allow me to live in peace," Ayah grumbled.

Muha took off his straw hat and threw it into the dangau. Rubbing his crooked mouth, he said, "I better go home," and pulled my hand.

Ayah nodded. He didn't seem to care.

I followed Muha, maneuvering between the collapsed turmeric plants with leaves that had yellowed. Half of the thick, orange rhizomes protruded from the ground, ready to be harvested. The current low selling price kept Ayah from harvesting them.

When we arrived at home, the succession of gunfire lessened until it finally disappeared. We could hear a small commotion coming from Leman's stall. Some men headed there, and I followed them, even though Ibu told me not to.

On the streets, people's excited whispers were occasionally interrupted by cheers supporting Arkam's attack. Only a few men were drinking coffee inside the stall. Most of the people were standing around outside. It seemed that everyone was waiting for something to happen. Meanwhile the thick, jungle-like growth of the plantations that spread from northwest to south now seemed peaceful.

I figured that Arkam and his men were now hiding from the soldiers who tried to retaliate.

After a while, Arkam appeared from the bushes by the downhill road. The leather strap of his M16 was slung on his shoulder. His thick brown shirt was soaked with sweat. The sides of his crumpled cap were also wet, and sweat streamed down his temples, forming waterlines by his ears. Panting, he repeatedly wiped his forehead with his arm and scanned the area behind him.

Breathing hard, he yelled, "Death to those dogs from Jakarta. We killed three of them today."

After Arkam and his men reunited, it was very noisy for a moment. Stomping around panting, their bodies drenched in sweat, they quickly retrieved the three motorbikes they had left hidden in the bushes earlier and drove off heading north.

We were left with the faint roar of their bikes as they disappeared into the hills.

The sun was getting hotter as noon arrived. A hawk hovered in the sky above a brood of chickens wandering around in an open space near the bicycle repair shop. When the hawk shrieked, the chicks quickly rushed to their mothers.

I left the people who stayed to have lunch in Leman's stall and went home.

Arkam had told the truth when he said they had shot three soldiers. However, later that afternoon, someone said that only one was dead, while the other two survived. Soon after that, a military unit arrived and beat up dozens of villagers in Lhok Jok and Ceumpeudak, where they set fire to five houses.

That noon incident also resulted in an intensive search in the villages in the vicinity of where the shooting had occurred. Of course, the culprits were nowhere to be found. Still, the military continued to check everyone they met, asking for names, number of family members, and their whereabouts at the time the incident occurred.

The next day, around mid-morning, some thirty soldiers appeared in Tamoun. It was *Meughang,* the day before the Ramadan fasting period started. On this day, the Acehnese bought beef or other meats to cook and share with family members, relatives, and orphans.

The soldiers ordered all villagers to gather on the open field in front of the mosque.

The women, who were in the midst of preparing the meal for Meughang, were forced to leave their houses with the doors wide open. The soldiers then freely entered and ransacked the empty houses. No one could avoid the soldiers, who stopped everyone on the street.

Ayah and Muha, who did not go to the field that day, were already herded outside.

I followed Ibu, Raziah, and Baiti.

Ibu carried Zuhra, while Raziah carried Akbar, who cried as soon as he was carried outside.

"What did I do wrong?" Baiti snapped defiantly when a soldier forced her to go outside.

The soldier threw her a grim look and growled, "Shut up, bitch."

Ignoring Ibu's look telling her to obey, Baiti continued to challenge the soldier.

Irritated, he shoved her with the tip of his rifle.

Baiti screamed, then walked trembling in the direction the soldier had shoved her.

All men and women — old and young — children, babies, the sick, and disabled were gathered in the open grassy field in front of the mosque. The morning sun soon stung everyone's skin, blinded everyone's eyes. The large field, usually used by the villagers to dry their padi grains and betel nuts, was now filled with hundreds of trembling villagers whose bare feet and rubber slippers crushed the young grass. Not one man was spared from being slapped, punched, and kicked. Ayah, Kakek, and Muha were no exception. Every time someone got hit, a commotion broke out, even though the villagers did not fight back.

I sat curled up near Ibu, Baiti, and Raziah, who carried her baby. The women covered their faces with their hands. Most of them were squatting. The old women sat on the ground.

The soldiers' shouting as they beat up the people sounded as if they were possessed. Every time a soldier threatened, kicked, or stabbed someone's back with a rifle handle, the women near the victim screamed hysterically before clamping their hands over their mouths while saying the name of God. There was crying and screaming everywhere.

Ayah's face was swollen from the punches he received. Muha's lower lip was split and his chin was bloody.

There was not one man who did not get hit. It was as if all the villagers of Alue Rambe were held responsible for Arkam's attack. It seemed that the soldiers thought that it would have been impossible for the rebellion to develop and attack the military without the villagers' support.

"Do you know where you went wrong?" yelled a sturdy man, who was referred to as commander and seemed to be more educated than the others. "You're raising rebels. You're supporting the country's enemy. You're cooperating with them. You're a bunch of losers." The commander continued his rant while kicking at the men who stood in the front row. "Don't try to fight the army. You'll all end up dead. For every soldier you dare to kill, we will kill an entire village. We will burn your houses down." He had a wild look in his eyes. "Where's Hasan

Tiro? The bastard is abroad, enjoying himself in Malaysia. You've all been cheated."

When the commander finally ran out of words, he fell silent.

A soldier with a thick mustache drew his bayonet and slashed off a young man's ear. The longhaired man screamed. He covered the left side of his head with his hand, moaning. Thick blood reddened his hand and temple, flowing to his neck and onto his clothes. Tears blended with his perspiration.

The soldier laughed and slashed off the man's other ear. Screaming, the man placed his hands over the places where his ears used to be. Blood seeped between his fingers onto his wrists.

After the soldier returned his bayonet to its case, he picked up the ears. Holding each ear between the thumb and index finger of each hand, he waved both ears at the people, who were horrified. The two bloody ears, separated from their owner's body, looked strangely disgusting.

That soldier took the ears to a corner of the field where the women crouched in fear. Their wailing filled the air.

"Shut up, you bitches," the soldier shouted.

The stench of urine and people passing gas filled the air. Some people pinched their noses while others did not seem to care.

"Ears," the soldier lectured, "are used to listen. But none of you listened to what we said. Therefore, these ears were useless."

After standing for hours, people's legs and feet were giving out and cramping.

The sky was very bright, the sunlight blinding. A hawk perched on a tree branch. Shrieking, the vulture identified food. The scorching heat added to the injuries of the tortured bodies. The blood on their faces and arms had dried out.

Past noon, the soldiers who had ransacked the empty houses replaced the soldiers who were guarding the villagers. One of the soldiers, in passing, hit Muha on the head with the handle of his gun, and blood seeped to Muha's forehead.

That was the beginning of my deep hatred of soldiers, which remained until I became an adult. If only I had supernatural powers, such as an immunity to weapons, or owned a magic weapon, I would surely have killed them all. But at that time, I did not even dare to look at a soldier's face. My whole body trembled each time a soldier passed me.

The second round of torture was delivered by the commander's deputy.

There were some villagers who could no longer stand; they could only sit or squat. Others had collapsed to the ground, but the soldiers forced them to stand again. Meanwhile, the man whose ears had been cut off was left cringing.

"This is what happens when you disobey us," shouted the deputy commander, with one hand on his hip. "This is nothing. Many of our soldiers were killed."

He continued to deliver a long speech about the uselessness of rebelling against the government. He pointed out that it was impossible to build a country within a country. He said the rebels had chosen the wrong road and were harming their own people. Their actions, he said, would bring suffering to the people of Aceh.

"If you're good, we'll be good to you as well," he said firmly and ended, "Do you understand?"

"Understood," the crowd answered in unison.

"Hey, you with the crooked mouth." The deputy commander turned to Muha. "What's your name?"

"Mu-Muha, sir," Muha stammered. The blood on his forehead had begun to dry.

"Are you a rebel?"

"No, sir," Muha answered weakly.

"Do you understand what I said?"
"I do, sir."
"What is it? Repeat."
"If you're good, we'll be good as well."
"Asshole," the deputy commander cursed. "How dare you mock me with your crooked mouth."

Muha stayed quiet.

The deputy commander walked closer and looked closely at Muha's mouth.

"Why's your mouth crooked?"

"Got slapped by Satan, sir."

The commander laughed. The other soldiers joined in.

However, none of the people who were being tortured laughed. They looked like young plants wilting in the heat. Aside from being deprived of food and drink, they could not move around. They were left to dry in the hot sun like padi grain and betel nut. Perspiration covered their entire bodies, and they could only wipe their faces repeatedly.

Ayah's left cheek was bruised and swollen, but he seemed to ignore it. He looked down, just like the other helpless men. No one dared to move, afraid to attract the attention of the soldiers and be beaten again. They looked stiff, filled with anxiety. No one could do anything, except wait for the next thing to unfold.

I could not bear to see Ayah's and everyone's condition. Feeling helpless, hurt, and broken, I turned away from them. Through it all, I was grateful that apparently the soldiers didn't know that Ayah was a camat in the resistance.

In the afternoon, the commander traded places again with his deputy. He repeated his previous speech incoherently to an inattentive audience. Suffering from thirst and hunger, the villagers merely listened without digesting anything he said.

Once in a while, the crowd answered a question in unison, while moving their legs. Half of them had already collapsed with no one ordering them to get up. It seemed the soldiers were actually tired as well. Some looked for shade under the trees; others went to Leman's stall.

When Zuhra whined that she was hungry, Ibu immediately put her hand over my sister's mouth, which made her curl back up in Ibu's arms.

Raziah kept Akbar's head and body covered under a batik cloth. Every time he made a sound, Raziah held him to her breast. The other women who carried their babies did the same. Meanwhile, their children were forced to remain in the scorching heat.

The odor of urine filled the air. Not only did small children and babies wet their pants, some of the women did, too. Some women stood in their urine-soaked skirts or sarongs.

When evening came, the people could no longer stand. Some chose to squat; others sat with their legs stretched out.

None of the soldiers, who sat in the shade under the trees, came to them.

The speaker now was the deputy. "Remember, if you continue to support the rebels, I'll kill all of you and burn down this village," he said with forced enthusiasm.

The commander took over again. He paced in the shadow of the trees, where his deputy and some soldiers were drinking coffee served by Leman's wife.

While the soldiers sipped their coffee, the thirsty and hungry people watched them, their mouths watering.

"Be law-abiding citizens and don't oppose us. We are defending the country. It's not right to be hostile toward us. We are good people. We don't like violence. We don't like to beat anyone up. We don't even have the heart to hurt an animal." The commander's speech was the opposite of what they had just done. "Do you understand?"

"Understood," the people, including Ayah, answered in unison.

After that, we were allowed to go home. Almost everyone walked with a limp.

When I began walking, my thighs were numb. I quickly moved away from the women, which freed me from the urine and fart odor. There were many men who had urinated in their pants, as well. Some people, who had not urinated while standing in the field, now rushed to the bushes behind Leman's stall to relieve themselves.

We found our house in complete disarray. Spilled rice dotted the floor from the kitchen to the living room. The pages from my textbooks were scattered between clothes, diapers, Ibu's shawl, and kitchen rags. Pots and pans were overturned. But we were too tired to clean everything up.

There was no water in the kettle. Our stomachs were empty, and intense thirst choked our throats.

We drank the unboiled water left in a pail. There was not even one spoonful of rice left inside the pot. The Meughang meat, which we did not have a chance to taste that afternoon, was gone, too. The soldiers had robbed us of all our food.

Raziah came out of her room, sobbing.

"Why are you crying?" Ayah asked.

"My necklace is gone." Raziah lamented the loss of her golden necklace, which Muha had given her as part of her dowry.

Ayah rushed into his room and checked his closet. He came back and said sluggishly, "They took all of my money."

Meanwhile, Ibu seemed to strengthen herself, trying not to care. She swept up the spilled rice and added it to the little bit of leftover rice in the sack.

The next day, almost all the villagers I met complained about missing money and valuables, which the soldiers had stolen. That was the miserable first day of fasting.

Even though gossiping was forbidden during fasting, the villagers still muttered about losing their valuables and not having any food. Moreover, their bodies still hurt from yesterday's torture. I heard that many villagers could not even get up that morning due to cramps in their calves, after standing for such a long time in the field. Some had a fever and could not get out of bed. Hence, they were forced to abandon their fasting.

# Chapter 7

On the third day of fasting, all of us – except Raziah and Akbar – went to the field to harvest turmeric. The dewdrops on leaves and grasses soon evaporated in the breezy, warm weather. Sunlight edged the dark green leaves. The mosquitoes and gnats hid in the lush cacao bushes, with yellowish and brownish-black pods dotting the branches.

For the turmeric harvest, Ayah and Ibu wore straw hats and old, long-sleeved shirts. After pulling the plants, they shook off the soil that still clung to the tubers, then cut the plant at its base to separate it from the tubers. They made separate mounds of tubers and brush as they moved along the rows.

Ayah's face was not swollen anymore, but he had lost his spirit, just like other men I met after the group of soldiers came to torture the villagers of Alue Rambe.

Muha collected the mounds of turmeric tubers in a used plastic rice sack. He didn't seem to care about the cut on his lip. His head wound was covered by his thick black hair and protected by the straw hat that shaded his face.

Baiti and I did the same. Filling our white plastic sacks with turmeric tubers, we estimated the weight. We carried the full bags home and poured our load onto the porch floor, in a square marked off by four wooden two-by-fours.

I could only carry sacks of around eleven to fifteen pounds of turmeric comfortably. I had to lug my load up a slanted, climbing road, which quickly tired me. Perspiration covered my back and face, and my mouth felt very dry.

Baiti walked right behind me.

We intentionally delayed our return to the field, and no one hurried us.

Only Muha quietly worked without breaks or any pretense.

During the fasting, we could neither eat nor drink. Not being able to eat did not bother me. But if I did not drink, my body felt weak, and my throat felt dry, which made me not want to speak. I had perspired so much that I felt as if my body was squeezed dry.

Baiti and I reluctantly returned to the field.

Unless it was necessary, Ayah, Ibu, Muha, and Baiti did not speak to each other while working.

Zuhra was the only one who gibbered to herself while playing with a piece of turmeric tuber behind Ibu. Her small face was covered by Raziah's straw hat, and she kept pushing up the rim with her yellow-stained hands. When she managed to lift the tip of the hat, the beads of perspiration dripping down her creamy cheeks glistened in the sunlight.

We startled when three soldiers appeared out of nowhere in the turmeric field.

Ayah was cutting a turmeric stem and was so shocked, his knife slipped and cut his thumb.

Once they saw we were busily at work, the soldiers returned to the pathway. Four other soldiers appeared at the corner of the street and joined them. Each carried a long-barreled gun.

"What do they want now?" Muha mumbled.

"They couldn't have looked for Ayah," Baiti said, staring at the soldiers' backs as they walked away. "They saw it themselves: Ayah is not a rebel."

While pinching his left thumb to prevent blood loss, Ayah ran to the dangau and took off his hat. A few drops of blood seeped to the base of his hurt thumb.

Nono, who was sleeping under the dangau, woke up and looked at him.

Ibu hurried to pick some young miracle leaves. The plants grew in the wild next to the mung bean field. She crushed the leaves by squeezing them between her palms as she turned them. She then placed the thick green pulp directly on the cut in Ayah's thumb.

Ayah groaned, "Ouch, that stings."

"Luckily, your finger isn't gone." Ibu tore a strip of the batik sling she always carried around in case Zuhra said she was too tired to walk.

Ayah sat in the dangau, drenched in perspiration. His thin hair clung to his scalp. He said, "If I lost it, I wouldn't be able to work anymore."

"Nazir, take the bag of turmeric you collected home," Ibu said.

Reluctantly, I hoisted the full bag of turmeric onto my shoulders. Staggering, I found my balance and started back on the slightly uphill pathway. Huffing and puffing with my whole body hurting, I made it home. After I emptied the bag, I sat down to rest under the guava tree.

I purposely did not return to the field. Instead, I headed to the end of the alley in the opposite direction of the field. I felt bad for slacking off, but I was very tired and my mouth was really dry. I so badly wanted to slip into the kitchen and gulp down a cup of water. However, although no one would know, I didn't dare do it.

Not far from the entrance of the alley, I suddenly saw a group of soldiers coming from the direction of Kakek's house. I stopped in my tracks. My heart throbbed. I stooped and crawled into the brush along the street to a palm tree surrounded by bushes that were waist-high. Peering between the branches, I watched the soldiers gather at Leman's stall.

After the last soldiers disappeared, I ran through the alleys behind the wooden houses, ignoring my fear. I pretended to be a rebel who was on a spying mission. Maybe this was the effect of the Saturday night war movies I had watched at Leman's coffee stall. My fear was overcome by my desire to fight back, something that lately helped me understand the reason behind the Acehnese's courage to fight the soldiers.

All the doors of the wooden houses I passed were closed. However, I was certain that the residents were home and peeking out. I concluded with much relief that the soldiers had not come to round up the villagers again but merely to show off their power.

I climbed into a jackfruit tree not far behind Leman's stall. A group of soldiers was fighting over a cluster of warangan banana, a type of banana that mainly grew in northern Sumatra, that they brought out from a stall. Even though it was the fasting month, the stalls were still open. The villagers still needed to buy rice, flour, cooking oil, and other daily necessities.

After the soldiers finished the bananas, they lumbered off in the direction they came from.

I dragged myself home in the burning heat. After taking off my sweaty shirt, I lay down on my bed. A gentle breeze soon put me fast to sleep.

When I woke up at dusk, I felt as if I had lost all my strength. I found Ibu in the backyard chopping up the dried coconut husk that Baiti had gathered earlier for kindling.

Muha and Ayah came back from the field carrying sacks of turmeric. Careful not to damage the rhizomes, they emptied the bags. The gathered turmeric formed a mound as high as my waist.

"You don't need to help carry the turmeric home," Ayah said before returning to the field with Muha. "Just clean up the goat shed and burn the trash. Don't forget to move the goats. They're not fasting."

Not only were the goats not fasting, but many of the Alue Rambe villagers were not fasting, as well. Those who were working the fields openly brought along food and water bottles. My family was religious and did not dare to disobey God's law.

Aside from Zuhra, who was still too young to participate in the daily five-time praying ritual, Baiti was the only one who was lax about it. When Ibu checked on her, she always claimed to be on her menstrual period. One time I noticed that despite her claim, there were no used sanitary napkins thrown into the trash hole behind the house. Even during the fasting month, Baiti, on several occasions, missed Zuhr and Asr prayers, and even often missed the Fajr prayer.

Breaking the fast was something I looked forward to the most. While my body got weaker and I lost my energy, I waited impatiently for the moment. The fresh, young coconut water and *kolak ubi*, a yam stew prepared with coconut milk, pandan leaves, and palm sugar — or mung bean porridge on other days — along with various delicious dishes Ibu had prepared, were so good. I didn't know of any food that tasted better than the food Ibu prepared to break the fast.

At sundown, some of the chickens went back into their coop while others flew into the jackfruit tree behind the house. The pile of trash in the goat shed was lit to chase away the mosquitoes and gnats.

My patience was really tried during the minutes just before the *bedug*, or mosque drum, was sounded. The served food made my mouth water, and I had to swallow several times to clear my mouth. Even though, unlike previous years, there were no meat dishes, and the rice was only served with *urap* — a salad of steamed vegetables mixed with seasoned coconut gratings — along with spinach soup, kolak ubi, and young coconut water — the very simple meal tasted delicious when someone was very thirsty and hungry.

As soon as the sound of the bedug was heard, I didn't know which dish to eat first. The quiet of Maghrib was soon exchanged with the clinking of glasses, bowls, and plates. Wars and other fears were forgotten as we broke the fast. None of us felt like talking, except for Zuhra, who exclaimed, "I want the kolak ubi, too!"

With a full stomach, I forced myself to perform the Maghrib prayer in my room. Then, with my back leaning against the headboard of my bed, I studied some textbooks, until the call for the Isha prayer came from the mosque.

During fasting month, I only twice joined the *tarawih* congregations, the optional congregational night prayers only performed during Ramadan, with twenty *raka'at*, or prayer units, excluding four raka'at of Isha and three raka'at of *witr*, or supererogatory night prayer with odd number of raka'at.

Some older people performed two raka'at of *rawatib*, a voluntary prayer offered before the main obligatory prayer, before and after Isha. This was followed by the *tadarus,* or reciting the Quran together by those who excelled in reciting the holy text.

During this year's fasting month, people did not perform the Quran recitation after the tarawih prayer. Due to the curfew, only a dozen people from around Tamoun joined the tarawih congregation. No one could predict what the soldiers in Simpang Mawak would do next. Those couriers of disaster kept moving closer to my village.

After an afternoon of hard work, everyone except Ayah fell asleep. In the dim light of a small oil lamp, he sat by himself in the kitchen quietly rolling his nipa palm leaf cigarette. He no longer cursed Arkam.

The next day, at Leman's stall, the village chief announced an order for villagers to install outdoor lights. He stated that he would not be responsible for the consequences for those who ignored the order. The Alue Rambe villagers were known to often disobey God's laws and ignore the mandatory cleanup around houses and mosques, but no one dared to defy orders issued by the military. Everyone was familiar with the beatings that the soldiers were capable of administering.

Soon after the village chief announced the warning, the village burst into a bustle of activities. The sounds of saws cutting wooden boards, axes chopping logs, and hammers hitting nails filled the air. Sometimes, the construction sounds were interrupted by people's conversation. That day, almost all men, including Ayah, left their work in the field.

Only Muha tended to the field. He gathered the turmeric that had been left in the field the day before and carried the load home.

Ayah chopped down one of the large trees near the cemetery. A long, straight branch, as thick as his arm, was going to be used as a post. Using a tape measure, Ayah then cut up the rest of the wood to size. While working on the frame of his lamp house, he told me to go to Kakek's house and fetch two pieces of woven sago palm leaf roofing.

"Tell your father to come here. I can't make that lamppost," Kakek said.

I nodded and picked up two pieces of woven roofing. With a lot of trouble, I carried the large mats under low-growing areca and candlenut trees, up the winding, uphill alley to my house.

I put down the two pieces of roofing and then helped Ayah hold the wood so it would not move while he sawed it. Ayah had designed a lamp house with a floor that was a twelve-inch square. The walls around it were about eighteen inches tall. He cut three triangles out of Kakek's woven roof panels and assembled them to cover the house. The lamp house rested on a pole that was my shoulder's height.

Overcome by a terrible thirst, I rushed to the kitchen. I took a plastic cup from the dish rack and filled it with water from the kettle. I gulped down all of it. Still unsatisfied, I poured another half cup and drank until nothing was left. The cool water flowed from my throat into my chest cavity and into my stomach.

"Did you just drink something?" Baiti asked, surprised.

Baiti's question confused me. *Why was she surprised to see me drink?* I said, "Yes. What's wrong with it?"

"Aren't you fasting?"

"Oh, my God!" I screamed. "I forgot."

Even though I had already been fasting for a few days, there were still times I forgot about it. Ayah told me that it was okay if one forgot. It would not invalidate his fast.

Now, Ayah had to go to Kakek's house, and I helped him carry his tools. On our way, Ayah cut off two large branches of trees growing in the wild near Kakek's fields. The wood of those branches was hard and would hold up in bad weather.

Kakek and Nenek were lying on the divan on their porch. Kakek complained about his flaring back pain. His left eye, which was injured when a soldier slapped him a few days ago, had healed. Lately, Kakek worried. It seemed that the soldiers had finally discovered that the rebellion leader in Alue Rambe was his son. Thus, he believed that every night, soldiers watched his house secretly.

"I can't live with soldiers spying on me," Kakek complained.

"What can we do about it?" Nenek asked.

"I don't know." Kakek watched Ayah saw a piece of wood under the mango tree. "I can't think. Every era has its own changes, has its own generation. This is not my era anymore."

"Can't you forbid Arkam?" Nenek asked.

"How can I?" Kakek answered with another question. "This is his struggle. That's all. What can I do? I'll just have to leave everything with Allah."

"But now, none of us can live in peace anymore," Nenek replied.

"I haven't been able to sleep well for the past month," Ayah suddenly interrupted and stopped working for a moment.

Kakek seemed cornered. After remaining quiet for a while, he replied, "At my age, I should be able to live in peace. So later, I can die in peace, too."

"I also don't want to live in constant fear," Ayah said, frustrated.

Because of Arkam, Ayah was now involved in the rebellion even though he had not done anything that warranted labeling him as a rebel. As an ordinary farmer, my father only worked in the field. Now he was listed not only as a member of the rebellion but also as a high-ranking official. At least in our village, a camat was considered that.

In Aceh, none of the high-ranking government officials ever visited the villages. Even the government's camat had never set foot in this village. That's why no one in our village knew what he looked like. The villagers believed that his only job was to sign papers.

Nenek repeatedly wiped her tears with her shawl and said, "I can't bear to see people beaten like that. Why did Allah send those demons to this village?"

Ayah didn't respond. He flattened the remaining small branches with his machete and measured them. Four planks were needed to build the frame of the walls and roof. For its base, Ayah used a board, as wide as the base of an oil lamp. Kakek's lamp house was exactly like the one Ayah had built for our house.

When we came home, Muha had finished attaching the roof to our lamp house, which was erected in the middle of our yard. I liked it and kept looking at it. In the evening, before it turned dark, I placed a small oil lamp inside the lamp house and lit it.

I should actually have used the big oil lamp. However, because the soldiers had stolen all of our money, we had to use kerosene sparingly.

As soon as we finished breaking the fast, the big oil lamp from the living room was moved to the lamp house, and I took the small lamp to my room. I enjoyed being in the well-lit yard. It was even brighter outside than in the house. Because other people's yards were also lit, the entire village looked bright at night instead of dark and gloomy like before. But there was a curfew, so no one could enjoy these beautiful bright nights except for the rebels who were spying on the military and the soldiers who were spying on the rebels.

The atmosphere of this year's Ramadan nights was very quiet and oppressive even though the illuminated yards made the nights more vibrant. No one dared to leave their house after nine o'clock. There was no sound coming from the tadarus activity. It was replaced with the sound of a lathe coming from the bushes. The oil lamps in the villagers' yards burned silently until the morning arrived; the flames dwindled, and the light dimmed because it ran out of oil, and the soot stained the glass chimney.

---

Due to Ayah's unwillingness to use the money earned from selling the turmeric harvest to buy rice, kerosene, and other necessities, no one wore new clothes during this year's *Eid al-Fitr*, the religious holiday marking the end of Ramadan, except for Zuhra and Akbar.

Ayah delivered his long-winded advice. "You need to replace your school uniform. Prioritize the more important things. Why would you buy new clothes when you can't go out freely? We *did* harvest a lot of turmeric, but it only made a little amount of money. We can't blame the wholesalers in the city for paying such a low price. They have to go through so many military posts during the transportation of the goods. Every post will ask for money. These are illegal charges. It's extortion. I don't believe the military are defending the people."

Actually, I really wanted to wear a pair of long jeans for this year's Eid al-Fitr, since I was already in middle school. Unfortunately, I had to wear my shorts again, with a shirt that Ibu had managed to hide and looked quite new. I was really embarrassed when we visited Kakek's house and met my visiting uncles, aunts, and cousins, who all wore new clothes.

I had seven maternal uncles and aunties. Except for Arkam, everyone came to visit this year. Most of them lived in North Aceh and in the suburbs of Lhokseumawe. Only a few of them lived in Lhokseumawe itself. Ibu never took me there to visit.

*Arafat Nur*

My uncles and aunts rode their motorbikes. They complained about the many checkpoints they needed to pass. They told us how they were bullied and insulted in front of their children. They said that the checkpoint at Simpang Mawak was the worst. They had to leave their IDs and were ordered to return before nighttime.

One of my aunts asked about Arkam.

When Kakek told them that Arkam was involved in the resistance movement, my uncles and aunts turned pale. After a long pause, they began whispering to each other nervously.

I understood their precarious situation if the soldiers found out that the rebellion leader of this village was their brother.

They left before the Asr, earlier than was planned. It seemed they tried to avoid meeting Arkam. They hugged Kakek and Nenek with tears in their eyes and hurried to leave.

That night, Ayah was once again plagued with anxiety. Pacing between the living room and the kitchen, he often peered through the windows while pressing his body against the wall as if he was afraid there was someone out there aiming a rifle at him. Ayah's behavior disturbed everyone. It seemed life no longer held any peace.

"You'll get sick if you continue to stress like this," Ibu warned.

Ayah replied, "Who can stay calm having to live under these threats?"

Ayah once told us that he had always hated violence. Since childhood, he avoided problems. The camat position terrified him, as it was related to the rebellion, and it was public knowledge that the military killed every rebel and often tortured his family.

When daylight tumbled into my room through the window, I got up.

In the kitchen, Ibu was cooking rice. She looked pale and her eyes were swollen, but she exuded a stubbornness. "We need to eat," she said.

After staying up all night long, Ayah's fatigue finally caught up with him and he had fallen asleep on the bench in the living room.

After Ibu made sure that he was asleep, she turned to me and, tapping her lips with her index finger, she whispered, "Be quiet. Let Ayah sleep."

# Chapter 8

The military violence during Meughang had turned Alue Rambe into a war zone like no other. Dozens of soldiers wandered everywhere with their rifles aimed at the villagers' homes.

In the field, Ayah and Muha cleared the brush under the areca and candlenut trees. The mung beans were harvested two months ago. Now, that field was fallow. In the dry season, it could not produce anything. The drought didn't seem to impact the wild grasses. They still thrived and reclaimed the land as if it should have been theirs in the first place.

The June sun forced its light through the foliage of the water apple tree in front of my house. The intense heat scorched the open area of the front yard around the lamp house. Suddenly, several soldiers appeared in front of our house. Two walked towards the cemetery, while the rest went to the stream. One of them entered the yard and shouted, "Get out. All of you, out to the street, pigs."

Startled, I started shaking. It was as if something drained my energy. I broke into a sweat. My heart pounded, and I was afraid I would faint.

"Everyone, get out." The shouting sapped the last of my energy.

Ibu walked out carrying Zuhra in her arms. Raziah followed with Akbar in her arms. Both looked ashen.

When the soldier grabbed Raziah's hand, she screamed, then quickly covered her mouth with her other hand.

Baiti shuffled out. She too had no color in her face. She screamed when the soldier tried to touch her.

The soldier then turned to me and poked me with the tip of his rifle. "Where are the others?" he asked.

Ibu, Raziah, and Baiti bowed, hiding their faces. Zuhra cried in Ibu's arms. Akbar was quiet. Raziah had probably slipped her breast into his mouth.

"Where are the others?" the soldier hollered.

Ibu and Raziah started to shake. Dark spots began to show on their skirts and soon liquid dripped from under those skirts onto the floor.

In the alley, soldiers stomped around, yelling profanities and curses.

Ayah and Muha came running from a side of the yard. They were barefoot and empty-handed. They probably had taken off their boots, which would easily attract the soldiers' attention, and left their machetes behind so they would not be considered armed.

"I'm sorry, sir, we just came from the field." Ayah bowed his head respectfully.

"Yeah, I bet you did," the soldier sneered.

Muha moved toward Raziah, but was stopped by a soldier who slapped him before turning to Ayah and slapping him as well.

When the soldier was about to hit Ayah again, Nono came running from behind the house and attacked the soldier, who quickly turned to Nono and kicked him with his combat boot.

Nono yelped as he tumbled.

The soldier raised his gun, and Ayah growled, "Stupid dog. Get lost."

As the gunshot cracked the air, Mother and Raziah shrieked, and all of us fell to the ground.

A loud yelp came from behind the house.

I imagined Nono's sprawled body after being hit by a hot bullet.

When Nono yelped, Ayah's face turned even whiter. Tears rolled down his cheeks.

I quickly turned around, pretending not to see it.

Meanwhile, the soldier rushed into the house. A few minutes later, he returned to the yard without closing the door. Another soldier, who was drenched in perspiration, herded us to the street, where a group of other villagers stood under guard.

On the main road, some people were herded at gunpoint to an open field in front of the same mosque that the same soldiers had used to torture people from my village.

Two soldiers came from the north end of the road, pushing Yasin, who was limping. Fresh blood dripped from his calf; his left eye was swollen shut.

"You were involved in the attack Arkam led, right?" a soldier yelled. "Admit it."

Yasin stayed silent. He took the beating as if he no longer felt any pain. Perhaps the many beatings had numbed his body. He did not cry; instead, he showed a terrifying rage. "Just shoot me," he shouted.

None of the soldiers moved. It seemed they intentionally made Yasin suffer and enjoyed watching him, as if he were a character in a theater performance.

It turned out that a lot of soldiers had infiltrated this place. Whenever the military were on a manhunt, they'd infiltrate the area from all directions. They'd leave their trucks and soundlessly slip into the village using footpaths and country roads. Even the farmers who were working in their fields would not realize their presence. Once I was told that they could not be heard even when they stepped on dried leaves and branches.

"How's that possible?" I asked in disbelief.

The storyteller only shook his head — he was just as flabbergasted as I was.

Usually, the arrival of soldiers could be detected by the sound of their trucks. As soon as they heard the approaching convoy, anyone involved with the rebellion would flee from the village. Apparently, the military who currently occupied the posts were shrewder. They secretly infiltrated the villages and captured a number of people they suspected were connected to Arkam.

While Yasin was being tortured, two soldiers appeared from the alley next to the mosque, dragging a young man whose body was riddled by bullets. A bullet hole in his waist exposed red flesh. Dried leaves and twigs were stuck in his gaping mouth, and his teeth were smeared with blood and soil.

Later, we were told that the young man was not a rebel. When he saw a group of soldiers walk in front of his house, he became scared and immediately ran away. Two soldiers shot him. The same fate befell three other men, whose bodies were left in the jungle.

"This is how a rebel ends up," said the commander who had lectured us during the Meughang horror, as he pointed at the young man's body. "Of course he's a rebel. Otherwise, why would he run from us? Only people who are guilty are afraid of soldiers."

As soon as the commander stopped talking, a soldier slammed his rifle handle on Yasin's bent back. Yasin staggered and fell to the ground. Some women screamed, then quickly covered their mouths. The men helplessly looked on.

"Where are you hiding your gun?" a dark-skinned soldier snarled.

Yasin, grimacing, raised his hands.

"Are you deaf, huh?" The soldier hit Yasin over the head with his rifle. The first time his rifle landed on Yasin's temple. The second time, he hit Yasin's ear and blood began to seep out of it. "Where's that son of a bitch Arkam?" the soldier yelled.

"Just shoot me," Yasin screamed back.

Wailing mingled with prayers, and recitations of *zikr*, the Muslim rosary, filled the air.

The intense, continued torture of Yasin was unbearable to watch. Even a soldier who was guarding the road turned away every time his comrade slammed his rifle into Yasin's body.

"You must be deaf." The soldier continued to kick Yasin, who lay cringing on the gravel road. "You need to be educated the hard way," he raged.

The commander shouted, "You, villagers of Alue Rambe, need to see this to learn a lesson. This is what will happen to you when you join the rebellion or support it. Do you understand?"

"Understood," a choir of trembling, hoarse, and stuttering voices responded.

"If the rebels were brave, they should show up and fight us rather than hide in the jungle. Cuh," the commander spat, then added, "They only dare to fight the poor."

I was fifteen and thought that the commander's words were contradictory to his actions. It was the military who didn't dare to follow the rebels into the jungles. Instead, they abused innocent villagers. They were the cause of our suffering. The rebels had never persecuted the villagers.

The arrival of two big trucks brought some relief to the tense atmosphere.

A soldier directed the drivers to turn the rickety trucks around at an off-road turnout and park them with the engines running. Not far from us, a thin soldier with a thick mustache stood watching.

I recognized him as the one who cut off the villager's ears during the Meughang day barbarity.

He shouted, "Drag him."

Two soldiers took a rope and tied Yasin's feet. At that time, the punishment for rebellion was death. The government had put a law in place that allowed the execution of rebels without trial. Yasin was sentenced to die.

After Yasin's feet were tied, all of the soldiers climbed onto the truck. Standing on the truck bed, they yelled, "Hey, you stupid villagers of Alue Rambe, watch this. Maybe you don't want to be rebels anymore."

They then drove off, dragging Yasin across the gravel road. The sharp gravel peeled his skin.

Women screamed and cried. Some men could not hold back their tears. Everyone seemed affected. Yasin was someone's son, nephew, cousin, relative, and neighbor.

We later found out that before Yasin was apprehended, around fifty soldiers from the Simpang Mawak and Buloh Blang Ara Military Base had sneaked into Alue Rambe. Because they had walked from Simpang Mawak, their presence went unnoticed by the villagers. Considering how fast they caught Yasin, a suspicion arose that a traitor had turned him in.

Meanwhile, other violent incidents had spread to other villages around ours. The military not only tortured and killed the rebels, they also raped the women. The rapists were protected by the law, and the authorities allowed it to happen to deter the rebels.

News about occurring atrocities was only spread by word of mouth. For instance, when Muha went visiting his relatives in Cot Meureubo, he told them what happened in Alue Rambe and brought back stories of incidents in his hometown to us.

When we came home after the latest bloodshed, the sun already hung slanted in the sky. Its scorching light was blocked by the candlenut and coconut trees, which created long shadows across the roof. The call for Asr prayer came from the mosque. Because our front door had been left open, the chickens had entered the house and wreaked havoc. They had helped themselves to the food on the table and had defecated everywhere.

Nono came to greet us, limping. His left front leg was hurt. Thankfully, the bullet had not hit his body.

Ayah quickly cleaned the wound and medicated it with some kerosene. "Smart dog," Ayah mumbled.

Afterwards, Ayah took a bath in the stream and changed his clothes, then went to visit the families of the four murder victims. Sitting quietly, with tears in his eyes, Ayah paid his respects and condolences.

Even though Ayah was very scared, he was relieved not to have been arrested. He was very grateful that no one in Alue Rambe called him Pak Camat anymore.

"Please be patient," Ayah said to the victim's family when he came to mourn. "This is a difficult test for all of us." He repeated himself to each family. There was nothing else to be said. There were no words meaningful enough to penetrate such a deep sadness. The pale, gloomy faces and the women's and children's sobs would break any heart.

It had gotten too late in the day to bathe and enshroud the deceased.

In the evening, Ayah went back once again to support the mourning families.

I followed Ayah like Nono followed him when he went to the field. It seemed that he felt comfortable having me around.

A few people recited the Quran, sitting next to the dead body, which was covered with a long batik cloth. Whispers and restrained sobs were interspersed with the humming of prayers.

Several times, tears filled Ayah's eyes.

Meanwhile, I was plagued by anxiety and sadness. Whatever I ate tasted bland, but at the same time, I was hungry.

I felt uneasy through the night. Unable to fall asleep, I kept tossing. The events during the day kept rolling through my brain like a continuous film. I blinked several times, hoping to erase the images. When that didn't work, I tried holding my breath. Finally, I closed my eyes and listened to my own breath in the silence that held me.

---

The next day, Ayah and Ibu visited the families of three other victims. The bodies of Yasin and the two young men whose bodies were dumped into the truck were found in different places along the roadside in Lhok Jok.

One of Yasin's hands was gone. The skin was peeled off the backside of his legs, and the white of his bones protruded from the open flesh. His face was a mere skull, and it was difficult to identify him.

Aside from Ayah, only a couple of others came to mourn at noon. Usually, visitors would bring some money and rice. This time, only a few people observed the custom.

The custom in Aceh was to attend the evening wake, but this night, no one came.

The soldiers would regard the wake as a secret meeting of rebels. An announcement — forbidding gatherings — had been pasted on the walls of all stalls.

A couple of nights after Yasin's murder, Arkam suddenly appeared with a man who brought a sack of rice for Yasin's parents. I happened to have accompanied Ibu, who had gone to visit Yasin's parents. I almost could not recognize Arkam. He wasn't dressed like usual. He wore neither his red cap nor his leather shoes. Instead, he wore loose cotton pants, a pair of rubber slippers, and a shirt similar to what other people wore.

He immediately shook the hand of Yasin's father, who stared at his face for quite a while. It seemed the old man had difficulty recognizing Arkam.

"I'm very sorry about what happened. Yasin should still have been with me. Instead, he too is gone —" Arkam halted when the old man turned away.

Yasin's father cleared his throat, as if wanting to say something but failing to do so. After a pause, he wiped his tears with his shirtsleeve and, looking away from Arkam, he said, "I never thought my child would die this soon."

"I will take revenge," Arkam exclaimed with a choked voice.

The old man remained silent, as if he was not listening.

Arkam looked awkward. What had happened was his responsibility. He was the one who had persuaded Yasin to take up arms.

"I swear, I will avenge those soldiers," Arkam repeated.

That old man remained silent, as if whatever Arkam would do was inconsequential.

Ibu's and Arkam's eyes were swollen.

Arkam looked very guilty, and he acted uncomfortable. Finally, he took Ibu's hand and kissed it.

"Please forgive me…" Arkam trembled and burst into tears.

Ibu also cried.

Both then held back their tears. They probably were embarrassed to have displayed their feelings in public.

A few people in the yard looked at them, touched.

I thought Arkam had taken responsibility for his part in all of this by coming to offer his condolences and bring a sack of rice. When he saw me, he came to me and slapped me on the back.

I could not bear to look at him and bowed my head.

Not long afterwards, Ayah appeared, which changed Arkam's facial expression. Unlike before, when he passionately convinced the people of Alue Rambe to join the rebellion, now his body language showed discomfort. He looked desperate. Ayah and Arkam exchanged uncomfortable looks. It was as if they had met unexpectedly under unpleasant circumstances.

"I have to leave," Arkam said after greeting Ayah.

Ayah nodded.

Ibu remained quiet. Words had lost their meaning.

# Chapter 9

"Tell me," Ayah said to Ibu at lunchtime, before returning to the field. "How can Arkam stand up for the rights of the Acehnese in this kind of a situation?"

Ibu sat on the front steps while delousing Zuhra's blond, shoulder-length hair. In our family, only Zuhra had blond hair, and her skin was lighter than the rest of us. A few other girls in this village had hair like Zuhra. Their hair color was a reminder that some Acehnese descended from the Portuguese. The blond hair didn't hide the presence of lice as well as black hair did.

Ibu, grumbling, wondered why the girl could not take care of herself and had allowed so many lice to breed on her head.

Zuhra, who now was five years old, often squealed when Ibu pulled out a few strands of her hair along with the lice or its eggs. She tried to get up several times, but Ibu quickly grabbed her shoulder and seated her again.

Ibu energetically took to the task of delousing. She impatiently pinched the louse and crushed it to death between her thumbnails. Both of her thumbnails were stained with the blood and corpses of the crushed lice.

Ibu glanced at Ayah. "I don't understand men and this country's affairs."

Ayah squatted on the porch floor, leaning against the wall not far from Ibu. He looked at the thin scab on the back of his thumb. Because he was constantly moving his thumb, it took a while for the wound to completely heal.

When a fly landed on the scab, Ayah slapped it with his other hand. The fly flew away, swirled, and returned. Ayah kept slapping at it, and the fly kept coming back. "The soldiers are like flies." Ayah rested his eyes on Zuhra's blond hair. "By landing on our wounds, they wound us even further."

"Why don't you put some medicine on it?" asked Ibu, looking at Ayah's wound. There were small white dots around the edges of the scab that could turn into pus.

"A wound," Ayah replied, "if it's too severe, can't be treated anymore."

"Yours is only a small wound. It hasn't turned bad yet."

"You're right," Ayah said, "and also wrong."

Ibu chuckled. "You've always liked to puzzle me."

"I did not mean to puzzle you," Ayah said seriously. "You're right; this is a small wound, but a severe one."

After applying a few drops of skin medication from a bottle with a label picturing a woman in a swimsuit showing her bare back, Ayah quickly left the house. Every so often, he raised his left arm to blow on his thumb. The lotion, which actually was not suitable for his type of wound, would make anyone scream when applied to an open wound. But it quickly dried any wound that would not heal.

---

In the afternoon, after carrying two pails of water from the stream, I went to Leman's stall. A man in his forties had just returned from the Buloh Blang Ara market, riding his bike. He told some people who were taking a break that a man had just been killed on the street. The people listened to him as if the victim was one of their relatives.

A Toyota Hiace stopped in front of Leman's and Basyah's stalls. A group of kids climbed on the pickup and jumped happily on the truck bed. Before I was circumcised and grew a thin mustache, I used to do the same thing.

A fat man climbed out of the pickup. He was a wholesaler of betel nut and candlenut and talked to Leman in front of the warehouse. Their conversation, once again, was about the military murder victim.

The television broadcast news about President Soeharto's activities. He stood, proudly waving, while the television announcer listed the accomplishments of the government during his tenure. The president's broad smile almost closed his eyes.

All of a sudden, I realized that the bloody assaults on the Acehnese were never reported. It was as if nothing had happened here. We were left to live in despair.

Meanwhile, toward the end of the news broadcast, an announcement was made about a corruptor who had embezzled billions of rupiahs of the nation's money. The people at the coffee stall, whispering, figured that the amount of money would feed seventeen future generations of descendants without them having to work.

As a math exercise, I tried visualizing the number of bills it would take to pay out the number shown on the television screen, below the picture of the embezzler. I imagined how the stacks of paper money would fill Leman's warehouse and coffee stall, and Basyah's workshop and warehouse. And even if Samaun's warehouse and grocery store were added to the list, there would still be money left to fill the remainder of the stalls and warehouses in Tamoun. The embezzler of that much money was not only one person. Every month would bring a new corrupter.

Some laborers took the betel nuts, candlenuts, and coconuts out of the three warehouses to be weighed and then loaded into the mini truck. The fat wholesaler recorded the weight of every load in his big book. For a moment, Tamoun came to life with sounds of the hanging, clanging metal scale, the shouts of laborers shouldering loads, the thuds of sacks thrown into the truck, and the creaking of the truck as it strained under the load. All of that, mixed with the television broadcast and short music sessions in between its programs, charged the air with energy.

---

In the month of August, the drought reached its climax. During that season, almost all of my family members were busy tending the backyard, except for Raziah and Akbar, who stayed inside the house. Ayah and Muha cleared the brush that prevented the growth of green grasses. I sometimes helped them after school or during the weekend. After the brush was cleared and burned in a fallow field, green grasses would sprout in the pasture where our five goats were tethered.

Ibu and Baiti helped each other, picking up the candlenuts and gathering firewood. They also picked up the dried palm leaves that had dropped between the candlenut trees.

Sometimes, Ibu would take Baiti to the riverbank, where the river ran along Seuneubok Drien village. The jungle there provided a lot of firewood, ranging from arm-sized logs to twigs. When dry, this wood made excellent kindling. Ibu purposefully stocked up on it for the rainy season. The wood logs behind our house were wet then, and the coconut leaf ribs and husks were difficult to dry out. Even when already thinly chopped, it needed weeks to dry.

The betel nut trees were only fifteen feet tall but already laden with clusters of deep yellow fruits.

Muha used a pole that had a small sickle tied to its end to bring down the clusters. He hooked the sickle around the cluster's stem. When he gave the pole a strong tug, the cluster fell to the ground. The fall broke some of the yellow fruit off the stalk.

Ayah gathered the betel nuts. The bright, dry-season sunrays bounced off the shiny betel nut skins and onto Ayah's face. While bagging the nuts, his lips formed a smile. It only lasted a moment; then, his face turned dark again.

I knew that Ayah, just like all of us, felt uneasy. Every day, there was something new to be anxious about. I noticed most of the villagers were also walking around with pale and gloomy faces. When we bumped into each other, there were no more jokes or laughter; we merely said hello before hurriedly going each our own way. Despite our worries, we still needed to go to work.

Suddenly, Nono barked.

Ayah's blush deepened when Mahmud appeared and approached him. Mahmud, a villager of Seuneubok Drien, held out his hand.

"Excuse me, sir," Mahmud politely greeted. "Arkam sent me to ask you about something important."

"Then ask. I'm very busy right now," Ayah replied.

"Arkam plans to attack the Simpang Mawak base and likes to have your opinion about it," Mahmud said cautiously.

"My opinion is that he does not need to attack anything or anyone," Ayah growled.

"Arkam thinks this is an important attack. It's not only about revenge. The military have defiled our dignity."

"Hey, why are you asking me?" Ayah yelled.

"Arkam says you're still a camat."

"Shut up."

"I'm sorry, sir, but that's why I came here," Mahmud said, startled.

"You can leave now," Ayah yelled.

"So, what should I say to Arkam?"

"If we don't capture and kill him, the soldiers will kill us, instead."

"So, you're agreeing with him?"

"Hey," Ayah shouted impatiently and grabbed Mahmud by his shirt collar. "Are you stupid or insane? Don't they have someone sane to send here?"

"Oh, sorry, sir." Mahmud trembled. "I'll let him know that you d-d-don't a-a-agree."

Ayah released Mahmud with a shove and said, "I hope I don't have to see you again, ever."

Mahmud trembled even more. Straightening his shirt, he glanced in the direction of our house.

"What are you waiting for?"

"I– I just want to know how your family is… Is Baiti okay?" Mahmud asked, hesitant.

"We're fine," Ayah grumbled, grabbing the nearest betel nut cluster.

Mahmud left, heading northeast. There was no main road that connected Alue Rambe and Seuneubok Drien. The farmers and wild chicken hunters used the dirt country roads. Our villages were separated by a river without a bridge. Both sides of the riverbank were unpopulated and covered by dense brush.

Before Mahmud's reappearance, Ayah's anxiety level had lowered considerably. Now he went back to cursing Arkam again. Despite the fact so many people had died and had to run away, that man still wanted to cause trouble.

---

A night watchman was always ill fated.

Two soldiers from Simpang Mawak, who were assigned to check on the night watchmen, found one of them fast asleep near dawn.

When the sleeping young man argued that he was not feeling well, a soldier slapped him. He then was ordered to take off his shirt and pants and marched to the river, where he was forced to soak. Meanwhile, the other seven night watchmen were slapped for allowing their colleague to fall asleep.

During another night, at a different post, when the soldiers paid the night watchmen a midnight visit, they found the watchers sitting around, sleepy.

The soldiers ordered the watchmen to line up and then take turns slapping each other.

Whoever did not slap the person standing next to him hard, would receive the correct slap himself.

That night, a young man and his father worked the same watch. The young man also happened to stand next to his father in line. When it was his turn to slap his own father, he did it softly. Despite being slapped repeatedly and each time harder, the young man never applied the example he received to his father's face. In the end, he wound up with a severely bruised face.

"This is an exercise that will keep you awake," the soldier said.

The soldiers did not check on the night watchmen every night. It happened only once or twice a week. Their appearances were always unexpected, and each time they brought disaster. They were always looking for mistakes.

Any night watchman who did not carry a machete, club, or flashlight would be kicked, slapped, or even trampled.

On the back wall of the night watch post hung a chalkboard with a roster of those on duty.

The soldiers always checked it carefully. They would fetch anyone absent at his home. Regardless of the reason he gave, they would drag him to the post.

"Now you know what it means to be a soldier."

On another night, two soldiers, who came riding their motorbikes, found all night watchmen wide awake and completely outfitted. However, the soldiers were still able to find fault. They bombarded the night watchmen with questions.

"Why are all of you standing guard here? Are you afraid someone will carry this post away?"

"Are you expecting the rebels attacking the village to come straight here? You're brainless pieces of shit. Disperse! You don't need to guard this post, morons."

And the night watchmen who were confident they would not get into trouble ended up all being slapped.

The night after, another group of night watchmen was on duty. The two soldiers, who again rode their motorbikes from Simpang Mawak, found an empty post.

As soon as the night watchmen heard the roar of the motorbikes, they went into the alleys and walked around shining their flashlights left and right. When they returned to the post, they found the two soldiers waiting for them.

"Good night, sir," the lead watchman greeted.

"Where have you been?" a soldier asked.

"We were patrolling the village, sir."

"Why didn't anyone stay here to watch the post? What would you do if the rebels came and burned it down?" the soldier yelled. "Line up, all of you."

After beating the men, the soldier became calmer. It almost seemed he wanted to make peace.

"Patrolling is important, but don't ever leave the checkpost empty. Always have four people guard the post while the other four are on patrol. In other words, take turns patrolling. Do you understand?"

"Understood."

After Ayah worked his turn as a night watchman, he returned in the morning with a swollen cheek. He cursed the soldier who beat him, and hoped his ship would sink on its way back to Jakarta. "In reality, the night patrol is not to prevent the rebels from entering the village, but an exercise in figuring out how not to get hit by the soldiers."

The soldiers from Simpang Mawak were changed with others, but their brutality never changed. The installation of the night watch and the increased intensity of the army's pursuit of the rebels, both openly and in secret, caused the rebels to scatter.

Everyone was certain that the murder of seven Alue Rambe villagers and the murders in other villages were caused by spies of the military. And the villagers wondered who amongst them were the traitors.

The military pressure continued to increase, and early in October 1992, word spread that some twenty rebels had left Aceh. Some young men who were known as Arkam's followers were never seen again in our village.

During that time, Ayah and Muha worked on clearing the land that had lain fallow after the turmeric harvest. During the dry season, the weeds had taken over the untended land. Just like the rebels who could not be broken by any military measures, the weeds thrived regardless of the heat and drought. The thick brush was now waist-high.

*Arafat Nur*

Ayah planted his field with mountain padi because there were no wet rice fields in this village. He predicted that in the coming months, the rain would fall regularly. Other villagers did the same to take care of their rice supply in the upcoming year.

During the next two months, the rain did not fall heavily, but enough fell to make the seedlings of our rice crop grow well. When the straight stems were as tall as my chest, the tips would form soft, flat buds.

While the grain was maturing, flocks of sparrows often came to feed. Ayah and Baiti and sometimes Ibu and I had to take turns shooing the birds to keep them from stealing our rice crop.

Nono also diligently watched over our crops day and night.

# Chapter 10

During the rainy season, we always caught the water runoff from the roof for our daily needs. Nono found shelter beneath the dangau while guarding the yellowing rice field. If there were one or two sparrows brave enough to perch in the rice field, Nono would immediately bark and chase them, ignoring the rain that soaked his body.

Ayah really loved Nono. I often felt that he paid more attention to the dog than to Zuhra and me, who were his real children.

"Smart dog," Ayah mumbled. Smiling, he watched Nono running through the rain and added, "He's second to none."

"Yeah, Nono is a smart dog," I agreed.

"I'm not sure if I can get another dog who's that smart, if he died." Ayah's gaze followed Nono affectionately.

Ayah always gave Nono enough to eat; hence, Nono was healthy and his fur thick and shiny. His eyes were sharp like Ayah's eyes when he was angry. The dog quickly understood Ayah's instructions and knew what he had to do without needing to be told repeatedly.

*Arafat Nur*

When the rain stopped, Ayah asked me to hurry home and cut grass to feed the goats. The sun breaking through the sky after the afternoon rain created a rainbow. For a moment, I looked at it, amazed.

A cool breeze blew through the melinjo, candlenut, and cacao trees and created a light drizzle. I walked to the stream carrying a plastic bag and a sickle.

Ibu, who had not been able to do laundry in the rain, now walked to the stream with Manis on her heels. The cat slinked along. She obviously did not like the wet brush alongside the path.

Zuhra was already six years old, but still followed Ibu around. She did not like to stay with Baiti, who often teased her. Actually, Zuhra was not fussy, unless she was sick.

Our parents did not spoil us. They merely taught us to take responsibility for our actions.

The sunbeams seemed to dance on the rapidly flowing water in the stream. Dark gray clouds that looked like smoke rising from the burning trash pile in the goat shed hid the rainbow. During the rain, the goats were confined in their shed. When they were hungry, they'd become restless. Their bleating and stomping often could be heard all the way to the stream.

"Zir, quickly cut the grass." Ibu placed her laundry pail on a rock that was almost as tall as the surface of the water trapped between stones that formed a dam.

The sound of water cascading from the dam was very loud. I liked watching the falling water and was always amazed how water would invariably move toward a lower place. It would not be held back by any obstacles. It would simply crash over and drown everything in its path.

I went to cut grass on top of a hill near the stream where clove tree saplings sprouted abundantly. Cloves did not grow well in this area. Therefore, many clove trees had been cut down, but the land was left to lie fallow.

Not far from there was a chasm in a hill that was filled with a dense jungle. Thorny vines that tightly tangled with each other formed a canopy on top of bent tree branches. From afar, the area appeared impossible to penetrate by anything except boars and snakes.

I sliced my sickle through the lush green growth and piled my cuttings until I had enough to fill my bag. The area I had cleared now looked like a field of green stubble. Perspiration dripped from my forehead as I pressed the cuttings tightly into the bag.

Dark clouds that looked like the shoals of the river that flowed below our rice field had replaced the rainbow.

Ibu was still doing the laundry. Her bent back moved with short jerks as she hurriedly scrubbed the clothes.

With her legs tucked under her body and her chin resting on her front paws, Manis patiently waited for Ibu on the gravel roadside.

Zuhra played in the water, only wearing her underwear, which had a flower on her bottom.

"Zuhra, hurry up," Ibu yelled. "People will be here, soon."

"Okay, I'm bathing."

"Weren't you just playing all this time? You can't even rinse a cloth."

When I crossed the bridge, Ibu called, "Don't forget to build a fire in the goat shed."

"Okay, Bu."

I emptied half of the grass cuttings into the trough in the goat shed. The goats were really hungry and devoured their feed. There were nine goats now. Two does had recently given birth to two kids that had started to eat grass. Yet their mothers' milk was still their staple food. When the kids suckled, they often poked their mothers' belly. The nanny in return would kick at them and make the kids leave.

When I grabbed my towel to take a bath in the stream, Muha had just returned from the Buloh Blang Ara market with a sack of rice and a plastic bag filled with miscellaneous items. His face was swollen, and a three-inch gash ran across his neck.

Raziah greeted him, taking the plastic bag from Muha's hand. When I passed by, I heard my sister ask her husband about his swollen face.

During dinner, Muha told us what had happened when he passed through the Simpang Mawak checkpoint. "A soldier blocked my way and slapped me. He accused me of helping the rebels and tried to confiscate the rice. In defense, I told him that my wife and children were hungry at home. This rice almost didn't make it home."

The wound on Muha's neck started to swell and turn black and blue. "They accused me of buying rice for the rebels. They said that Alue Rambe was a rebels' nest." Muha paused. "Luckily, another soldier apparently felt sorry for me and pulled his friend aside to finish checking me out." Muha ended his story.

Muha's experience was nothing new. It seemed that the military's sole duty was to abuse the villagers. It was as if they had not performed their duty if they did not engage in acts of violence.

"The angel of death can rest now," Ayah said in response to Muha's story. "Too many of his helpers are sent to Aceh."

After Muha's incident, Ayah refused to go to the Buloh Blang Ara market, because there was no way to avoid going through the Simpang Mawak checkpoint.

The soldiers would arrest anyone they suspected of being a supporter of the rebellion and take him to a base that was specifically built as a torture chamber.

The continuous brutality suffocated me. Anger, sadness, and despair filled my heart to the point that I felt my chest would explode.

---

When the rice haulms began to bloom, Muha spent more time in Kakek's fields, where he cleaned the betel nut and banana orchards. Ayah took care of the rice field. Ibu, Baiti, and I every so often helped him.

Ayah sometimes asked me to give Kakek and Nenek a hand. Nenek often sent me shopping for kerosene or other household items. I also helped her draw water from a very deep well next to their house. Kakek said that the well was dug a year before my birth, because they could no longer walk to the stream to fetch water.

Kakek was very old and became slower and weaker by the day. He was no longer able to swing the machete strongly anymore, and this caused his betel nut orchard to turn into a small jungle. His banana farm was still well maintained. After he finished his daily task of weaving palm leaf roof tiles, he would take down the old banana leaves with his machete.

Once every three months, a banana wholesaler would come in a Chevrolet pickup with two workers dressed in dark uniforms. The workers would walk through the orchard, looking for banana clusters that were ready to be harvested. With their sharp machetes, they expertly cut through the soft trunks of banana plants. The first slash was applied with measured strength, in the middle of the trunk, and left the plant still erect.

The slanted, second slash caused the plant to bend slowly, as if offering its fruit respectfully.

The third slash, at the base of the cluster, was done with one hand gripping the cluster tip that had lost its banana heart, thus preventing the cluster from hitting the ground. The fourth, strongest slash, right at the base, chopped the cluster off the trunk.

After all the clusters were gathered in the front yard, the wholesaler quickly counted the tiers in each cluster in front of Kakek, who could no longer see very well. In his count, the man often skipped the last tiers at the end of a cluster.

Fully trusting the honesty of human beings, Kakek watched the bananas he had planted with such great effort being loaded on the truck bed. Then, he counted the money the wholesaler handed him.

"Is this enough or did I miscount?" The wholesaler glanced at Kakek, who had to put on his glasses.

"I trust you," Kakek said.

The wholesaler handed Kakek another five-hundred-rupiah bill. "This is from me," he said, "as alms."

"You're too kind," Kakek exclaimed.

The man smiled, then left in a hurry. He drove himself, as if he were not a boss. The two workers in the back put down their machetes and held on to the sides of the truck. They would collect bananas at other farms until the truck was full. Ropes that were diagonally tied to the sides of the truck prevented the load from rolling to the ground. Some factory workers said that those bananas were transported to the city and sold in various markets.

Other than helping Kakek with cleaning his orchard, Muha also cut the sago palm branches. After trimming the leaves with his machete, he bundled them and then carried them home. On certain days, Kakek taught him to weave roof tiles. Muha was a quick learner, and it didn't take long before his tiles were even better than those Kakek made.

In the evening, Muha took Akbar, who was now three years old, with him to bathe in the stream.

Zuhra joined them. She ran around happily, as if there were no war.

At dusk, I lit all the lamps in the house, and then lit the lamp inside the lamp house in the yard. The wind scattered the thick smoke rising from the burning trash in the goat shed. The mixture of burning wood, coconut shells, and husks, smothered by wet dung, filled the air with an odor typical of burning dung. The thick smoke kept the mosquitoes and gnats away.

The chickens gathered, their chicks and returned to their coop.

Ayah hurried to the field to feed Nono.

Before I went back into the house, I looked for a moment at the setting sun. The rays of light were unable to permeate the trees' dense canopies. The tall, vigorous trees shaded the scattered villagers' houses that were built on their respective farms.

The light of a small oil lamp in the lamp house illuminated its surroundings with a reddish light. It created its own festive world, but with no one to enjoy it. The lamp would remain lit through the silent night. An occasional night watchman passing it on his rounds would be the only one seeing it. Despite their lit porches and yards, the houses appeared as if they were uninhabited.

That night, I slept wrapped in a thick blanket. I pulled it closer around me when I was awakened in the middle of the night by the sound of raindrops falling on the roof. I thought I was having a nightmare when the raindrops turned into gunshots. The continuous sound woke me completely. The sound was real and came from up north. Because the nights were usually very quiet, any noise, even if it came from far away, could be heard everywhere.

Ayah coughed in the living room and then everything turned silent again.

It was very cold, and I fell back asleep until daylight.

Baiti sat yawning on the kitchen bench. She stared at me with a knowing look but didn't say a word.

After turning off the oil lamp in the yard, I went back inside. Through the wide-open bedroom door, I saw Ayah sitting in bed, his back leaning against the headboard. His eyes were closed.

It turned out that last night's gunshots in my nightmare were actually real. Soldiers had attacked a neighboring village but did not make it to ours.

After breakfast, Ibu told Baiti to take the dirty laundry to the stream, while she stayed home to take care of other chores. In the event that soldiers showed up and, under pretense of searching the house for rebels, ransacked the house again, she would claim to be taking care of her sick husband.

The chickens were making a lot of noise in the coop. When I opened the coop door, they rushed out and, in a frenzy, pecked at the handfuls of chopped-up sago stems I scattered for them to eat. Some of them moved to the backyard, where there was an abundance of grasshoppers, crickets, and worms. Perhaps, just like humans who became bored of eating rice, they occasionally needed some snacks.

Birds tweeted and chirped in the trees while I walked to Leman's stall. People there were talking about last night's shooting. Ayah was apparently mistaken. They believed it was Arkam who recklessly took revenge for the deaths of his friends and rebelled against the soldiers' brutality. Alue Rambe village and the neighboring villages were wrapped in anxiety.

Muha passed Leman's stall on his roadster bike with Raziah and their son. They probably were evacuating to his mother's house in Cot Meureubo.

Soon afterwards, the roar of motorbikes approached Alue Rambe. Some people quickly went home.

Three motorbikes carrying six soldiers came to a halt in front of Leman's stall.

The soldiers headed straight to the village chief's house, which was not far from mine. Two of the soldiers immediately entered the house. They slapped the thin man, in his fifties, then herded him outside. With a gun barrel poked in his back, the village chief led the soldiers to Kakek's house.

According to Nenek, Kakek was weaving sago palm leaves when the soldier who arrived first slammed his rifle into Kakek's thin chest, knocking the air out of him. When the other soldiers arrived, they yelled curses and profanities while kicking around Kakek's supply of leaves.

Nenek was fetching water and walked outside when she heard the commotion. She screamed when she saw Kakek being beaten by a group of soldiers that behaved like robbers.

One of the soldiers pushed Nenek. She fell and hit her head against the wall.

The young man shouted in her ear, "Where's your son? Where's that rebel?"

"I don't know," Nenek answered, trembling.

"You old hag." The soldier, followed by his comrades, went into the house.

The noise of falling furniture and breaking items, along with the soldiers' swearing, could be heard outside.

Nenek, whose rheumatic knees were swollen, was unable to get up. She lay on the floor crying, "*Allah, Allah, Allahu ya Rabbi*... Allah is my God."

A tall, muscular soldier lifted Kakek by his shirt collar. He held Kakek so high off the ground, Kakek looked like a butchered goat.

Kakek gasped for air.

"Where is Arkam?" the soldier yelled.

Kakek shook his head, spluttering.

The soldier shoved Kakek head first to the ground and then trampled him.

Nenek screamed when another soldier lifted Kakek off the floor. She dragged herself to a broom and weakly waved it at the soldier. When she threw the broom at him, she missed, and the handle hit her head. "Treat your parents like this when you go home," she cursed in Acehnese.

Meanwhile, the village chief could not do anything, as he too was a victim of the soldiers' brutality. "You're just like one of the rebels," a soldier exclaimed.

After they tortured Kakek until he no longer moved, the soldiers left Alue Rambe, cursing the villagers as they released gunshots in the air.

The village chief asked several people to help him carry Kakek into the house. They lay Kakek on a pandan mat and placed his head on two cotton pillows.

When Ibu heard that Kakek had been beaten by a group of soldiers acting like rogues, she ran hollering to her parents' house with her waist-length hair fluttering in the wind.

Nenek wailed, wiping her eyes with her shawl. She ignored her bleeding left nostril, which she only noticed when she wiped her nose with her shawl.

Kakek finally showed some life in the afternoon. He still had great difficulty breathing. Blood spurted from his mouth when he coughed. Someone spooned saline water into his mouth, but he was unable to swallow it. Kakek's condition remained the same until nightfall.

Meanwhile, Ayah ran around asking everyone for help. He paid a young man to pick up a medicine man from Seuneubok Drien, using back roads.

The medicine man, known as an expert in herbal medicines, arrived in the evening. He brought a bottle of some potion and checked every part of Kakek's body. Kakek could not even swallow a sip of water, let alone drink the medicine.

"He has serious internal injuries," the middle-aged medicine man said.

"So what should we do?" Ayah asked anxiously.

"We have to make him drink."

Even as the next morning arrived, when his heart stopped beating and he exhaled his last breath, Kakek still had not swallowed a single drop of water. Perhaps Kakek passed away thirsty.

After spending the whole night crying, Nenek and Ibu had no more tears left in the morning. They merely sniffled.

Ayah punched the trunk of the rose apple tree.

I did not cry out, but my eyes kept shedding tears.

Now Kakek was gone. I could not believe it. My chest hurt very much. I felt as if everything inside my body had been crushed.

# Chapter 11

The mixed scent of sandalwood powder, lime, camphor, *cempaka* and *kenanga* spread across the room. Kakek's small house was crowded by mourners who wished to pay their last tribute. Teungku Imam Masjid's wife recited the *Surah Yaseen* verses, accompanied by small hums of the mourners who whispered to each other, while the others walked back and forth preparing for the enshrouding ceremony. Meanwhile, Teungku Imam Masjid and five other people prepared a bathing place outside the house. Water was drawn from the well and poured into a plastic drum.

Other than Ibu, none of Kakek's other children – including Arkam – attended the wake. None of them saw Kakek for the last time before he was buried. Their absence tainted Kakek's death. He had many children, yet it felt as if he only had one child, my mother.

Since no one could rely on Nenek, Ibu assumed the responsibility of taking care of the mourners, while Ayah and Muha took care of the enshrouding.

At that time, Alue Rambe, known as a meeting place of rebels, was very dangerous to visit. Other than at Simpang Mawak, there were many other posts visitors had to pass through before reaching Alue Rambe. The soldiers were always suspicious of anyone who came to a village carrying an ID with an address in another village.

Nevertheless, it was our responsibility to tell my uncles and aunts that Kakek had passed away. It was then their choice to come or not. But Ayah had a difficult time trying to contact them because there was no one he could send to deliver the sad news to his in-laws in Lhokseumawe — if they still lived there.

"Why does it seem that everything is farther away?" Ayah mumbled.

Muha offered, "Let me go to Lhokseumawe."

"Do you know where they live?" Ayah asked.

Muha shook his head.

"Then why would you go there?"

Embarrassed, Muha lowered his head, then walked away.

Ayah could only leave a message with Leman, who went shopping at the Buloh Blang Ara market that morning. He hoped Leman would meet someone who could help pass the sad news to his wife's siblings who lived in Lhokseumawe.

Leman easily passed the Simpang Mawak checkpoint because he bribed the soldiers with a loaf of bread or some cigarettes.

Meanwhile, other villagers were unable to do anything or go anywhere. If the soldiers found someone roaming around the village, they would immediately suspect him of being a rebel. That person could be held for an all-day interrogation at the soldiers' post, or could even be shot in the head on the spot if he was considered defiant in any way. It was a very difficult time to travel, even if it was to visit friends and relatives who happened to live in another village.

Ibu was the only one who was able to be with her father when he breathed his last breath. She sat sobbing with Nenek and Raziah.

Teungku Imam Masjid bathed Kakek's body with the help of four other men. The body was then placed in the main room again. Teungku Imam Masjid's hands trembled as he plugged Kakek's ears and eyes with pieces of cotton that were sprinkled with talcum and camphor powder. Kakek's body was later enshrouded in a white cloth that was purchased from Samaun's stall.

Dozens of people came to perform *salah* for Kakek. His body was carried on a bier to the rapidly expanding cemetery. There were eight new graves.

"Be careful," Teungku Imam Masjid cautioned.

Two workers had dug a grave, and Kakek's enshrouded body was lowered into the hole. Ayah and Muha received Kakek's body with red eyes and pale, sad faces.

After the hole was filled and soil mounded on the grave, Teungku Imam Masjid led the prayer, which dozens of people answered with, "Aame-e-en." The afternoon sun penetrated the remaining coolness under the shady banyan tree at the cemetery and evaporated the dampness in the soil. Some mosquitoes and gnats flew around and landed on the mourners' feet. The insects flew away when they failed to follow the mourners, who left the cemetery one by one.

Ayah was the only one who stayed. I waited for him by the road. He seemed to be unaware that I was watching him. With both of his hands on his back, he stood for a while near the wet, yellowish clay mound. The wind blowing from the direction of the field ruffled his uncombed hair.

*Arafat Nur*

At the start of the new academic year in mid-1992, I often saw soldiers at the soccer field, across from the Buloh Blang Ara Military Base. The field was usually used for the flag ceremony on August 17, Indonesia's Independence Day. Now, the soldiers used it for all kinds of military exercises.

One of the soldiers chased me off. He yelled, "Keep moving. Go on home. This is not some sidewalk entertainment, stupid."

I was sixteen and a senior in middle school. I began to realize that the only things soldiers did were march, carry guns, yell, and sing. Once in a while, after an informant tipped them off, they'd arrest a rebel who was visiting his wife and children. And sometimes, they would engage in a shootout with rebels who blocked the road.

In those days, school was open irregularly. I had some basic knowledge of mathematics, religious studies, language, and history. But I had a problem understanding why people would die to defend a flag — which was actually nothing but a colored piece of cloth — and why they had to kill each other over it.

My heart throbbed every time I had to go through the Simpang Mawak checkpoint on my way to and from school.

The soldiers took turns searching individuals who passed through. Even though they still scoffed at school children, they usually left students alone. But one time, after finding out that I was from Alue Rambe, they searched me.

At first, I thought the soldier was merely joking when he yelled, "Open your bag. What do you have in it?"

I took off my shoulder bag and lifted the flap. "Only books," I stammered. Holding the bag wide open, I tried to force a smile and added, "pens and a ruler." Even though I did not feel guilty, I was scared they would bodily search me like they were known to do to adults.

For a while, the soldier stared grimly at me. Then he lowered the tip of his rifle but kept staring at my open bag.

I did not dare to close the bag.

After a while, it seemed he became bored and growled, "Go on, get lost, little rascal," and added, "If you stand there for another second, I'll shoot you."

That was the friendliest treatment I had ever witnessed of all inspections.

Alue Rambe villagers were reluctant to go to Buloh Blang Ara market unless they had to. And there was always something that was needed but unavailable at any of the Tamoun stalls. There was always someone who would hand me a few thousand-rupiah bills — I would hide them inside my sock — to buy something. Ayah, Ibu, Muha, Raziah, Baiti, Zuhra, Akbar, and even Nenek always had an errand or two for me to run.

After Kakek's passing, Nenek became ill and I was often asked to buy her medications at a pharmacy in Buloh Blang Ara, on my way home from school. The market now was quiet; even on market days, there were no street peddlers putting up tents to display merchandise along the roadside. Market days were just like any other day. There were only a few cars and trucks that stopped to load or unload merchandise.

Because Nenek was ill and there was no one to take care of her, Muha and Raziah moved in with her. Muha resumed taking care of all the chores Kakek had done while alive. He tended the areca and banana orchards and spent his free time weaving roof tiles. He also tidied the yard, pruned mango trees, and burned the trash pile in the corner of the yard.

Ibu visited Nenek several times a day. Sometimes she went during the morning, other times in the afternoon. A few times she even visited during the evening. She went whenever she could break away from her own chores at home.

With her head lying on a pillow, Nenek lay on the same pandan mat where Kakek had lain. For days, she refused to eat.

Other than rice, Raziah also cooked mung bean porridge, kolak ubi, yam stew, and *kolak pisang,* banana stew.

Nenek finally ate, but only a little bit. "I think I'll be dying soon," Nenek said calmly, as a tear filled the corner of her eye.

Ibu pulled her shawl across her face and wiped her eyes. "Please don't say that. You have to get well. You have to eat."

"I don't want anything. Everything tastes bitter."

I avoided looking into Nenek's eyes. I didn't quite know how to handle my feelings. I hated myself for becoming teary-eyed, as well.

The fragrance of sandalwood, lime, camphor, cempaka and kenanga flowers, and the lingering scent of Kakek's body mixed with the odor of Nenek's urine. She could no longer get up and was barely able to sit. Even when Kakek was buried two weeks ago, her legs were already half paralyzed, and she sat in front of the kitchen door, crying and staring outside.

After Kakek's passing, the house was wrapped in silence day and night.

Nenek lay on the pandan mat on the floor without being able to do anything. She only took some of the pills I bought for her, after swallowing a few spoonfuls of rice Raziah fed her.

Ibu, who came to cheer her up, was engulfed in sadness herself.

Every time I went along with Ibu, I listened to their long, halted conversations. It became harder and harder to hear what Nenek was saying.

Ayah was at his wit's end trying to notify his in-laws, who were nowhere to be found. No one had shown up, even though a month had elapsed since Kakek's passing.

Meanwhile, Nenek's condition worsened, and she could not even take a sip of water.

Then, one afternoon Mahmud, the curly-haired man from Seuneubok Drien, passed our field.

Ayah, who was cutting down the rice haulms, immediately threw down his sickle and the bundle of rice haulms he held in his hand. "Hey! Wait!" Ayah called out, running toward Mahmud.

Startled, Mahmud stopped cautiously. "Please, Pak Camat, don't be mad at me." Mahmud looked scared.

"Where have you been?"

"I was in the Nisam Forest with some other rebels."

"Do you know where Arkam is?"

"Oh, him?" Mahmud paused, then said, "I can't tell you."

"Why?" Ayah frowned.

"It's a secret."

"You don't trust me?" Ayah asked, irritated.

"Pang Arkam is being hunted. No one is allowed to know his hideout."

"But this is very important."

"What's the matter?"

"It's a family problem."

Mahmud remained silent for a while, then said, "I'm sorry, Pak Camat. Family problems don't matter anymore. The nation's problem and the rebellion are now the most important issues and come before anything else."

Ayah's face was drenched in perspiration as he grabbed Mahmud by the collar and said, "Listen, Arkam's mother has been very ill for a long time. She's dying. None of her children, except for my wife, is around. You've got to find Arkam right now. It's up to him to visit her or not," Ayah yelled.

"B-b-but, Pak Camat —," Mahmud stuttered.

"There's no but," Ayah yelled again. He let go of Mahmud's collar and, shoving him away, Ayah added, "Or else, you'll regret it."

"B-but I've got to go home first. I can only go back tomorrow morning. It … it's impossible for me to sleep in the jungle tonight. You have to understand." Mahmud wiped Ayah's spittle from his face.

"It's up to you," Ayah snorted and turned away.

Nono appeared from the jungle and barked at Mahmud.

Ayah instructed the dog to stop and go back. He ignored Mahmud, who was walking away.

Meanwhile, Muha, Baiti, and I gathered the bundles of dry rice stalks in a heap next to the dangau. Before going home, we covered the heap with a large, thick tarp. The next day, we'd thresh the grain by beating the rice stalks against a wired wooden box.

The job of cutting and threshing the rice grains could take up to five days. The unhulled grain was collected in fifty-pound bags and later dried in the sun, before being stored for months.

Every two weeks, Muha would bring a sack of rice to the rice mill in Blang Riek, not far from where a new high school was being built. Each time he passed through Simpang Mawak, the soldiers at the checkpoint only held him in temporary custody and asked such irrelevant questions like, "Why is your mouth still crooked?"

The rice that Ibu cooked from the newly harvested grain produced a delicious fragrance. The rice was soft and sweet. It was very different from the cheap, *catu* rice that Muha bought at the Buloh Blang Ara market. This inferior-quality rice was hard and tasteless. I often ended up biting the small stones it contained. The catu rice was sold by the teachers and government employees who refused to eat it. The poor farmers, like most of the villagers of Alue Rambe, were the ones who ate it when they did not plant the mountain padi.

Nono also seemed to be happy when he ate our rice laced with a piece of salted fish.

Ayah's gloomy face lightened when he watched the dog eat. Lately, there were so many things that made him sad. I noticed Ayah preferred to be with the dog over being with human beings, especially people who only brought him problems.

"As long as I live, I'll never let you go hungry; you'll eat whatever I eat," Ayah told Nono when he fed him at the side of the house.

I watched him through the kitchen window without him knowing.

The dog circled Ayah, who was squatting. At mealtimes, Ayah always made sure his wife and children had enough food before he served himself. If there was only a little fried fish on the table, he would take just bits of it, and sometimes he would only take the head. Secretly, he would then dip his finger into the used cooking oil in the pan, drizzle it over the rice on his plate, and add a dash of salt. And he would even share the fish head with Nono.

Ayah had found Nono on his way home from the Buloh Blang Ara market. Nono was a sick puppy, lying in the street. At that time, I was a fourth-grader, and that would make the dog around six years old now.

Ayah would intentionally set some money aside to buy two cans of milk — one for us and one for Nono. When Nono ran out of milk — and our milk would run out before his — Ayah would buy two more cans. Ayah took care of him really well and fed him food mixed with a pill he bought from the drugstore. Nono grew into a healthy, agile dog. He loved chasing after quail, and took his catch to the dangau to eat.

I never knew how Ayah chose Nono's name. I'm sure he must have had a reason for it. Perhaps it was simply that the name was easy and there was no other dog going by the same name.

Other than Nono, Ibu was the one Ayah shared his thoughts and feelings with. I knew that my parents were close, but Ayah never showed his affection for Ibu in front of us, his children.

Nono always kept some distance between him and Ayah. It seemed the dog somehow knew he was considered unclean by humans.

Ayah never touched him either, except for when he treated the wound on the dog's front leg where he got shot by the soldier.

"If I die," Ayah whispered, "you always have to protect my children."

---

When Arkam finally appeared at Nenek's house, he was very thin, unshaven, and had sunken eyes. He was dressed in a long-sleeved, stained shirt, an old pair of blue jeans, and work boots. He no longer wore a red cap; instead, he wore a straw hat, the kind farmers wore.

As soon as he entered the house, he dropped to his knees at Nenek's side and bowed to kiss her hand. Sobbing, he held the hand that was now merely skin and bones, with raised veins running like ropes across it.

Nenek could only look at him.

I hardly recognized my uncle. The man who used to be so self-assured and filled with enthusiasm now looked beaten and seemed to have lost all of his authority.

"Forgive me," Arkam sobbed. "It's all my fault."

Ayah and Ibu, who were present, could not keep themselves from feeling sad. Arkam was no longer the leader who promised to protect the villagers. Instead, it was he who needed protection from the people.

Ayah, who wanted to reprimand him, could not bear to do so.

Arkam looked deeply shaken when he heard about Kakek's death, while sitting next to Nenek as she was dying. He gently rubbed her hand on his arm.

The situation seemed to force Ayah to drop the issue of resigning as camat and forget his fear of being recorded as an official in the rebellion.

I saw anger and pity in Ayah's eyes when he looked at Arkam. Ayah turned away when Arkam met his look and their eyes connected.

I understood that a quarrel between siblings would worsen a sick parent's condition.

It was starting to get dark when my parents and I went home. Everywhere, the outside lighting was already turned on. Baiti had lit ours. Once home, we immediately took care of the goats and chickens, then walked to the stream to bathe.

When we returned to Nenek's house after dinner, Arkam was no longer there. Soon afterwards, we heard a volley of gunshots coming from the area of Cot Meureubo.

Arkam's thin body was riddled by bullet holes. One of his eyes was missing. To spare Nenek, Arkam's body was laid out in our house.

## Chapter 12

In early 1993, our village was still under military surveillance. The soldiers not only watched those they suspected to be rebels, they also kept a close eye on the family of the suspected rebel. The night watch patrols intensified.

Ayah decided it was useless to hide out in the dangau at night because he had to report for duty as a night watchman every ten days. At that time, he had to face soldiers who bombarded him with questions that could pose a trap. It didn't matter if or how he answered the questions. He always ended up getting beaten.

The same happened when Ayah was on night watch duty two days after Arkam was shot dead in Cot Meureubo. The light from the torches lit the faces of the eight night watchmen lined up in front of the checkpost.

"Did you know that Arkam was a rebel?" the soldier asked the night watchmen.

"We didn't," answered a young man at the end of the line.

"Liars," the soldier yelled, slapping the man. "How dare you lie. Does your religion teach you to lie?"

The man staggered then straightened himself while rubbing his cheek.

"Hey, you," the soldier yelled to the next man, a thin man in his thirties. "Did you know that Arkam was a rebel?"

The man lifted his face and looked scared.

"Why didn't you catch him?" the soldier yelled furiously. Punching the man in his stomach, he repeated, "Why didn't you catch him, huh?"

The soldier landed another punch on the man's face. "Answer me. Why didn't you report him to us?"

That man rubbed his cheek, quietly.

When the soldier repeated his question again, the fair-skinned man remained quiet and simply lowered his head.

The night watchman who stood next to him in line started to say, "Sir, he —" but was immediately interrupted by a slap in the face.

"I didn't ask you, stupid," the soldier roared and proceeded to drag the man who didn't answer him to the street. Beating the man with his gun, he kept yelling, "Answer me." When the man lay crumpled on the street, the soldier kicked and trampled him with his heavy army boots. He finally yelled, "I'll shoot you if you don't open your mouth."

When the soldier pushed the end of his rifle against the man's temple, Ayah said, "He's mute."

That soldier slung his rifle back on his shoulder and walked back to the line of night watchmen. "He's mute?" he snorted.

"Yes, sir, he's mute," the young man standing next to Ayah said.

"Why are you telling me this just now? Stupid!" the soldier yelled and slapped his face.

The man who had been interrupted by the soldier earlier on interrupted and said, "I tried telling you, but you wouldn't let me, sir."

"Hey, I didn't ask you." The soldier punched the man's face again. "How dare you interrupt me."

"Hey, old man," the soldier turned to Ayah. "Did you know that Arkam was a rebel?"

"Yes, I did," Ayah answered.

"Why didn't you report it to us?" The soldier slapped Ayah in the face.

"I was afraid."

"If you're afraid of the rebels, what's the purpose of serving as a night watchman?"

Ayah silently lowered his head.

The soldier then moved to the man next to Ayah. "It's useless to question stupid people like you," he grumbled while randomly slapping the lined-up night watchmen.

"Damn rebels," the soldiers cursed as they returned to Simpang Mawak.

Two night watchmen walked the mute man home, where his wife burst out screaming as soon as she saw her husband's battered body.

---

A few days after Arkam was buried, Nenek let out her last breath.

Just like when Kakek passed away, people came to mourn and helped with all preparations for the burial. It seemed sorrow continued to surround us, while neither fear nor anxiety subsided.

Ibu looked pale, tired, and sad. So did Ayah, whose eyes were red and sunken.

Because none of Kakek and Nenek's children came, Ayah had to host the guests who came in the evening to recite the *samadiyah* prayer. Ever since there was a curfew, the villagers performed the samadiyah in the afternoon after the Asr prayer with a zikr.

From morning until noon, Ayah and Muha walked around Kakek's orchards with sharp machetes. After they picked up debris, they picked betel nuts and coconuts. Then in the afternoon, after taking a bath, Ayah boiled water in the large kettle and prepared hot tea while waiting for dozens of guests who would come to pray.

Some women helped to arrange the *kue basah*, or traditional cakes, on a tray. Those cakes were brought by the women who followed the prayers — led by Teungku Imam Masjid — from the kitchen.

Now that Ayah was temporarily the head of the family in Kakek's house, he spent most of his time there. All of us had breakfast, lunch, and dinner there.

In the afternoon, Ibu went home to feed the chickens. Sometimes, Baiti would do it. We would only return home at night to sleep.

Three days after Nenek passed away, I found Manis, neglected and starving. I was suddenly reminded of Nono. It had been a while since I last saw him. I doubted he was in the field. After we harvested the rice, there was nothing he needed to watch over, neither during day nor nighttime.

The next afternoon, I took home a coconut shell filled with some rice with a little bit of fish mixed in. When I could find neither Manis nor Nono, I placed the food under the jackfruit tree and went back to Kakek's house to help wherever needed.

On another afternoon, after I untied the goats, I saw Manis sleeping near the kitchen. Her stomach was very flat. Suddenly, Nono appeared with a dead bird in his mouth. He walked up to Manis, who woke. Nono put the dead bird down near Manis and shoved it toward the cat.

Manis eyed the dead bird, then slowly rose and went to sniff it a few times while looking at Nono. After meowing a few times, Manis took the bird and carried it to the pineapple bushes while Nono watched.

Nono looked fit. I figured that at night, he watched over the chickens in the coop and protected them from weasels and minks.

Six days after Nenek's passing, the rain fell for a while and created puddles everywhere. That afternoon, I let the hungry goats out of their pen, took a plastic sack and a sickle, and went to cut grass for their night feed. Because they had not eaten all morning, I had to provide them with food for the night.

When I tied up the goats in the backyard, Manis followed Nono on the footpath to the dormant rice field. There was no sign of awkwardness between them. While Nono and Manis were always on friendly terms, they were never as close as now.

I headed to an open field next to the cemetery to find fresh grass that the goats would like. I stopped in my tracks when I saw a man standing amidst the graves with his back toward me. It was Ayah.

He stood looking at Kakek's, Nenek's, and Arkam's graves. Arkam was placed in between Kakek and Nenek. The clay soil was wet and sticky from the heavy rain, and the green grasses around it were flattened by human footsteps.

---

By mid-May 1993, there was a change of guard at the Simpang Mawak checkpoint, and they no longer watched my village. Tamoun was once more crowded until the evening. After doing all of my day chores after school, I often watched television at Leman's in the late afternoon to chase away the boredom at home.

In the evening, I liked to read the school textbooks and do my homework, until I was sleepy. Because there was not enough room in the kitchen to store all the rice we harvested earlier in the month, my room was now crowded with piles of rice sacks.

―•―

I was helping Muha clean Kakek's front yard when an old Chevrolet truck stopped at the entrance of the alley leading to Kakek's house, where Muha, Raziah, and Akbar now lived. A thin man and two workers, who each carried a sharp machete, stepped out of the truck. The two workers immediately went to the banana orchard. Muha greeted the thin man, who was a banana wholesaler. He asked for Kakek, and when Muha told him that Kakek had died, the man bowed his head.

"Please tell Ayah that someone's here to buy the bananas," Muha told me.

I ran home and found Ayah cleaning the goat pen. The afternoon sun shone on the yard where the lamp house silently stood.

"Why should I be there?" Ayah asked when I relayed Muha's message.

"Maybe he doesn't want you to think him dishonest." Ibu stood in the backdoor opening.

"Who would accuse him of such a thing?" Ayah walked out of the goat pen and added, "Did I ever distrust him before? Why is everyone always thinking poorly of me?"

"Who is thinking poorly of you? No one is," Ibu calmed him.

Ayah did not respond. He went to the backyard, with Nono on his heels. When he returned with a wood log and went back into the goat pen to start the trash fire, Nono waited for him outside the pen.

In the evening, Muha came over with Raziah and their son.

Muha handed Ayah the money he had received from the banana wholesaler.

"This money is actually neither all mine nor your mother's," Ayah replied. By *your mother*, Ayah meant Ibu, who was Muha's mother-in-law. Referring to Muha's mother-in-law as if she were his own birth mother was a way to show closeness. "That money partly belongs to my brothers-in-law, your maternal uncles. But, none of them is here. How am I supposed to give them their share? So, let's just use the money together."

"Yes, I understand," Muha answered.

"I can't blame anyone. What good would it do anyway? Even if we blamed the soldiers?" Ayah remained pensive for a while, then added, "I've never visited my mother, either. But I have an older brother and sister who can take care of her. Just like you, I lost my father when I was still young. Maybe, by now, my mother has also passed away."

Muha nodded slowly and cleared his throat.

Ayah picked up the money Muha had laid on a bench, counted it, and then gave it all back to Muha, without taking even one rupiah. "This money is for you. You need to buy some rice and fish."

Muha was speechless for a moment, then protested, "But we eat from the rice in the sacks that are stored in Nazir's room."

"Then, just buy whatever you want. Don't you, Raziah, and Akbar need new clothes?"

Muha was touched by Ayah's generosity. Behind his rough exterior, Ayah hid a soft heart. It was true that Ayah often grumbled and said something embarrassing, but in the end, he was always right.

One afternoon, Ayah and Muha went to clear up the areca orchard near the river.

While Ayah gathered and put the areca nut clusters into a sack, Muha cut down the palm midribs for roofing materials. Suddenly, the sharp machete slipped from his hand and hit his leg. Muha screamed. He had hacked into his leg bone. Blood seeped through his pants.

Ayah came running and quickly tore his shirt to make a tourniquet. The machete had cut into the leg bone rather deeply.

Muha groaned with pain.

When Muha was unable to get up after several attempts, Ayah told him to climb on his back so he could carry him home.

When Muha hesitated, Ayah yelled, "Hurry, stupid."

Ayah carried Muha, who was smaller than him, to Kakek's house. He moved as quickly as he could along the uphill road between the shrubbery among the areca and cacao trees while supporting Muha's bottom with both of his hands.

Muha held on to Ayah's shoulders, grimacing. His wounded right leg hung off to the side like a wooden log. Blood and mud stained his pants.

## Chapter 13

Around June 1993, I had already registered at the new high school in Blang Riek. I had also enrolled Zuhra, who was now seven years old, at the elementary school I used to attend, near Simpang Mawak.

In order to pay for Zuhra's and my schooling, we had to sell five goats at the Buloh Blang Ara market. The money went to pay for our application fees and tuition, as well as to buy our uniforms and school supplies.

Even though we owned a big piece of land that included Kakek's orchards, which Muha now took care of, it only provided enough to cover our daily necessities. The prices for agricultural commodities were very low, while the prices of basic necessities continued to increase. The price of kerosene kept climbing. Kerosene to us was just as important as any other basic necessity. We used it to light the oil lamps in front of our houses.

The new soldiers, who were sent to replace the old batch in Simpang Mawak, rarely entered the villages. According to rumors, these soldiers acted as security guards at some government projects to earn additional money. They were also known to ask the contractors for a share in their profit.

A bulldozer that belonged to the Ministry of Public Works came to Simpang Mawak to level the roadside. The heavy equipment roared back and forth on the road, shaking the surrounding areas. The engine's rumble was easily heard from afar.

The monkeys moved away from the road that the bulldozer flattened from Ceumpeudak to the south of Alue Rambe.

About a dozen dump trucks came down from the northeastern hills near the Mobil Gas refinery in Lhokseumawe and poured a mixture of soil and yellowish gravel on the flattened road. Then another elongated vehicle, which looked like a compactor with a giant metal plate in the middle of it, pounded the material into the ground.

A group of shirtless boys in shorts, who were out of school, ran happily toward the heavy equipment, but were immediately yelled at by several workers. "Hey, this is not a toy. Get away. You'll get hurt."

The boys ran laughing to the roadside. Some climbed up a tree along the roadside and, quietly sitting on the branches, watched everything from above while thick dust clouds filled the surrounding area. It became a festive show, and my village was suddenly crowded.

The stall owners in Tamoun moved their merchandise aside when the bulldozer came to clear the road in front of their stalls.

I often saw a few soldiers guard the area around the trucks that brought coconut tree–sized concrete pillars. When a crane arrived to help unload them along the main road of Buloh Blang Ara, soldiers busily regulated the foot traffic but did not search anyone.

A few months later, the concrete pillars were erected along the district's asphalt road.

The people of Seuneubok Drien, Ceumpeudak, Alue Rambe, and Lhok Jok were often spared from the inspections at the Simpang Mawak checkpoint on their way to and from the Buloh Blang Ara market. However, others who wished to enter those four villages to visit their relatives or for any other reason were required to report first and leave their identification cards at the checkpoint. They were also often searched, and some were even arrested because they looked suspicious.

Until then none of my maternal uncles and aunts came to visit Kakek's, Nenek's, and Arkam's graves. At that time, it was perceived that coming to Alue Rambe meant you were looking for disaster.

I was happy when the main road in my village was leveled, even though it had not been paved with asphalt yet. The road looked wide when Zuhra and I passed it every morning on our way to school. Once I passed Simpang Mawak, my old bicycle moved fast across the smooth road to the high school in Blang Riek.

Unfortunately, in less than a year, the road was full of holes again. The quick deterioration of the road was not only due to poor workmanship. According to rumors, the contractors had to pay one-third of the budget to the military as dues for security services.

I expected the Years of Massacre to end soon, because development and road construction was taking place everywhere, under the control of the all-powerful military. The gravel sub-district roads — starting from Lhokseumawe — were now finished with asphalt. The erected utility poles had electrical cables spread on the crossbars, providing electricity to the surrounding houses, which motivated people to buy color televisions.

Light rains began to fall in early November. The parts of the road that were flat and elevated could be traveled on without trouble, like any other asphalt road. But all the roads that went through the hills were eroded. The lower parts of the road were flooded, and the water dragged some of the yellowish, gravelly soil onto the villagers' farmland.

The mini-trucks that came to buy agricultural products in Alue Rambe often got stuck and had to be pushed by lots of people. The spinning wheels created big holes in the road. If it were not for the truck drivers, who filled the holes themselves by shoveling soil and gravel that had washed down from the hills, the road damage would have remained unattended.

When cars became trapped in the mudholes, their churning engines sounded like a person grunting as he tried to lift or pull something far beyond his strength. The spinning tires left black marks from their peeled-off rubber. The black smoke from the vehicles' exhaust was similar to the oil lamp's soot, and it blackened the clothes and faces of the men who tried moving the vehicle.

On rainy days, the hill under Leman's stall was always muddy and slippery. Because half of the road was completely eroded, truck drivers were forced to drive their vehicle over and into holes. The engine would roar noisily once it was forced to rise from the depression. Every time a truck got stuck, farmers helped push it to the road in front of the open field that was occasionally used by the military as a gathering place to torture the people of my village.

The villagers who used motorcycles and bicycles did not experience the same problems. For them, the patched road around the holes was like an asphalt road. However, the riders who were unable to maneuver around the holes and ride through them would bounce on their saddles as if they were riding a horse.

The hard road around Ceumpeudak was in much better shape. The road was flat, and the few small holes that appeared were easily filled with the loose gravel compacted by passing cars. Bikers had a smooth ride on this road, northwest to the Buloh Blang Ara market and south to Simpang Keuramat.

At the intersection of Simpang Mawak, the roads leading to Lhok Jok and Seuneubok Drien converged. Those narrow roads, only ten feet wide, often confused the military headed to Alue Rambe. They often took the wrong road when chasing after rebels, which had often enabled Arkam to escape.

The five stalls in Simpang Mawak had been renovated. They had new walls, and a coffee stall had been expanded. The stalls were surrounded by a densely built housing complex. A large stretch of rice field unfolded behind the houses.

After Arkam's death, the military ignored our village. Arkam's remaining followers never appeared again. Other than busying themselves with various construction supervisions, the present military presence was merely an effort to prevent the reoccurrence of rebellion. Only once in a while would they act on a tip from an informant and arrest someone.

Ayah had regained the weight he lost. He was calmer now, and even though his hair was thinning and showed silver strands, he still looked handsome. He looked strong and healthy. He still tended his orchards and occasionally worked in the field to plant peanuts. The only time Ayah became restless was when it was his turn to do the night watch.

One day, I overheard Ayah talking to Nono.

Ayah was sitting on a porch chair with Nono seated in front of him.

"Remember, if someone comes to arrest me, you must not attack him," Ayah said.

Nono cocked his head. His pink tongue hung out of his mouth, and his quick breath sounded like someone snoring.

"Remember, don't attack them," Ayah repeated. He fastened his eyes on the dog and added, "It's no use. If you try to attack them, you'll die before they do."

Nono stared at Ayah without blinking, as if he understood what Ayah had said.

I believed that Nono was able to understand Ayah. Dogs had sharp instincts.

Ayah had developed a habit of talking to his dog, just like Ibu sometimes talked to her cat, and Baiti talked to the chickens and goats.

Perhaps the loss of *Partai Golkar*, The Party of The Functional Groups, in last year's general election was to blame for Ayah's reoccurring anxiety. After the loss of the President Soeharto-owned, military-supported party, with their yellow logo that depicted a banyan tree, the soldiers resumed making trouble for the night watchmen.

The soldiers still acted unfriendly towards our village because we always voted for *Partai Persatuan Pembangunan*, or The United Development Party, which had a green logo depicting a Kaaba symbol. No one had voted for the *Partai Demokrasi Indonesia*, or The Indonesian Democratic Party, which had a red logo depicting a bull's head.

None of the rebels ever surfaced again. The soldiers stationed at checkpoints along the way were rotated every year, just like the roster of the night watchmen.

It was impossible for the rebels who had fled to return home. Those who did would be immediately apprehended at their houses.

The military had a list of rebels' addresses compiled from information obtained from files confiscated during previous raids. This list, combined with the information from villagers who worked as informants, enabled the military to easily arrest anyone involved with the rebellion. And even though, at that time, the illusion of imminent peace had been created, the soldiers were still watching the homes of villagers they suspected to be sympathizers of the rebellion.

A number of young men in my village, who had secretly become Arkam's supporters, moved away from Aceh under the pretense of looking for employment. However, many of them failed to cross the Aceh borders. Some were found dead; others simply disappeared.

There was nothing else to be done in this village, other than to work in the field. And because the wholesalers always bought the agricultural products at a very low price, the farmers remained poor. Meanwhile, the government eliminated job opportunities at the gas liquefaction plants, fertilizer factories, and paper mills. Those who wished to work as civil servants had to prepare money amounting to millions of rupiahs. Farmers were not able to do this. It was hard enough for them to pay for their children's education through high school.

At that time, only a few children could finish elementary school. Hardly anyone finished middle school, let alone high school. A lot of my friends in this village were illiterate. The same situation applied to other youth of my age in other villages. They could not read, let alone write, which created a shortage of eligible males to marry, and girls had difficulty finding a suitable husband.

A lot of girls started to have secret affairs with soldiers stationed at nearby checkposts. Many of these shallow-minded Acehnese girls became pregnant, and their illegitimate children, who were born and raised without a father, would become Aceh's future generations.

---

When I was in my sophomore year of high school, the soldiers from Simpang Mawak checkpoint often wandered around, carefully observing everyone's face. On my way home from school, or any other time I biked along that road to buy something at Buloh Blang Ara market, I would notice a group of girls mingling with a number of soldiers. They would sit in the checkpost, or on the front porch of the villagers' house, and, on some occasions, I saw a few girls go to the checkpost. It was strange that the checkpost made any man tremble but made those sixteen- and seventeen-year-old girls giggle happily.

Oftentimes, I heard people refer to them as *cheap girls.*
*Corrupted girls.*
*Naughty girls and bitches.*

Those girls usually came from Blang Riek, and some of them were my classmates. One of them was Yeni, a beautiful girl with light, yellowish skin. She was my first love. However, because I thought that she was too beautiful for me — although I never once thought I was less attractive than my classmates — I never told her about it.

Once, I was determined to greet her. Before approaching her, I looked at my face in the window glass several times. I had already prepared several simple greetings to create an impression that it was just a normal, friendly greeting. However, once I faced her, I could not remember any of those words, and even if I could have, the words would probably not be appropriate for the situation at that time.

When I faced her, my tongue became numb and my body stiffened. I imagined I must be as pale as I had been when facing the soldiers. My heartbeats punched the inner wall of my chest. If Yeni were able to see it, she would have seen my chest move uncontrollably.

"Do you want to talk to me?" Yeni asked.

My body trembled.

"Yes," I stuttered.

"What's the matter?"

"I'd like to borrow your notebook." I first thought that was a good reason, but when I said it, it sounded fake.

"Which one?"

I could not stand to look into her beautiful eyes, which rested on me. Yeni didn't seem to be suspicious. After all, borrowing a book was important business. Her attitude calmed me.

"The notes from this class," I said and looked outside.

"Didn't you take notes?" she asked, confused.

Her question exposed my lie. "Y-y-you're right. But I don't have all of it. I-I missed some parts," I stuttered.

Yeni smiled and dug into her bag. She looked calm, as if she had not noticed any of my awkward behavior.

I was relieved.

"My handwriting is bad." She handed me a notebook wrapped in a plastic sleeve. "I hope you can read it."

I nodded, not knowing what else to say other than to thank her.

All I could think about on my way home was Yeni's notebook. I could not wait to get home to see her handwriting, and I peddled fast. No longer able to contain my impatience, I decided to stop in the middle of a quiet road after passing through Simpang Mawak. I reached into my bag for the notebook. For a moment, I enjoyed holding that beautiful girl's notebook. After turning it a couple of times, I pressed it against my chest.

I closed my eyes and took a deep breath, hoping the book would hold some traces of the fragrance of her hair. I was imagining her soft breasts pressing against my chest when a passing motorcycle spoiled my daydream. I put Yeni's notebook back in my bag and jumped on my bike. During the remainder of my ride home, I had to adjust my seating position on the saddle several times because my penis kept throbbing.

Once home, I locked my door. I kept looking at Yeni's handwriting in her notebook and imagined the movement of her beautiful hand as she wrote. To me, those notes were the most important writing in the world.

That was my first experience approaching Yeni. It turned out that Yeni was the one who often borrowed my notebooks, especially when she had not finished her homework. She even invited me to her house, several times. Of course, I was only happy to help her.

Yeni was weak in mathematics, physics, chemistry, and biology.

I always did my homework diligently, and Yeni often came to my desk after class. Sometimes, she would unreservedly flirt with me while touching my hand. Her touch wildly excited me, and her scent caused me to have several wet dreams.

In our senior year, Yeni was not chosen to attend the accelerated class, and she began to avoid me.

I was brokenhearted. I only then realized that my feelings had blinded me. Even though she was not rich herself, Yeni was actually never interested in a quiet and poor man. She had only used me to get her homework done.

During that time, Yeni openly visited the soldiers' checkpost and flirted with them. Her parents turned a deaf ear to their neighbors' mockery.

I did not want to think about Yeni anymore but regretted her reckless attitude. Perhaps she never thought of the consequences. Yeni was not alone. I heard that there were several other girls who liked to visit the military post.

I hated those promiscuous girls and their ignorant parents. Or, perhaps Yeni's parents had prohibited their daughter from going, but she did not care. It also could be that her parents did not dare to prevent their daughter's relationship with the soldiers, because they were afraid of being accused of being rebels.

Because I could not do anything, I only sighed. "You'll bear the consequences of recklessly indulging lonely soldiers."

---

When I came home from school, I changed my uniform and ate a late lunch alone in the kitchen. During the entire month of December, I did not need to carry water to the house. The big plastic drum used to contain the runoff from the roof would be covered with a wooden lid once it was full.

The rain made me feel lazy. I especially did not like to cut grass after Asr in the pouring rain that made the air stinging cold. But I didn't want the goats to go hungry at night, so I braved the weather. If I finished my job early, before the heavy rain, there would be time to sit by the window, wrapped in my sarong, and watch the falling rain. I really liked watching the rain; it made me feel very comfortable and allowed my imagination to fly freely.

The rain that fell that afternoon continued until Isha, and turned the weather very cool. After finishing my homework, I slept soundly under my blanket.

In my high school years, the school hours were longer. The last class would finish at two in the afternoon, and I would get home around half past two.

School did not just take my time when I was confined there for the better part of the day with various rules. Even at home, I had to think about answers to problems that I had no idea if they would be useful someday. Every day, the teacher sent us home with problems to solve. He collected the answers the next day. I could not even find *one* ray of hope in this desperate situation of people living under pressures and with fear as a result of the rebellion.

My goals were simple: I just wanted this land to be a safe place, so if I grew up to be a farmer one day, I could work in peace. I would build a house, own a motorcycle, marry, and have children. Every weekend, I would take my wife and children to Buloh Blang Ara market and, at the end of every month, I would take them around the city of Lhokseumawe. How beautiful this life would be if there were no shootings and no search holdups along the road.

I continued to fantasize until I fell asleep. Maybe some of those fantasies turned into my beautiful dream. But then, that beautiful dream soon turned into a nightmare. And the nightmare became a reality I had to face when, that night, there was pounding on the front door accompanied by screams and yelling.

Startled, I listened to the yelling, stomping boots, and sounds of people fighting, with the racket of objects falling and being thrown against walls, along with the shuffle of bodies hitting the floor and walls.

I was still at the threshold of sleep and wakefulness, having a hard time determining if I was living a nightmare or if the moment was real. As soon as I got out of bed, I was dragged outside by a soldier who had broken into my room. In the yard, I was met with beatings. The cold wind chilled me to the bone.

In the dim light of the oil lamp, I faintly saw Ayah lying on the wet and sticky ground.

Two soldiers held Ibu back.

Zuhra, crying, grabbed onto Ibu.

Ibu was crying, too.

I was confused and terrified.

Some soldiers were still inside the house, rummaging through our belongings.

I heard Baiti scream out loud before her voice was muffled and someone snapped, "Shut up, bitch."

I wanted to see what was happening, but a soldier stopped me with his rifle. "Don't move," he said.

There was no use fighting back, and I trembled in fear.

Ayah lay face down on the ground. He remained motionless, like a dead person. Perhaps he was unconscious. I did not see any blood, nor had I heard any gunshots. His brown-striped shirt was soiled with mud.

Some time later, three soldiers walked out of the house. Two other soldiers pulled Ayah up and made him stand.

Ayah staggered and groaned.

"Damn rebel," one of the soldiers snapped.

Then two soldiers dragged Ayah to the street.

Ignoring my own fear and the biting cold, I ran after them.

A soldier who saw me chasing after Ayah immediately turned toward me and pushed me down. Behind me, Ibu screamed.

"If you get any closer, I'll shoot you," the soldier growled.

Through the darkness, I saw the shadows of those armed men drag Ayah to the street. The sound of their footsteps and rustle of their rifles was so loud. I listened to the wind traveling through the wet leaves after the rain.

Trembling, I clasped the wooden fence and gritted my teeth. I had a hard time standing. My knees were wobbly. Standing in muddy soil, it was difficult to move my feet. Having no idea what to do, I burst into sobs.

Soon afterwards, I heard the roaring sound of a truck that slowly became distant.

They were taking Ayah to only God knew where.

I stayed outside for a while. I could not bear to go inside to see what had happened there. I looked around me — everything was a blur. The night was so dark, cold, and cruel.

# Chapter 14

Except for Zuhra, none of us could sleep that night.

Three soldiers had raped Baiti. She and Ibu sat huddled together, sobbing.

I sat alone in the living room, trembling. I was immobilized by cold and exhaustion. A buzz filled my entire body; the sound continued to become louder, building pressure in my head and chest, making me feel I could explode at any time. Instead, I endured and the moment passed in silence.

*Ayah did not resist, yet they beat him unconscious, threw him into the yard, and dragged him into a truck parked on the main road.*

At daybreak, I went outside and looked for Nono, who was nowhere to be found. I ran to Kakek's house and anxiously knocked on the door.

Muha, shirtless, answered the door. "What are you doing here? It's only dawn."

"Ayah," I panted. "Last night… he was kidnapped by the soldiers."

Muha hurriedly dressed. Without saying a word, he put on his boots and ran out. His footsteps soon faded.

Raziah, who was pregnant with Akbar's sibling, walked into the room looking perplexed. "What's wrong?" she asked.

"Ayah was kidnapped by the soldiers last night," I answered, regaining my composure.

Raziah slumped against the wall and slowly slipped to the floor. Shaking, she took a sip from the glass of water I handed her.

For a moment, we sat quietly.

When Akbar called for her, Raziah slowly rose and said, "You better go home now. I'll be there in a while."

I left.

Baiti, still deeply shaken, had wrapped her face and body with a blanket and crouched by the door.

I went to the kitchen.

Ibu grieved silently while cooking rice and boiling water.

"Did Muha come here?" I asked.

"He left already."

"Where did he go?"

"I don't know."

I looked for Nono in the backyard, but like last night, he was still nowhere to be seen. Grabbing my bike, I wondered if he had left. I walked my bike up a small hill before getting on it.

I quickly pedaled across the much-damaged main road. Riding through the potholes and over bumps made my entire body shake, but I didn't care. I continued to pedal, as fast as I could, ignoring the cold.

The sound of my fluttering shirttails accompanied the rattling of the bike chain and the creaking of steel balls on the bicycle's axle when I stopped pedaling.

Before I reached the Simpang Mawak checkpoint, I stopped and dropped my bicycle's chain. Holding my breath, I anxiously walked my bike to the front of the post and pretended to fix my bicycle's chain while trying to see what was going on at the post.

Usually there was a commotion at the post when they were holding a farmer suspected of subversive activities, but today, it was strangely quiet. I began to doubt that Ayah was being held there.

Two soldiers glanced at me and then went inside. Another one yelled at me from behind a sandbag bunker, "Don't stop there, stupid."

I quickly rose and walked away with my bike chain dangling.

The soldier immediately chased me, repeatedly kicking my bike.

"The chain was loose," I mumbled.

"You, stupid."

Once the post was out of sight, I put the bike chain back on with a stick. Both of my hands were smeared with motor oil, which was very difficult to remove, but I didn't care. I quickly pedaled across the paved road, passing my still-quiet school. I crossed a small bridge between two rice fields before reaching the Buloh Bridge, where I took off my bike chain again. At the Buloh Blang Ara Military Base, I pretended once again to be fixing my bike while trying to get a glimpse of what was happening on the base. Other than a couple of soldiers pacing the entryway of the building, the base looked pretty quiet. The side area where three blue tents had been set up, looked deserted.

When I noticed two soldiers watching me from behind their sandbag bunkers, I pretended to be totally absorbed in fixing my bike chain. The few times I looked up, I took great care to make it look unintentional. Meanwhile, I tried my best to get a glimpse at the inside of the base.

"Hey, you," a soldier yelled. "Move on. Hurry."

*Arafat Nur*

When one of the soldiers approached me, I quickly rose and dragged my bike to a rickety truck parked alongside the road. The soldier hurled a rock at me but missed.

"If you ever hang around this base again, I'll shoot you," he threatened before turning back.

Exhausted, I sat down in front of a stall in the Buloh Blang Ara market. Perspiration stuck my shirt to my back. I had no idea where to look for Ayah. I was pretty sure that the soldiers based in Buloh Blang Ara were the ones who had arrested him last night, but I could not begin to guess where they had driven him with the truck.

People passed by, heading towards the market's greengrocers and fishmongers. Some of the merchants who had just opened their stalls already had a few customers waiting. As time passed, it became more crowded, and it was as if nothing had happened last night. Several motorbikes loaded with big baskets filled with merchandise entered the market. It started to get busy, and I decided to go home. My lips were dry and I was hungry, yet, I had no appetite.

As soon as I arrived home, I rushed to the kitchen and poured myself several glasses of cool water. I drank until I was bloated.

The door to Baiti's room was open. Ibu tried to spoon-feed her. My sister sat in a stupor and refused to eat. She acted like someone who had lost her mind. Meanwhile, Zuhra sat on the edge of the bed looking at her sister.

I went out looking for Nono, hoping that he could help me. I tried to find him in the dangau and looked around the young peanut field that did not need to be tended. I became irritated when I could not find him there either. I wondered if he had abandoned us.

"Where did you go?" Ibu asked when I came back into the house and sat on the dirt floor.

"To Simpang Mawak and Buloh Blang Ara."

"What did you do there?"

"Looked for Ayah."

For a moment, we were both silent. Then Ibu burst into tears and went back into Baiti's room.

I went back outside to look after the animals.

---

When Muha had left our house early that morning, Nono had met him on the road, barking, as if he were trying to tell him something. Muha, who often worked in the fields with Ayah and Nono, understood that the dog was trying to tell him something.

He immediately followed Nono, who ran down the yellow gravel road. No one was around that early in the morning, and all the stalls in Tamoun were still closed.

Nono kept running ahead of Muha.

When they reached Simpang Mawak, Muha asked Nono to stop.

Nono, whimpering, tilted his head. His ears erect, he kept his eyes on Muha. Several times, he started to run away but came back when Muha did not follow him.

Finally, Muha paid attention to the dog's strange behavior. His breath quickened when he squatted near Nono and whispered, "It's impossible to go through Simpang Mawak. There are a lot of soldiers there. Take me through the back roads."

Nono was silent for a while. Then, all of a sudden, he ran off. Every so often, he looked back, as if asking Muha to follow him.

Nono ran in the direction of Lhok Jok.

Muha had difficulty following the dog, who maneuvered surefooted along the narrow footpaths and weaved through thick brush.

The path led to the main asphalt road near Blang Riek. Nono quickly crossed the road and walked into a large area of *sawahs*, wet rice fields that were recently harvested. It had been raining all night and the fields were flooded. Nono made sure to stay on the dikes.

Muha, who followed him closely, would have looked like a fisherman going fishing with his dog, had he carried a fishing rod. A narrow strip of land with a stream running through it divided the sawahs.

Nono ran, whimpering, through the small grove of coconut trees and shrubbery to the riverbank. At the base of a large *ketapang* tree that touched the water's edge with its branches, the dog halted and howled while anxiously looking over his shoulder.

Ayah's body floated, wedged between a large log and the bank of the river.

Once he saw Ayah's body, Muha rushed to pull the body out of the water.

Ayah's body was torn by bullets. He had a broken nose, and his cheeks were swollen. His brown shirt and black cotton pants were ripped, but there were no bloodstains. It seemed that all of Ayah's blood had drained through his gaping wounds into the river and was now one with the brownish river water.

After he dragged Ayah's body to the riverbank, Muha sat down and burst into sobs. After a while, he picked up Ayah's body and headed home. Nono, who now was the one following, yelped once in a while.

Muha kept walking while carrying Ayah's body, which was bigger and heavier than his own. Muha's grief had awakened a great strength inside him. When he reached the paved road near Blang Riek, he moved Ayah's body onto his back, as if Ayah were still alive. He carried Ayah the way Ayah had carried him home from the field when he cut himself with a machete.

Muha hurriedly crossed the still-deserted road and turned into a wooded area.

Even though Ayah was dead, the soldiers would still arrest Muha if they found him. They also might throw Ayah's body back into the river or dump it somewhere in the jungle.

For the military, even dead rebels represented evil and a threat and were unworthy of a decent burial.

Nono followed Muha closely.

When he arrived at a rubber plantation, Muha slowly lowered Ayah's body to the ground. Weeds and shrubbery choked the saplings that were barely five feet tall. Mosquitoes and gnats swarmed around Muha's head and Ayah's body. Muha swatted the buzzing mosquitoes that attacked his face and arms.

Nono watched him, whimpering.

"Nono," Muha mumbled, "We're only halfway… go on."

The dog yelped softly.

Muha lifted Ayah's body again. With Ayah's head resting on his shoulder, and his hands and feet dangling, Muha could no longer hold back his tears. No longer dammed by anger, the tears streamed out of Muha's eyes as he resumed walking, with Nono close behind him, till they arrived at the street in front of Leman's stall.

Muha was unable to answer the questions of people crowding around them. Fatigue and sorrow tightened his chest. "They killed Ayah," was all he could stammer.

Without paying further attention to the crowd, Muha limped home.

Some people followed him. Others went to inform the village chief and Teungku Imam Masjid and his wife.

---

While Muha and I were looking for Ayah, Ibu, Raziah, and Zuhra were trying to comfort Baiti, and no one had taken care of the chickens and goats. I quickly grabbed some chicken feed. The fowl scurried, fluttering out of the coop as soon as I opened it and settled down pecking at the feed I scattered.

The goats quieted as soon as I unlatched the gate of their shed, and they trotted ahead of me to the spot where they knew they'd be tethered for the day. I was tethering the last one when I heard commotion coming from the alley.

A small group of people headed toward our house. Muha, with the village chief and Imam on either side of him, headed the procession.

I went to meet them, then froze in my tracks.

Muha carried Ayah's body on his back. Part of an arm hung over Muha's shoulder. For a moment, everything around me spun and turned pitch black.

Nono nervously circled Muha, whimpering. Every so often, he ran toward me, only to immediately return to Muha.

I walked ahead of everyone into the house.

Baiti's door was ajar, and Ibu walked out of the room looking bewildered.

Raziah and Zuhra, who held Akbar by the hand, were right behind her.

Ibu screamed as soon as the procession entered the house. She staggered toward Muha, who carried Ayah's body but then collapsed, shaking.

Several women who had just arrived steadied Raziah, who was on the verge of fainting, while Baiti and Zuhra, sobbing, held Ibu's hands.

Ayah's bruised face and gaping wounds were proof of the torture he must have endured before the soldiers riddled his body with gunshots. Unable to move or utter a single word, I stared at Ayah's body, with my ears ringing and heat filling my head. Something was very, very wrong.

The murder of my father changed my view of the world. I hated the soldiers who claimed they had the people's interest at heart, while the truth was they hurt and killed people. And I, who happened to live during this time, was forced to accept the unacceptable. They had killed the people I loved the most. And they would always be able to find a reason to kill me.

---

The strong scent of sandalwood powder, kieffer lime, camphor, cempaka, and kenanga filled my nostrils and settled in my chest, where my being was frozen in silence. As was customary, Ayah's body was bathed, enshrouded, and prayed over, then carried to the cemetery. Standing at the bottom of the freshly dug grave that was as deep as I was tall, Muha and I received Ayah's body. We carefully laid it on the ground and placed Ayah's head on a small mound of dirt that served as a pillow. We then untied every single knot of the cloth he was wrapped in.

Muha and I climbed out of the hole. Clumps of soil dropped onto two wooden boards that were nailed together and laid over Ayah's body to protect it from direct contact with the soil as people filled the grave. The sound of soil being shoveled into the grave filled the afternoon.

Ibu and Zuhra, who were among the mourners, wiped their tears several times with their shawls.

Baiti, who was still very much shaken, stayed home with Raziah.

After the closing prayer, the mourners left the graveside. Imam Masjid's wife embraced Ibu, who slowly left the cemetery with Zuhra.

For a while, I stood alone, staring at the fresh grave that held Ayah's body. Scattered around it were Nenek's, Arkam's, Kakek's and the other eight victims' graves.

Standing in the scorching afternoon sun, which now hung tilted in the sky and was no longer blocked by the lofty old banyan tree, I was lost in my own thoughts. *Why was everything suddenly so silent, and why was I suddenly all alone in this world?* When I started to walk home, Nono went to Ayah's grave and looked at it sadly.

I could not stop wondering why I could not cry like Ibu, Raziah, Baiti, Zuhra, and Muha. All of our neighbors were also crying. Even Nono howled. *Am I not as loyal as the others? Are Muha and Nono more loyal to Ayah than I?* I overheard some people whisper, "Nazir didn't cry when his father died. His heart is as hard as stone."

That night, when I sat by myself on the long bench on the porch, Muha joined me. The dim light of the lamp house was able to reach the place where we sat. The voices of some women who were about to go home traveled outside.

Ibu, still stunned, stood in front of the bedroom's door and responded to condolences from the mourners.

Baiti sat curled up next to Zuhra, who was sleeping.

After sitting for a while silently next to me, Muha said finally, "He was like my own father." Muha broke into sobs. It seemed he had been trying to hold his tears by not talking. "Maybe he was more than my own father, since I haven't had a father since I was your age."

I was quiet, gripped by uncertainty. I cleared my throat a few times and fidgeted uncomfortably. It was difficult to respond to Muha's statement appropriately.

"I love him," Muha continued between sobs, "Just the way I love my own mother."

I knew that he loved Ayah like he loved his own mother. Because he had lived without a father, Muha could not compare his love for Ayah with that for his own father.

I did not say anything. I felt guilty because I could not cry like him. Maybe in his eyes, I looked like a son who did not love his parents, who did not even shed a tear when his father died.

"I'm very sad," said Muha again, still sobbing.

I remained quiet.

After all the guests had left, Muha, too, went home.

Ibu told me to come in and closed the door.

I quietly stayed in my room until nothing other than a gentle snore broke the silence of the night. I didn't know who made the noise, whether it was Ibu or Baiti or even Zuhra. Of all the family members at home, which now were only the four, I was the only one who remained awake until deep into the night.

Suddenly, I burst out crying with uncontrolled sobs. I cried for a long time while anger and a deep resentment took a hold of me. I felt my muscles tighten, and in the blurry mirror hanging on a wall in my room, I saw my reddened face, my wild eyes, and my unkempt curly hair.

Ayah was the kindest person I had ever known; even the dog loved him. But he was tortured and killed in a cruel way because of his alleged involvement in a rebellion against the nation in which he actually took no part.

The strong fragrance of sandalwood powder, lime, camphor, cempaka, and kenanga in my room lingered in my memory until decades later. The scent aroused the passion in me to fight against the brutal people who had killed Ayah and raped my sister. Neither Ayah nor my sister were even linked to the insurgency.

I had never hated the Indonesian government, or wanted to rebel against them, or fight against their soldiers. I also did not care if we, the people of Aceh, could be freed from oppression one day.

What I hated were those cursed individuals who had killed Ayah, who had massacred thousands of innocent men, who had raped Baiti and hundreds of other innocent women. I had no idea how much anger I would have to contain in the years to come.

# Chapter 15

On the first and second day after Ayah passed away, only about fifteen people came to mourn — to pray and perform zikr for him. No food was served to the guests, except for some cookies that people had brought, along with a few pounds of sugar to be served with tea. All of us were still in shock and drowning in our grief. We only had rice with salted fish and wild spinach curry, which Raziah brought from her house. None of us had an appetite, and the food was tasteless.

I did not see Nono for those two days. Because he wasn't wandering around the house or in the alley, I thought he was in the dangau, watching over the peanut crop.

During the long dry season that followed the rice harvest, Ayah had planted peanuts, which were now only a month and a half old. The young plants did not need to be watched closely because the monkeys would only come once in a while.

Nono was surely starving because no one brought him food. He should have come home. Because grieving people had no appetite, there were many leftovers. After the mourners left that afternoon on the second day, I flavored a scoop of cold rice with some salted fish and took it to the dangau. The peanuts Ayah had planted were doing well. The occasional rain freshened the plants. The lush field reminded me of Ayah, and I became even sadder. While it was Ayah's sweat that had made these plants grow, he now lay buried in a dark hole in the ground.

I did not find Nono in either the dangau or the field. In the shade of the candlenut tree next to the dangau, I stood tall and looked across the field while shouting his name. My voice broke when, after a while, Nono was still nowhere to be seen. I did not know why, but I suddenly missed him. Perhaps Ayah's passing did not only sadden us, but also hurt that dog very much. After I was sure that Nono would not show up, I left the bowl with rice at the dangau. That way he could eat as soon as he came back.

Perhaps the dog went hunting and lost track of distance while chasing his prey.

The bank of gray clouds in the western sky slowly began to redden.

Sadness once again filled me when I looked over the field of peanuts Ayah had planted, and I suddenly was compelled to go to the cemetery, which was not far from away.

I was shocked to find Nono lying on Ayah's grave. He didn't get up to greet me; softly whining, his tail tapped the ground every so often. His ears were pulled back, and when he looked up at me, his eyes were filled with sadness.

I wondered if Nono had something to eat in the past three days. He looked like he had lost a lot of weight. His belly was flat and his fur matted. *Does a grieving animal lose his appetite like a human being? How long can a dog endure starvation?*

After praying to God to provide Ayah with a large piece of heaven, I asked Nono to come home with me, but the dog did not budge.

"You've got to come home," I said, sadly. "I looked for you in the field and left food for you there."

The dog stretched his right front leg and, whimpering, scratched the ground.

I didn't understand why he was doing that. I didn't know how to interpret a dog's sign language.

Nono let out another soft yelp.

"All right, then," I said, wiping my wet eyes. "If you don't want to go home, you can go to the dangau and eat the food I left for you there."

---

On the third day after Ayah's passing, Ibu asked me to catch the two roosters and three hens that had not left the coop that morning.

Teungku Imam Masjid came over with a sharp knife. He asked me to hold each chicken with its wings folded and legs together while he butchered it, facing the direction of Mecca.

The dying chickens made a lot of noise flapping their wings and kicked up a lot of dust flip-flopping on the ground with bleeding necks.

Three women of our neighborhood came to help Ibu dress the chickens.

Muha and I built a furnace from banana stems, large enough to hold a large kettle to cook the chicken curry and a large steamer to cook the rice. The large kettle and steamer were community property and kept in a storage room at the mosque. While I watched the fire, Muha went to collect dried bamboo stems from the riverbank.

The heat from the burning furnace, combined with the scorching heat from the sunlight, coated my whole body with perspiration. Our tasks forced us to bury our sorrow for a while and showed others how strong our family was as we faced the ordeal of Ayah's brutal murder by the beastly soldiers. While it appeared we simply accepted it all, the fire inside me raged even bigger.

The delicious aroma of simmering chicken curry spread everywhere. Not long after noon, people started to arrive. Men and women, old and young, including children, flocked to our yard, as if we were having a party.

Muha and I had to unfold a plastic tarp so the people could sit where we used to store our bagged rice.

While Imam Masjid led the prayer, the hum of prayers and dhikr filled every corner of our house. It seemed to bother the old rooster. He stretched his neck and crowed a warning, as if he saw a hawk flying in the sky.

Imam Masjid's wife worried that there would not be enough food and asked me to count the guests so that the amount of food placed on each plate could be proportioned appropriately.

There were more than sixty guests, excluding children. Flustered, Imam Masjid's wife instructed the kitchen help to cut the portions of rice in half and break up the small pieces of chicken in two or even three pieces. To make sure everyone got something to eat, plates of rice and dishes were prepared and arranged on the kitchen floor. After the prayer was recited, the plates were distributed, followed by glasses of water.

After Teungku Imam Masjid invited everyone to eat, they finished their meal in about five bites and immediately emptied their glasses of water. Perhaps they didn't have enough food. Everyone was smacking their lips and making sucking sounds while holding their tongue against their teeth, as if trying to extract the last bits of food that were stuck between their teeth. The empty plates were definitely a testament to the advice of

Prophet Muhammad to not leave even a single grain of rice on one's plate.

When I tried to find some leftover rice and a piece of meat in the kitchen, I could not find anything.

Ibu, who saw me walking between the women who were cleaning up, called, "Have you eaten, Nazir?"

"I had my lunch, but now I'm hungry again."

"I saved you a plate. Look under my bed."

Under Ibu's bed, I found a plate of rice covered with a tray. When I walked out of the house with it, I came upon Muha standing behind the kitchen.

Muha looked at the rice plate in my hand as if he had not eaten and asked, "Didn't you have your lunch already?"

"This is for Nono," I replied.

"Where is Nono?" he asked, surprised.

I shook my head. "Maybe in the dangau."

"Nono also needs to eat well," he replied and turned away.

I poured half of the food on the plate into a coconut shell and devoured the other half. Then I rushed to the dangau where I found the rice and salted fish I brought yesterday covered by a group of fire ants.

I walked to the cemetery and found Nono lying on Ayah's grave. The dog most likely had stayed there all this time without food or drink, without any regard to his own weakening condition.

"Can you pray?" I half-joked.

My casual words somehow saddened me. Teungku Imam Masjid once said that plants and stones could pray for people who had passed away. I did not know if dogs could also pray. *If they could, would Allah accept a prayer recited in a dog's own language?* I believed that Nono prayed for Ayah day and night.

"Eat this." I put the coconut shell under his nose.

Nono stared at me for a while. Then he blinked his eyes and rose. He staggered before starting to eat the rice and chicken meat in the coconut shell.

Watching Nono eat made me happy. I had no idea why I could feel happy in the current situation. Apparently, a feeling would always present itself and sometimes even when not desired.

Nono finished the food but I was sure he wasn't full yet. When I tried to persuade him to come home, he only let out a soft yelp and curled up on Ayah's grave.

I was flabbergasted at Nono's loyalty to Ayah even after he was buried. Nono continued to ignore me and, not wanting to force him, I went home alone.

Dogs were considered unclean beings. From a religious study book, I learned that Satan spit on Adam's body during the process of his creation. A dog was created from that spit to protect Adam's body. Therefore, dogs were considered unclean.

Even though dogs were created from Satan's spit, they were very loyal toward humans. Their loyalty exceeded the loyalty of humans amongst themselves. If Allah was willing, the dogs that faithfully defended humans would be placed in heaven, just like the dog that protected seven men, as told in the "Companions of the Cave," a Quranic story. I was sure that one day, Nono would be reunited with Ayah in heaven.

---

On the sixth day after Ayah's passing, some heavy equipment, including flatbed trucks, tow trucks, and a crane, entered the village to deliver some long concrete poles to install electrical wiring for Alue Rambe. When I was at Kakek's house — I still called it Kakek's house even though Kakek and Nenek had both passed away and now Muha, Raziah, and their child occupied the house — to pick a cluster of half-ripened bananas, I saw a worker, who wore a yellow hard hat, scold children who wandered around the crane.

Along the roadside around Ceumpeudak, the concrete poles had already been erected, with their bases buried deep into the ground and set in concrete.

The crowd at Leman's stall watched the whole process, ignoring the heat from sunlight that suddenly became strong. Scattered clouds covered the sun once in a while. A southeastern breeze cooled my sweaty face while I struggled with the weight of the big cluster of bananas. I had to put my load down several times to switch hands before I reached home.

In the afternoon, Imam Masjid arrived at our house with a sharp knife to butcher a goat. Tomorrow, a ceremony to commemorate the seventh day of Ayah's passing would be held.

I followed Muha, who dragged a male goat to the jackfruit tree in our backyard. The fat goat's four legs were hog-tied with a rope. The animal wriggled with all its might.

Muha and Teungku Imam Masjid ignored the loud bleating that stopped as soon as the goat's throat was slit, and thick blood poured into a hole in the ground near the jackfruit tree.

Some women helped Ibu and Raziah in the kitchen while Baiti stayed in her room, only coming out to urinate behind the house or defecate in a public toilet in the stream. Ibu carried Baiti's food to her and forced her to eat so that my sister would not starve. Baiti ate very little, and she quickly lost a lot of weight. Some women who looked in on her could not bear to watch her and quickly left.

Teungku Imam Masjid untied the dead goat and proceeded to hang the carcass off a sturdy branch of the jackfruit tree to dress it. Muha helped lift the goat. Meanwhile, I went to fetch two big bowls, which I put on top of a wooden table that had been prepared. After the goat's body was hung with its head down, Teungku Imam deftly skinned the dead animal with a small knife he carried wrapped in its sheath in the folds of his sarong. He started by dissecting the skin of one leg.

Muha followed his example with much slower movements on the other leg.

Before it turned dark, the goat was cut up. A flock of chickens crowded around the intestines.

Nono was nowhere to be seen; he was supposed to get his portion of fresh meat before it was marinated with salt and limejuice.

When Teungku Imam Masjid and Muha were not looking, I took three pieces of meat from the bowl and took it to the cemetery.

Nono still lay on the same spot. There was no headstone. Two castor bean branches marked the head and foot ends of the grave. The vegetation of the spot where Nono lay was trampled.

I put down three pieces of fresh goat meat in the coconut shell.

Nono sniffed it and immediately ate it.

I sat down. This very quiet place was now where Ayah, Kakek, Nenek, and Arkam rested. It was as if their graves were spread across my being, and I felt quiet.

"Become smart and useful," Ayah had said repeatedly, and those words were imprinted in my mind.

I was a high school student. None of the other kids in Alue Rambe had the same level of education as me. Most of them did not finish their elementary school and were illiterate. Only a few could read, and most of them had left the village. Now, there were only five young men in this village who could read, and they only showed up for their night watch duty. Like most villagers, they were busy working in their orchards and fields.

"Nono, you have to go home," I said, wiping my wet eyes. "There's no use to wait here for Ayah. He won't come back to life again."

That dog stared at me, puzzled.

I sighed. I stretched both of my legs and placed my hands on my knees. Once again, I gazed at Kakek's, Arkam's, Nenek's, and Ayah's graves. The four graves were only mounds of dirt with coral stone, which was believed to have the ability to send up a prayer for the person buried.

"You can't be like this," I said to the dog lying at my right side. "If you continue like this, you'll soon die, too."

Nono whimpered. I found it difficult to understand him, and perhaps he couldn't understand me either. I wanted to explain to him that there was no need to lament death for too long. I rose and said, "All right then." Annoyed, I added, "Stay here if you don't want to come home," and I left him.

---

At dawn, when the day was still young, my house was already bustling with various activities. Several women were cooking rice, boiling water, and preparing the goat curry. Everything had to be done by noon. Ibu had purposefully planned this big *kenduri*, ceremonial meal, in addition to the previous one for Ayah's spirit. During his lifetime he had done so much for our family, from working hard in the field to providing us with an education and raising us with so much love.

At first, Ibu wanted to slaughter three goats, but that would trouble a lot of people. After talking it over with Muha and me, it was finally decided to butcher only one male goat. Considering the wealth Ayah left us, three goats for the seventh day of Ayah's passing ceremony was not excessive. But during these uncertain times, butchering just one goat already made this kenduri the most luxurious festivity held in this village for the past six years.

At midday, after the *Zuhr* prayers reverberated from the mosque, people started to come to partake in the meal. They headed for the small tent that was set up near the porch, where the food was being served.

Everyone was served a scoop of rice, a piece of goat curry, and two pieces of jackfruit stew.

We purposely served the meal this way so everyone would get an equal amount to eat. If we allowed people to help themselves, some gluttonous folks would take as much as they wanted without consideration for others.

The guests, who were invited by an announcement in the mosque, flocked to our house in a continuous flow. After getting their food, they looked for a seat on the porch, which was already covered with a mat. Some went to sit on mats under the coconut tree, and the rest spread mats under a Malay apple tree near the lamp house.

This commemoration ceremony of Ayah's passing did not differ from Raziah's past wedding ceremony. The guests were neither somber nor sad. Instead they happily joked with each other before and after eating their meals.

After finishing their meals, they immediately excused themselves. They, indeed, were not required to perform a prayer. All the food was gone before sunset.

Muha and I had to cook another pot of rice. In the kitchen, the women were boiling chicken eggs that Ibu had gathered. There were fifteen special guests who came in the afternoon after the Asr prayers to read the samadiyah prayer for Ayah. There was no more goat curry left for them. Nevertheless, they had already attended the event at noon.

Fortunately, Ibu had hidden some of the goat curry under her bed for our dinner.

I had been too busy during the day to think about Nono. During dinner, I secretly set some rice and a piece of meat aside for that dog. Muha and Raziah went back to Kakek's house, with a small care package of a handful of rice and some pieces of goat curry that Ibu gave them.

Ibu looked sad and tired. But she tried to keep it to herself.

There was not one guest left in my house. The bustle that started at noon suddenly was gone. Ibu quietly started to put away some scattered utensils.

Ibu's silence cut through my heart. Ayah was no longer with us, Baiti was drowning in her never-ending sadness, Zuhra had fallen asleep, exhausted, without Ibu. Raziah no longer lived with us. Now everything was very different, and the house resembled a cemetery.

I lit the lamp in the yard and then walked to the cemetery. I carried a plastic bag with a large fistful of rice and goat curry in one hand and held a flashlight in the other. I pointed the light at the clay dirt road flanked by thick growth. Only the parts I pointed my flashlight at were lit. It was as if the light could not spread, as if there were a wall blocking it.

The cemetery felt like a dark jungle. There was no one around. Even during daytime, farmers rarely used this street, let alone at night.

"Nono," I sighed, hoping that the dog was there.

Everything remained eerily silent.

I walked into the cemetery, pointing my flashlight towards the graves. I believed in the existence of spirits. Muha's crooked mouth and the villager's swollen genitals were proof they existed. Thinking about the incidents made me even more scared, especially because I now was standing alone in a dark cemetery.

I sighed with relief when I saw Nono. I quickly put the flashlight on the ground and put the food into the coconut shell.

"You're now causing a lot of trouble," I told the dog. "You can't take care of yourself. No one will take care of you. Don't be counting on me. I won't live forever."

Nono didn't seem to care. He continued to eat.

I picked up the flashlight and took a deep breath. "If you keep acting this way, you'll die here from starvation," I said, irritated.

Even though I only brought Nono food once a day, it seemed that lately I talked more to dogs than humans.

"All right, then," I said, walking away slowly. "Tonight is the last night I'm bringing you food. Tomorrow, you must come home, or else I will beat you."

## Chapter 16

The large, open grass field across from the Buloh Blang Ara Military Base was crowded with students and teachers from the elementary, middle, and high schools, government employees, and a row of armed soldiers. The U-shaped assembly faced an empty pole.

I was at a flag ceremony to commemorate Independence Day. After Kakek and Nenek were persecuted and died as a result of it, after Arkam was slaughtered, after Baiti was raped and Ayah was brutally murdered, I began to lose my understanding of many things that happened in this world.

The midday heat on the 17th of August 1994 stung my skin. The steamy air made my whole body perspire even though we were not marching. The entire crowd stood impatiently waiting to move through the parts of the ceremony. Each part took a very long time. And this was a repeated misery every year.

Some girls who fainted in the assembly were carried by the teachers to the shade of a banyan tree at the corner of the field.

The others, with perspiration streaming down their faces, did not dare to move under the watchful eyes of soldiers who stood behind the assembly lines with rifles hanging from their shoulders.

The headmaster had warned us several times: If we did not attend this ceremony, we would be punished severely. Our names were checked from the attendance list before we marched to the field. The presence of students at the ceremony had become a benchmark of success for the soldiers. They felt the ceremony awakened the spirit of resistance against insubordination, especially for teenagers whose fathers had experienced the pain from the kick of a soldier's boot.

While I harbored a great hatred towards the military, I did not want to fight against them or show my dislike for them. However, two students who stood in the line next to mine were apparently born in a family of ill repute and were looking for trouble. While everyone solemnly followed the ceremony, one of them poked the other in the ribs, which solicited the response, "You shithead." Several students started to giggle, which caused the teachers to throw us fearful, warning looks.

Just a moment before the flag was raised, one of the students let out a stinker, as if it were a command for the national anthem to be sung. Chuckles broke the silence as the flag was slowly raised while everyone saluted.

One of the students, a thin boy who wore a shabby uniform and worn shoes, saluted the flag with his right hand while the other scratched his butt.

After the ceremony, the soldiers dragged the students who had disrupted the ceremony with their behavior to the side of the field for a beating.

I deliberately walked away. I did not want to deal with either the soldiers or those kids. But the excessive treatment from the soldiers sparked my anger. I intensely disliked their army uniforms and their weapons. My anger flared every time I saw a soldier.

I changed during that time. I became very quiet. At school, I avoided troublemakers and generally stayed away from everything that could turn into a problem.

———•———

Ayah's passing put our family in a state of uproar. Ibu was often drowning in her sadness, and Zuhra often had to remind her that the fish in the frying pan was almost burnt.

Meanwhile, Baiti continued to drown in her misery. A few times, I caught her staring out of her window. She would look away when I talked to her. It seemed that keeping to herself was the most comfortable for her.

I had an impression that her swelling belly, which was getting more difficult to hide, bothered her the most. She even refused to see the girlfriends who came to visit her.

An eerie silence greeted me when I came home from school in the afternoon. It felt as if all vitality had been sapped out of life. However, something inside me was still burning, reminding me I had to move through these tough days, without drowning myself in endless sadness. I always reminded myself that I needed to be strong and healthy, so I could take care of the field and the orchard and do Ayah's jobs. If I were to get sick, I would burden Ibu. Illness became the scariest thing for me.

After I finished my meal, I grabbed my straw hat and headed for the field. I took along a jar of drinking water and a sickle. Now, I was the only man in the family and the breadwinner.

I left the drinking water jar and the sickle under a candlenut tree at the roadside and picked up a hoe from the dangau. I dug up the ground as fast as possible, until I ran out of breath.

*Arafat Nur*

The scorching afternoon sun burned my skin, and soon I was soaked in perspiration. The thirsty soil quickly absorbed the droplets of my sweat. Now I really understood how hard Ayah worked in the field to provide for all of us. This is how it felt to be a man who provided for his family.

Exhausted, I let go of my hoe and walked to the candlenut tree to get a drink. The mouth of the container felt warm against my dry lips. The water, even though it was warm, quenched my thirst.

I sat down and leaned against the tree trunk. My arms were dark and my hands rough. The skin was peeled at several spots from gripping the hoe handle. The thought that I had to finish digging up almost an acre of land before September sent me back to the field. I hoped for heavy rainfall that would prepare the soil for planting.

At twilight, I cut a sack of fresh grass for the goats' night feed. White clouds floated in a clear blue sky. I cleaned up the pen and built the fire while Ibu herded the goats home from the backyard.

It was dark before I reached the stream to bathe. When I returned with a towel wrapped around my waist and carrying the bucket in one hand, the smoke from the lit garbage and dung in the goat pen filled the air and irritated my eyes.

I lit the lamp in the yard, and its beautiful sparkling light pierced my heart. Ayah's unconscious body had lain there before he was dragged to the truck that was parked at the entrance of the alley.

For a moment, I stared at the spot and wondered what was wrong with Ayah, what was wrong with me, what was wrong with this world. The sounds of buzzing cicadas and chirping crickets drifted from the candlenut and melinjo orchard across the street. I walked into the house and locked the door, as if forbidding the darkness of the world to enter the house.

"You've been working too hard," Ibu told me when I sat down at the kitchen table.

I stopped chewing for a while. "I'm not sick, Bu."

"I'm worried that you'll get sick if you work too hard and push yourself like that."

Apparently, Ibu had been worrying about me. However, with enough food and sleep, work had made me stronger and healthier. Each day, my muscles became stronger, harder, and more resilient. At first, the work was definitely torturing, but then my body adjusted. I grew taller and gained weight. Most of the time, I was so exhausted I slept soundly through the night and never heard the sound of nightingales or owls anymore.

Ibu told me that a weasel had been stealing chickens. "Only feathers and innards were left," she said and added, "Nono is never home anymore."

The dog still kept his vigil at Ayah's grave. I no longer brought him food, so he hunted birds, snakes, or whatever other animals he could. I had not seen him during the past week, as I was too busy preparing the field for planting before the first rains would fall in September.

However, I could no longer leave Nono to his own devices and have him wind up being a stray dog. One afternoon, on my way back to the field, I brought along some rice and fish and went to Ayah's grave.

The dog still lay curled up on the grave. The ground at the head of the grave was completely trampled. Nono's dull fur was thinned, and he had sores at several bald spots.

Seeing how thin Nono was made me angry and sad at the same time. Though I was angry with his stubbornness, I tried to persuade him, gently.

I put the rice into the coconut shell, which had rolled all the way to Kakek's grave. I noticed that the other three graves were covered with greenery.

While waiting for Nono to finish his food, I weeded the three graves. It was easy because the roots were buried in soft soil. I recalled everyone as I weeded their graves. The only one I was not close to was Uncle Arkam. The most vivid memory I had from the six years we spent together was his dream to free Aceh from oppression. Now, he was buried deep under this ground. His rebellion had not created freedom. Instead, it had worsened the oppression and increased our calamities.

When Nono finished eating, I immediately ordered, "Nono, go home."

The dog looked at me with his pink tongue hanging out of his mouth.

"You must come home," I repeated. "You must protect my house and the chickens. That miserable weasel is on the prowl again. You must kill it."

Nono cowered, whimpering, as if not wanting to obey me.

"I've never forbidden you to love Ayah. I love him as much as you do," I said. "But you can't stay here forever. Your duty is to protect the house, protect the livestock, and the field. This grave will only make you suffer."

When Nono continued to whimper and still didn't move, I lost my patience. I picked up a broken tree branch and waved it at him. "If you don't go home, I'll hit you," I shouted and added, "Hurry."

When I hit the ground with the branch, it made a loud thud, and broken twigs flew around when I waved it at Nono again.

Nono rose, startled. He moved away, yelping, with his tail between his legs.

"Go on home," I snapped. Breathing hard, I pounded the ground again and added, "Right now," as I raised the branch and waved it at him.

Terrified, Nono ran yelping to the street. He stopped near the cemetery gate, and turned, looking for me.

I pointed the branch in the direction of our house and yelled, "Go on."

For a moment, Nono stood staring at me. His eyes were filled with deep sadness. He finally seemed to understand that he could not defy me. Whimpering, he trotted toward the alley of our house.

I gazed at the clear sky filled with thin clouds that looked like scattered smoke. The bright afternoon sun above the canopies of the trees around the cemetery blinded me.

When I came home from the field in the evening, Nono lay curled up against a wall at the eastern side of the house, not far from where he used to lie. He looked at me cautiously when I passed him, carrying a sack of grass on top of my head, but he didn't get up.

Before I took a bath, I fed him. This mended our relationship.

Nono ate his food without hesitation.

I happily praised him, "Smart dog."

That night, I heard the dog's light steps as he walked around the house. After Ayah passed away, I moved to the front bedroom. Ibu and Zuhra moved to the middle bedroom, where Muha and Raziah used to stay. Baiti now stayed in my old bedroom and sometimes slept with Ibu and Zuhra.

After Nono came home, Ibu stopped complaining about the weasel stealing the chickens.

The dog's body regained its strength. The sores on his skin slowly healed on their own, and his fur now looked shinier than before. Overall, the dog looked bigger and healthy.

One day, Nono brought home a dead weasel almost as large as a quarter of his own body. The weasel's head bled from holes of canine teeth that had penetrated deeply. One of Nono's hind legs was wounded and the wound had crusted.

I buried the weasel by the banana trees near a soursop tree. I was sure that this old weasel was the one who always preyed on our chickens and had killed many of them. As long as Nono was around, the chickens would be protected from wild animals.

Nowadays, Nono spent more time close to home. He would have to move to the field once the peanut plants started to bear pods. I knew that Nono often secretly went to Ayah's grave. He would stand there for a while and stare at the mound, his eyes filled with sadness.

---

Not long after the army abandoned the Simpang Mawak checkpoint and the soldiers were transferred to Buloh Blang Ara Military Base, Raziah gave birth to a baby girl. While the midwife was tending to Raziah, Ibu walked busily between the kitchen and bedroom to prepare the diapers and other necessities.

Baiti, drowned in her own silence, sat in front of the stove tending the fire that boiled water for the baby's bath. Meanwhile, Muha tried to shush Akbar, who was crying for his mother.

I glanced at Baiti, who was drawing in the ashes of the firewood with her index finger. She had trouble sitting on the small stool with her bulging belly, which she could no longer hide. Every time she bumped into me or our eyes happened to meet, she looked away.

I realized she was ashamed of herself, so I chose to avoid her. If she passed me, I looked away as if she were not there.

I really pitied my sister and could not bear to watch her suffer. Yet I was disgusted by her bulging belly that carried the soldier's bastard child.

Baiti, who covered her body with loose clothes and wore a long batik skirt, never left the house. She never saw the widened asphalt road with the utility poles alongside it, nor did she know that Leman's stall now had a new color television.

I very seldom spoke with her. Every time she came out from her room, she covered her face with a batik cloth, as if she were walking in a crowded street and tried to avoid other people's looks. She looked very pale when she came to greet our maternal uncles and aunts who visited us with their children.

Now that the soldiers were no longer at Simpang Mawak, our relatives were finally able to visit. They visited Kakek's, Nenek's, Arkam's and Ayah's graves with somber faces. They were overcome by grief when they found out that their father, mother, brother, and brother-in-law were already buried.

But when they returned from the cemetery, while still wiping their tears, one of them said, "Now that Ayah has passed away, we have a right to our share of his wealth, as stated by the Islamic law."

Ibu, who had been swept into the crowd's grief, had not recovered fully and immediately fell silent.

I watched the look on her face change and wondered if she was having the same startling experience as me.

It appeared that the passing of Kakek, Nenek, Uncle Arkam, and Ayah didn't mean anything to them and the deaths had been immediately forgotten. All they worried about was the wealth Kakek had left behind.

I asked myself, *Where were they when their father and mother were still alive? Who was the one who took care of their parents when they were ill? Why didn't they regret and feel guilty that they could not see their parents while they were sick? Why did they come only to claim their inheritance?*

Ibu's face was taut as she explained, "Muha and Raziah now live in that house. If you want it, you can take it. Muha and Raziah can live with us."

None of them replied. My uncles and aunts, who sat in a circle on a mat spread out on the porch, exchanged glances.

"It's not that we want to move into Kakek's house," an uncle replied. "We have our own house in the city. We also won't be able to take care of Ayah's orchards. Muha and Raziah can continue to live there, but we have a right to the harvest of Ayah's farm."

"Of course," Ibu quickly interrupted and looked at them one by one. "As stated in this village's law, half of the yield belongs to the caretaker. Not only will he share in the harvest, he will also receive a fee for taking care of the land."

"Well, yeah, that's what we meant, half of the net proceeds."

"I set the amount aside." Ibu rose and walked to her room. She returned, holding a few bills that had been earmarked to pay for the installation of electricity in our house. The small sum was money Muha had given to Ibu each time he sold a harvest, and she now handed the money to my uncle.

The man who had a slightly bulging belly and was around Ayah's age took the money from Ibu and counted it.

It was obvious that Ibu's siblings did not care about her sorrow. They only came to claim their inheritance. They ignored how difficult our life was. Those people from the city — who were never close to us — had never experienced the wrath of the military like we had. The rebels mostly operated in the villages and jungles; they rarely went into the city.

So Ibu had to be patient and postpone the installation of electricity in our house. Most of the Alue Rambe villagers had already installed the electric meter on their house walls and thrown away the oil lamp that smelled of kerosene and covered their house with soot.

At night, Leman's stall was crowded. The remaining villagers acted like moths drawn by the bright light from Leman's lamp.

The absence of soldiers in Simpang Mawak greatly reduced the villagers' fear about the military. Because the curfew had been lifted, the stalls stayed open till midnight. Once in a while, two soldiers from the base in Buloh Blang Ara came with their motorbikes to check on the night watchmen.

In our house, which was still dimly lit by oil lamps, I listened to songs from a transistor radio I had bought at the Buloh Blang Ara market. For a while, the music transported me away from my gloomy environment.

The melancholy that our house was wrapped in made me feel like a stranger in my own home. The silence always evoked sad memories. It often felt like everything had turned into a cemetery. At night, I listened to pop and *dangdut,* Indonesian folk music, while flipping through the pages of my school textbooks. I liked the songs the radio played.

When I turned the radio off, night sounds outside permeated my room. There were the crickets' insistent chirping and dogs barking in the distance, the song of the nightingale and the hooting of owls. And then, when the night reached its moment of deepest silence and clearest stillness, I could hear the wind sigh through the soft rustle of the leaves. The old fears had disappeared and were replaced by a new restlessness. Meanwhile, the night kept moving like time that never stopped.

My memories of Ayah and seeing Baiti suffer always filled my chest with unbearable rage. At such moments, I would leave the house and go to Leman's stall to order a cup of coffee and enjoy the show on the color television — an object that amazed the villagers of Alue Rambe as a miracle they never imagined before.

In color, the people on the screen looked as real as the people around us. The TV showed us a wide variety of incidents happening around the world: the rise of the United States as the world's superpower, the never-ending war between Israel and Palestine, the threat of Russian nuclear weapons, the heated situation in the Middle East, as well as many other events. However, everything happened in countries far away, and this made me feel even more isolated.

# Chapter 17

A group of girls who were about to enter Leman's stall giggled with each other when they saw me. Every time I walked on the street or sat down in Leman's stall, I always felt one or two girls watching me. They'd pretend to joke with each other while throwing glances at me. The braver ones openly made their advances, which made me feel awkward. Usually, I would respond in passing, as if I was not interested.

There were too many girls between the age of seventeen and twenty in Alue Rambe. They had reached their marriageable age, and their families eagerly waited for someone to propose to them. Some of their mothers tried to befriend my mother, hoping to make me their son-in-law. One of them, Aminah, even followed Ibu home a few times.

In general, Ibu was happy with the attention from the neighbors who wanted to make her a part of their family. Their attention consoled her and helped her cope with the death of her husband and the rape of her daughter. But sometimes, they were so insistent, they irritated Ibu. Because she could not ask them to leave, she instead half-heartedly engaged them in conversation.

"I'd be very happy to have in-laws like you," said Aminah, who lived across the river.

I was in my room, trying to finish the homework I had to submit on Monday, and overheard the conversation.

Ibu replied, "Nazir is still a kid. He's just tall. He hasn't even finished school."

"Isn't he going to graduate next year?"

"He's still a kid."

"He seems to be a competent farmer already. Surely he'll be able to feed his wife and children," the woman pressured. "Furthermore, didn't Muha marry Raziah when he was in his twenties?"

"What are you getting at?" Ibu asked, straightforwardly.

"It's 1994 now. Next year, Nazir is going to turn twenty, and he will reach a marriageable age. A lot of men in our village get married around that age."

"If I'm not mistaken, Nazir will only be nineteen next year."

"It's not a problem, is it?"

Ibu remained silent for a while.

"So, what do you think?"

"About what?"

"About matching Nazir with Zulaiha?"

"I don't know if Nazir likes her. I'll ask him first, okay?"

Once the woman left, Ibu came inside.

I was about to go to the field.

Ibu seemed startled when we passed each other. Perhaps she thought I had already gone.

"Did you hear my conversation with Zulaiha's mother?" Ibu asked.

I pretended not to know anything and said, "I didn't hear anything, Bu."

"Do you like Zulaiha?"

"Argh. I don't want to talk about it."

"But her mother keeps needling me. The mothers of other girls also keep asking about you."

"I'm a guy, Bu," I replied, looking away.

"They're worried because there are no men available to propose to their daughters," Ibu said.

It didn't seem to cross her mind that a lot of young men had left Aceh during the past four years. Some had disappeared quietly, while others were kidnapped and massacred.

I was able to stay because I was a student. The military did not consider students to be a part of the rebellion. The unemployed and uneducated young men were the ones they were concerned about.

"Maybe Nono will do," I joked.

"What?"

When Nono heard his name, he immediately rose and came to me with his tail wagging, and we headed for the field.

After the peanut harvest in June, around two months ago, I planted the plot with turmeric, and now the stems were about an inch tall. The southern part of my field, which previously was filled with shrubbery, now showed a lush green of mung bean plants. Thick clumps of lemongrass served as a border between the plots.

Thin gray clouds filled the overcast sky. The wind blew the tips of the turmeric leaves against my naked ankles.

Nono was still following me around. He looked healthier since he stopped sleeping on Ayah's grave.

Every time I found a bent stem, I straightened it by pushing some soil against it. Some collapsed stems looked as if they had been stepped on by passing boars or dogs. I was sure Nono was not the culprit. He knew these plants were planted on purpose.

When I reached the southern part of the field, Samsul, Zulaiha's father, was working in his field, which was adjacent to mine.

After we exchanged polite smiles and greetings, he started a conversation. "Your turmeric plants look really good," he said.

I replied with a smile and a nod.

Apparently, he felt the need to add, "Your plants look better than any of the turmeric plants in this village."

"Hopefully."

I didn't understand why this man, who usually kept to himself, suddenly was so talkative. When he came toward me, I looked up as if observing the weather, then quickly walked to the dangau. I swept up wood and bamboo debris from termites. The wind blew hard while I gathered the garbage under the dangau, and soon it started to drizzle.

Nono curled up near me when I sat down on the bench and, swinging my legs, surveyed the large field of turmeric. For the time being, the plants didn't need much care. I didn't have to start weeding the plot until next month. Meanwhile, I only needed to check on the plants every so often. Now I could use my time to take care of the coconut and areca orchard at the back of the house. I no longer needed to weed the candlenut orchard. The shade and dense foliage of the trees discouraged the growth of wild grasses.

When the drizzle turned into rain and the wind became colder, Samsul came running to my dangau. He flicked the raindrops off his hair as soon as he was under the roof. His presence made me uncomfortable. At a time like this, I preferred to be alone.

"Can I sit here?" Samsul asked.

"Go ahead," I said and moved over.
"This rain will refresh our plants," he said, sitting down.
"Hopefully, it won't come down too heavy," I responded.
"I don't think so. This is September rain. It's usually light."
I nodded and then fell silent for a long time.

When Samsul picked up the conversation, he startled me. He said, "I heard that you already have a future wife."

"Who said that?" I growled. "I'm still a student."

"Oh, then I was given the wrong information."

"Who gave you the information?"

"Zulaiha." He seemed embarrassed. "You know her, right? My daughter is paying attention to you."

"Of course I know her."

"She's sixteen. She's a good girl and doesn't like to wander around Tamoun at night. She is also a very good cook. I prefer her cooking to that of her mother's."

"Oh."

"Why don't you ever visit us?" he asked and turned to face me. "We're close neighbors. We can even become a good family."

"Hmm." My throat suddenly felt itchy. I rose and said, "I'm too busy. I'm busy studying and taking care of the field." I excused myself while walking away. "And now, I have to cut grass for the goats."

"If you don't have time in the afternoon, you're welcome to come in the evening." Samsul's voice trailed after me.

---

On a Sunday at the end of September 1994, Ibu quietly went to fetch an old woman who lived at the southern end of the village. The woman had been a midwife since Arkam was born.

Baiti gave birth to a baby boy, who was named Muslim. I had no clue whose idea it was to give the baby this name. I also was very surprised that the name disguised the fact that the child was illegitimate.

Just before the baby was born, Baiti groaned like someone under great duress.

Ibu walked in and out of the room and tried to calm her. She held Baiti and rubbed her back.

After it was born, the baby screamed so loud, I was sure he could be heard at the end of our alley. Our neighbors probably guessed that my sister had given birth to a bastard child. There were not many people who knew about Baiti's pregnancy. Some of them might have forgotten about the rape, because Baiti had been hiding for the past nine months.

I suddenly found myself dragged into a vortex of feelings; I pitied Baiti and Ibu, I hurt from losing Ayah, I hated the soldiers, and I was disgusted by Muslim. All those feelings churned inside me and made me feel as if I was going to explode. Unable to stand being under the same roof with the baby who represented Ayah's murderer, I staggered to the door.

In Samaun's stall, I worked off my anger. Together with a middle-aged man, I helped carry sacks of betel nuts, which Samaun had purchased from a farmer, to the scale and then loaded the sacks on a mini truck owned by a wholesaler from the city.

---

Ibu often laid Muslim down in the living room. When she changed his diaper, I coincidentally glanced at the small, wrinkly lump in his crotch. The baby had a round face and flat nose. There was a small resemblance to the soldiers who murdered Ayah. His crying often disturbed my sleep, which made me hate him even more.

I was just as disgusted with the baby as I had been with Baiti's pregnant belly. The baby came from the seed of the man who had killed Ayah — or had participated in Ayah's murder.

Sometimes, I pitied Baiti, who was busy caring for a baby she did not ask for. She had not worked since the onset of her pregnancy and had to rely on Ibu. She took some money from the sale of my peanut harvest to buy the baby's diapers and clothes. She could only use a few of Akbar's hand-me-downs for Muslim.

---

The sale of a male goat, combined with the proceeds of the betel nut harvest, finally enabled us to pay for the connection to the electric circuit in Buloh Blang Ara. When the installers came, Baiti was changing the baby's diaper.

Ibu quickly removed the dirty diaper. She didn't have a chance to greet the two men at the door and buried her annoyance in silence.

I showed the electricians where the meter should be installed. The two men, who had come riding their motorbikes with their cables and tools, immediately went to work.

I helped them run a cable between a pole in the alley in front of our house and a breaker panel they nailed to an outer wall of the house. After that, they installed switches and plugs in every room.

"Is that your firstborn?" one of the electricians asked me while Baiti dressed the baby.

"No." It felt as if I had screamed my answer. I quickly continued, "He's my nephew. I'm still a student." I was insulted that he thought the baby was my child and ashamed that the baby was a part of my family. The man had quickly jumped to the conclusion that I was the baby's father. *Did I look that old?*

When the installation was finished, I kept flipping the switch, repeatedly turning the light on and off. I was amazed by the blinding brightness that came from the light bulb.

I moved all oil lamps to a corner of the kitchen. The light in my room was so bright, I had to turn it off before going to bed.

---

One afternoon, when I checked on an outside light that was burned out, the village chief came to ask me to take part in the night watch. He said that the older watchmen were often sick. Therefore, those who were over sixty years old were excused from the night watch duty.

The number of men in my village kept decreasing. Some who owned land or had relatives elsewhere, moved. Others simply wandered off and left their wives. It seemed that people left the village because they worried about being the military's next victim and experiencing the same ordeal as Ayah.

Soldiers would arrest anyone who had given a rebel a plate of rice or a cigarette. They said that giving anything to a rebel was the same as supporting the rebels' efforts to undermine the government.

With the decrease in the number of men in my village, the number of night watchmen had also decreased. Even though I was still a student, I was put on the roster three times in a month. I was the only teenager among middle-aged and old men. While they often nodded off, their eyes would immediately open wide once they heard the roar of motorbikes in the distance.

Because I was still in school, the village chief placed me only on Saturday night rosters. I therefore moved among the different groups and didn't always have to report for duty every ten nights like other night watchmen.

During the first month, I was put on the roster three times, but not a single soldier came. In the second month, two friendly-faced soldiers greeted us with a *salaam,* the Arabic Islamic greeting, and chitchatted with us. My intense dislike for them made me stiffen when they questioned me.

"So, are you a student?"

"Yes."

"Gentlemen," a soldier kindly addressed the platoon of night watchmen. "I'm sure that after working hard during the day, having to do your night watch duty makes you very tired — especially when you have to go to work again the next day. But during the night watch, not everyone needs to be awake all the time. There are eight of you. Four can do the watch while the rest can go to sleep. Among the four of you who do the watch, two can stay at the post, and the other two can make the rounds. Meanwhile, the other four can sleep. That way, you can take turns sleeping. Right?"

The soldier's words brought me great comfort. I started to think that not all soldiers were bad, and after that night, the raging flame of hatred inside me began to die. As soon as the two soldiers left, three men and I immediately went to sleep, even though I did not have to go to school the next day because it was Sunday.

We passed the new rules on to the night watchmen of the next shift. It so happened that the same soldiers came to check.

During my next turn, I slept peacefully with three other members while the other four were on watch duty till two in the morning. That night, the soldiers who came to check on us were two different soldiers. They immediately dragged those of us who were sleeping, out of our cots and beat all eight night watchmen until we were black and blue.

I was wrapped in my sarong when I was dragged off my cot. At first, I thought one of my fellow night watchmen was playing a prank on me. The first two hard slaps on my face disoriented me. Only the third slap made me realize that the one hitting me was an enraged soldier.

"What good will you do here if you're asleep, huh?" the soldier yelled. "This is called a night watch — you're not supposed to be sleeping."

"But the inspector who came yesterday said that half of us could go to sleep," one of the watchmen interrupted.

The interrupter was immediately slapped. "Who was yesterday's inspector? Is he your father?"

My head hurt, and the hard slaps made me dizzy.

A soldier pushed me down.

Another yelled, "Hey, you. Straighten up."

"You don't need to beat us anymore," I said weakly.

A rifle handle slammed my back with a loud thud.

"What did you say?"

"I hurt," I answered.

A punch landed on my face, followed by a knee to my stomach and repetitive slams on my back with the butt of the soldier's rifle. I collapsed. When I touched my temple, I was bleeding. However, I did not feel anything. I did not feel any pain; I only felt hot. The fire inside me raged again.

"You're a rebel, right?"

"I'm still a student."

My hatred for the military resurfaced. I promised myself I would be a rebel like Arkam and kill all those barbaric people. As dawn neared, I went home with a bleeding face and head and bruises on my back and thighs.

Ibu was shocked and started screaming when she opened the front door and saw me.

"It's okay, Bu," I said, trying to walk straight. "It only hurts a little."

While she cleaned my wounds with cotton pads dipped into warm water, Ibu scolded me for talking back to the soldiers. She said, "You're lucky they didn't take you away."

# Chapter 18

During the long rainy days in January 1995, I often sat on the daybed in the living room looking at the rain. The sound of rain hitting the hard ground and the rustling, windswept leaves brought me peace. Some chickens took shelter beside the porch, some were in the coop, and others were in the goat shed. I always cut grass for the goats after school.

Muslim was now three months old. I always avoided him.

Ibu or Baiti usually put him on the daybed in the living room after bathing him in the afternoon. The baby's face reminded me of the soldiers' faces and Darwin's monkeys in my biology class. The chubby baby was healthy and had a good appetite. He was able to turn over and babbled on the daybed Muha and I had built.

Baiti, who had returned to do house chores, watched her baby as she walked back and forth. Every time the baby was near me, I cringed as if there was a strange presence bothering me.

Baiti did not dare to ask me to watch Muslim. However, Ibu, who chose to ignore my dislike of the child, said, "Please watch Muslim. Don't let him get too close to the edge."

"I can't," I replied curtly, while walking away. "I have to check on the goats and chickens." For a moment, I stood on the side porch, looking at the seven goats we had left after some of the kids and their mothers had been sold. The goats were like money in the bank that could be withdrawn when needed.

Meanwhile, Muslim rolled over to the edge of the daybed and dropped to the floor. His screaming alerted Ibu and Baiti, who rushed to him in a panic.

Ibu rubbed Muslim's back while blaming me for his fall.

The baby's frantic screams were deafening and terrified me. Muslim's face was so red, his screams so shrill.

"How did he wrong you to make you dislike him so much?" Ibu cornered me.

Baiti silently stroked the baby's face with the corner of her sling as if she accepted the bad hand of cards life had dealt her. And this made me feel terribly guilty.

---

During the turmeric harvest in March, Baiti took the now six-month-old Muslim to the field. She made a hammock for him in the dangau with her sling and had Nono watch the baby.

Ibu, Zuhra, and Baiti pulled the old turmeric stems out of the ground, and I carried the harvest home in a plastic sack. Because I was the only one who carried the turmeric home, and there were three women who harvested the roots, I quickly fell behind.

Baiti immediately ran to the dangau when the baby cried. She lifted Muslim from his sling and brought him to her breast while softly patting his butt.

Muslim always made me feel unsure. When I was around him, my feelings alternated between disgust and pity. It was undeniable that the baby came from the seed of one of the savages involved in Ayah's torture and murder. The flesh and blood of that brutal individual was now a part of my family, and we were obliged to care for him regardless of our own needs. I swore to kill him one day.

Muslim was seldom sick and grew up facing the world with an innocent, carefree attitude.

When I began to turn over the ground in preparation of planting rice, Muslim started to walk. Holding on to the walls, he toddled around the house. Several times, he reached for his mother's back while Baiti sat cracking betel nuts on the porch.

One afternoon, Baiti let him amble into the yard without support. The toddler, who only wore a pair of faded, worn shorts, came to me, laughing with outstretched hands.

I was putting a dressing of ground turmeric on a wounded chicken's thigh after it survived a weasel's attack.

When Muslim came near me, he reached for me to help support himself. I pretended not to see him and moved away to return the limp chicken to his coop.

When the support he had counted on was not there, Muslim fell flat on his face. Crying, he scrambled in an effort to get up. After several failed attempts, he finally managed to rise and again started toward me. However, when he saw Baiti on the porch, he changed directions and moved toward her.

I watched him quietly while feeling guilty. I actually felt very sorry him, but my disgust over the fact that he was the seed of that godforsaken man was much stronger.

One morning, after it had rained the whole night, I decided to skip school to plant rice. Sitting on the stoop in the door opening, I hurriedly finished my breakfast of fried yams and a cup of coffee.

Muslim, who was already up, toddled happily around the living room, babbling. For some reason, the child's cheerful jabbering really irritated me. When Muslim came to me and reached for my arm, I roughly pushed my elbow toward him. Muslim staggered and fell on his bottom, hitting my hot coffee, which burned his right leg.

Ibu, who walked into the room just as my elbow touched Muslim, rushed to grab the screaming child. "How did he wrong you?" Ibu attacked me. "Why do you hate him so much?"

"He's the seed of Ayah's murderer," I shouted. As I quickly left the house, I glanced at Ibu, who held Muslim up under his armpits. Some of her hair fell on her forehead, and a pensive look settled in her eyes.

I walked to the field carrying a quarter bag of rice seed with Nono on my heels. I agreed with Ibu and was bothered by her question. I kept asking myself, *What had the child done wrong to deserve my cruel behavior?*

Unable to shake my guilty feelings, I buried two small poles, one at the northern part of the field and one at the southern part. Between them, I strung a strap of raffia as my guide so I would not stray too far to the left or right when making the seed holes. Then I grabbed my trowel and started digging.

Plagued by my guilt over my behavior toward Muslim, my mind was muddled, and I felt restless. Muslim, a one-year-old baby, was supposed to be showered with affection. Instead, I was hurting him. Baiti, who had been violated by three men and had suffered from deep shame, was still able to accept the baby and treat him with compassion and fortitude.

The dark clouds that still lingered in the sky blocked the morning sun. I wiped the sweat off my forehead, no longer expecting Ibu and Baiti to come help me. It was entirely my fault. Muslim had no idea of the calamity that had resulted in his birth.

"Hi." Zulaiha suddenly appeared from the field next to mine.

I looked up, holding the trowel midair.

The girl walked gracefully towards me with her head bowed. She looked embarrassed when I turned to her. Because I rarely wandered around the streets and only went to the stream to take a bath, I hadn't seen her for a while. Even though she was rather shy, she looked quite pretty holding a glass bowl that was covered with a small banana leaf.

"Are you watching your field?" I asked, trying to cover up my awkwardness.

"That has always been my job," she answered. Resting her eyes on me, she added, "I noticed how hard you're working."

"I'm a guy," I answered.

"I brought you a bowl of sticky rice with grated coconut. Do you like it?" She held out a small bowl.

"You're too kind," I replied, but did not move.

"If you haven't had your breakfast, you can eat it now."

"I just ate my breakfast. I'll eat it when I'm on my break."

She nodded and smiled. "I'll put this in your dangau," she said.

Zulaiha walked away gracefully in her calf-length skirt. The wind played with her straight, long hair. Zulaiha's skin was darker than Yeni's, but she was prettier than most girls in this village. My dream to get a girl as pretty as Yeni was like wishing a pig could fly. I realized that beautiful girls always left a scar.

I went back to work. After I finished ten rows running lengthwise from north to south, Ibu and Baiti were still nowhere to be seen. I would have to fill the holes with rice seed myself. Having to work by myself was my punishment.

"May I help you?" Zulaiha suddenly appeared behind me.

Her question flustered me. But she did not wait for my answer. She went straight to the seed bag, loosened up the tie, and scooped up seed with a plastic bowl in the sack. Then she walked to the first row at the northern end of the field and proceeded to fill the holes with a pinch of seed. She took charge of the situation as if she were working on her own field.

For a moment, I watched Zulaiha, amazed. She continued to fill the holes to her left and right with rice seed. When we came to the southern border, I moved the poles with the raffia strap to create another seedbed. When I passed by her while digging the holes, I asked, "Won't your parents be angry if you're helping me here?"

"Of course not," she answered shyly.

Zulaiha never stopped working while she talked to me. She kept moving forward, placing five to six seeds in every hole.

I knew Zulaiha acted that way because she was embarrassed. By coming to my field, it was as if she was offering herself to be my wife.

But because she sincerely came to help me, her actions did not come off as the actions of a girl who could not get a date. Her attitude was truly touching and stirred up other feelings inside of me.

When I took a break, Zulaiha joined me. She drank some water in the dangau, but kept her distance. After drinking from a plastic cup I had brought from home, she immediately returned to fill the holes I had dug with rice seed.

In the dangau, I ate the sticky rice with grated coconut and sprinkled with palm sugar. It was one of my favorite dishes. I did not know whether this was a coincidence or if her mother had pried the information about my favorite food out of my mother.

"I'm sure you were the one who cooked that sticky rice," I said when I returned to the field to continue working on the seedbed.

Zulaiha lifted her head. When she glanced at me, she looked even more beautiful than before. "Why?"

"It's delicious," I replied.

She could not hide her smile, even though she quickly lowered her head. "Really?" her voice was filled with joy. She tried to cover it up with humility by saying, "My mother taught me how to cook it."

To other people who watched us work in the large field between the neat rows of freshly worked land, we might have looked like a pair of newlyweds. Perhaps that was the impression of Ibu and Baiti, who carried Muslim in her sling, when they showed up after the sun had passed the noon mark in the sky.

Zulaiha quickly put down the seed bowl and ran to her parents' mung bean field in the adjacent plot.

I pretended to be consumed in my work with no idea of any girl who had come to help me. I also ignored Ibu and Baiti's presence, even when they chitchatted with each other, as if they, too, had not seen a girl helping me in the field.

Ibu picked up the seed bowl and, filling a hole near me, she said, "I never thought that one could dig seed holes and fill them at the same time."

"But that's the way it is," I said and set my jaw.

---

The following week, after cutting grass for the goats in the late afternoon, I walked to Samsul's field to return Zulaiha's glass bowl she forgot to take home.

Zulaiha sat in her dangau embroidering a flower motif on a piece of cloth, which looked like a pillowcase. I had heard that the girl liked to embroider, and she was also able to sew with a sewing machine that was operated with a foot pedal.

Before I reached the dangau, two puppies came running to me and barked noisily. I ignored them, but prepared to kick them if they dared to bite me. However, the dogs only tried to intimidate me.

Zulaiha reprimanded the two dogs and told them to be quiet and go away.

Samsul was cutting down a banana tree. He quickly picked up a cluster of bananas and walked away.

Zulaiha moved back to the edge of the wall when I walked up the stairs and sat down in the dangau's door opening.

"I'm returning your bowl," I said, handing her the bowl.

Zulaiha's lips quivered. "Thank you," she said, blushing.

"I'm the one who should thank you," I smiled. "You helped me plant the rice."

"Ah, I didn't help much."

"I should've helped you, too," I said.

Zulaiha did not answer and tried to hide her face behind her embroidery.

For a moment, I turned my attention to two puppies I had never seen before. The dog I usually saw was a black-and-golden female.

"This is the first time I've seen these puppies." I turned to Zulaiha, who seemed to be engrossed in her embroidery work.

"Ayah told me they were Nono's children," she said.

"Really?" I asked, skeptically.

"It's true," Zulaiha tried to convince me. "They're almost a year old. They used to stay home before. I'm just now bringing them here."

"Is the yellow one a male or female?" I asked.

"Both of them are males," Zulaiha said and asked, "Do you like them?"

I nodded.

Ibu's scolding about my attitude toward Muslim kept gnawing at me. The next day, after school, I bought a set of new clothes for Muslim and put them in Baiti's room. I had been very cruel to him. I realized now that he was an innocent child.

I was wrong to act hostile towards him. After all, he was a child with feelings and, just like any other child, he needed affection and attention.

It made me happy to see Muslim wear his new outfit. The child now could walk pretty well. He toddled toward me, and I grabbed his outstretched hand as soon as he reached me.

While I played with the boy, Samsul walked into the yard with the yellow puppy I saw in the field the day before.

"I brought you a present," Samsul said and tied the pup to the Malay apple tree in front of our house. Straightening himself, he rested his eyes on Muslim. Suddenly in a hurry to tend to his goats, Samsul hurried home.

When I held the pup to check its genitals, Muslim waved both of his hands in the direction of the dog, as if giving it his blessing. When I gave the dog a plate of rice and salted fish, Muha appeared and exclaimed, "Wow. A puppy."

"It's Nono's pup," I said.

"I never knew," he said in passing, "that male dogs could give birth."

"Nono is the father," I corrected. "The mother is still a female dog."

"Such a good coincidence," he said. "Last week, I found Kakek's old dog dead in the back yard."

I was stunned and unable to say anything when Muha untied the dog and took him home. Muha named the dog Situng and trained him to be a boar hunter.

Situng had a very sharp nose and became the smartest, strongest dog in the village. He became the pack leader of all dogs in Simpang Mawak and always announced the presence of soldiers to the rebels when his shrill howl penetrated the jungle.

## Chapter 19

On a hot Sunday afternoon in April 1996, while we threshed the rice grains by beating them against the wooden box with wire sides, Mahmud showed up out of nowhere. Even though five years had gone by, he did not look any older. But he looked very different now. His curly hair was cut short. Unlike before, the pants and shirt he wore looked new.

I almost did not recognize him, but Nono greeted him with angry barking.

"Has your dog not eaten?" Mahmud asked fearfully.

I told Nono to stop barking and leave.

"Thank God, it seems he has eaten." Mahmud sighed awkwardly as Nono headed for the dangau. He then asked to speak to Muha.

Lately, Muha helped us with the rice harvest process, cutting and piling the stalks, then threshing the grains.

I didn't care why Mahmud wanted to see Muha and returned to threshing the grain.

Meanwhile, Ibu spread a plastic tarp to catch the rice grains, which Baiti separated from the hull. After laying the unhulled grains on a rattan tray, Baiti would lift the tray above her head. By tilting the tray, she'd slowly drop the grains. The wind blew away the empty hulls while the grain fell around Baiti's feet.

Zuhra then gathered the grain.

Beating the rice haulms against the wire caused the grain to fall into the box, while the dry, empty hull and leaves blew away. My head and face were covered by an old T-shirt with eyeholes. The particles of beaten rice haulms created a fine, sharp dust.

The intense heat quickly dried the cut top part of the haulms. For a moment, I looked up into the glittering sky. The light was so bright that I became dizzy when I looked down again.

Between beating the rice haulms, I noticed Mahmud and Baiti exchanging glances.

While I threw a bundle of threshed haulms on the large heap next to me, Mahmud came to me. He picked up a rake and moved the heap of threshed haulms slightly away from me, then offered me his hand as if I were an adult.

"I'm very sorry about the incident that killed Pak Camat," he said pensively, as if talking to himself. "Too many people have died during the past seven years, and too many women have been raped by the soldiers. It's truly very sad."

I took off the T-shirt that covered my head so he could see my face and said, "I don't want to be reminded of that."

"I'm sorry, Nazir," he said, looking guilty. "I didn't mean to reopen your old wounds. I came here only to acknowledge that Pak Camat was a part of us. We will never forget him. He has contributed a lot to our cause."

"What has he done?" I asked, looking closely at Mahmud. "As far as I know, Ayah was never involved in any attack against the military."

"You're right," he replied and quickly continued, "But, he brought a lot of good ideas to the meetings, even though toward the end, he refused to attend them due to worsening conditions."

"Whatever," I snapped.

Mahmud mumbled a few words before he excused himself.

I noticed him looking at my sister while walking away from the field.

A few days later, Mahmud reappeared in front of my house. I had just come home from buying a plastic sack of rice and a sack of chicken feed. I untied the sacks from my bicycle's rear rack and invited him to come in. But he chose to sit on the long porch bench next to a pile of unpeeled betel nuts. I noticed that he kept looking at the kitchen door and remembered that in the past, I had caught him watching Baiti peeling the betel nuts near there.

The aroma of fried banana and the sizzling sound of hot oil came from the kitchen and made my mouth water. I took the rice to the kitchen. Wiping the sweat off my forehead, I drank a glass of water.

Ibu, squatting in front of the furnace with a scoop in her right hand, tended the sizzling frying pan. Meanwhile, Baiti brewed a pot of sweetened tea at the table.

I returned to the porch to chat with Mahmud.

A short while later, Baiti brought out a tray with two cups of sweetened tea and a small plate of fried banana.

Mahmud openly looked at my sister, and his eyes followed her as she walked back to the kitchen.

"It was not only Ayah," I sighed, after the kitchen door closed behind Baiti. "My sister, too, was victimized by the soldiers' brutality."

"You mean, your sister who was just here?"

"Yes." I paused and looked at Muslim, who was sleeping in his hammock, then replied, "The soldiers raped her that night."

"Oh." Mahmud's face reddened and his breath quickened. "I did not know about that," he said as his jaw set.

We fell into a long silence. It seemed there was nothing else we needed to talk about.

Mahmud sipped his tea and picked up a piece of fried banana without taking his eyes off Muslim. After we finished the last piece, he took another sip of his tea and said, "I just want to know if you have any resentment about your father's murder and want to take revenge."

"What do you mean?"

"I don't mean anything. I just want to know if you want to avenge your father."

"What if I do? What do I need to do?"

"Maybe I can help you."

"When?"

"As soon as we're given a chance."

---

Around the end of April 1996, I prepared to take the high school graduation test. People seemed to forget about the presence of the military, who lately seldom patrolled the village. Even the night watchmen did not seem to worry anymore. Even if they were caught sleeping during their watch, the new soldiers, at worst, would slap them.

What kept us wondering was the disappearance of several soldiers, which was never reported in newspapers or on the radio. The military kept this information under wraps because it would contradict their boasting about how successful they'd been in eliminating thousands of rebels. How embarrassing it would be if the military were to announce that members of their fierce legions were kidnapped.

Most likely, many people would burst out laughing and say that the news sounded like the screeching of a hawk that watched his friend being preyed on by a chicken.

Around that time, a man named Ahmad Kandang suddenly appeared at Leman's stall. He had never left the country during the past years of massive killings. He was not suspected of being a rebel because his father had recently retired from the military.

I did not really know Ahmad Kandang. He lived in a different part of Aceh. I had only heard about him from other people in Leman's stall. During his own visit to Leman's, Ahmad shared, in animated conversations with other coffee drinkers, his hatred towards the military that had caused the Acehnese to suffer. His friendliness and generosity drew many people. Several villagers fully supported his plans to fight the soldiers with their own strategy of kidnapping and killing.

Only a few of the people knew him well. People said that he was an expert in assembling bombs and had exploded several in front of police stations and military bases in Lhokseumawe. But, later he had to stop these bombings because the enraged military and police units took their anger out on innocent bystanders.

The safest act of resistance with the smallest possibility of getting caught was kidnapping and killing the military spies who infiltrated the villages. Disguised as street peddlers, the villagers sold everything from kitchen knives, perfumes, and massage oil to plastic pails and ceramic plates.

Ahmad and some of his followers asked a few women to disguise themselves as customers. They lured their suspect to a quiet place, then captured and searched him. If the man's ID card proved him to be a soldier, they would torture him and bury him in the jungle.

## Arafat Nur

When Mahmud came back in September, I understood what he meant when he said that he might be able to help me take revenge for Ayah's death and Baiti's rape. I had just graduated from high school, and I never thought of continuing to university. Only the rich and government officials' children could continue to university in Banda Aceh. I was the only breadwinner of my family. It was my responsibility to take care of Ibu and my siblings.

"Your body looks more muscular now," Mahmud said, looking at me.

I was bigger and taller than most soldiers who were sent from Jakarta. My daily chores and the raging fire inside me had built my muscles and made me stand tall. Whenever I was reminded of Ayah, I felt like a giant who was about to jump into a crowd of soldiers and crush them to death as if they were lice; that was how angry I was.

"Too much Acehnese blood has been shed," I said. Mahmud sent me a puzzled look.

I was twenty-one. Most of the youth around my age, especially the girls, were already married. Some of them had two or three children. Some had finished elementary school, a few graduated from middle school, but none graduated from high school.

Zulaiha often visited my mung bean field, which was in bud. There had not been much rain since July, and the crop was not doing too well.

"The time for revenge has almost come," Mahmud said.

I left Mahmud with Baiti, who had just finished nursing Muslim.

Unlike before, this time Mahmud brought sugar, bread, and coffee.

Ibu took Muslim and Zuhra to visit Raziah, who now lived in Kakek's house with her family. Apparently, she wanted to give Mahmud an opportunity to have time with Baiti, who still acted shy around him.

Mahmud came back a week later. He came to see me in the field where I was weeding the mung bean beds. "I want to marry Baiti," he said, earnestly.

From the first time I noticed him eyeing my sister until now, I did not understand Mahmud. He was very different from most men. At that time, there were a lot of girls who were having trouble finding a husband. Most of them were prettier than Baiti and were still virgins. Yet, Mahmud had just asked for Baiti's hand in marriage. I gave him my blessings without reservations, especially because Baiti seemed to like him.

When his family came carrying five trays filled with sweet cakes, Nono did not bark at them.

I took Ayah's place and married off my sister. The ceremony was not followed by a party. The celebration at Mahmud's parents' house in Seuneubok Drien was just as simple. In their dilapidated wooden house, we were only served a meal of some chicken meat. After staying a week with her in-laws, Baiti came back home with Mahmud, who brought along some of his clothes.

During Baiti's stay with her in-laws, Muslim stayed home with us. He often cried for his mother. Ibu, Zuhra, and I patiently shushed him until he fell asleep, exhausted, with beads of perspiration on his chubby cheeks. I now loved him as much as I loved my other nephew and niece, Raziah's children.

In the afternoon, I heard from someone at Leman's stall that a soldier, disguised as a peddler of wallets and belts, was captured by a group of men near Lhokseumawe. I hoped that the captured soldier was one of the men who had raped Baiti or killed Ayah.

After moving in with us, Mahmud and Baiti occupied the middle room that once was Raziah and Muha's room. Unlike Muha, Mahmud was unwilling to go to the field. It was true that he didn't have the muscles a farmer needed to do the work. However, he was able to walk for miles through thick jungles and mountainous terrain.

Mahmud often woke up late and then wandered off to only God knew where. Even after living with us for several months, no one, including Baiti, knew what he did for a living or where he had gone when he came home late in the afternoon or evening.

Mahmud quickly avoided me whenever he saw me carry a big sack of grass on top of my head. When he saw me put on my straw hat, he looked away and went back inside the house. I never asked him to go with me to the field.

When all of us were busy, he would take our five goats and tether them in our backyard. He probably did easy jobs like that so he would not look like a freeloader in our house.

However, Mahmud always had enough money to provide for his own needs, so he didn't need to use his wife's savings. Occasionally, he'd return in the evening with a plastic bag filled with fresh fish he said he bought at the Buloh Blang Ara market.

Sometimes he'd bring new clothes for Muslim, whom he had accepted as his own child. Our whole family was touched by this, and we easily forgave him for never working in the field. Mahmud's love for Muslim made me realize even more that I did not have any reason to dislike the child.

Mahmud was not clever. He was unable to stay focused during a conversation. He didn't seem to understand the real cause of the rebellion. He had no idea what the importance was of keeping notes of important meetings and what the leaders of the rebellion had to do to solicit support from foreign countries.

All he knew was that Aceh had to be liberated from the abuse and tyranny of the government in Jakarta. Just as simple as his train of thought was, the same went for Baiti. She, too, didn't seem to care about what happened outside of her immediate environment. This probably made them a harmonious couple, even though Mahmud looked like a lazy bum, while Baiti always worked hard.

"Actually, I do have a job," Mahmud said one evening when we had our dinner in the kitchen. "My work has to do with issues of the rebellion."

I remained quiet because I did not know what he was trying to say.

Ibu and Baiti nodded hesitantly.

However, Zuhra, who had listened to him carefully, asked, "So you work in the rebels' field, right?"

Mahmud nervously coughed and a few grains of rice spurted from his mouth.

Baiti rushed to clean up the rice on her husband's arms and the table while giving Zuhra the evil eye.

"What did I do wrong?" Zuhra barked. "I was only asking."

I had found out that Mahmud handled parts of the resistance's finances. Some businessmen and rich people were willing to help the resistance movement, now led by Ahmad Kandang. Other than to finance the movement's needs, the money was also distributed among the families of the victims of the soldiers' brutality. After their husbands and sons were killed, these families lived in poverty.

Next, Mahmud took me to meet Ahmad Kandang.

About fifteen men sat in a circle on a mat, as if we were participating in a ceremony. Some smoked, which made the room stuffy. I did not smoke. Having to breathe the smoke that people around me exhaled made me uncomfortable.

Ahmad Kandang was smaller than I expected. He wore a pair of blue jeans and a longsleeved denim shirt. A black cap covered his hair. People would never have thought that he was the man who led a dangerous movement against armed soldiers.

"We have to resurrect our fight," he said, addressing the crowd gathered in the room. His voice was not as deep or loud as I had expected. His demeanor made the impression that he would not have the heart to kill a pig, much less human beings. "Not only do we need to fight for our rights, we also need to oppose the army's atrocities that surpass the devil's."

The audience nodded in agreement.

Ahmad pulled on his clove cigarette, which came from a yellow box made in China, an expensive brand at that time. After he took a few more drags, he spoke again.

"There's no end to their kidnapping, killing, and raping. If we don't fight them now, we will end up being massacred. They plan to kill all the residents here, and then send people from their island to inhabit this land. You can see it now."

It was true that some parts of Aceh were now inhabited by people from Java. The military had barracks around the properties so the rebels could not chase them away.

Ahmad's speech reignited the fire in my chest that had started to die for some time. If I looked at what was happening around me, it was really difficult to argue with Ahmad's statement. The military apparently had arrived at a plan to kill all Acehnese, even though at the onset of the reign of President Soekarno, the people of Aceh had donated an airplane to the government while the rest of the country could not even breathe.

"Only we can save ourselves," Ahmad continued. "Don't expect too much help from other nations. They do not see how much we suffer. The Acehnese are a great nation whose wealth is being robbed and whose people are being annihilated. We never thought the people we helped in the past, the people incapable of driving away the Dutch and the Japanese, would turn against us."

"Look at our brother, Nazir," Ahmad pointed at me and made everyone turn toward me. "His father was killed, and his sister raped."

After he paused for a while, he pointed at Mahmud and said, "It's not shameful to marry a girl who has been raped. She was raped against her will. The men who marry girls who are rape victims are the men who are willing to help our suffering girls."

Some people nodded their heads; others whispered. Cigarette smoke billowed and filled the room.

"We have to unite and support each other. Other than uniting to fight the soldiers, we also must gather money, to help the families of victims who lost their breadwinner. Remember, we don't fight out of revenge; we fight against injustice. Our dignity has been trampled, our religion violated. We now have to fight all of them, dead or alive."

After a brief silence, Ahmad glanced at the door.

"Please come in, Brother Muha." Ahmad welcomed my brother-in-law and continued, "He's a new member of our police force."

I was shocked. I didn't know Muha would be involved in this kind of secret gathering.

Not long after the small meeting disbanded, a group of police officers drove up in a truck. They were met by a number of women carrying babies and small children who were gathered around the house and kept the police from entering.

Meanwhile, inside the house, many people worked quickly to disguise Ahmad. Some shaved his thin mustache, others helped him put on a skirt and a blouse. They completed the female clothing with a shawl.

Then, Ahmad, who now looked like a woman with his lipstick-stained lips and carrying a baby, walked right by the police officers, who were busy trying to move aside the women gathered around the house.

When the police finally entered the house, they did not find a single man. Ahmad Kandang, who at that time was the Vice-Commander of the Pasai Area for the resistance movement, was saved from the ambush by the villagers who loved him dearly.

## Chapter 20

Units under command of the resistance movement's Vice-Commander for the Pasai Area, Ahmad Kandang, attacked small groups of soldiers that passed by the main road and threw homemade bombs in front of the police stations in Lhokseumawe.

On Tuesday, February 4, 1997, radios broadcast news about a robbery at the Bank Central Asia at the heart of Lhokseumawe. Three armed rebels had shot dead a security officer and cashier. A driver and three military police officers were wounded.

I could not get get tired listening to the repeating broadcast and brought along my radio to the field. I sat for a while in the dangau contemplating the situation. I was afraid the government would send the military to the villages again.

When I saw Zulaiha walk into her field, I immediately turned off the radio and jumped down from the dangau.

Zulaiha smiled sweetly.

We went to pick mung beans together. I looked at the cluster of pods I had just picked. Each pod was about the size of my index finger and held ten to fifteen beans. When I looked up, gray clouds filled the overcast sky and a flock of birds fluttered between the treetops.

Suddenly, Zulaiha asked, "What are your plans for the future?"

I did not understand her question. "What do you mean?"

"Doesn't everyone have a plan?"

I thought for a while, trying to figure out what she meant. Finally I said, "I don't know what my plans for the future are."

"Don't you plan to propose to someone?" Zulaiha's voice trembled, and the hand that continued to break off clusters of mung beans shook.

Guessing what she was driving at, I answered, "Of course I do," and continued, "but I can't right now."

Zulaiha bowed her head. The rim of her straw hat covered her face.

I watched her nervously roll a mung bean pod between her thumb and index finger. I wanted to say something to her that weighed heavy on my heart, but I did not know how to say it. There were too many problems I had to face but could not talk about now. I did not feel prepared to enter into a marriage. Other than being too young, I planned to join Ahmad Kandang's unit.

I was compelled to drive away the criminals who had killed Ayah, raped Baiti, and murdered thousands of villagers. There was no way I would tell Zulaiha this. Also, if I were to take up arms against the military, I would always be chased by the police officers and soldiers. *How would that affect her, Ibu, and Zuhra? Who would take care of the orchards and work in the field?*

After a long silence, she asked, "When will you?"

Zulaiha's question was not answered until mid-March.

After my meeting with Ahmad Kandang, I began to understand the nature of Mahmud's employment. It turned out that he did odd jobs on an as-needed basis. Sometimes he was asked to take provisions such as rice and fish to a hideout; at other times, he worked as a courier, delivering messages from one rebel to another, and sometimes he was asked to pick up or deliver money. He did not know anything about weapons, let alone carry one. The only time he touched a weapon was when he was told to wipe the disassembled parts.

Ahmad Kandang paid Mahmud by the job. That income was enough to meet his daily needs for a week or two.

A group of soldiers came to Alue Rambe, looking for two fugitives involved in the Lhokseumawe bank robbery. They arrested five men at Leman's stall.

While chasing a villager in the alley in front of my house, they released some shots in the sky.

Baiti, who had only recently recovered from her trauma, huddled with Ibu in the kitchen.

Mahmud, who was home, rushed out through the back door and headed for his parents' house in Seuneubok Drien. He stayed there until the next day.

When Mahmud returned, he said, "I can't be seen too often by the soldiers."

I thought he was correct to stay away from the soldiers, even though he had such an innocent face, the soldiers most likely would overlook him. During a road inspection, people like Mahmud were usually ignored by the soldiers.

Meanwhile, early in 1997, some people from political parties started preparing their campaigns for the election of delegates to the central and regional House of Representatives at the Buloh Blang Ara market. Most villagers favored the Green Party with a Kaaba cubic logo even though the Yellow Party, with the banyan tree logo, put a lot of pressure on them. While the soldiers by rights could not be involved in political matters, they played a big role in promoting the Yellow Party, which I heard was under the direct command of President Soeharto.

---

During the campaign activities for the General Election, the soldiers no longer roamed around Alue Rambe. The farmers were now bothered by boars that destroyed the plants. Muha took out his spear and, together with a dozen other men, went on a boar hunt. Nono and Situng came along together with other dogs that were usually watching over the farms and the houses. The soldiers from Jakarta chose to ignore the ruckus of hunting cries from the men and barking from the dogs that carried from the jungle to their base near the Buloh Blang Ara market.

The wild boars destroyed the farmers' plants. Many plots of cassava, yams, and the newly planted coconut saplings were uprooted and trampled. During the day, the boars hid in the forest without leaving any trace of where they had gone. But the boars could not deceive Situng, who could find even the most hidden boar's nest.

During the entire afternoon, noise of the hunt filled the air.

Zulaiha and I often were in our respective fields; sometimes we visited to help each other. Working my field filled the passing time and brought me quasi-happiness.

Once in a while, I joined the hunters along with Nono, who was getting older and was not as agile as he used to be. Now it was young Situng who led the pack with relentless determination. Once he picked up the boar's scent, he quickly followed the trail with the rest of the pack right behind him.

Nono, who was known as the smartest of all dogs, did not seem bothered by Situng taking on the leadership of the pack.

Perhaps he knew that the younger dog was his own flesh and blood, and heir to his father's intelligence.

At that time, it was a particular boar that plagued Alue Rambe, Seuneubok Drien, and Cot Meureubo. The animal was once wounded in the stomach by a spear. While the encounter did not kill the boar, it turned him into a ferocious, vengeful animal that would charge anyone he met in the field. Two of the five people he had butted almost died, and the others were severely wounded.

The soldiers and police officers in Buloh Blang Ara knew about the problem but chose to ignore it. Perhaps they were even happy that a boar killed the villagers. Several strong men from the three villages agreed to bring along their dogs and go after the boar.

The jungle that surrounded the villages was quiet, until a dog found a boar in hiding and, barking, alerted the other dogs, which would respond.

The barking of dogs was followed by the yelling of hunters, who split up in order to signal which direction the boar was moving. The farmers who were still in their fields quickly climbed into a tree or their dangau. It was common knowledge that a hunted, angry boar would charge anyone who crossed his path.

It was quiet for a while. The boar apparently had managed to get away. Some men cautiously followed their dogs.

The hunters and their dogs headed toward the stream. But when they arrived at the riverbank, the dogs lost the boar's scent. They ran in different directions, agitated, sniffing the ground and checking out clumps of vegetation.

Meanwhile, Nono sniffed the ground around him before following Situng who, with his nose to the ground, headed towards a bend of the river where there was a small marsh.

Situng and Nono stalked the muddy thicket when suddenly the boar jumped out of the thick growth and grabbed Situng's hind leg.

Nono immediately started barking, which brought everyone running to the marsh.

Under sudden attack by so many dogs, the enraged boar was forced to let go of Situng. Growling and groaning, the boar faced the attacking dogs. Charging randomly, it threw and wounded several dogs.

Muha, who was ahead of the other men, was the first one to throw a spear, which hit the boar in its front leg and made it stumble.

When three other spears almost simultaneously stabbed its neck, head, and stomach, the boar collapsed with wide-open eyes and fresh blood seeping out of its mouth.

Situng's leg was severely wounded.

Muha wrapped the dog in a plastic sack and carried him home.

Raziah made a turmeric paste to medicate the deep wound on Situng's leg.

That night, Nono and Situng feasted on fresh boar meat.

---

When the General Election day arrived, on May 29, 1997, the village chief and his staff were busy arranging three tins containing ballot papers. Situng limped behind Muha, as if he wanted to participate in the election. I was now old enough to vote. I really hated the Yellow Party because I knew it represented the military. And it was impossible to vote for the Red Party, which seemed to be affiliated with communism. As far as the Acehnese were concerned, communism was to be shunned like dogs and pigs. Thus, I had no other choice but to vote for the Green Party.

People thronged to the voting booth. The men congregated, drinking coffee while enjoying the rare hubbub. That day, almost everyone, including the disabled, came to vote.

In the mosque's yard, not far from the voting kiosk, Zulaiha approached me. "Why are you avoiding me?" she asked, looking down.

I looked down, too, and answered, "I'm not avoiding you. I'm busy."

She was silent for a long while, as if she regretted her own fate. Her passive attitude annoyed me without reason. But I could not avoid her.

"You didn't tell me when you plan to propose to me."

After remaining silent for a while, I said, "Maybe next year."

When Zulaiha walked away without saying anything, she left me feeling guilty.

Perhaps Yeni's behavior had changed my attitude toward women. I suddenly realized that I still carried a torch for Yeni.

Not long after the votes were counted and the Green Party won the election in Alue Rambe, two soldiers came in the middle of the night and herded all the night watchmen to the stream to be soaked. This also happened the next night. In the end, a lot of Alue Rambe villagers suffered from a continuous fever. But ironically, their hardship turned into something people joked about in the coffee stall.

The same thing happened on the night I had night watch duty. I obeyed the soldiers' order to walk to the stream. The cold pierced my body when I entered the water. We were forced to squat, so only our heads were above the water. Anyone who tried to stand was hit on the head with a long piece of wood.

"Cool down the ardor you harbor for the Green Party," a soldier snarled.

The other soldier waved his gun and said, "The party that you chose will never be able to defend you."

"You stupid villagers will never learn."

"If the Yellow Party had won, your village would be protected."

"You'll never understand."

"Now, cool off."

At that time, Jakarta increased the number of soldiers they dispatched to Aceh. Ahmad Kandang and his followers were forced to hide. Baiti was worried because Mahmud did not come home.

# Chapter 21

On a hot Thursday afternoon in mid-May 1998, a year after the General Election, I went to have a cup of coffee at Leman's stall.

During the previous two weeks, the radio and television broadcast news about the university students' demonstrations in Jakarta, which resulted in street riots, burning buildings, and looting.

Soldiers and police officers shot at the unarmed crowds, who demanded that President Soeharto resign. The armed forces used real bullets — not rubber bullets or tear gas. People collapsed from gunshot wounds and soon, blood colored the black asphalt.

Now the people in Jakarta realized how brutal the soldiers and police officers were. What happened in Jakarta was nothing compared to the killings that happened almost every day in Aceh, but because the uprising happened in Jakarta, the radio and television broadcasts treated it differently. They magnified the incident to the extent that it became something that could lead Indonesia to massive destruction.

On May 21, 1998, after ruling the country with an iron fist for some thirty years, Soeharto was forced to resign.

While sipping my cup of coffee, I witnessed his resignation. There were only a dozen or so others who witnessed it. I never imagined that anything could be more powerful than Soeharto and could force him to surrender. *Would this bring a change to Aceh?*

Some men cheered as President Soeharto stepped down. Overjoyed, they shouted curses at the man, who was one of the main figures who had caused the deaths of thousands of Acehnese.

"He'll be damned," a thin man shouted.

"I hope he'll die soon," a short man added.

I, too, was happy with the fall of Soeharto's government. He would now reap what he had sown.

---

After working in the field, I took a break by having a cup of coffee in Leman's stall. A shadow fell on my table and I looked up. A young man filled the door opening.

It took me a while before I recognized Raiyan, a middle school classmate. He now sported a thick mustache under his sharp nose and sideburns on his cheeks. He wore a cap and was dressed in a T-shirt, a pair of jeans, and black leather shoes.

I rose and he walked to my table.

"Raiyan?"

"Nazir!"

We shook hands and slapped each other's shoulder.

I invited him to sit down and ordered coffee.

"How are you? Can't believe five years have passed since we last saw each other. You look healthy, but your skin seems to be much darker," he said, scrutinizing me.

"I'm always out in the sun." I grinned.

During our childhood, Raiyan and I were not close friends. Raiyan only made it to the third grade of middle school. When he did not pass that grade, he chose to help his parents in the field. The only time Raiyan and I encountered each other during our childhood was when we both happened to be fishing in the river. Since then, we had become occupied by our own work.

Our warm meeting suddenly drew us closer.

"I just heard what happened to several of our unfortunate comrades and your father. My condolences." Raiyan sipped his coffee and continued, "Trust me, the end of our suffering is imminent." Raiyan sounded very reassuring, trying to console those whose parents and siblings had been killed.

I nodded.

There was a brief silence before I asked, "How about you? What do you do now?"

Raiyan cleared his throat and then went on to say that he was close to Ahmad Kandang. He expected to become the Panglima Sagoe of Buloh Blang Ara, a position that had been vacant since Arkam died. Together with other young men who had recently returned from their escape, he spent his time with Ahmad at their hideout, perfecting his shooting and martial arts skills.

Rebellion leaders like Sofyan Dawood and Ishak Daud, who had fled, had now returned to Aceh and disguised themselves.

These days, the military stayed closer to Lhokseumawe and the capitals of other sub-district areas. Raiyan said that, in the weeks nearing the fall of President Soeharto, upheaval in the administration of the central government had discouraged the military from openly continuing their hunt for the remaining rebels. However, they never let up on pursuing Ahmad Kandang. This forced Ahmad to go into hiding and use the situation to amass power and train his new recruits.

Raiyan told me that Ishak Daud, who was involved in the 1990 attack on the Buloh Blang Ara Military Base, when Arkam was still alive, had been caught by the police after his disguise as a fishmonger was revealed. He was immediately brought to the Lhokseumawe Regional Court, where his trial created quite a scene.

Ishak was later moved to the Sabang Regional Court. On Sabang, a small island off Sumatra's most northern shore, no one paid attention, and then the judge sentenced him to twenty years behind bars.

"There are still so many things to take care of." Raiyan rose and held my eyes. "Are you ready to fight?"

My throat closed up. My tongue stiffened. Unable to utter a word, I vehemently nodded.

Raiyan shook my hand. "I'll see you again," he said, then quickly left.

---

It was time to harvest our coconuts. Muha and I climbed the thirty-foot-high trees that carried racks of eight to a dozen coconuts at the base of each leaf. We threw the picked coconuts to the ground, where they bounced in all directions.

Ibu and Baiti gathered the coconuts while Zuhra, who had just finished elementary school, held Muslim's hand and made sure the four-year-old stayed clear of the falling coconuts. Mosquitoes swarmed around them, and Muslim's arms and legs were covered with bites.

When the goats' bleating reached us from the backyard, Ibu asked Zuhra to check on them. Perhaps one of them was snared by the tether rope.

From my vantage point in the top of a coconut tree, I watched Zuhra drag a goat to the edge of the areca orchard where grass grew abundantly. After throwing the last ripe coconut to the ground, I climbed down.

"Mosquitoes," Muslim complained, scratching his neck. "I'm itchy."

Baiti wiped Muslim's nose with the tip of her long-sleeved shirt, then picked up a small eucalyptus oil bottle that now contained kerosene. She poured a small amount of kersosene into her hand and rubbed it on Muslim's legs, arms, and face.

"Don't whine," Baiti scolded softly.

Muslim continued to pout. "I want to go home," he cried.

"Don't act like a spoiled brat."

"I want to go home."

"If you keep whining, I'll smack you."

Muslim moved away and squatted under the tree I had just harvested.

Baiti built a fire of dried leaves and twigs, along with midribs and coconut shell pieces that still had some husk on them. She lit the fire with a torch made of bundled dry coconut leaves, the tips of which were dipped in kerosene. The thick smoke chased away the mosquitoes and gnats.

I climbed up my seventh tree and slashed three racks of ripe coconuts. So far, I had cut about twenty racks, three or four from each tree. I left the remaining three trees to Muha and helped Ibu take the dropped fruit to Baiti, who sat next to a pile of coconuts, splitting them.

While taking a rest, I sat down and removed the meat from the coconut shells that Baiti had split.

Zuhra, who had finished moving the goats, joined me in removing the coconut meat. The tip of her brown skirt was muddied by the dark soil. After finishing elementary school, Zuhra did not continue her education because the school was too far away and traveling that far was too dangerous for a girl.

"If only Ayah was still alive, I'd be able to go to middle school," Zuhra said, looking down.

Baiti stopped swinging her machete. For a moment, she looked at her sister, who sat crumpled up, and sighed. When Baiti returned to her work, she brought down her machete onto the coconut shells with all her strength. Her hair bounced during her repeated movement. Some strands fell onto her forehead and temple and stuck to her perspiring face.

This was the third day we worked on the coconut harvest. Each day started at sunrise and was only interrupted by a prayer and lunch break at noon. We then continued until evening.

Before the sun reached its zenith, Ibu placed a full sack of coconut meat on her head and took Zuhra home to tend to the household chores.

Soon afterwards, Baiti followed, carrying Muslim on her back.

Now only Muha and I remained. We continued removing coconut meat from the shells and put it into the sacks. The only sounds came from our knives scraping the soft shell, an occasional cough or throat-clearing, and the rustling leaves. The wind dried the perspiration on my skin and clothes. To quench our thirst and keep from getting hungry, we drank the water from the young coconuts and chewed on coconut meat.

"I might be leaving soon." Muha suddenly stopped scraping. He rose and, while taking out his nipa palm cigarette box, moved to sit on a small mound of dirt. For a minute, he focused on rolling his cigarette, as if the words he had just said were meant only for himself.

I was shocked. After all, he had a wife and two children. "Where will you go?"

"I'm going to join Pang Ahmad."

It had been a long time since I had heard about Ahmad Kandang. Even during the time the military was still persecuting the rebels, Ahmad continued coming to the villages to recruit rebels. However, because he was now hunted by a special unit, he was no longer able to wander freely around the villages. Now, his followers came to meet him in his hideout.

Raiyan had told me that Ahmad used his hideout to assemble bombs. He only shared this knowledge with very few people. And no one ever equaled Ahmad in bomb-making skills. Ahmad also used the place to train his recruits to shoot and discuss various strategies.

At first, I thought that Muha's involvement with Ahmad Kandang was no different than that of the other villagers. Many of them supported Ahmad in different ways. Some of them acted as spies, others were radio operators, others collected dues for the movement, and still others supplied the rebels with their basic needs. None of these activities required the supporter to leave his family. But if Muha was to be directly involved as a rebel, he definitely would have to leave Raziah and their two children.

Although I knew that all Acehnese — except those traitors who worked for the Jakarta military — hated the military, I could not understand how Muha could arrive at such a decision while he was responsible for protecting and providing for his family.

"I'm thinking of Ayah," Muha said, looking down.

I slowly put down my knife and sat down on a nearby wooden log, holding my knees.

"Actually, I don't want to fight," Muha said. "I have a wife and two small children. I've never been influenced by any of their propaganda. But each time I think of how cruelly they treated Ayah, I can't keep from crying. I've sworn to avenge his death."

For a moment, the world around us was so still. The early afternoon wind swept my face and fingered my hair. I finally said, "But you don't even know Ayah's murderer."

"Nazir," Muha looked straight at me. "They're all the same. Every soldier is a murderer, a kidnapper, and a rapist. Even though there might be some who didn't actually do those things, they are all involved in what their friends have done. Don't tell me that they wouldn't know about the atrocities."

What Muha said silenced me.

---

Finally, Muha left with some young men to go to a secret place in the Nisam jungle.

Around that same time, Mahmud left without telling anyone, including Baiti, where he was going. It seemed to bother him that although he'd been born a farmer's son, he couldn't perform the day-to-day tasks of a farmer. It was true that we thought of him as a lazy fool.

Two days after Muha left, Raziah came with her two children to live with us. The silence draping Kakek's house, along with the sound of footsteps at night, made her anxious and unable to sleep.

"Where is Situng?" Ibu looked at Raziah's pale face and added, "It's probably just Situng wandering around."

"You can't hear a dog's footsteps; only his breathing."

"Situng would definitely bark if someone came to the house."

Raziah was quiet for a while, then said, "I don't know. It seemed that Situng was somewhere else at that time."

"Does that dog no longer stay home?" Ibu probed.

"Situng never goes very far. But I don't know what he does at night. Maybe he wanders around the backyard."

"If there was someone around, Situng would've known it immediately," I interrupted. "He has a very keen sense of smell; it's much sharper than other dogs."

When Raziah and her children moved in with us, Situng stayed behind to guard Kakek's house. I took him food when I went there to clean the banana orchard and cut down bushes in the backyard. Raziah had left the property in good condition, and Muha's woven roof tiles were stacked neatly on the porch. The yard was swept; broom scratches marked the ground. But the place felt like it was left by its dead owners.

The house, actually, indeed belonged to deceased people. I had only gone there to feed Situng and clean the banana orchard and cut bushes. But a week later, the shrubbery started to take over again. The bushes flourished even thought they grew in the deep shade of the trees. The orchards showed no signs of human presence since I had been there. There was no trace of human footsteps around the house.

Now my chores increased. I had to take care of the orchard in my backyard, as well as Kakek's orchard that Muha had left. I had neglected my field for almost a month, and now, it was impossible to catch up. If I were to leave Kakek's orchards, the shrubbery would take over. In less than three months, the soft twigs would harden and turn into twisted wooden branches that were difficult to remove. During the past three years, too many orchards had reverted to wildland.

I worked without giving my body any time to rest. My shoulder and arm muscles grew bigger and hardened. I no longer felt the itchy mosquito bites. The gnats on my skin felt like dust. It seemed that I had lost my sensitivity for anything but the exhaustion I felt at night. Meanwhile, I was still tortured by the memory of Ayah's death.

I took along a transistor radio to the field and turned it on under a papaya tree. I listened to popular dangdut and pop songs, which did not differ much to my ears. I did not pay any attention to the lyrics, but the music drove away the sense of loneliness that came with being by myself in the field. Sometimes, the radio signal was not good, and the sound was like a voice in the middle of a storm.

I stopped cutting down the bushes as soon as Waldi, one of the announcers for Adi Maja Lhokseumawe Radio, read the daytime news. "Ladies and gentlemen, the demonstration led by the university students in Jakarta is still ongoing. They urged the central government to stop the war and massacres in Aceh and withdraw all of the soldiers from Aceh. In their demonstration, they cited the incidents of murder, torture, and rape that soldiers inflicted daily on the Acehnese.

"The House of Representatives in Jakarta responded to the students' demonstration by forming several teams to find evidence of the soldiers' crimes in Aceh. Those teams are currently conducting their investigation. At several places used as army checkpoints, mass graves containing dozens of human skulls and bones were found. The forensic report states that the broken skulls and bones and ropes not rotted by the soil were proof that the victims experienced severe torture before they were killed."

The announcer's voice ceased and was replaced by a song titled "Goodbye My Past," which was sung by a band called Five Minutes.

I closed my eyes. My scalp felt like it was being stabbed by thousands of needles. When I opened my eyes, I felt the breeze that passed through the tall grasses between the papaya trees. I continued to cut down the brush. *Were we headed for the end of this tunnel of misery?*

During the following days, I heard a lot of people talk about the discovery of criminal evidence. The military commander in charge at that time denied the accusation, saying that hundreds of bones from the buried bodies in several killing fields resulted from the atrocities perpetrated by the Dutch soldiers that attacked Aceh hundreds of years ago. However, the investigation results released by those teams revealed that some of the victims were killed just five years ago.

On the streets, in the Tamoun stalls and other places, villagers busily discussed the matter when they met each other. When I went to the Buloh Blang Ara market, everyone in the coffee stall was discussing the grave excavations and the supporting testimony of the victims' families. Radio stations and newspapers endlessly aired broadcasts about the barbaric and cruel behavior of the military in Aceh.

## Chapter 22

Nono lay curled up under the jackfruit tree, sleeping. He was twelve now and often showed signs of being tired or not feeling well. Despite his graying muzzle, the dog still looked handsome. I wondered how long a dog was able to retain a memory, to feel a loss. It seemed that Ayah's passing had taken all the joy out of his life. A sad, longing look was engraved in his eyes.

I now realized that even a dog would always remember someone's good deeds.

When I squatted near him, Nono looked up and thumped his tail a couple of times.

"You're a good dog," I said, looking at him.

In response, Nono let out a few short barks and thumped his tail again.

I smiled and said, "You don't have to guard the field anymore. Just guard the house."

After Muha left and I was saddled with caring for Kakek's and my own orchards, I was forced to abandon my field. I now was the only male adult in this household. No one counted on Mahmud. His presence, or lack thereof, didn't affect any of us, including Baiti. If Mahmud was at home, she took care of him in a wifely manner, and when he left, she acted as if he were a stranger she did not care about.

"Nazir!" Ibu called from the side yard. "Please help me set down these candlenuts."

I jumped up and ran to Ibu to relieve her from the sack of candlenuts on top of her head. I could not bear to see how she pushed herself to work.

"Why are you carrying such a heavy load?" I carefully placed the sack on the porch. Handled roughly, the worn plastic bag would break and the candlenuts spill.

"I don't want to make two trips just to get these nuts home." Ibu scowled.

"You can ask me to help you," I grumbled. "Or else, you can ask Baiti or Raziah."

"Don't worry," Ibu shushed. "Each of us has something to do. You're also very busy."

The sun was already high in the sky. The heat had baked the soil. The places not hardened by constant traffic were turning into dust bowls. After a while, I went to my room and took a few ten-thousand-rupiah bills out of the closet and put them in my pants pocket.

I walked straight to Leman's stall and ordered a cup of coffee. Sipping my coffee, I picked up a few pieces of sweets and sticky rice, and added it to my order. I also bought four batteries for my radio, a can of milk, and a bag of cookies.

Back home, I handed the cakes to Akbar, Siti, and Muslim. Then, I placed the sticky rice in a coconut shell and poured some milk over it. I had seen Ayah feed Nono this concoction several times and remembered how much the dog liked it.

As soon as I put down the coconut shell, Nono pounced on it. He ate heartily, lifting his head between bites to throw me a thankful glance. Dogs might not have a human vocabulary, but they sure knew how to show their gratitude.

---

In July 1998, I was overjoyed when I heard the news about the withdrawal of all the military troops from Aceh. Apparently, the pressure on the government to withdraw intensified due to the investigation committee's proof of the atrocities the soldiers had committed. In the last week of July 1998, I wanted to go to Lhokseumawe to watch the parade of trucks that transported the soldiers, but Ibu did not allow me to go.

"What's the good of going there?" she grumbled. "What if there's a clash? No one can predict everything will remain peaceful. Please don't get involved."

So I ended up not going to the city. Instead, I stayed in my room, listening to the radio reports about the troop withdrawal ceremonies, which were designed to create the impression that the departing soldiers were heroes. The radio station definitely sided with the military because, after all, it was owned by the government. But even private radio stations were mouthpieces for government propaganda.

When I became bored with the radio, I went to the yard.

Akbar, riding my old bicycle, came to the gate. He wore his red-and-white school uniform. He was a second-grader now.

Muslim and Siti ran outside to greet him.

Akbar often brought snacks home for his sister and cousin. He did not look like his father. Maybe this was because he didn't have Muha's crooked mouth. I often wondered what would become of Akbar. He didn't seem to worry about his future. It made me happy that, aside from being a good student, he was also close to his sister and cousin.

Raziah walked up to him while tying her hair back with a rubber band. "What kind of a snack did you bring home?"

"Bread," he answered, looking at Siti's and Muslim's outstretched hands.

Raziah smiled. "Change your clothes. Don't get your school clothes dirty."

I turned and walked away, as if not caring about the small, intimate interaction between my family members.

On the land adjacent to the yard, I had planted a papaya orchard. The variety I grew was very popular. It was especially sought after by city folks. Although the fruit was not very high-priced, growing it was still profitable. Every three days or so, a buyer came and loaded the large baskets he carried on the rear rack of his motorbike.

From afar, I saw Samsul in his orchard, watching a buyer fill his baskets.

I sauntered over to the well-maintained fields adjacent to mine. I was surprised to spot Zulaiha, in her dangau. Although we lived in the same village and our fields were adjacent to one another, we had not seen each other since last year's General Election. Zulaiha looked up, startled, when I walked closer. She dropped her embroidery into her lap as we awkwardly exchanged glances.

Zulaiha had changed a lot. She looked slimmer. Her features had matured, and there was an elegance about her. Her hands looked smooth and soft like those of a city girl who had never touched a machete or hoe handle.

"Are you embroidering something?" I felt foolish asking the question but couldn't come up with anything else to start the conversation.

"Yes, I... I am," she stammered.

I smiled and wrung my hands, wondering whether to remain standing there or sit in the dangau with her. I had never been in such an awkward situation before. In the end, I decided to climb up and sit down in the dangau's door opening.

"What brings you here?" she asked.

I pointed at the adjacent plot of land and said, "My field has turned into a jungle."

"What are you going to plant it with?"

"If I have enough time, I'll grow a crop of papaya," I answered and threw her a quick glance.

Zulaiha smiled. She ran a finger across the embroidered rose on the cloth in her embroidery hoop. She was almost finished. There were only a few penciled petals left.

"Are you not working today?" she asked.

"I'm not," I answered. "I planned to go to the city, but Ibu wouldn't let me. She was worried there'd be trouble."

"I also heard that today all soldiers will be withdrawn from Aceh," Zulaiha said softly and returned to her needlework.

The news about the military withdrawal had spread through the village like wildfire. Some of Ahmad Kandang's followers, who had come home to take care of miscellaneous matters, shouted victory and openly waved the star-and-moon red flag, the flag of the resistance movement that Hasan Tiro raised twenty years ago.

I wondered if it just might be possible that we would finally be able to live peacefully. That we had finally entered a time during which the Acehnese could farm their fields without hindrance, and parents could raise their children without being bothered by futilities.

Zulaiha looked pretty, sitting there embroidering. The afternoon sunlight put a beautiful sheen on her straight black hair.

"I think I better go on home," I said and rose.

Zulaiha smiled.

After silently standing there for a while, I stammered, "Hopefully, we soon will live in peace."

As I walked away, Zulaiha said, "That would be lovely. Wouldn't it?"

---

A week later, during the second troop withdrawal, I secretly peddled my bicycle to the Buloh Blang Ara market. Heading north, I rode between rice fields, orchards, and villagers' houses. My back was soaked in perspiration.

When I arrived at the crossroad at the entrance of the Buloh Blang Ara market, the street was crowded by various vehicles. Bicycles, motorbikes, cars, buses, and trucks of all kinds and sizes moved in all directions and made me dizzy. Not long afterwards, a string of regular-sized and mini-sized yellow trucks, filled with soldiers, headed south to the city center, where the largest military base was located.

After drinking a cup of coffee in one of the stalls at the crossroad, I walked my bike across the street, then rode it across a big bridge to the bus terminal. I got off my bike close to the terminal and, for a while, watched the two-way congested traffic try to cross the road.

It was already noon when the sound of a big explosion in the eastern part of town startled me. People walking on the street stopped. Several people came out of the coffee stall and, for a moment, the traffic halted. The first explosion was followed by several others. Some ten minutes later, a long line of trucks rolled by with roaring engines. Hundreds of soldiers pointed their guns at people on the street as they drove by.

Some people from the crowd threw rocks at the passing trucks while yelling curses and profanities. The soldiers responded with swear words. The exchange of yelling, cussing, and blaring sirens filled the air with a cacophonic chaos.

After the last truck passed, there was a lull in the noise. Some people who arrived on motorbikes told us that there was a big riot in progress at the city center. People were looting and destroying buildings.

At the small park near the market, a group of people drove by in a truck, shouting, "*Merdeka,* freedom." I recognized one of Ahmad Kandang's followers among them. The truck moved on, and I turned my bicycle toward home.

When I was back at the southern part of Buloh Blang Ara market again, I found it difficult to cross the very crowded bridge. There was neither police nor soldiers to stop them. People broke into a large, two-story building that had several movie posters attached to its outside walls. One of the posters depicted a flying man kicking the air; another showed a woman clad in a bikini, showing off her cleavage.

People kept on going in and out of the building, carrying many things. Some of them carried boxes, some carried televisions. Some held boxes close to their chests, others carried large plastic bags. I broke free from the crowd only after I got a hold of myself and overcame being overwhelmed by all that was happening around me — things that I could not understand at all.

After that day, there were no more night watches in the villages, and there were no more soldiers who came to inspect. On the nights that followed, the light at the checkpost was turned off.

---

At the end of September, Muha and other men who had left with him returned to their respective houses. Raziah and her children returned to Kakek's house. I was busy clearing up my field. Zulaiha often accompanied me and brought me food. I was happy and didn't pay any attention to any ruckus on the streets.

Three days after Muha's return, Ahmad Kandang, with five of his loyal followers, appeared briefly at Leman's stall. I did not have an opportunity to see him. From Mahmud, who returned home that day, I heard that Ahmad planned to revive his old tactic, which was to kidnap the soldiers. He was not convinced that the soldiers had withdrawn from Aceh entirely.

At that time, construction of gigantic electricity towers that belonged to the Electric Utility Board had commenced in the northern Aceh area. The line ran from Medan to Banda Aceh. The giant poles were built in a parallel line, with a measured distance that passed through agricultural fields, rice fields, and over hills. Northern Aceh was often without electricity at all hours of the day and night. These poles were designed to solve this problem. Most of the construction workers came from Medan.

Ahmad and his followers found out that three of the construction workers were soldiers in disguise. They captured the three men and drove them to Alue Rambe, where they threw them on a field in front of the mosque. The villagers used the field to dry betel nuts, and, during the Years of the Killings, the military had used the field to torture the villagers.

Another unit of rebels captured a palm oil plantation owner and his overseer. The two men turned out to be government informants.

Ahmad's men gathered the five men in the middle of the field. The soldiers wore workers' clothes and dirty jeans; the plantation owner wore a shirt, and his overseer wore a T-shirt. The five disguised soldiers looked like ordinary people, not like fierce soldiers. They looked even more pitiful than the farmers they used to persecute.

Suddenly, Tamoun turned noisy and crowded. Men surrounded the five cuffed and shackled traitors. A villager took a piece of wood and slammed it against the bleeding face of one of the captives. The women who witnessed the scene screamed, then covered their mouths and faces while hurrying away.

Even though I was filled with anger, I did not have the heart to participate in the torture. The soldiers who were sent to Aceh, especially those who were tasked with infiltrating the villages, were soldiers who had received special training that taught them to be merciless. They would be more than capable of administering even worse torture. But when the villagers beat those five men, I was unable to witness it and looked away.

"Why are you just standing there?" someone holding a bloodied club asked me. "Don't you remember what they did to your father?"

The man shoved his club towards me, but I ignored him. Suddenly, my body trembled from anger and pity.

"They're all *kafir*, unbelievers," the man snorted, staring at my sweaty, dusty face. I had come from the field, where I had just cut down brush that was knee-high.

"Don't feel sorry for them," the man with the club shouted, watching me shake.

"But," I sighed, "they're dead."

"Beat them. Even if they're dead."

"I can't."

"You must."

"I cannot."

"Remember what they did to your father."

"I cannot."

"You're a weakling," the man snapped and hit the men's heads with his club until their skulls split open.

The five battered, dead bodies were left out in the sun, with their hands and feet still tied.

Some men came by to check them and then left. Others went to the cemetery. They dug two holes at the edge of the cemetery, away from the villagers' graves and far away from Kakek's, Arkam's, Nenek's and Ayah's graves. In the afternoon, four bodies were moved to the cemetery. They left the commander's body lying in the field. Two dead soldiers were put into one hole; the plantation owner and his overseer in the other. The two corpses in each hole were stacked on top of each other.

At the end of the day, some men who were the followers of Ahmad shouted, "Death to the soldiers," and carried the dried-out, dead body of the commander into a jeep and drove it to Buloh Blang Ara, where they threw it on the paved road near the military base.

But Ahmad Kandang's troops did not stop there.

His troops, who were gifted with a natural talent sharpened by training, continued to kidnap soldiers. The soldiers who were sent to Aceh under cover, one by one, disappeared without a trace. Even the military themselves did not realize that the spies they had sent out were being murdered. Only a few dead bodies could be found.

Ahmad Kandang had separated his men into small groups that worked in various regions. They moved swiftly and cunningly. Ahmad, who looked like an ordinary Acehnese, was difficult to pick out of a crowd. The soldiers did not suspect him of apprehending and killing several of their comrades.

The soldiers who hunted Ahmad Kandang came several times to the Buloh Blang Ara market. His name was mentioned everywhere, as if he was the main figure who led the rebellion.

# Chapter 23

I had started transplanting the papaya seedlings to the field I had cleared. Nono, who was not as agile as he used to be, often followed me. His presence would be needed in the orchard when, in about three to four months, the trees started to bear. At that time, he needed to keep away the monkeys that were attracted to the fruit.

While waiting for the papaya to grow, I worked on the dangau. I cleaned up the dangau's floor. After replacing the broken bamboo slats in the walls, I oiled the walls. Then I gathered the scattered garbage and burned it. I also replaced the dangau's old thatched roof with new panels that Muha had woven. Since his return from his combat training with Ahmad Kandang, Muha sometimes went out with Raiyan. The two of them joined Ahmad in his subversive activities. Other than that, Muha returned to tending to Kakek's orchards. He cleared the brush in the areca orchard, and removed the old banana leaves so the air could flow freely through the grove.

Zulaiha brought me a drink and a bowl of peeled, ripe papaya. I had promised to propose to her several times, but now I was sure that I would propose to her after the papaya harvest, in about six or seven months. Hopefully, the yield would be good.

"This time I'm really going to do it," I said and then added, "as long as the war doesn't break out again."

"What if it does?" Zulaiha asked, blushing.

I thought for a while. "I don't know."

Since January 1999, too many soldiers and police officers drove around the streets with their trucks. They wandered around the markets, and the villages. It felt as if the soldiers that had been withdrawn from Aceh were sent back. Their main purpose was to capture Ahmad Kandang, who never appeared in Alue Rambe anymore.

With the arrival of these new soldiers, riots started to occur again in some areas. I heard that in East Aceh, people walking home from a religious assembly in an open field were fired on when they passed a nearby military base. The crowd responded by throwing rocks at the soldiers.

---

The weather in April 1999 was very sunny. As early as sunrise, the repeated sound of machetes splitting betel nuts on small logs interspersed with conversation and laughter filled the air around our side porch. Ibu, Baiti, Raziah, Zuhra, Muslim, and three neighbor girls worked to remove meat from the shell.

I helped collect the nuts that still lay scattered on the orchard's ground and peeled nuts that had been left unpeeled in the sack after the harvest.

The price of betel nuts, cacao, coconut, palm oil, and other agricultural products soared. Samaun was even willing to buy unpeeled betel nuts. Even the young betel nuts that were still green and had to be peeled and cut into two before the meat could be scooped out and dried were quite valuable. Sometimes, these young nuts were even more expensive than older, whole betel nuts.

About eleven farmers from Alue Rambe bought motorbikes with the money they earned selling betel nuts and cacao beans. Some landlords, who lived in Buloh Blang Ara and owned vast farmland in other villages, bought new cars.

Once in a while, I went to the field to check on the papaya trees and feed Nono. Once a week, I fed him sticky rice and milk. I always looked for Zulaiha, but she was never around. Every so often, I only saw her father or her mother in their field.

During the last few weeks, I spent more time in the areca orchard near our backyard. I looked for clusters that had been overlooked during the harvest and collected the ripe fruit in a large plastic bag. Later, I carried the bag home and poured the contents in the front yard around the clothesline pole.

When there were no more clusters left, I returned to the side porch to help peel the fruit. But the presence of the three neighbor girls, who had struck up a friendship with Ibu and Baiti in recent months, made me go to my room, where I listened to my radio while revisiting old textbooks. After a short while, I decided to go to the field. There were always weeds to pull between the growing papaya trees. In the kitchen, I was filling up a container with drinking water when I overheard one of the girls ask Ibu, "Is Nazir going to get married this year?"

"Only if the price of betel nuts doesn't fall."

I did not know what was funny about Ibu's answer, but everyone started to chuckle.

The papaya trees now almost reached my waist. Nono still guarded the field. When he tired from wandering around, he would lie down in the shade of the candlenut tree near the dangau. Furthermore, Samsul's dogs also guarded the fields. But sometimes the monkeys still outsmarted the dogs and managed to get into a guarded field.

While I moved down the rows of papaya trees weeding, I heard someone cough behind me. When I turned, Zulaiha stood in the path.

"You're quite busy, aren't you?" she quipped.

I looked at her, puzzled. "What is that supposed to mean?"

"I know that many girls are peeling areca nuts at your house now," she replied coldly. "That's why you probably prefer to stay home."

"There are not many girls," I tried to explain. "There are only three or four of them, including Zuhra."

"It must be fun to be surrounded by females, right?" she said, sarcastically.

"Except for Muslim and me, everyone in my house is a female."

"Hmmm…. Do you like them?"

"Who?"

"Those girls."

"Are you jealous?"

She blushed.

"Listen," I said, "I don't care about any of those girls."

"Then why are you ignoring me?"

"I've been busy with the harvest of my areca orchard, but I've still been coming here to feed Nono and check on my field. I always look for you, but you've not been around."

"I was in the dangau."

"Then why didn't you call to me?"

"It's inappropriate," she snapped. "It's inappropriate for a girl to be calling a man."

"You didn't have to call out. All you had to do was make some noise."

"Noise?"

"You could have coughed or pretended to shoo the birds."

Zulaiha chuckled gently. Her sour face turned cheerful. When she chuckled, she covered her mouth and then covered her face with both hands.

I liked her smile and cheerfulness.

"I thought you had forgotten me," she said.

"How can I forget you? Aren't we getting married soon?"

"I'm worried some other girl will change your mind."

"You're the only girl I know well enough to be close to."

She blushed again. "You're a good flirt."

---

Leman went every morning to the Buloh Blang Ara market to get the newspaper. At times, a lack of funding to reach areas outside Lhokseumawe made the television and radio stations unreliable. Because there were only a few people who could read in this village, I was assigned to read the news aloud. Suddenly, Leman's stall was crowded with people who came to listen carefully to every sentence I read, as if the words I read were a magic spell to ward off danger.

On May 3, 1999, the newspaper reported a massacre at the intersection by the Krueng Geukueh paper mill, about twenty-five miles southwest of our village.

The soldiers killed some two hundred villagers. This atrocity was worse than any that had happened during the Years of Killings. Now the soldiers, without hesitation, shot at an unarmed crowd, children, and those who fled. They even shot at those who were lying on the ground.

During their discussions, villagers concluded that the soldiers' barbaric acts were clearly aimed at annihilating the Acehnese. My anger started raging again. I wanted to take up arms immediately. I went to the field to think things through. If I joined the resistance, I surely would not be able to marry Zulaiha. I also worried about what would happen to Ibu, Baiti, Zuhra, and Muslim.

The papaya trees had now started to fruit. The small fruit was shaded by wide leaves. Sunlight made the dark green leaves glow. A grasshopper eating a papaya leaf jumped on another leaf when I shook the branch.

Nono must have picked up my scent, and he trotted toward me.

I slapped my forehead when he sat down near me. "Sorry, I forgot to bring you sticky rice."

Nono left me and went to lie in the shade by the dangau.

After weeding several rows, I went to the dangau to get a drink of water. I hoped Zulaiha would show up. When, after a while, she still didn't, I headed for the stream with Nono on my heels.

On a path near the stream, I met Raiyan. After exchanging some chitchat, he said, "Those soldiers are vermin. I will kill them all."

"I agree," I said.

"We can join the same troop," he offered.

"I don't know how to use a weapon."

"We're Acehnese, Nazir," Raiyan said. "We don't need a lot of special training. Weapons will quickly merge with our body and soul."

"I don't understand."

"Someone like you only needs a little instruction. Trust me, in just a day, you'll be a sharpshooter."

"All right," I answered nonchalantly. "When the soldiers attack this place, I'll join you."

Raiyan nodded and shouted, "Merdeka."

"Merdeka," I replied.

By the last week of July, the papayas had grown as big as my fist. It had now become a habit for the people of Alue Rambe to gather in Leman's stall, waiting for the newspaper he would bring. On July 23, 1999, the newspaper reported that soldiers had killed an *ulama*, an Islamic scholar, and sixty of his students in a *pesantren*, an Islamic boarding school, in Beutong Ateuh, West Aceh. More than two hundred soldiers surrounded and shot Teungku Bantaqiah while he was teaching the Quran to his students, many of whom were apprehended or shot.

After I finished reading the newspaper, the crowd immediately engaged in conversation, and the stall was soon filled with their voices. When the illiterate crowd cursed the soldiers, it was as if a radio's volume had been turned up.

"Beastly devils."

"They killed an Acehnese ulama. Cursed heathens."

"Damned killers."

At the end of October 1999, a week after Abdurrahman Wahid was elected as president of Indonesia — replacing B.J. Habibie, who had only served a year — three trucks transporting some two hundred soldiers arrived in Alue Rambe. The sun was high in the sky, and I was in the field harvesting papaya with Ibu.

Muha and Baiti carried the fruit and stacked it on the side of the alley near the cemetery. Later in the afternoon, a buyer would come to pick up the load.

Noise from the roadside made me stop my work and leave the field to see what was going on.

Close to my house, people ran by me, panting. One of them mimed slashing his throat with his index finger. Pointing toward the road, he shouted, "Soldiers!" He kept running, and I automatically followed him.

---

By the time the military trucks stopped in Tamoun and all the soldiers had jumped out, all the dogs and workingmen had fled. The villages were suddenly deserted and devoid of capable men. Only old men, women, and children remained.

Imam Masjid, who was now in his sixties and suffered from swollen, rheumatic knees, was forced to limp to the graves of the two soldiers who had been tortured and killed by the rebels and buried about a year prior.

Meanwhile, three other villagers were ordered at gunpoint to carry hoes to the cemetery.

The soldiers rounded up everyone in the village and herded them to the cemetery, where they were forced to watch the grave digging. The air filled with shouting from the angry soldiers and crying from the frightened women and children.

Some of the soldiers ransacked the empty houses, looking for the men who seemed to have been swallowed by the earth.

---

Together with five other men, I hid on the hill near the stream. When two soldiers herded Zulaiha, with her mother and sister, to the gravel road, I held my breath, hiding inside brush that covered my head.

The yelling of the soldiers and crying of the women drove me mad. I was very worried about Ibu and Zuhra, the two people I worried about the most, and stayed behind when the other five men with me fled. Two soldiers arrived at a junction in front of my house, where they gathered the remaining villagers they found.

It was impossible to stand tall and stick my head out of the brush when they herded Ibu, Baiti, and Zuhra out of the house. I couldn't see their faces. I only heard the soldiers' yelling.

"Hurry, stupid."

"Damned villagers."

"Where did they go?"

"How dare you kidnap people."

---

The three unfortunate villagers tasked with digging up the graves worked while shivering in fear.

The women who were forced to see the corpses looked away. When a soldier forced them to look, they could not stop screaming. Some people cried, others moaned. The old people chanted prayers, as if hoping for a miracle to set them free from danger.

When the corpses were laid bare, the commander asked Imam Masjid, "Is this the Muslim way to bury a human?"

That old man stammered, "Islam does not condone such act."

"Then, who did this?"

"Those people."

"Who are those people?"

"The rebels."

"What did they do?"

"Beat them to death and then buried them."

"They're very cruel."

"True," Imam Masjid replied, "they're cruel."

"Were any of these villagers involved?"

"None as far as I know."

"Where are those rebels now?"

"They haven't been here for a long time."

"Why?"

"I don't know," answered the old man. "Perhaps, they have been captured somewhere else."

Imam Masjid's answers were honest. That honesty saved the villagers. In wars, too much honesty could kill everyone, but honesty imbued with little lies would save us and the rebels. If he had lied from the start, Imam Masjid might not have limped home but rather would have been carried home dead instead.

The two fully clothed corpses were put into a body bag, placed in the truck, and driven away.

Only after the roaring engines of the two army trucks died off did the men come out of the hillside bushes. Some went back to their respective houses, others gathered at Leman's stall. They compared notes and asked the women what the soldiers had done. Their soft voices were all that was heard, and soon, quiet settled over Tamoun.

## Chapter 24

The dirt road to the field was cracked and dusty. I was on my way to take Nono to the papaya orchard. Because Samsul's field was between crops and mine was in full fruit, mine became the monkeys' main target.

Earlier, there had been plots of long beans, tomatoes, cucumbers, squash, corn, and eggplant. But all these crops had been harvested.

Nono was no longer able to keep away hungry, destructive monkeys by himself. If he warded one tribe off in one corner of the field, another would already be at another corner. The monkeys came to the field as soon as dawn broke, and if I came late, the yellow, ripe papayas still hanging off the stem would be punctured, the black seeds falling out of the holes.

I could not wait to bring Situng with me and went to Kakek's house to find Muha.

Muha called Situng as soon as I told him my plight. When Situng did not respond, we went to Kakek's banana orchard looking for him, to no avail. The dog was nowhere to be found. "This is strange," Muha said. "He usually stays around."

We had made a full circle and were standing at the roadside in front of Kakek's house. Muha suggested, "Why don't you go back to the field. I'll keep looking for Situng and take him to you."

I agreed and started to walk back when, suddenly, Situng came running from the neighbor's orchard. He stopped to look at us, then ran barking past us.

"Situng!" Muha shouted.

Situng looked back but continued to run toward the jungle.

"Crazy dog," Muha cursed.

I shook my head, puzzled.

Not long afterwards, other dogs ran by us in the same direction as Situng. They usually behaved that way when military trucks arrived in the village.

But this time, neither Muha nor I had heard any truck drive up. The rain had stopped since January, and the dry roads enabled trucks to drive fast and create thick dust clouds as they roared by.

"I'm wondering if I'm turning deaf," Muha mumbled. Turning to me, he asked, "Do you hear any trucks?"

I listened carefully. All I heard was the wind traveling through the treetops. There was not even the sound of the mini trucks that usually came to transport agricultural products. We could distinguish the sound of military trucks.

"I don't hear anything," I answered.

We continued walking in the direction Situng had gone, while Muha kept calling him. When we arrived at the end of the road, I turned toward the field when, all of a sudden, a group of soldiers ambushed me and ordered me to go to the field in front of the mosque.

I trembled, helplessly. I knew that if I made a suspicious move or ran, they would shoot me on the spot.

"Now you don't have time to run. Move it," a soldier snapped and poked me with his rifle.

"If you run, I'll shoot you," another soldier added.

I walked with both of my hands behind my head. The bright sunlight on the open field blinded me.

Some soldiers found a number of men weeding their orchards and others who were carrying water from the stream. They, too, were herded to the field. Next, they had captured every adult male in the village and gathered them at the field in front of the mosque.

Five soldiers guarded us at gunpoint. We were told to line up.

I was very scared that one of those guns would be fired accidentally. The guns were loaded, and the soldiers had their fingers on the triggers. All it took to pull the trigger was for any of them to get startled or run into something.

There was not a single truck parked anywhere in Tamoun, yet there were hundreds of fully armed soldiers everywhere in Alue Rambe. They most likely came in on foot so that no one would hear them come and make an escape.

The soldiers did not bother the women. They only had it out for the men, adults as well as teenagers. They went down the line slapping and intimidating us. Those who looked defiant or stood tall were treated worse than those with a calm and meek demeanor. Someone as demure as Raiyan, even though he had a beard, was only slapped once.

I was only slapped across the mouth. I tasted something salty, and when I spit, I saw blood.

"We know you protect the rebels," the commander accused us. "Am I correct?"

No one dared to answer. It was very quiet on the field. The only sound was that of the soldiers' boots stomping across the hardened ground, crushing dried areca nuts.

"Is it true?" The commander's face hardened. The perspiration on his forehead glistened in the sun. While adjusting the strap of his long-barreled rifle, he slowly walked toward Raiyan and looked at him closely for some time.

Raiyan bowed his head as if he were a child being reprimanded by his parents.

"Hey, you. Are you protecting the rebels?"

Raiyan shook his head. "No," he answered, sounding like someone guilty of doing something wrong.

"If not, then why are there rebels in this village?" The commander moved towards an old man.

The man fearfully stuttered, "We're scared."

"You can't be scared," the commander interrupted. "You have to fight back. Those rebels are the nation's enemy, they will bring you trouble."

The forty-some villagers dutifully listened to the ranting commander, who paced the ground.

"Who among you is a rebel?"

No one answered. The silence intensified.

"Hey, why isn't anyone answering?" Are you all deaf?" The commander stomped the ground. "Who is Raiyan? Point him out. Don't be afraid."

None of us spoke.

"All right then." The commander was visibly annoyed. "Are there any rebels here?"

The commander approached one of the boys in the group. He didn't beat the lad but kept his eyes on him, visually demanding an answer.

I saw the boy's hand tremble as it hung by his side.

Finally, the boy answered, "Yes, there is."

"Where?" the commander yelled. "Where is he? Show me."

"He ran away."

"Where to?"

The boy pointed south while looking down.

"If they want war, why do they run away when we come?" the commander barked. "Why? Maybe all of you are rebels, too." The commander, overcome by anger, slapped everyone standing near him. "Answer me!"

A man answered, trembling, "We're scared of getting beaten."

"Why would you be afraid if you didn't do anything wrong?" the commander shouted.

Everyone was silent again.

"Hey, you, what's your name?" The commander turned and approached me.

"Nazir," I answered.

"Have you ever seen any rebels?"

I nodded. "I have."

"How many were there?"

"I didn't count them."

"Hey, that's not the answer I need," he snapped and lifted my chin with the end of his rifle. "How many of them are there?"

"There used to be twenty of them, but there are only six now."

"Where did the rest go?"

I shook my head. "I don't know."

"So there are only six of them left?"

I nodded.

"Why don't you fight back if there are only six of them? There are so many of you. Why do you let six people beat you?"

The commander continued yelling a stream of curses until he was hoarse and looked exhausted. When it started to turn dark, he suddenly softened. In a much calmer tone, he said, "We wouldn't hit you if only you weren't so stubborn. We have been forced to beat up innocent people. We don't hate you. Our only purpose in coming here is to protect you from the rebels. They are evil."

The commander's behavior was like that of a pleading child. It signaled that they were through with us for that day, and soon thereafter we were allowed to go home.

---

On a Thursday morning in mid-February, all of Alue Rambe was awakened at dawn by the sound of gunshots from the west. Startled, I jumped out of bed and rushed outside. I climbed up the hill near the stream. At first, I thought the shots came from somewhere nearby, but it turned out they came from the border between Alue Rambe and Cot Meureubo, about a mile and a half away.

I hid quite some time behind a durian tree by the bushes near the stream. I was cold and covered myself with a sarong that I brought along. When two figures came toward me from the field, I pressed myself against the tree. At first, I thought they were disguised soldiers, but it turned out that they were merely villagers who were also on the run.

At the sound of a loud explosion, I dropped to the ground. The grenade explosion was followed by screams. A moment later, there were repeated gunshots. The sounds were different. The self-assembled guns that belonged to the rebels sounded different than the factory-made weapons of the soldiers.

Before the day turned bright, numerous men from our village were already working in their fields. They had just set out the saplings of rubber, areca, and durian trees. I saw columns of smoke rising from five spots in the vicinity of Cot Meureubo.

Later on, I heard that soldiers on a rampage had beat a number of people and then burned the houses around the orchards.

Some villagers who managed to escape told us that a platoon of soldiers and police officers appeared in Lhok Jok, Alue Rambe, and Seuneubok Drien. They battered every man they could find and questioned women and children about the men's whereabouts.

A dozen other people and I hid in the orchards. Others hid in the foothills. Around noon, a villager from Cot Meureubo told us that two rebels and two villagers had been shot dead. He said that the soldiers had been spying on the rebels for some time.

Raiyan and his five men deliberately stayed in a house on a rubber plantation that was owned by a factory worker in the city. They knew the house was being watched and intentionally chose the place for a skirmish. The house was isolated from other houses, and their encounter would not affect innocent villagers.

When a platoon of soldiers and police officers approached the house, there was no sign that anyone was inside, and the door was locked from the outside. Suddenly, two rebels fired a round of gunshots from inside the house. At the same time, other rebels hurled grenades at the group of soldiers standing guard.

Other soldiers, surrounding the house, responded to the rebels' fire.

One of the rebels, who had been shot and collapsed but was still breathing, pulled out the safety pin of his grenade and threw it on the ground near the soldiers who moved towards him. The rebel's body was instantly shattered, but the explosion also wounded eight soldiers.

Afterward, Raiyan told us that the conflict had killed sixteen soldiers and police officers and wounded dozens of other soldiers.

"We had baited the soldiers to come to such a suitable place," he said. "Hence, we only had two casualties."

After the incident, some villages in the Buloh Blang Ara district looked deserted. Not a single man was seen walking in the streets, and the fields were empty.

About five hundred soldiers and police officers patrolled the streets of the district. Helicopters hovered over the area but dared not fly low.

―――•―――

The dense jungles around the hills and valleys now became our world. The military quickly took over the villages, which were now only occupied by women, children, and old men. In Simpang Mawak, the soldiers re-erected their checkpoints; hence, it was easy for them to reach Alue Rambe, Seuneubok Drien, Lhok Jok, and Cot Meureubo.

In almost every part of Aceh, the war was raging. Jakarta sent many soldiers to Aceh, but this never deterred the rebels. We considered the casualties as a part of our fate. Every fallen rebel was immediately replaced by another. According to Raiyan, most of our weapons were smuggled in by boat, but some came from military generals in Jakarta. They sold the weapons to leaders of the resistance movement who had connections with them.

Ishak Daud, who had been sentenced to twenty years behind bars, had been released and was now back leading his men in the fight against the government's injustice.

Sofyan Dawood and Ahmad Kandang were also back on the scene. Each of them was in charge of several platoons of men who were ready to die. Skirmishes happened every day. Soldiers and police officers roaming the streets were easy targets.

The rebels did not hesitate to attack military checkpoints in various places. They threw grenades and sprayed police stations and military bases with gunfire.

The soldiers then retaliated by persecuting the men and burning down villages.

Every time Raiyan's troops or other troops were involved in shootouts with soldiers on the roads, in the village outskirts, or on abandoned farms, other men and I ran to the jungle, climbed up to the hills, ran down to the valleys, and stayed for weeks in empty shacks on abandoned farms. We returned once we received news that the soldiers had left the villages.

"Nazir," asked one of my comrades during a boring night we spent in a shack in the middle of a farm. "When will you marry Zulaiha?"

"I don't know," I answered with a sigh.

I had failed to propose to Zulaiha several times. Every time a date for our engagement was agreed on, the soldiers would appear to pursue the fighters. I had not seen Zulaiha during the past month. I did not have a chance to visit her house. In this kind of situation, the elderly men, women, and children stayed at home. They were scared to leave the house, as there was no one to protect them.

I did not know how my papaya trees and the orchard behind the house were doing. During the few times I was able to come home, the shrubbery had started taking over the papaya field. The orchards behind our house were quite clean because Baiti and Raziah kept an eye on them. Ibu had grown weaker and was often ill. Muha had joined Raiyan about two months ago, and I had not seen him since.

After Muha left, Raziah and her two children moved in with Ibu. The soldiers in Simpang Mawak had found out about Muha's involvement in the attacks against their checkpoints.

But, they were unable to recognize Muha, because there was not a single photograph of him around in either our house or Kakek's house. There was no photographer at Muha and Raziah's wedding, and we did not own any photographs, except for Zuhra's, Akbar's, and my school pictures.

From the newspaper that Leman always brought home, we were informed that on May 12, 2000, a Humanitarian Pause for Aceh was declared; it was an agreement between the fighters of Aceh and the Indonesian government, signed in Switzerland. The Humanitarian Pause, which mandated a cease-fire, seemed unenforceable in Buloh Blang Ara, as well as in Alue Rambe. That agreement was only implemented in the big cities, and even then, only for a short while. The soldiers in sub-districts still hunted for rebels who, in turn, fought back.

"That Humanitarian Pause isn't our business," a commander who attacked Alue Rambe said to the women there. "Our duty is to hunt and eliminate the rebels."

Every time those soldiers came to Alue Rambe, they either yelled at Raziah or tried to flirt with her. This also happened to other women, especially the pretty ones. The soldiers did not care if the women were married or still virgins.

Zulaiha also experienced such treatment. When I met her more than a month ago, she said, "They groped my thighs…"

I was furious, but I could not do anything. I was ashamed of my own impotence. I felt useless. All I could do was flee to the jungle when the soldiers came to harass the women.

"I'll propose to you immediately," I said.

Zulaiha ran inside, crying. Her sobs pierced my heart. I left her house and headed for the stream with my head down.

# CHAPTER 25

At the end of January 2001, we were shocked by the news of Ahmad Kandang's death, caused by an explosion of one of his homemade bombs in a jungle. According to some people at Leman's stall, on January 27, Ahmad was assembling a high-explosive bomb. To test the bomb, he asked his men to dig a deep hole.

He threw the bomb into the hole and waited with everyone for it to explode. When, after a while, the bomb did not detonate, Ahmad offered one hundred thousand rupiahs to anyone who dared to take out the bomb. When no one stepped forward, he increased his offer to two hundred thousand rupiahs. With still no one willing to retrieve the bomb, Ahmad himself went into the hole. Soon afterwards, there was a big explosion. His body completely torn, Ahmad died instantly.

Raiyan and his followers went to mourn and perform prayers. For a few days, samadiyah prayer was performed at a hideout.

Meanwhile, soldiers and police officers took turns going to the villages to capture men suspected of being among Ahmad Kandang's followers.

At the same time, the rebels rode their motorbikes into the city at night. They threw grenades and opened fire at random. The military responded, of course, and for several hours, the noise of artillery fire filled the air. Ahmad Kandang's death did not affect the rebels' spirit at all; they continued to attack the military at any opportunity.

The soldiers who occupied the villages hid in orchards and fields around the houses, waiting for the rebels to come out of hiding. But when a week passed and none of the rebels returned from the jungle, the soldiers went back to their posts or bases.

During my absence, the situation at home had taken a turn for the worse. All the chickens were gone. The soldiers had taken some for food while hiding in our field, some had died from a bout with tapeworm, and Ibu had killed some to feed the family. There were no food peddlers, and the trucks that transported agricultural products no longer came to Tamoun. There was a shortage of rice everywhere. The three stalls in Tamoun looked like they would go bankrupt soon.

To survive with her three children and three grandchildren, Ibu had sold three goats. The remaining four looked very thin. Zuhra and Baiti tethered them only around our house, where there was hardly any grass growing. Also, with me gone, no one cut grass for their night feeding.

In the orchards around the house, the weeds had grown tall. The ground of the areca and candlenut orchards was littered with fruit that had dropped and begun to rot. Coconuts lay scattered around the trees.

No one had dared to go to the orchards for fear of running into soldiers who were watching the villagers' houses.

The warehouses in Tamoun refused to store any produce, as there were no buyers.

My papaya trees barely survived the invasion of weeds.

Samsul's and my dangau were burned down.

Samsul's field had turned into a jungle.

Zulaiha was not around. I suddenly missed her and hoped to see her.

At the cemetery, I went to Ayah's, Kakek's, Nenek's, and Arkam's graves and found Nono there. He was thin. He rose when he saw me and just stood there with his tail wagging and eyes filled with a sadness that cut through me.

"Go home," I said. "Guard the house."

The cemetery had also turned into a jungle. Weeds covered the graves, and the headstones could barely be seen. I cleaned my loved ones' graves. The clay and sap from the weeds stuck to my hands.

Finally, I went to Kakek's house. It had been almost a year since Muha left to join Ahmad and Raziah had moved back home with her children. I had not heard anything about Muha and Mahmud and did not know where either could be.

Some of the roof panels were detached; one of the walls was broken open. I peeked through the hole and saw that the room was littered with garbage.

I walked around the house, hoping to find Situng. The dog had probably left because no one was feeding him. The dogs that used to guard the orchards and fields now roamed the streets. After the men who usually took care of them left, the dogs started to forage for food. They looked for scraps around the villagers' houses and hunted. Because the villagers' themselves had a food shortage, scraps were scarce, and the dogs migrated to Simpang Mawak, where some were adopted by soldiers. No one I asked had seen Situng.

It started raining mid-May. Zulaiha and I met several times near the strea or on her porch.

"If no soldiers appear during the rest of this week, I'll ask for your hand," I said.

Zulaiha immediately broke into a big smile.

I suddenly realized how deeply I cared about her and how much I wanted her.

"I always pray that this war will end soon," she said. Her voice was filled with hope.

"We'll have a small party."

"Ayah said that it's all right not to have a party. The situation now is very difficult."

"I've prepared a dowry of seven gold nuggets."

Zulaiha only nodded.

One nugget weighed three point three grams. It was customary for a dowry to be ten nuggets. However, for us farmers, seven would do.

After meeting Zulaiha, I went home to see Ibu.

Lately, Ibu often complained about her swollen right knee. The old midwife had massaged it for her, but the swelling got even bigger, and she had difficulty moving around. Apparently, the swelling in her knee was not caused by a sprain but was brought on by rheumatism. The pain would spike in the morning and make her limp to the kitchen.

"Bu, please ask for Zulaiha's hand for me," I said.

Ibu did not reply.

"What's wrong, Bu?" I asked, surprised by her reaction. "Do you disagree?"

Ibu looked away silently.

Uneasy, I waited for her answer.

"What will you use for a dowry?" Ibu asked suddenly.

"Don't you have the gold nuggets I gave you for my dowry?" I now was totally confused.

"The soldiers took it, son." Ibu burst into tears. "A week ago, they came to search the house. They took everything. Also, all of Baiti's, Raziah's and Zuhra's money."

I was dumbstruck. My head hurt and my ears felt hot. I had saved up for that gold for a long time. And now what little money I had saved from every harvest sale was gone. My means to propose to Zulaiha had vanished.

I walked out to the backyard. It would be impossible to air my feelings at home. In the banana orchard near the house, I repeatedly drove my fist into a plant until it collapsed and the skin of my knuckles was red and chafed.

"I'll go to war," I hissed and gritted my teeth. "Now, I really want to go to war."

I had a cup of coffee at Leman's stall and silently cursed the soldiers who had destroyed my life.

———•———

Time moved monotonously as days flowed into each other. If I did not work in the field, I watched television at Leman's stall. One night, the broadcast reported news from the Presidential Palace in Jakarta. In the live report on July 23, 2001, President Abdurrahman, dressed in a pair of shorts, waved at the crowd from the palace's yard. With spotlights shining on him, he was unceremoniously escorted out of the palace as if he were a beggar. He was immediately succeeded by his vice-president, Megawati Soekarnoputri, who was the daughter of Soekarno, Indonesia's first president.

During her inauguration, a group of soldiers came to search our village again, looking for Sofyan Dawood, Raiyan, Muha, and other rebels who had vanished during the past six months. Despite being wanted by the military, Muha occasionally came home. In the middle of the night, he'd sneak to Raziah's bedroom window and let his presence be known with soft knocks and whispers. If I happened to be awake, I would hear the thud of his rifle when he placed the weapon on the ground.

I was tired of constantly being on the run. Because I had no weapon, I was forced to follow those who did. We moved through the jungle and climbed up into the hills that surrounded our valley. From the top of the highest hill, we could see what was happening around us.

My village had turned into a jungle; there were no more fields, no more open space. Everything was overgrown. I could not detect a single house among the dense growth. On top of the hill, the wind blew through my long hair. I no longer had the time to get a haircut.

"There are so many of them," a man panted as he climbed up the ridge.

Another thin man who was with him chimed in, "This time, they might stay longer."

We continued to cross the jungle while watching for snakes that might be hiding under the bushes. Around noon, we came upon an abandoned papaya field. Unfortunately, birds had been there ahead of us and had pecked large holes in the ripe fruit.

I picked a half-ripened fruit, cut it up with the jackknife I carried in my pocket, and ate it, sitting away from the others. *How did I land in this deplorable situation?*

We dispersed in the evening. Some found abandoned houses, others stayed in the dangaus they found still standing in the fields. Some farmers who lived around Simpang Keuramat warned us not to move in the southeastern direction. They had seen many soldiers walk into the jungle there.

I stayed with eight other men in a dangau near the river. I built a fire from garbage to use as lighting. Hunger kept me awake on my watch. Around midnight, I woke up one of the others to take over my watch and fell fast asleep.

Around noon, when our hunger was getting the better of us, someone found a machete under the dangau, and we went looking for a sugar palm. We took turns climbing to the top to cut out the heart of the tree. The milky white heart of the palm tree was invigorating.

The nine of us were gorging on the palm's heart when a man walked up to us and said, "The soldiers chased us into the jungle. They pitched a tent at Tamoun and built a checkpost."

"Oh, my God. What if they find us here?" someone panicked.

"They won't be able to get past the hill," the man who brought the news replied. "They will only roam the farmland and the jungle along the roadside."

"If they set up a post there, we won't be able to go home," one of the men said, terrified.

Other than contemplating our uncertain fate in the jungle, we also worried about our families we had left behind.

I thought about Ibu, Zuhra, Baiti, Raziah, Muslim, Akbar, and Siti. I also thought about Zulaiha, her mother, and sister. I had not seen Samsul, Zulaiha's father. He and a few other men had supposedly gone southwest of the village.

One afternoon, we heard faint gunshots in the east. In the evening, it came from the southeast, where there were oil palm plantations. We were trapped in the middle of a thick jungle and did not know where to go. There was no way we could leave this jungle. The soldiers would not be able to cross the river and penetrate the thick bushes.

By August, our clothes had turned shabby and smelled bad. Mosquitoes and gnats surrounded us. They followed us everywhere with their annoying buzz. The heart of the sugar palm was all we had to eat. Sometimes, we'd stumble on a papaya tree or old coconuts. We would even eat the heart of a coconut tree. Those among us with a weak stomach suffered from diarrhea.

After being on the run for more than a week, three of us came down with a high fever, which we suspected to be malaria. When they could no longer endure the hardship of living in the jungle, they snuck home. Their wives hid their sick husbands under the bed and covered them with banana clusters.

On the ninth night, the soldiers who camped out in Tamoun disassembled their tent and left Alue Rambe. As usual, all of us went home to our respective houses, ate, took a bath, and changed our clothes.

Ibu, my sisters, nephews, and niece, were all fine, but Ibu kept looking at me sadly.

"What's wrong?" I asked.

"Please, eat first."

I was hungry and wolfed my food down. Afterwards, I returned to Ibu with my question. "What happened, Bu? Why are you so sad?"

"Go take a bath and change your clothes," she said. "You really smell."

I rushed to grab my towel and walked to the stream where I took a long bath. While bathing, I thought of Zulaiha. *How could I propose to her without a dowry?* I really wanted to see her, but what good would it do?

I felt refreshed after bathing and putting on clean clothes. I sat down on the daybed, near Ibu, who showed me her swollen knee. I probed, "What's wrong, Ibu?"

"Zulaiha," she paused for a moment. "Have you heard about it?"

"I haven't heard anything," I answered. "I just returned from the jungle."

Ibu fell into a silence, which made me even more anxious. "What's going on, Bu?" I asked impatiently.

Ibu remained silent.

"Please tell me, Bu," I urged. "What happened to Zulaiha?"

"The soldiers raped her."

---

In October, I found Raiyan in his hideout. I had prepared myself to join him. I no longer cared what was going to happen. Even if I did not join the rebellion, the soldiers would still hunt me. Every time they came to my village, the other men and I had to flee. No one was willing to endure the soldiers' beatings.

"I'm really happy that you're finally joining me." Raiyan threw me a big smile.

"Then give me a gun," I replied impatiently.

Raiyan burst out laughing.

I felt insulted and asked, "Why are you laughing?"

Raiyan continued to chuckle but stopped when I gave him the evil eye. He slapped some dirt off his arm and said, "You're very passionate, my friend."

"So, what's wrong with that?" I asked, looking at him closely. "Can't I be passionate about it?"

"I know how angry you are. I know," he replied. "Now you understand what kind of people those soldiers really are. I really want to give you a gun, right now."

"Then give it to me," I said straightforwardly.

Raiyan was silent. "My friend," he said, "right now, we have a shortage of guns. A lot of our weapons have been seized by the soldiers."

"Then, what's going to happen?" I was disappointed. "Do I have to fight with a machete?"

Raiyan chuckled softly. "No. You'll still get a gun. You only need to be patient."

"How long do I need to be patient?"

"I don't know. I'll try to get one as fast as possible. Maybe it'll take a month, maybe two. And maybe I can get one as soon as next week."

Neither of us said anything for a long time. I looked at the five other men who lived in that shanty in the middle of the jungle. They were drinking coffee and chain-smoking endlessly.

I did not know them, other than having seen them several times when they visited Leman's stall. A young man, younger than the rest, poured coffee into glasses and brought it to us.

"By the way," Raiyan said, "What made you decide to join me?"

I thought for a moment. "Is that important?"

Raiyan, who looked older than his age, chuckled. The world that had turned him into a fugitive had broadened his mind and made him wiser than people his age. Those traits earned him the position of Panglima Sagoe.

"It's not important," he answered. "I just wanted to know."

"I fight for many things," I answered.

"Such as?"

"For Allah, for Ayah, for Kakek, for Nenek, for Baiti, for Arkam, for Zulaiha, for the people who have fallen as victims and those who're still alive, and for Aceh." I halted. "But I can't fight a war without a gun."

Raiyan was quiet. He sat cross-legged in front of me. Resting his elbows on his thighs, he held his chin in his cupped hands. His eyes pierced mine when he said, "I promise to get you a gun, soon."

The rain came down harder. Water dripping from leaks soaked the floor. We moved to a drier spot and wound up scattered. Some remained standing, others curled up, and still others sat on a wooden log in the corner of the hut.

It rained through the night. I fell asleep in a hammock with both ends tied to a pole. Two men stood guard outside.

I woke up in the morning and washed my face with rainwater in a big drum. On top of a brick furnace, I found the leftover of last night's coffee and picked up a piece of bread. As soon as Raiyan woke up, I went back to my village. I walked through the jungle using footpaths and cutting through brush. I was always on the alert about the situation around me. I was now a rebel, albeit one without a weapon.

Aside from spending my time escaping when soldiers invaded the villages, I was familiar enough with the jungle here. Everything around me seemed to be draped by sadness. I did not want to surrender myself to the situation, nor did I want to die without having done something worthwhile.

When I reached the main road of Alue Rambe, I did not go home immediately. I turned onto a footpath and followed the stream and then continued to Zulaiha's house after walking through a grove of banana plants. I walked to her bedroom window and called her name. When there was no response, I walked to the porch.

Zulaiha's mother answered the door and invited me to come in. "Zulaiha won't come out of her room." The woman looked pale; she looked at me sadly, then left me standing there.

I waited for a while, but when Zulaiha did not come out, I shouted, "I came to see you. Whatever happened to you, I still love you."

There was no reply.

I remembered how, after Baiti's rape, she had refused to come out of her room, other than to use the bathroom. I could only imagine how much a rape victim had to endure.

"Do what you want," I continued. "I swear I'll propose and marry you. I'll love you as long as I live."

For a while, it remained quiet. Then sobbing broke the silence, but no one appeared. Each sob pierced my heart. "I swear I'll kill the person who hurt you," I shouted before leaving.

# Chapter 26

At the end of January 2002, I heard the sad news of the death of Abdullah Syafi'i, the Supreme Commander of the rebels in Aceh. Previously, he was the commander of Pidie Area. He was known and liked for being well mannered, simple, and kind, while also being a well-respected soldier.

In an old hut with a sago palm roof, in the foothills between Alue Rambe and Cot Meureubo, dozens of rebels under Raiyan's command gathered for a wake. Since morning, several villagers had come to cook rice and prepare the goat curry and drinking water. Muha brought along five orphans from Cot Meureubo.

The service dedicated to the Supreme Commander of the Aceh Resistance Movement was held in secret, but some people still stood guard outside. After the meal, with lighting only from flashlights and oil lamps, the village Imam led everyone in prayers, and soon the chanting penetrated the silent jungle.

Raiyan said that he had to hold the event to honor his leader no matter how difficult the situation was at that time.

After the prayers, Raiyan shared a short biography of Abdullah Syafi'i, who had led the guerilla movement for twenty years in the Pidie area. He had never received military training like Ahmad Kandang or Ishak Daud. He was the one who appointed all area commanders in the Aceh Freedom Movement. When taking their oaths, he always reminded the new leaders to be loyal to Aceh, to protect its people, and to hurt no one. Abdullah Syafi'i was succeeded by his vice-commander, Muzakir Manaf.

I returned home after a few days went by without the sound of gunshots. Muha came with me but left his gun behind. Some four months had passed since I last saw him. He had lost a lot of weight.

"I'm sad about what happened to Zulaiha," he said, stopping for a while.

I did not answer him. Dawn was breaking as we moved along a footpath that weaved through thickets and sometimes disappeared. When that happened, we'd simply move on until we came upon another path. We would not get lost, because the surrounding hills guided us.

"How's Mahmud?" Muha asked.

"I don't know," I slightly panted. "He hasn't been home in a long time."

"Hopefully, he's still alive."

None of us thought too much about Mahmud. Even Baiti didn't seem to think about him that much. What baffled me was that she never got pregnant, even after being married to Mahmud for many years, but it had taken only one encounter with those cursed soldiers to make her belly swell.

Muha was only home for three days before the soldiers detected his presence and arrived in a truck at Tamoun. Muha headed for the Nisam forest. I heard that Muha and other rebels escaped to the jungle of Simpang Keuramat.

Leman's now was the only stall on Tamoun that was still in business.

One day, a buyer for the remaining betel nuts in the warehouse drove up in a mini truck. The thin man who wore eyeglasses complained about the road fees the soldiers at Simpang Mawak leveled. He said that every delivery truck that passed the post was stopped, inspected, and asked for money. Along the main road between Medan and Banda Aceh, roadblocks of barbed wire forced the trucks to stop. There were about thirty posts, and drivers had to pay a passing fee at every one.

At night, some rebels managed to attack those checkpoints with gunfire and grenades. Enraged, the soldiers retaliated. They searched everyone who passed their posts, and every day, dozens of people were arrested, beaten, or shot.

Despite the escalated tension between the rebels and the military, the daily routine of the farmers continued. After that mini truck appeared in Alue Rambe, other mini trucks appeared with buyers for betel nuts, coconuts, candlenuts, and rubber, and I started to clear the brush around the house while Raziah and Baiti gathered areca on the ground.

Ibu, who could not walk anymore, sat on the porch, peeling the areca fruit. Zuhra filled the water container from the stream, cooked, and tethered the goats.

During the following days, I gathered coconuts that lay scattered on the ground. After splitting them, I removed the flesh from the shell. I took the copra to Tamoun when the buyers were there. The small trading activities in Tamoun revived the starving villagers.

I continued to clear the land. Raziah, Baiti, and Akbar helped me. Akbar was twelve now, and no longer went to school. I stacked the cut brush at a marshy lot. I worked every day. When a troop of soldiers arrived, I ran and hid in the jungle.

There seemed to be no change in my daily routine other than that now I anxiously waited to hear from Raiyan about my gun.

One late afternoon, I realized I had not seen Nono for a while. I asked Akbar, Raziah, Baiti, and Zuhra, but none of them had seen him either. When I called for him at the cemetery and he didn't show up, I continued to look for him there. After a while, I found his dead body lying under a banyan tree. Ants and flies covered his eyes and mouth.

I took my hoe and buried Nono. I sat for a while next to his grave wondering why I felt so sad about the death of a dog. I kept to myself for the rest of the evening. So much had been taken from me.

I went to Samsul's house several times, but because Zulaiha would not see me, I did not know how she was doing. Perhaps she didn't want me to see her pregnant belly. She should be about seven or eight months along now. I tried to calm myself in preparation to face even the bitterest reality.

Sometimes I would walk to her house and, standing by her window, shout, "Zulaiha, I don't care about your pregnant belly. I still love you. I miss you."

Through the closed window, I heard her sobbing. I balled my fists and tried to calm my racing heart. After a while, I left with heavy steps.

---

In the early afternoon of July 7, a dozen men walked up the path from the field carrying Muha. He had bullet holes in his shoulder and neck; his chest was laid open. They laid him on the daybed in the living room. Raziah screamed as soon as she entered the room with Ibu, Baiti, Zuhra, and Siti on her heels. Akbar was still in the field, and Muslim had not yet come from school.

Not long afterwards, several women and men came by. They gasped and covered their mouths when they saw the body.

Imam Masjid, who came with his wife, quickly instructed us to prepare everything for the burial. While we took care of the bathing and shrouding, three men went to the cemetery to dig the grave.

Someone was sent to Cot Meureubo to fetch Muha's mother.

I seethed, looking at Muha's mutilated body. *Even after his death they treated him with such cruelty.* After we enshrouded and prayed for him, we carried Muha to the cemetery. I was one of the pallbearers.

"They took his heart," one of the other pallbearers said, wiping the sweat off his forehead.

"What for?" I asked, stupefied.

The man did not answer.

Later, he told me that Muha was shot during a siege on the plantation area of Simpang Keuramat. He was the only one who died. The other five men who were with him managed to escape.

During that incident, Muha shot one soldier dead and wounded three others.

After they shot Muha dead, the soldiers cut his chest open, took his heart, and then threw the body by the roadside.

Lately, the soldiers often engaged in such cruelty to discourage the rebels.

I gritted my teeth as I received Muha's body and laid him in his grave.

We buried Muha next to Ayah. Now this cemetery was dominated by my family's graves. It might very well be that the one to be buried next to Muha would be me.

Soon after the funeral ended, a troop of soldiers surrounded my house. I ran to the jungle with a few other men. I felt like killing them all. *They didn't even allow us to grieve.*

Some soldiers stayed around the orchards and guarded the alley in front of my house. Ibu, Raziah, and Baiti ignored them because they mostly stayed outside and only once in a while came into the house. Some of them then glanced at Zuhra, who had turned into a beautiful seventeen-year-old.

The soldiers asked Imam Masjid where Mahmud was.

"I haven't seen him for three or four years," Imam Masjid answered.

"Where did he go?"

"I don't know. Maybe he's already dead. I haven't heard anything about him." Imam Masjid might have tried to persuade the soldiers to leave. However, the soldiers, counting on Mahmud to come home now that Muha was dead, stuck around. But when no one showed up after a while, they left, and I eased home.

Now, there was no other man in this house to target than me, and I always came home because I did not have any other home. I knew Ayah was listed as one of the rebels' government officials. Arkam, his brother-in-law, during his lifetime was known as the most dangerous rebel in this village. And now I, who was Ayah's only son, had joined the movement. It was difficult for a woman to become a rebel. But Ayah's daughters ended up marrying rebels. Raziah was married to Muha, who became a rebel. Baiti married Mahmud. Though God only knew who Zuhra would marry, it was clear that we were a rebellious family.

We did not commemorate Muha's death with a ceremony, zikr, and prayers. Ibu canceled her plan to butcher a goat when no one would come to help us. Imam Masjid, who now walked with a limp, couldn't possibly help us by himself.

That evening, after returning home briefly, I left the house again. My intuition said that my house was being spied on, even though people saw soldiers leave the village. I believed that another unit was still hiding, somewhere behind my house, waiting for me or Mahmud.

Dressed in a pair of jeans, a T-shirt, a jacket, and boots, I headed for the jungle by myself. My sarong hung off my shoulder, and I carried a pocketknife and flashlight. The village was not safe anymore. I was sure that even if I did not join Raiyan, the soldiers would still capture me, and I would end up being tortured to death. I did not want to die like Ayah.

I could only turn on my flashlight after ensuring that the light could not be seen from afar.

Almost everyone I loved had died. And those who were still alive would continue to live in misery. *Oh, Ibu, Baiti, Raziah, Zuhra, my nephews and niece, what kind of fate will you face? Zulaiha. Why do you always refuse to see me?*

When I arrived at the top of the hill, I stood still in the middle of tall grasses blowing in the wind and felt like a wandering ghost, floating in the air, unable to touch the clouds but also unable to touch the ground. I did not know where to go. The dogs' howling followed by gunshots seemed so far away.

---

In the morning, I woke curled up in my sarong in the middle of nowhere on top of a hill. The light of the sunrise blinded me. I rubbed my eyes and tied my sarong around my waist, then started to walk in the southwestern direction. After I passed through some patches of brush, I came upon a grove of banana plants alongside a marsh.

I pulled down a branch with a cluster of ripe bananas that had been pecked at by birds.

The branch bent and brought some of the plant with it. The cluster now lay in front of me as if offered by the plant. Some of the lower bunches had ripe bananas. I cut a few and ate them for breakfast.

After I was full, I continued my walk through the brush. A plump piglet crossed my path and scurried into a nearby thicket. By the time the sun was noon high, I walked into a coconut grove. I looked but couldn't see any houses. Three oxen peacefully grazed in the shade of the coconut trees. I was thirsty and climbed up a tree to pick a young coconut. I made sure to throw it into some bushes so it would not break open when it hit the ground.

I made a hole in the top of the coconut by stabbing my knife repeatedly into its soft shell. After I quenched my thirst, I walked quickly through a dry rice field and some more abandoned fields, and finally entered an oil palm plantation. On the plantation, where the weeds were already knee-high, I found an abandoned, dilapidated hut with half of its roof caved in.

There was no sign of any humans. Water inside a big tin drum had spilled over and was covered with debris from the roof. I scooped up some water with my hands and washed my face. Some mosquito larvae floated on the water's surface. I wiped my face with my sarong, then sat on the ground to rest while thinking about my next move.

I reflected for a while. Muha was no longer around. His life had ended, like Ayah, Kakek, Nenek, Arkam, and Nono. Clearly, I would meet my fate at my own house. It was impossible for me to go home, but neither could I be seen in the streets. Only the jungle and the orchards with their fruit offered me shelter.

I continued my journey. Climbing down the hill, I found a brook, whose bed was lined with pebbles. The clear water flowed steadily. I squatted near a rock and scooped up the cold water. I washed my face and drank. A gravel path went uphill between bushes.

I had to stay in the jungle if I wanted to look for Raiyan. Going back home now would be like signing my own death sentence. Now, only a gun could keep me alive.

When the sun started to descend, I was trapped amid brush in a humid cacao plantation. Under heavy attack of buzzing mosquitoes, I quickened my step. I stumbled several times as my steps got caught in the tall grass.

Next, I walked into an areca orchard and surprised two young men with my sudden presence. They immediately put their guns to my head.

"Who are you?"

I breathed hard and perspiration rolled from my head down my neck and onto my shirt collar.

"Nazir," I stammered, "One of Pang Raiyan's recruits."

"Nazir?" one of them asked while looking at his friend without lowering his gun.

"There's no one called Nazir in Pang Raiyan's unit. I know every one of them."

"Yes," I answered, calming myself, "but you don't know me."

The two men herded me to a small hut by the river. A young man slapped me, accusing me of being a spy for the military. They would not listen to anything I said and tied me to an areca tree near the hut.

I struggled and threatened to get even with them.

"You're just the same as the soldiers who killed my family," I shouted furiously. "Muha was my brother-in-law. You must know him. You don't need to tie me up. I'm one of you."

"Shut up, or else we'll zip your mouth."

They burned garbage to chase away the mosquitoes, but the insects continued to land on my arms and neck. The rope around my wrist was so tight it numbed me. I was very hungry and my mouth felt dry. I finally fell asleep leaning against the areca tree.

The next morning, Raiyan appeared with two other men.

"Nazir," Raiyan yelled once he saw me tied to the areca tree. "Why did they tie you up?"

I did not answer and shot him an unhappy glance.

Raiyan struggled to untie my hands. "You guys are assholes," he cursed the two men, who immediately stepped back.

One of them walked up to me and said, "I'm sorry. It's just a misunderstanding."

"One day, I'll be tying you up," I replied and left him.

After we finished our coffee and bread, we left the hut. I walked between three armed men. Even though they did not point their rifles at me, I looked like their prisoner.

By noon, we arrived in a jungle between Alue Rambe and Cot Meureubo. In a small dangau, two men were cooking rice and making coffee on a stone furnace.

Raiyan and I went into the dangau and sat down, facing each other.

Outside, someone fried some salted fish. The sound of the sizzling oil and pungent scent of the frying salted fish spread.

"Biram," Raiyan called. "Get me the gun."

"Yes, Pang." A man with a spiky haircut moved aside a crumpled fishing net and some clothes that covered a gun. He laid the gun in front of me.

I stared at the AK-47, which had a few scratches on its body. I had never touched a gun like that.

"This gun belonged to Muha — may Allah grant him a place in heaven — and you will follow in his footsteps. You will inherit his gun. But before you can claim it, you need to be prepared to join the movement. This means you have to be as ready to die as you're ready to kill."

The other four men had left their activities and now stood around us, as if this were a sacred ceremony. They watched us in solemn silence.

"I've been ready for a long time," I said, holding Raiyan's eyes.

"All right, then," Raiyan continued and shook my hand. "I initiate you, Nazir bin Dahli, as a soldier of Aceh. Now repeat after me, I, Nazir bin Dahli, swear in the name of Allah, to be faithful to Negara Aceh and the Wali Negara, Hasan Muhammad Tiro."

Raiyan immediately embraced me, and so did the four other men.

I spent the rest of the day paying attention to Raiyan's instructions on how to operate the weapon, locking and releasing the trigger, and how to reload the bullets and shoot accurately.

When I held the gun, I felt on fire. The weapon was much lighter than I thought. I could not wait to go down the streets and hold up a squad of soldiers.

"Tomorrow, we'll have a party," exclaimed Raiyan passionately.

"We're ready," everyone replied.

## Chapter 27

The first time I shot the gun, I did not expect the weapon to recoil, and my entire body trembled. I was pretty shaken up too. Raiyan, Biram, and I ambushed a passing military truck at the border of Ceumpeudak and Simpang Keuramat. The soldiers decided not to engage. They fired back but kept moving.

Soon afterwards, we heard shots coming from the direction of the Simpang Mawak checkpoint. I responded eagerly with several gunshots.

"You're just wasting bullets," Raiyan growled.

During the month of August, we spent a week in that jungle. At night, we snuck into Seuneubok Drien, and slept there on plastic tarps.

We were planning to attack the military base at Buloh Blang Ara when a centipede bit Raiyan in the foot. The centipede must have crept into his leather shoe while he sat in the bushes. His right ankle was so swollen, he could not wear his shoe. I took his gun and carried it for him. Limping, he held onto my shoulder while moving along the jungle path. Because Raiyan couldn't put hardly any weight on his right foot, he put pressure on my shoulder with each step he took. The terrain was difficult, and Biram and I took turns supporting Raiyan, who groaned as he leaned on us. Biram and I were soon exhausted.

"It's amazing how much damage the bite of a small centipede can do," Raiyan moaned.

Because it was impossible to take him to his home in Alue Rambe, I took him to my dangau. The weeds in my field were already waist high. I snuck home and asked Raziah to grind up some nutmeg. It was too dangerous to wait, so I filled a jerry can with drinking water and returned to the dangau.

Raiyan was smoking a cigarette when Raziah showed up with the nutmeg paste wrapped in a banana leaf. I washed Raiyan's swollen foot and applied the paste.

Meanwhile, Biram stood guard, hiding in the brush near the alley.

After Baiti brought us some food, I replaced Biram. I asked everyone to keep my presence a secret. I didn't want to be seen by anyone other than my family.

Coming home was very dangerous. Soldiers could suddenly appear out of nowhere and search the house. Some people were shot in the morning when they opened their door to start their day. For us, home was a more dangerous place than the battlefield.

The next day, Raiyan's foot was still swollen and throbbing. However, we had to move on. The longer we stayed in one place, the more dangerous it was for us. We left around noon. Biram and I again took turns supporting Raiyan. By nightfall, we reached another abandoned field and decided to spend the night in what was left of the dangau. Biram went to see a villager he knew to ask for food.

It took seven days for Raiyan's foot to heal from the centipede's bite.

In mid-September, Raiyan left us in the jungle of Simpang Keuramat to join an important meeting with some leaders of the movement at a secret location. Biram and I contacted someone in Simpang Keuramat to help us buy daily necessities, such as rice, eggs, salted fish, cooking oil, and bread at the market.

Raiyan was gone till early October. During his absence, Biram and I practiced our martial arts skills in the jungle. Besides our agility, the training was also to increase our endurance.

In late November, we moved northwest toward Buloh Blang Ara. Through his handheld radio, Biram contacted a group of rebels in Bereunghang, an area a little more than a mile west of Buloh Blang Ara. As planned in the meeting that Raiyan had attended, we were to launch simultaneous attacks on every military post in the Buloh Blang Ara District.

We had finished the two sacks of rice and did not want to wait any longer. Via radio contact, we agreed with some other groups to attack the Buloh Blang Ara Military Base and the police station that night from different directions.

Two platoons, from the south and east, were to attack the police station. Those coming from the west could not possibly enter the heart of the city because it was blocked by a police station.

Therefore, Raiyan, Biram, and I would have to attack the base. The fight would be very imbalanced, because there were forty soldiers against the three of us. However, this was not a confirmation of strength, but more of a meeting of the minds. We were to attack and fight the best we could and then retreat as carefully as possible.

By midnight, when not a single vehicle or person was on the street, the three of us approached the back side of the military base.

Biram hurled a grenade at the building with all his strength, then immediately ran toward a gravel path that led to Cot Meureubo. Raiyan and I sprayed the building with rounds of ammunition from across the street. The soldiers returned our fire with equal fury. Bullets whizzed back and forth. The guns produced a deafening noise.

Not long afterwards, there were explosions in the area of the market. Although a little late, the rebels coming from the west had apparently joined us. The noise of the gunfire and exploding grenades made it sound as if we had destroyed the whole town.

The soldiers' fire was ineffective because they did not know exactly where we were. Between rounds of fire, Raiyan and I ran south toward the jungle.

As soon as there was no response to their fire, the soldiers stopped shooting. While the shooting still continued around the market area, I walked into the jungle. The three of us met up in the Blang Riek jungle. Together we headed toward Lhok Jok.

We could not return to Alue Rambe because we heard that dozens of soldiers already waited there for our return.

After walking for a while through a dense forest of tall trees, we realized we were lost. Meanwhile, the November rain had started to fall. Raiyan turned on his flashlight but could not find his bearings. He finally decided to move deeper into the jungle and turned into an area where roots as large as our thighs popped out of the ground and lay across the path. The thick tree canopies that touched each other above kept the rain from falling straight on us.

Suddenly, we could not move any farther; our way was blocked by a massive dirt wall with trees growing on top of it. We could only move sideways. Meanwhile, the rain came down harder and the wind shook the tree branches, scattering leaves. Some stuck to my wet face.

We never came to the end of the dirt wall. Instead, we suddenly found ourselves facing a huge gap.

Raiyan shined his flashlight into the gap; the floor was covered with scattered leaves and dried branches.

"This is a cave," Raiyan exclaimed, catching his breath.

I was amazed that there was a cave in this jungle. No one had ever mentioned it. I had no idea where we were. The three of us went inside. After Raiyan made sure the cave was safe, we put our weapons on the ground.

I picked up a branch that had many twigs and, using it as a broom, I swept the garbage together. The cave was quite roomy; it could easily contain ten people or so.

Biram picked up another branch and helped me. Raiyan moved the garbage to the cave's entrance. He failed several times to ignite his lighter. The strong wind blew out the flame as soon as he lit it. Every so often, the wind blew a spray of rain into the cove.

Finally, the garbage caught fire. The smoke immediately filled the cave. Raiyan kept poking through the fire to keep it burning.

Biram found a few decaying branches as big as our arms. The fire kept lapping at them until they ignited. The flames of the fire were brighter than the light of Raiyan's flashlight.

Biram took a plastic tarp, three sarongs, and bread out of his bag. We spread the tarp out on the floor.

"I hope we killed some soldiers during our attack." Raiyan leaned his back against the cave wall while lighting a cigarette.

Biram rose and took a cigarette from the box Raiyan put down and chimed in, "I heard the screaming." He turned to me and asked, "Did you hear it, Nazir?"

"I could only hear them scream and curse," I answered.

Raiyan chuckled. He took the box of cigarettes from Biram and gave it to me.

"I don't smoke," I said.

"No wonder you're so healthy."

We chuckled.

The next morning, I was awakened by the trickling of water. The rain had stopped. I walked out of the cave and found a small stream only a few steps away from the cave, whose entrance was covered by bushes that were chest-high. Some big rocks obstructed the water flow. The water of the shallow stream was murky, but I still drank from it and used it to wash my face.

So did Raiyan and Biram.

When we returned to the cave, the handheld radio newscast reported that Lhok Jok, Cot Meureubo, Alue Rambe, and Seuneubok Drien were surrounded by hundreds of soldiers and police officers. The men from the three villages had run away to the jungle. The radio broadcaster also informed us that during last night's attack, five police officers were wounded by gunshots, one soldier died and two were wounded by the grenade explosion.

Because the villages around us were besieged, the three of us were trapped here. I predicted that this cave was located along the border of three villages: Lhok Jok, Cot Meureubo, and Alue Rambe. We could not move anywhere.

If a shootout happened, the soldiers would shoot the villagers. Finally, we prepared ourselves with weapons, ready to shoot, and waited for the soldiers' arrival, in case they hunted us all the way to this cave.

When night fell, I hung a hammock between two trees next to the cave. I lay down in the net. The moonlit sky behind those leaves looked so bright. The moon also appeared up there in a golden glow. I kept looking at it. Between my sleepiness and alertness, between my pain and helplessness, I heard a dog howling. Sometimes the sound was so near and sometimes it moved away, far, far away, almost as if the dog were howling at the moon.

———•———

The enemy we waited for never found us. They only hunted us for two days, then had to return to their bases because these were being attacked by other small groups of rebels. When this happened, the three of us left the cave and went home.

The front door creaked when I eased it open and woke Ibu up from her nap on a mat in the living room. I quickly knelt next to her and kissed her skinny hand. The skin of her hand was wrinkled and her veins were raised, but her grip was still strong and felt like that of an industrial worker. Ibu looked pale and her eyes were more sunken than before.

"You're home." She smiled. "I heard that the soldiers and police had to leave."

"Maybe they'll come back one day, Bu." I tried to repress my deep sadness upon seeing Ibu's condition.

Ibu's happy face turned sad. She covered her face with her batik shawl and burst into tears. "I was so scared they'd find you," she sobbed, "and shoot you like Ayah."

I could only let Ibu cry. I was a rebel who had to be strong and resilient. I had made the decision to take up arms and be prepared to be shot dead. I of course did not tell Ibu this.

"I'm so afraid to lose you," Ibu continued.

"They won't find me, Bu," I said firmly, trying to convince her. "If they come after me, I'll run far away."

Ibu wiped her wet eyes with her batik cloth.

Baiti and Zuhra came out from their room, and Raziah appeared from the kitchen. I knew they must have heard Ibu cry and had purposely stayed away. Before I could walk up to my two older sisters, Zuhra, who had grown into a teenage girl, quickly came to greet me. Siti and Muslim froze when they saw me.

I greeted them and rubbed their heads and hugged them. They were both eight now; Muslim's nose looked even flatter than before.

They suddenly turned awkward and went to their rooms.

Their behavior amused me for a minute but then, suddenly, it was as if a big hand squeezed my heart. The house seemed to be draped in perpetual gloominess. The wooden walls seemed duller, termites had bored holes in the studs, and sawdust filled the corners of the room. The table had a broken leg and was held up by a piece of wood. The door curtains were worn out.

Everyone seemed to be wearing the same clothes they had been wearing for years. I was saddened when I noticed that Muslim wore a pair of pants that were too small for him. In order to still be able to wear the pants, he used a piece of string to hold them up. But the string was so worn that it broke. Everyone broke out laughing while Muslim scrambled to pull his pants up and cover his genitals.

What hurt even more was to find out that there was no food in our house. There was neither rice nor fish. According to Ibu, Akbar could only go in the afternoon to Simpang Mawak to buy two pounds of rice and some fish. That amount of rice was not enough to feed a family of seven for a day. I knew they didn't have the money to buy more. They often ate boiled bananas or yams to appease their hunger.

I met Akbar in the yard. He carried a cluster of bananas and had just returned from Kakek's house. His clothes were stained by sap, and his shirt had a tear on a shoulder and a hole in his armpit. Even though he was thin, he looked handsome with his thin mustache.

Akbar put down his banana cluster as soon as he saw me and shook my hand. I slapped him on the shoulder and said a few words of encouragement. He nodded and picked up the banana cluster again.

The mild drizzle didn't prevent me from going to Zulaiha's house. I hoped to see her this time. But when I knocked on the door, the girl still did not want to see me. Her parents and sister didn't have anything to say. All they could do was bow their heads. But I was no longer embarrassed to speak out my feelings. I didn't care if they heard what I told Zulaiha.

"I'm here because I still love you," I said standing by her window. "I never hated you. But why do you hate me?"

"I don't hate you," a hoarse voice said softly.

I walked closer to the window to make sure it was Zulaiha's voice. I sighed and said, "Why don't you want to meet me? I really want to see you. Please c'mon out and meet me now," I urged then shouted, "see me now."

"I'm ashamed," she sobbed. "I'm not a virgin anymore. I'm no longer a good match for you."

"You don't need to feel guilty, Zulaiha. It's not your fault. And to me, you're still a virgin."

"Are you telling the truth?"

"I swear," I exclaimed and gritted my teeth. "What else do you want me to say?" I whispered desperately.

The window slowly opened.

She lifted her pale face for a moment then lowered her head again and cried. One of her hands gripped the windowsill while the other covered her mouth. Her thin body shook.

When I covered her hand that gripped the windowsill with mine, she cried even more. "Please," I sighed. "Please don't cry anymore. I'll propose to you soon. I don't have the gold anymore, but I'm offering you my soul and my life as my dowry for you." I slowly let go of her hand.

Her body shook even harder. She let go of the windowsill, and her slender fingers gripped my arm. "I'm not asking for any dowry." Zulaiha stopped crying and finally looked at me.

I leaned into the window and looked at the bed in her room. There was nothing on the faded pink bedsheet.

"Where's the baby?" I said. "I want to see him."

She lifted her head after rubbing both of her eyes. "What baby?" she asked with a hoarse voice.

"The baby you conceived," I answered.

Zulaiha stared at me, puzzled. "I wasn't pregnant."

"You weren't?" I asked in disbelief.

"Who said I was pregnant?"

"I thought you were pregnant."

"I was never pregnant," she stated firmly.

"Why didn't you tell me earlier?" I sulked. "Why wouldn't you see me?"

"I was scared," she stammered, "that I disappointed you."

"Trust me, Zulaiha, my love is only for you. No other girl can have my heart."

---

Raiyan, Biram, and I continued to collaborate with other groups of rebels to launch attacks and set up roadblocks. The three of us were considered the cleverest, most cunning and most agile fighters who were the most difficult to hunt. When the victims fell from the enemy's side, they beat any man they could find and burned the villagers' houses. The war was cruel and deaths were unavoidable. This was my fate, I could not avoid it; I had no choice, because wars never gave a choice.

Now, weapons for demolition had been created, hostility had been fostered; crime was everywhere. The greediness of the ruler had created this war, these destructions, and I was dragged into it and expected to perform the role I was dealt. I was forced to do it, whether I liked it or not.

We tried not to attack the soldiers in villagers' settlement areas. We chose the bushes, waiting for their trucks to pass, and then fired some shots and threw grenades.

One day, I wanted to launch an attack alone at a group of soldiers who often passed by while laughing in the street of Blang Riek, but Raiyan prevented me. The last time he went to the city, Raiyan received news that a cease-fire between the government and the fighters had been signed in an agreement abroad. He insisted that we obey the Cessation of Hostilities Agreement between the Indonesian government and the Fighters of Aceh, which was signed on December 9 in Geneva, Switzerland. In that agreement, both sides agreed not to attack each other.

We spent the rest of the day storing our weapons.

"Do you believe in that agreement?" I asked while we hid our weapons inside the cave.

"No."

"Then why are we hiding our weapons?" I asked.

"I just don't want to violate it."

"What if they violate it?"

"We will destroy them."

# Chapter 28

During the Cessation of Hostilities, the soldiers no longer came to the village, and I used the opportunity to take care of my field. I removed brush, picked coconuts, and harvested the areca fruit. Akbar was twelve now and growing into a lanky teenager. He diligently helped me.

Zuhra often joined Raziah or Baiti when they collected areca or removed coconut flesh from the shells.

Meanwhile, Ibu became weaker. She now spent her days sitting on the daybed or tinkering in the kitchen. Her thinning gray hair and the heavy bags under her eyes made her look older. Every time Ibu saw me, she asked, "When will you marry?"

I cleared my throat and tried to deal with Ibu's question. I was torn by uncertainty. I wanted to marry Zulaiha. If it were possible, I'd marry her right then. But the reality was that, at this moment, there wasn't anything I could do.

"I only have a short time left to live," Ibu said.

"We don't know when we will die, Bu," I responded.

"That's why I keep asking."

I cleared my throat.

"You're the only son and the heir of Ayah's family line. If you die before you marry, the line of Dahli will end."

I could only bow my head. *How could I marry a girl without a dowry?*

---

I often stopped by a coffee stall in Simpang Mawak. Outside of the stall I saw Situng wandering around among other dogs. It had been a long time since I saw him last. He still limped, but other than that, he looked healthy and still seemed to lead the pack.

I bought three pieces of grilled sticky rice and called Situng. He came, wagging his tail. When I placed the rice on the ground near him, he tilted his head, looked at me, then ate the rice. I was sure he still remembered me.

"Do you still remember Muha?" I squatted near Situng. "Your master died under miserable conditions. Hopefully, we're at the end of this war." I had no idea what compelled me to share my sadness and hope with a dog.

Situng looked up at me; he snorted and wagged his tail.

Suddenly, I was overwhelmed by anxiety and fear. "But if it turns out that the war continues, you must help us," I said. "Will you?"

Situng fixed his eyes on me and tilted his head as if trying to understand what I had just said.

"All right," I said, looking at the dog sitting in front of me, "I now initiate you as a rebel."

Situng wagged his tail, let out a few short barks, then trotted away.

I watched his wagging tail until it disappeared into the distance.

During my absence, my field and orchard were neglected. I now tried to catch up on the work.

The coconut harvest didn't make much money. The amount, combined with the proceeds from the sale of two goats, was only enough to buy three nuggets of gold.

I often met Raiyan and some of my friends for coffee at Leman's stall or in Simpang Mawak. They somehow found out about my predicament.

One day, Raiyan invited me to have a cup of coffee at Leman's stall. He really surprised me when he gave me two nuggets of gold.

"Don't think serving the resistance means working for free," he chuckled. "This is your pay for serving the resistance."

After years of endless adversity, I finally was able to smile that day.

Without waiting for the proceeds of the areca harvest that was still being peeled, I married Zulaiha in mid-December 2002, with five nuggets of gold for the dowry. The small party was attended by relatives and close neighbors.

Zulaiha looked very elegant in her traditional dress. After the *akad nikah*, the Islamic marriage ceremony, she kissed my hand, knelt in front of me and, for the first time, I kissed a girl. I kissed her on the forehead.

It was the most beautiful moment in my twenty-six years of a life lived under a dark cloud. Before sitting on the small bridal stage that was set up in her parents' living room, we toasted each other. Zulaiha blushed as we held each other's hand. But when no one looked, we tightened our handhold.

Zulaiha lowered her eyes and smiled shyly when I looked at her. "Don't keep looking at me," she murmured.

"Why?" I whispered.

"I'm shy…"

Her girlfriends, and my battle buddies who came to celebrate with us, could not stop teasing us with naughty jokes. The room was filled with the sound of happy conversation interspersed with the clinking of glasses and plates.

A photographer from Buloh Blang Ara never stopped taking pictures of us. After he made sure to have photographed us in various poses and had documented items specific to the occasion, such as the bridal stage and the bed, he went on to take pictures of the guests enjoying themselves and the food, both inside the wedding room and in the tent outside.

Later that night, we indulged in our happiness. I had never seen Zulaiha that happy. I never tired of looking at her glowing face. I liked touching her cheeks and stroking her hair.

And she treated me with such tenderness.

It was the first time in my whole life, I felt completely peaceful.

"I hope the soldiers won't attack us anymore," I said, looking at her. "I want this war to stop."

"I also don't like to live with fear and under constant pressure," she replied.

Even though there was a possibility that the Cessation of Hostilities Agreement would not be implemented to its fullest, for the time being, the Acehnese could breathe freely after having lived for almost twenty-five years in a state of war. At least for now, we could be happy.

And so, we kissed.

# Glossary

## Chapter 1

*Asr*: afternoon prayer time for Muslims
*Ayah:* father
*Ibu:* mother
*Kakek:* grandfather
*Melinjo* tree: *Gnetum gnemon,* a medium-size tree with oval evergreen leaves. The seeds and leaves are widely used in Indonesian cuisine.
*Panglima Sagoe:* a rank of an insurgency fighter in a sub-district; short form is "Pang"
*Quran:* the central religious text of Islam

## Chapter 2

*Adik:* little sister; polite way of addressing a younger female
*Broti:* giant wooden nutcracker
*Bupati:* county manager
*Camat:* district supervisor

*Dangau:* small, temporary hut in a rice field
*Imam:* worship leader at a mosque
*Isha:* night prayer time (approximately two hours after Maghrib) for Muslims
*Maghrib:* prayer time for Muslims right after sunset
*Nenek:* grandmother

## Chapter 3

*Beras-padi:* a mixture of rice and unhulled grain
*Peusijuek:* a traditional Acehnese ritual performed to ask for blessings at important occasions such as births, weddings, moving into a new home, etc.
*Pulut:* glutinous rice
*Sajadah:* prayer mat
*Salawat:* a special Arabic phrase used by Muslims in their five daily prayers as a salutation upon the prophet Muhammad

## Chapter 4

*Fajr:* prayer time for Muslims at dawn

## Chapter 5

*Gubernur:* governor

## Chapter 6

*Meughang:* an Islamic religious and traditional (Acehnese) ritual of slaughtering and consuming a cow or goat at three times during the Islamic calendar year: 1) on the day before *Ramadan* (the month of fasting); 2) on Idul Fitr (the feast of breaking the fast of Ramadan on the first day of Syawal, the tenth month

of the Islamic calendar year); and 3) Idul Adha (the festival of sacrifice).
*Padi:* rice grain
*Ramadan:* the ninth month of the Islamic calendar, which is the fasting month for Muslims

## Chapter 7

*Bedug:* mosque drum
*Eid al-Fitr:* (known in Indonesia as Hari Raya Idul Fitri or Lebaran) an Islamic religious holiday to celebrate the end of Ramadan — the fasting month.
*Kolak Ubi:* a yam stew prepared with coconut milk, pandan leaves, and palm sugar
Miracle leaves: *Bryophyllum pinnatum:* popular plant in tropical and subtropical regions
*Raka'at:* Islamic prayer units
*Rawatib:* a voluntary Islamic prayer offered immediately before or after the main obligatory prayer
*Tadarus:* group recitation of the Quran
*Tarawih congregations:* optional Islamic congregational night prayers only performed during Ramadan
*Urap:* a salad of steamed vegetables mixed with seasoned coconut gratings
*Witr:* supererogatory Islamic prayer performed at night between Isha and Fajr

## Chapter 8

*Zikr:* devotional Islamic act of reciting (silently or aloud) repetitive, short sentences glorifying God; optional use of prayer beads

## Chapter 9

*Allah, Allah, Allahu ya Rabbi:* Allah is my God.

## Chapter 11

*Catu rice:* inferior quality rice that is hard and tasteless
*Cempaka: Magnolia champaca* – a large evergreen tree known for its fragrant flowers
*Kenanga: Cananga odorata* – a native, tropical tree valued for the perfume extracted from its flowers
*Kolak pisang:* banana stew
*Salah:* Islamic ritual that Muslims perform during the daily five prayer times
*Surah Yaseen verses:* Chapter 36 of the Quran

## Chapter 12

*Kue basah:* Indonesian traditional cakes
*Samadiyah:* ritual prayer for someone who has just passed away.

## Chapter 13

*Partai Demokrasi Indonesia:* The Indonesian Democratic Party
*Partai Golkar:* The Party of The Functional Groups
*Partai Persatuan Pembangunan:* The United Development Party

## Chapter 14

*Ketapang tree: Terminalia catappa* – a large tropical shade tree that produces edible fruit with a stony core known as Indian almonds
*Sawah:* wet rice field

## Chapter 15

*Kenduri:* traditional ceremonial meal
*Zuhr:* midday prayer time for Muslims

## Chapter 16

*Dangdut:* Indonesian folk music

## Chapter 17

*Salaam:* Arabic word for a greeting

## Chapter 22

*Kafir:* Arabic word for unbeliever of the Islam faith
*Merdeka:* freedom

## Chapter 23

*Pesantren:* an Islamic boarding school
*Ulama:* Islamic scholar

## Chapter 28

*Akad nikah:* ceremony to legalize an Islamic marriage

# *ABOUT THE AUTHOR*

Arafat Nur, a prominent Indonesian writer, was born in Medan, North Sumatra, on December 22, 1974. He grew up during the political turmoil and military violence that plagued Aceh between 1976 and 2007.

Nur has written short stories and poetry since he was a teenager. As an adult, Nur was subjected to military violence as a consequence of his controversial newspaper articles. Today, Nur lives in East Java, farming rice and other agricultural products.

Nur is a prolific writer. Aside from numerous widely-published short stories, Nur has four published novels. *Lampuki* (Serambi, 2011), won the 2010 Jakarta Arts Council Novel Writing Competition and the Khatulistiwa Literary Award in 2011. Four years later, his novel *Burung Terbang di Kelam Malam* (Bentang, 2015) was published and translated into the English language, under the title *A Bird Flies in the Dark of Night* (Bentang, 2015). Nur established himself as an Indonesian novelist with *Tempat Yang Paling Sunyi* (Gramedia, 2015). After once again winning the Jakarta Arts Council Novel Writing Competition in 2016 with his novel *Tanah Surga Merah* (Gramedia, 2017), Nur claims a special place in his readers' hearts.

While *Blood Moon over Aceh*, the translation of *Lolong Anjing di Bulan* (Sanata Dharma University Press, 2018), is based on historical facts and testimonies of witnesses, Nur did not write the novel to judge or dwell on past injustices and misjudgments that led to a thirty-year tragedy. He hopes to spark a desire in his readers to do everything possible to prevent a repeat of the past by unveiling often still-obscure data in his writing. Nur states that experience is a wise and powerful teacher.

# *ABOUT THE TRANSLATOR*

Maya Denisa Saputra was born on July 30, 1990, in Denpasar, the capital of Bali, and grew up on Indonesia's "island of the gods." She spent a brief time in Singapore to obtain a bachelor's degree in accounting and finance at the UK-based University of Bradford. While holding a position in the accounting department of a family business, she pursues her interests in writing, literary translation, and photography.

Maya's writings and translation work have appeared in the Buddhist Fellowship Singapore's newsletter, Connection, an online platform that gathers writings about physical and mental wellness; B.Philosophy and LitSync, online communities of aspiring fiction writers; and InterSastra, a literary translation initiative.

Maya's translations can also be found in the archives of the Your Stories page of Dalang Publishing's website. For the Your Stories page, Maya translated: *The Golden Shackle / Belenggu Emas* / by Iksaka Banu, and *Lord, Whose Prayer Will You Listen To? / Gusti, Doa Siapa Yang Akan Kaudengar?* by Junaedi Setiyono. This work introduced her to further collaboration with Setiyono and Dalang Publishing that manifested in the translation of *Dasamuka* (Dalang 2017 – ISBN 978-0-9836273-1-9).

Maya currently lives in Surabaya, East Java, with her husband and can be reached at maya.saputra@gmail.com.

# MORE STORYTELLERS FROM DALANG PUBLISHING

*Only a Girl*
Lian Gouw

Three generations of Chinese women struggle for identity against the political backdrop of the World Depression, World War II, and the Indonesian Revolution. Nanna, the matriarch of the family, strives to preserve the family's traditional Chinese values while her children are eager to assimilate into Dutch colonial society. Carolien, Nanna's youngest daughter, is fixated on the advantages to be gained by adopting a western lifestyle. But when she raises her own daughter Jenny by colonial standards, it puts the girl at a disadvantage in new, independent Indonesia, where Dutch culture is no longer revered. The unique ways in which Nanna, Carolien, and Jenny face their own challenges reveal the complexity of Chinese society in Indonesia between 1930 and 1952.

Price: $17.95
Paperback: 298 pages
ISBN: 978-0-9836273-7-1

*Arafat Nur*

***My Name is Mata Hari***
Remy Sylado
Translated from the Indonesian by Dewi Anggraeni

*My Name is Mata Hari* tells the story of Margaretha Geertruida Zelle, a young Dutch woman married to an older military officer assigned to the Dutch East Indies. Claiming her mother's Javanese ancestry, she changed her name to Mata Hari, Malay for "eye of the day."

As Mata Hari, she danced on stages across Europe and the Middle East, and took many high-ranking military and government officials as her lovers. Convicted of espionage during World War I, she said at the end of her tumultuous life, "I am a genuine courtesan. And I am a dancer in the true sense."

Price: $17.95
Paperback: 334 pages
ISBN: 978-0-9836273-0-2

***Potions and Paper Cranes***
Lan Fang
Translated from the Indonesian by Elisabet Titik Murtisari

In Lan Fang's award-winning novel, Sulis is a young woman selling potions in Surabaya's harbor district. She meets Sujono, a day laborer with dreams of becoming a freedom fighter, and whose passion for Matsumi, a geisha called to Java by a Japanese general, is destined to ruin all of them. Each tells the story of their lives during the Japanese occupation of Java and Indonesia's transition from a Dutch colony to an independent republic.

Price: $17.95
Paperback: 252 pages
ISBN: 978-0-9836273-3-3

# BLOOD MOON OVER ACEH

*Kei*
Erni Aladjai
Translated from the Indonesian by Nurhayat Indriyatno Mohamed

At the end of Suharto's New Order, the Kei people hold on to their traditions as they flee the violence that divides Muslim from Christian and destroys the villages. Namira, a Muslim girl, works as a volunteer in a refugee camp when she meets Sala, a young Protestant man. Grounded in the islander's belief of "We drink from the same spring and eat from the same land, the land of Kei," the two fall in love amid the chaos that will soon separate them.

Price: $17.95
Paperback: 224 pages
ISBN: 978-0-9836273-6-4

*Daughters of Papua*
Anindita Siswanto Thayf
Translated from the Indonesian by Stefanny Irawan

Seven-year-old Leksi lives in modern-day Papua with her grandmother Mabel and her mother, Mace. Her companions are Pum, an old dog of unknown ancestry, and Kwee, a pig. Together they look back at the past, as they face an uncertain future. In *Daughters of Papua*, the present is marked by a contentious election, with the gold company that wants to rob Papuans of their heritage the only winner.

Price: $17.95
Paperback: 224 pages
ISBN: 978-0-9836273-9-5

# *Arafat Nur*

***The Red Bekisar***
Ahmad Tohari
Translated from the Indonesian by Nurhayat Indriyatno Mohamed

The *bekisar* is a fine crossbreed between jungle fowl and domestic chicken that adorns the houses of the wealthy. Lasi, whose father was a Japanese soldier, fair skinned and beautiful, is such an acquisition for a rich man in Jakarta. She is born in a village where the main source of income is tapping coconut palms for their rich sap, or nira. Her life takes an unexpected turn when she is betrayed by her husband and flees to Jakarta. She meets Mrs. Lanting, procuress of companions for men in high government and social circles, who sells her to the rich Handarbeni. Lasi enjoys her new splendor as a much-desired ornament, but is alarmed when she discovers the marriage is a sham. When she reconnects with Kanjat, a childhood friend now grown into a man, Lasi and Kanjat rediscover their affection for each other. Their bond is the village, its people and traditions. Together they struggle to free Lasi from a net of power, corruption, and deceit.

Price: $17.95
Paperback: 294 pages
ISBN: 978-0-9836273-2-6

***Love Death, and Revolution***
Mochtar Lubis
Translated from the Indonesian by Stefanny Irawan

During the early days of their nation's revolution, Indonesians were driven by passion and built a future on dreams. In a world still reeling from World War II, Major Sadeli of the Indonesian Army Intelligence travels to Singapore tasked with establishing naval and air routes to Sumatra and Java as well as securing weapons and radio equipment vital to the revolution. His desire for Indonesia to be prosperously independent, and independently prosperous, forces him to choose between personal happiness and commitment to a higher cause.

Price: $17.95
Paperback: 298 pages
ISBN: 978-0-9836273-5-7

# BLOOD MOON OVER ACEH

*Cloves for Kolosia*
Hanna Rambe
Translated from the Indonesian by Miagina Amal

Elderly widower Gamati swears to save his family line from extinction when he and his family fall victim to the infamous plunder expeditions of the VOC, the Dutch East India Company. To escape the colonialists' cruelties, he leads his orphaned grandchildren and a small group of fellow villagers to the safety of another, more remote, island north of their current location. The birth of his great-grandson Kolosia during the voyage assures Gamati of his family's ability to sail the Moluccan seas freely for generations to come.

Price: $17.95
Paperback: 298 pages
ISBN: 978-0-9836273-5-7

*Dasamuka*
Junaedi Setiyono
Translated from the Indonesian by Maya Denisa Saputra

Willem Kappers, an Edinburgh scientist, learns about intrigue in nineteenth century royal Javanese court and witnesses colonialism change powerful kings into puppets of the Dutch and English authorities. Kappers' involvement with an ambitious nobleman, Dasamuka, gives the reader an intimate glimpse into the struggle of the Javanese commoner against the oppression of the reigning sultan as well as the colonial powers.

Price: $17.95
Paperback: 265 pages
ISBN:978-0-9836273-1-9

www.ingramcontent.com/pod-product-compliance
Lightning Source LLC
LaVergne TN
LVHW041619060526
838200LV00040B/1351